By the same author:

   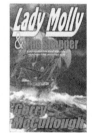

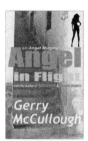  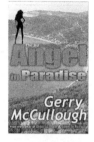 

Roundabout

a modern day Vanity Fair

Gerry McCullough

Published by

www.preciousoil.com/publications

ISBN 13: 978-0-9955404 7 7

ISBN 10:   0-9955404 7 0

First published **2020**

10a Listooder Road, Crossgar,
Downpatrick, Northern Ireland BT30 9JE

Come and watch the Roundabout. The people are beginning to climb on board. They sit on horseback, on lions, in motorcars.

Listen! – the music is starting. The roundabout begins – round and round, back to the start then round again. The people are clinging on tightly, afraid to let go – except for those who know what's coming next for them.

Most of them start off expecting good things – expecting to enjoy themselves. But after a round or two, they realise something is missing. They are no longer sure if the ride alone is something to enjoy or not.

Chapter One

Millicent Brennan and Susan O'Leary left St Bernadette's Convent School for Girls in Belfast on the same day. It was the end of June. The sun was bright, the beds were full of fragrant smelling flowers, sweet peas, tulips, pansies, marigolds. They had both turned eighteen in the last year and had now completed their A Level exams. The results would not be out for a couple of months yet.

Millie was a tall, slim, red haired girl with green eyes which had a wicked gleam. She was dressed in the Saint Bernadette's school uniform, not by choice but for lack of anything else. Her uniform didn't fit her very well. It was too big, and the skirt draggled round her slim, excellent legs.

Sooze was shorter, stockier, but nevertheless attractive, dark haired and blue eyed, with a sweet face hard to resist. She was also wearing school uniform, but in her case it was because she felt it was appropriate to wear it until she had actually left. In any case, hers, made to measure by an excellent dressmaker, fitted perfectly.

They had not previously been close friends, but recently Millie had made an effort to develop some sort of friendship with Sooze.

'Sooze, I do love the way you're doing your hair recently. It really suits you.'

'Oh, Millie, do you really think so?'

'Of course! I never say things I don't mean. You should know that by now, Sooze!'

After a week or two of that sort of thing she said, looking sad but brave, 'Oh, Sooze, I wish I knew where I was going to stay when they chuck us out of school. After boarding for years here – and now that my Dad's passed on – I really have nowhere to go. Och, well,' – with a tearful smile – 'I'm sure I'll find somewhere!'

Sooze had a tender heart. She felt a pang for Millie at once, and burst out without thinking, 'Why don't you come to stay with us for a while until you get yourself sorted, Millie? We have tons of room.'

'Oh, Sooze, do you really mean it? But would your parents want me? You'd have to ask them first, wouldn't you?'

'Well, I suppose I'd better. But I'm sure they'd be happy to have you.' Having Millie in the house wouldn't be a problem for Sooze, who wouldn't even think of doing any of the extra work. What else were the staff for? And she didn't expect her parents to object. All her life she'd been used to them giving her everything she'd ever wanted.

Millie pressed her friend's hand gratefully. She knew a little about Sooze's parents. Enough to think that an invitation to stay with them might open a few doors for her. John O'Leary was a high flying businessman, well off and powerful. His wife was in a position to buy the latest fashions and to appear regularly in photographs in the *Ulster Tatler.* They had a lifestyle which Sooze took for granted, but which Millie envied with all her heart.

Millie's parents were a very different story. Her father, Charlie Brennan – an unsuccessful rock musician who had been killed when he crashed his motorbike a year ago – had taught music to the girls of St Bernadette's two days a week, and had made himself so popular with the nuns – in particular the Mother Superior, headmistress of the school – that he had managed to persuade her to take in his little Millie as a pupil without charge, and to continue to keep her even after his own death. Charlie had been a man of great charm, but since he had never been able to keep a pound in his pocket for more than a few hours or so, he had left Millie equally penniless.

She had been glad enough to have her education continued in a school which ranked as one of the best girls' schools in Northern Ireland. As for Millie's mother, who had died when Millie was still a child, the less said about her the better, according to the Reverend Mother. She had been a singer who had met Charlie Brennan on tour, and had lived with him until the drug habit she had been unable to shake off finished her. Millie had inherited her singing voice but not, she was glad to say, her addictions.

Before girls left St Bernadette's, it was the custom for the headmistress to call each leaver into her study, and give them a little lecture on what was expected from every St Bernadette's girl going out into the world, and how she should conduct herself to bring honour to the school. Then Mother Veronica would solemnly present each one with a copy of a DVD she had had specially made, with a sermon from Father Connelly, who supervised the religious teaching of the school, together with a speech she herself had delivered at the preceding prize giving day.

'If you listen to this regularly, my dear,' she said to each girl, 'it will keep you on the right track.'

Chapter One

Sooze received her DVD with appropriate awe. Her habit had been to respect the Reverend Mother and to swallow everything she said.

'Oh, thank you, Mother Veronica!' she said earnestly. 'I'll treasure this.'

And Mother Veronica beamed benignly.

As Sooze left the study, the headmistress turned majestically to her assistant, the meek, rabbit like Sister Angelica.

'And I think that was the last of this year's school leavers, sister,' she said.

'Oh, but, Mother Superior ...' Sister Angelica murmured in a small frightened voice, 'what about Millicent Brennan?'

'Millicent Brennan?' The headmistress's frown was awe inspiring. 'Millicent Brennan does not deserve a copy of my DVD. It would be impossible to give that girl anything which would prevent her from going from bad to worse. Mark my words, sister, whenever we hear any-thing about that girl in the future, it will be all bad. I kept her here for her father's sake, but I'll be only too glad to see the back of her.'

Millie had committed the unforgivable crime of being rude to the Reverend Mother, and had even been caught imitating her to a group of girls, behind Mother Veronica's back.

Sister Angelica was near to tears. Much as she had had to suffer from Millie's cheekiness herself, she couldn't bear to see the girl sent off into the world without the support of the precious DVD. Dear Charlie Brennan's daughter, too! Charlie had been such a sweet man.

So when the Reverend Mother had departed to carry out some further duty, Sister Angelica slipped back into the study, opened the cup-board where the DVD's were kept, and removed one from the top of the enormous pile. One would not be missed.

She hurried out to the entrance hall, and was glad to see Millie and Sooze, their luggage piled around them, still waiting for John O'Leary's limousine to collect them.

'Millicent, dear! The Reverend Mother has had to hurry off to see to something – an emergency which has come up suddenly. So she asked me to see that you got a copy of her DVD. We couldn't allow you to leave without one. Susan already has hers, don't you dear?'

Sister Angelica soothed her conscience for the white lie by telling herself that she couldn't allow the poor child to be so hurt.

Millie took the DVD from Sister Angelica's outstretched hand. Her expression was hard to read.

'Please listen to it regularly, Millicent,' Sister Angelica said earnestly. 'As the Reverend Mother always says, it will help to keep you on the right path.'

A uniformed chauffeur came in through the main door as she finished speaking.

Sooze hurried over to him, followed by Millie.

'Hello, Kelly!' she greeted him smilingly. 'You're in great time. This is my friend Millie who's coming to stay with me for a while.'

'Hello, Millie,' said Tommy Kelly. The chauffeur was a tall, good looking man with dark hair and a sexy smile. Millie liked the look of him. She gave him her best smile in return, and to her pleasure he returned it with a wink. 'Now, let's get these suitcases out to the car.'

By the time they had everything loaded, Mother Veronica had come out onto the steps which led to the huge, impressive entrance door of St Bernadette's, ready to wave graciously to her best – i.e. most wealthy – pupil (although not, she was disappointed to see, to either of her distinguished parents).

She waved regally, noticing with disapproval that Millicent Brennan had apparently managed to wriggle her way into Susan O'Leary's car and must be getting a lift with her. She stood for a moment while the car began to move. A window rolled down and a hand was thrust out of it. The hand was holding a small object.

A second later, the object came whizzing through the air to strike Mother Veronica on her chest. Mother Veronica gasped with horror as the thing slid down her front and smashed onto the top step. She took an involuntary step backwards and looked down at the ruined object.

It was her DVD.

Chapter Two

It was already late in the afternoon by the time the car drew up at John O'Leary's luxurious country mansion. O'Leary had shops and offices in Belfast City Centre as well as in many other locations, but for his family life he preferred to stay away from the city noise and to live quietly in the heart of the Antrim hills.

Since all four members of his family – himself, his wife Samantha, his son Johnny and his daughter Susan – owned at least one car, the distance was rarely a problem. If the roads were occasionally snow-bound, which might happen once or twice a year, there was always the helicopter, which O'Leary mostly used for business purposes, but which came in useful for family trips often enough to have interested the tax man, if he had ever known about this.

Sooze took Millie by the arm and led her into the house, leaving Tommy Kelly to pick up the luggage, and Samantha O'Leary (Sammy to the gossip columns, Sam to her husband and friends) came drifting out into the hallway and kissed her daughter lightly on one cheek.

'So you're back already, darling?' she murmured. Her languid gaze ran over Millie coldly.

'This is my friend Millie, Mum,' Sooze said earnestly, drawing Millie forward and offering her to Samantha rather in the manner of a kitten presenting its owner with a mouse which it half knows may not be eagerly received.

Millie was aware of the coldness of Mrs O'Leary's attitude, as she nodded and said, 'Hello, Millie,' but she was determined to make a good impression.

'It's so very kind of you to invite me to your lovely house, Mrs O'Leary,' she said with an eager air. Then, as Samantha turned away, she whispered to Sooze, loud enough to be clearly heard, 'I thought it must be your sister, Sooze. Surely this lady isn't old enough to be your mum? Oh, how lucky you are!'

Mrs O'Leary smiled faintly. She was used to flattery. But she still liked it, and felt more friendly towards this stray girl than she had done before. Maybe she wouldn't be such a nuisance after all.

'Darling, take Millie up and show her her room, why don't you? And I expect you'll both want to shower and change before dinner time. That awful school uniform!' She shuddered visibly, and drifted back to the room where she had been flicking through a fashion magazine and sipping a cocktail when the sound of their arrival had interrupted her.

Millie followed Sooze up the wide staircase.

'Shouldn't we bring up our luggage, Sooze, if we're going to need to change?' she murmured to Sooze, but Sooze said, 'Shush, Millie! One of the help will bring it up. In fact, they must have done already – you can see it's not in the hall where Kelly left it.'

And Millie, looking round, could see that Sooze's two large suitcases and her own small holdall had disappeared.

The room which Sooze took her into was, to Millie's eyes, enormous. Used to her cubicle in the school dormitory, and before that to the tiny, squalid back room in the lodging house she had shared with her father, Millie felt as if she was living in a movie.

Apart from the sheer size of the place, she was impressed by the comfortable looking bed with its luxurious duvet and pillows matching the window curtains, the picture on all of them clearly designed by a celebrated artist, the wardrobe which ran along one wall with mirrors covering its sliding doors, the en suite bathroom, the comfortable armchairs upholstered to match the duvet and curtains, the desk and dressing table of a silvery looking ash, and the wide windows with their view out over the spreading gardens and grounds.

But Sooze was apologising for the lack of computer and television. 'It's really a guest room for grown ups,' she explained shyly. 'Mum doesn't realise that people our age expect these things now. But you can always use the stuff in my room, any time you want to, dear Millie,' she added.

Millie gulped. She noticed her shabby looking holdall placed on a chair beside the bed, and turned to Sooze with a woebegone expression. 'Oh, Sooze, you're so kind! But – oh dear!' She raised her hand to her eyes and dabbed at them. 'Sooze, I don't know what I should wear tonight. Your Mum expects us to change. But, Sooze – I don't really have anything except my school uniform and the dress I wore for church, and I don't know if that would be good enough. I didn't realise how well off your parents were, or what high standards they'd have. Oh, well.' She gulped bravely, and dashed imaginary tears from her eyes. 'I suppose I'm just being silly. Probably my church dress will do.'

Sooze's warm heart was touched. 'Millie, I want you to come right along to my room and we'll find you something you'd really like to wear tonight. You're slimmer than me, and I have a lot of really nice things still hanging in my wardrobe that I could wear last year but can't get into now. You can have your pick – in fact you might as well have them all, because I'll never be able to wear them again!' She grabbed Millie by the hand and began to hustle her out of the room and along the corridor.

Sooze's room was twice the size of the guest room allocated to Millie, for a start, and so much more luxurious that Millie could hardly believe it. She noted, among the expensive looking furnishings, a desk with the laptop, music system, and television that Sooze had mentioned earlier. But before she had time to cast more than one envious glance around the room, Sooze had slid open the wardrobe doors and was pulling frocks and skirts out of it and throwing them on her queen sized bed. T-shirts, shorts and shirts followed, as Sooze opened drawer after drawer.

Millie sat down abruptly in the nearest chair, in a state of genuine shock.

'But Sooze, you can't give all this stuff to me!' she exclaimed, when at last she was able to speak. 'What would your mother say?'

'Oh, pooh! Sam doesn't keep check on my clothes – she gives me a free hand to get rid of things and buy new ones,' Sooze said, laughing. 'She has enough to keep her busy supervising my Dad's wardrobe and getting new clothes herself, without worrying about me. She knows I have good taste – she trained me herself.'

She picked up a dress in olive green satin and held it out to Millie. 'Stand up, Mil!' she commanded. Then as Millie struggled out of the deep armchair, she held it against her and said in satisfaction, 'Wow! That looks as if it would be a great fit, and the colour is perfect with your green eyes. Try it on.'

Millie lost no time in discarding the hated school uniform and getting into the dress, which was a dream come true. She'd never had any-thing that came remotely close to it. And she could see, as she looked at the result in Sooze's mirrors, that, yes, the colour was exactly right with her green eyes and her long red hair.

'Sooze, may I really borrow this for tonight?' she breathed, gazing at her friend with wide eyes. Susan was not to know how much of Millie's reaction was avarice and how little was gratitude.

'You can not only wear it tonight, you can keep it, dear Millie,' Sooze said, her heart touched by Millie's response to what she felt herself was a not especially nice old frock. 'And everything else here that you like. I've already told you that. None of these things fit me any more. That's the worst of being still growing – although I'm sure I must have stopped by now. And that olive green colour never suited me. I can't think why I ever bought it. I've only worn it about twice, so it should be in good condition.'

And Millie, her arms full of clothes, presently returned to her own room to shower and to dress again in the olive green frock, with Sooze's promise to call for her and take her downstairs when it was time for dinner – 'For,' Millie said pathetically, 'this house is so enormous that I'm sure I should get completely lost, otherwise!'

Chapter Three

Dinner was at half past seven. Millie had paid a lot of attention to her hair, face and clothes, and was satisfied that she was looking her best. But she had to admit that Sooze, in a blue dress which matched her eyes and flattered her well developed figure, was looking really pretty. Prettier than Millie had expected, in spite of her regular compliments to her new friend.

'I expect my brother Johnny will be here, as well as my Mum and Dad,' Sooze told her as they went downstairs and into the drawing room. 'I hope you'll like him. He's very sweet, but quite shy with girls.'

'Is he as good looking as the rest of your family?' asked Millie rather loudly as they came into the room and she saw a young man standing by the drinks tray. 'Oh, yes, indeed he is!' Then she put a hand over her mouth and pretended to be embarrassed. 'Oh, Sooze, I do hope he didn't hear me!'

Sooze laughed. 'Hi, Johnny,' she said, 'good to see you! This is my friend Millie.'

Johnny, who had Sooze's dark hair and blue eyes and might have been good looking if he hadn't been so overweight, blushed and nodded shyly to Millie. 'Um – hi, Millie. Hi, Sooze. Um – can I get you something to drink, girls?'

'Indeed you can, Johnny dear,' Sooze told him. 'Millie, what would you like?'

Millie was in a quandary. A strong drink would have helped her considerably. But would it go with her shy, little girl, act? And would Sooze's parents approve of it if they saw her?

'Just whatever you and Johnny suggest, Sooze,' she murmured finally, looking up at Johnny from under her long eyelashes.

'Well, I was just going to have a pure orange,' Sooze said, to Millie's annoyance, but she was saved.

'Millie, I'm sure you'd rather have a G&T,' Johnny said, pouring out the orange for Sooze. He was trying to appear a man of the world like his father, who often said something like that to his guests.

'A G&T?' Millie asked. 'If it's something you recommend, I'm sure I'd like it, Johnny, although I don't think I've ever had one before. But a clever guy like you is bound to know what's best.'

In this she was speaking a little less than the truth, for most of her drinking had been done while she was living with her father, whose musician friends preferred gin, whiskey or vodka, and who had been amused to see the little girl knocking back drinks like their own. By the time she joined St Bernadette's Millie had been well accustomed to strong drinks, although gin with the addition of tonic had been a rarity. It seemed to Millie much longer ago than five drink free years in the convent boarding school, since those happy days.

Johnny, delighted with himself and with Millie, measured out the gin into Millie's glass, and had just added the tonic in spite of his sister's admonitions when they heard the sound of Sam O'Leary approaching. She was laughing and calling back to her husband as he came down the stairs behind her, still working with his bow tie.

Millie took the glass from Johnny, gulping down as much as possible before the O'Learys could see, and retreated behind her friend in order to finish up the rest before they could identify what she was drinking.

Sam came in, gorgeous in a clinging red dress, and immediately said, 'Johnny, since you seem to be acting barman, give me a strong vodka martini, darling!'

John O'Leary, coming behind her, said, 'And a whiskey and soda for me, my boy.' Then he turned to survey his daughter and her guest.

'Susan, my dear!' he exclaimed. 'How well you're looking!'

Sooze smiled, and murmured, 'Hi, Dad.'

'And is this your friend Millicent?' John O'Leary asked, turning to Millie, who was glad she had finished her drink by now.

'Oh, Dad, don't call her Millicent. You sound like Mother Veronica. She's Millie. And, Dad, no one but you and Sam call me Susan now. It's Sooze!'

'Susan, I don't like to hear you call your mother Sam,' O'Leary said.

'I don't mind, John,' Sam O'Leary said. 'In fact I like it.'

'Well, that's neither here nor there,' O'Leary said, clearly restraining his annoyance. 'But, Susan, your mother and I chose your name because we liked it, and we didn't choose Sooze! However,' he forced a friendly smile, 'if your friend would rather be called, Millie, then Millie it is. Glad to meet one of Susan's friends, Millie.'

He moved towards Millie and held out his hand. 'I hope we can make your short stay with us pleasant. Tonight will be rather boring, I'm afraid, but tomorrow we must see if we can line up a few more young people. Tennis, perhaps? You can see to that, I'm sure, Sam.'

'Oh, it's not boring, Mr O'Leary!' Millie assured him breathlessly, with a shy smile. 'It's lovely to meet Sooze's parents. And of course her brother. I've heard such good things about you all.' She shared an admiring smile between Sam and John, ending up with Johnny, and staying focused on him for rather a long time.

It was just as well that Zofia, the Polish girl who did a lot of the work in the house, opened the door of the drawing room at that moment to announce that dinner was served, before Johnny's fond parents had time to notice Millie's smile lingering on him.

But Johnny had certainly noticed, and as they sat down in the dining room round the mahogany table which could be extended to three times its size, as necessary, for guests, he made sure of getting a place beside this very sweet little girl who seemed to like and admire him, and who wasn't nearly as hard to talk to as most of the girls he'd met.

'Did you enjoy your drink?' he asked softly.

'Oh, yes! I'll know what to ask you for next time, Johnny,' Millie said, equally quietly. 'But Sooze says you shouldn't have given it to me, and your parents wouldn't be pleased if they knew, so let's say nothing, okay?'

'Sooze is far too interfering, Millie!' Johnny said rather too loudly. Sooze hastily distracted her mother's attention.

John O'Leary wasn't listening to anyone. He was too busy telling the girl how to serve the chicken soup.

'Sam, I thought it would be nice to invite Josh Gillespie to tennis, what do you think? And maybe Liam and Moira Bannon?'

'That sounds fine, darling,' Sam drawled. 'Why not give them a ring yourself?'

'Well, I'll probably text them,' Sooze answered.

'Will that be an even number?' Sam asked. 'Is Johnny going to play? Johnny, are you planning to play tennis tomorrow with Sooze and her friends?'

'Oh, certainly, Mum,' Johnny said. Then he added quietly to Millie, 'That is, if you're going to play, Millie?'

'I'd love to,' Millie said enthusiastically. 'Not that I'm much good – you'll have to help me, if we play as partners, Johnny.'

She noticed a rather annoyed glance coming her way from Johnny's mother, and added hastily, 'I'm not nearly as good as Sooze. I'm sure you all play much better than me.'

She had to fight hard to keep herself from giggling as she realised how much more annoyed Sam O'Leary would be if she knew that underneath the damask table cloth, Johnny's left foot was busily rubbing against Millie's right ankle.

Chapter Four

The sun shone brightly the next day, boding well for the proposed tennis. Millie woke up in her lovely bedroom and stretched luxuriously. Things had gone well yesterday, especially with Johnny. She thought if she put a little bit more work into it, she could get him. It would be nice to marry into a wealthy family and live this sort of lifestyle every day. But she needed to be careful. Mrs O'Leary – or Sam, as she would rather be called – was already suspicious. She probably didn't want her only son to marry someone like Millie.

Not that she hadn't been friendly enough. Millie had paid her a few more compliments and had seen that she was softening towards her. She had even invited Millie to join her, John Senior, and Sooze for a game of bridge. Sooze had already told her that Sam was a bridge fanatic. That was okay, because Millie was fairly expert at the game, having played often with her father's friends in happier days.

'Johnny doesn't know one card from another,' Sam had said indulgently. 'He always takes himself off to listen to his music downloads when I bring out the cards. I normally have to rely on Zofia, if we have no guests. So, off you go, Johnny. I don't need you tonight – Millie will make up the four.'

Looking back on it, Millie was sure this had been a deliberate move on Sam's part to separate her from Johnny. But she didn't mind. She couldn't have moved matters much further that night, in the presence of all Johnny's family. Besides, it would do him good to be kept waiting to see more of her. Today, at the tennis, would be a good opportunity.

Meanwhile, she had moved herself further into Sam O'Leary's good books by her skill at bridge. In fact, after cutting for partners for the first round, Sam had announced that she would have Millie as partner for the rest of the evening.

'No point in keeping cutting for partners,' she announced. 'It just disrupts the flow.'

There was no one there who didn't know quite well that Sam wanted to keep on having Millie as a partner for a very different reason, but no one said so. And by the end of the evening, Millie felt she had made definite progress, especially when Sam gave her a friendly smile and complimented her on her play. 'And please call me Sam, not that stuffy "Mrs O'Leary",' she told Millie graciously. 'We're all friends, aren't we?'

Millie retired to bed well satisfied with her day's work, and looking forward to the tennis the next afternoon.

Sooze was also looking forward to the tennis. She had texted Josh Gillespie, and then her other friends Liam and Moira Bannon, had decided to ask two more people, Stevie Thompson and Katie Morrison, and had got answers back from all of them saying they'd be there. But the only one who mattered really, in Sooze's view, was Josh Gillespie.

Josh was the son of Stephen Gillespie, a business associate of John O'Leary. John and Stephen had known each other since their university days, and they regularly met at business conferences, and considered each other friends, although neither would have hesitated to do the other down in a business deal if it had seemed a good idea. Josh had been encouraged to visit the O'Leary house with his parents, and to see himself as a special friend of Sooze, since they were toddlers.

Sooze was well aware that both Sam and John would be very pleased to see the friendship develop into marriage. She didn't care about that. What mattered to her was that she knew she had fallen flat for Josh a few years ago, and that he had shown every sign of feeling the same way about her. It seemed forever since she had seen him – not since the Christmas holidays – for at Easter John O'Leary had taken his family away for a holiday in the Seychelles.

Sooze shivered with pleasure at the thought of seeing the drop dead gorgeous Josh this afternoon. The memory of his kisses filled her thoughts every night before she fell asleep. She hoped very much that he hadn't changed his mind about her.

When Millie finally decided to roll out of bed, she dressed herself in one of the T-shirts and skirts Sooze had given her, and wandered downstairs in search of breakfast, not bothering to visit Sooze's room first. The smell of coffee led her to the kitchen, where she found the cook, whose name was Maria, the Polish girl Zofia, and Kelly the chauffeur sitting round the kitchen table eating and enjoying the coffee.

'Oh, that smells good!' Millie exclaimed. 'Would there be a cup going for me?'

Maria looked at her severely.

'Coffee is served for the family and their guests in the breakfast room,' she said, frowning.

'Oh, but I'd like to make friends with you three!' Millie exclaimed. To tell the truth, she was mainly interested in making friends with the chauffeur, Kelly, whom she fancied, but it never did any harm to get the staff on your side. She had experience of doing this successfully back at St Bernadette's, and it had meant she'd been able to beg extra food often, when the healthy but meagre food available to the girls had failed to satisfy her.

Zofia got up and fetched a cup from one of the cupboards and handed it to Millie with a smile. 'Help yourself,' she said, indicating the coffee machine. 'And come and join us if you really want to.'

'Oh, I do!' Millie said fervently, helping herself to a cup of coffee with generous amounts of cream and sugar. 'The family, apart from my friend Sooze, scare me to death. What are they like to work for? Is it okay here? And Zofia, do you do *all* the work in the house?'

'Oh, no,' Zofia reassured her. 'There's a cleaning company comes in twice a week. I have it fairly easy. We three, Tommy, Maria and I, are the live-in staff, but it's not a hard place, at all.'

'So, Tommy, do you spend all your time just driving around in that lovely Merc?' Millie said in a teasing way. 'And drinking coffee in between?'

'No, you see before you, Millie, the O'Leary chauffeur, gardener, handyman and anti-burglar device, all in one person,' announced Tommy Kelly with a grin.

'Oh, Tommy, how can you say such a thing!' Maria said in a shocked manner. 'When you know fine well there's a gardening company comes in regular, and most of the jobs a handyman might do get farmed out to local businesses!'

'Just joking, Maria! Our Maria takes life seriously, Millie. And so she has a right to do, being such a good cook. She deserves to take things whatever way she wants to,' said Tommy Kelly, giving Maria a big smile and a hug which immediately won back her approval. In fact, it was clear to Millie that Tommy was a favourite with both the women.

'So, do you all get plenty of time off, or what?' she asked, pretending a sympathetic interest.

'Oh, we do that, Millie,' Tommy answered, giving Millie the same smile.

'Aha! So you can take me out for a spin in the Merc sometime when it's not being used, then?' Millie responded, pretending to joke. But she had never been more serious. The two women laughed, and Zofia said, 'It would be as much as his job's worth to do that, Millie!'

But Tommy Kelly caught Millie's eye, smiled again, and winked. She knew that it wouldn't be hard to arrange the hoped for drive.

Just then she heard footsteps, and stood up. 'Well, it's been great to meet you guys and chat, but I expect I'd better report for duty now!' she laughed. 'How do I find this breakfast room you mentioned?'

'Back down the corridor the way you came, and turn left at the foot of the stairs. You'll see the door.' It was Zofia who spoke, and Millie said, 'Thanks!' again, and lifted her now empty coffee cup. 'I'll put this in the dishwasher for you, will I?' she asked.

Zofia took it from her hand. 'I'll do it,' she said. Millie smiled and gave a little wave as she made for the door and headed for the breakfast room.

There she found Sooze standing by the hot plates on the sideboard, choosing her food.

'Hi, Millie!' she said. 'Where did you get to? I called for you but you weren't in your room.'

'Oh, Sooze, I didn't want to be a pest!' Millie said. 'I thought you might not be awake, so I tried to find my own way down – but I got hopelessly lost. Then I bumped into Zofia, and she gave me directions.'

'Oh, I see,' Sooze said, her face clearing. 'Well, breakfast here is help yourself, usually. Come and see what you want. Then I'll take you out to see the garden and the tennis court.'

'Lovely!' said Millie enthusiastically.

Chapter Five

The sun was still beaming down when Sooze took Millie for a stroll round the gardens.

The roses were in full bloom, and their colour and scent lifted Millie into ecstasy. The rhododendrons lined the walks and flourished in purples and whites and palest pinks to darkest reds.

The tennis courts were at the farthest end of the spreading lawns and flower beds, and Millie was delighted to see the smooth, grassy spaces outlined in white paint to indicate the boundaries, and the nets spread across each court taut and ready.

'So, Sooze,' Millie said, 'tell me about these guys who you've invited to play this afternoon? Am I wrong,' she added slyly, ' or is there one of them you're specially interested in?'

Sooze blushed. 'Oh, Millie, how did you know?'

'Sooze, you're my friend, I'm interested in you. And I think I know you well enough by now to tell when something – or someone! – matters to you.'

'Oh, Millie, you've guessed right!' Sooze burst out. 'It's Josh Gillespie. His dad's a business friend of my dad – but that's not the point. Oh –' she sighed and blushed again – 'Oh, I don't mind telling you, Millie – I know you'll keep it to yourself. I've known Josh all my life, more or less, but it's just this last year or so that I've realised how much I fancy him. Oh, Millie, he's a real hunk! He has fair hair and blue eyes and he looks so strong. I'd die for him, Millie! There – I've told you!'

'And he loves you, too, doesn't he, Sooze?' Millie said softly. 'Oh, I can tell from how you look. This isn't a hopeless love sort of thing. You know he wants you, don't you?'

'Well – oh, Millie, yes, I think he does! But I haven't seen him since Christmas, so suppose he's changed? I don't know what I'd do if he has!'

'C'mon, Sooze, you don't really think he has!' encouraged Millie. 'Why should he? Sure, you're prettier than ever, girl! Loosen up! As soon as he sees you, he'll fall flat all over again!'

Sooze's face brightened up. 'Oh, Millie, you're such an encouragement. I'm so glad you're my friend.'

Then, it occurred to her that she should ask about Millie's own emotional prospects. 'So, Millie, I suppose you've noticed that Johnny's really mad about you. What do you think about him? Don't be shy! I've noticed you liking him!'

Millie had been listening with envy to Sooze's description of Josh Gillespie. A good looking guy with a rich father – who could beat it? By comparison, Johnny, rich or not, wasn't much of a catch. Still, he was probably as good as she could get – if she actually could get him, that was. It wouldn't do to let go of the bird in the hand for the sake of others in the bush whom she might not have much chance of grabbing.

So, trying to blush in her turn, she hung her head and murmured, 'Oh, Sooze, do you really think Johnny likes me? He's so clever and so good looking. I don't see how he could be interested in someone like me.'

'He's interested, all right,' Sooze said gaily. 'I've hardly ever seen him offer to play tennis before – it's not Johnny's style. And I bet you he'd have been happy to stay and play bridge last night if Mum hadn't chased him.'

Millie sighed happily, or tried to give that impression. 'I'm so glad you've lent me some shorts to wear, dear Sooze,' she said. 'Otherwise I'd have had to wear that awful tennis dress I wore at St Bernadette's. It was really kind of Sister Angelica to give it to me, since she never plays tennis herself now, but, Sooze, I've always felt so awful in it. A sort of Cinderella figure!'

'Well, you won't need to wear it today,' Sooze said, her heart touched again as she remembered the truly awful outfit Millie had worn for tennis at school. Long, drooping, much too big – the list of criticisms was endless. 'You'll be looking good in the shorts I gave you – not lent you! I'm sure Johnny will think so!'

And Josh and the other guys, Millie hoped.

'Hey, do you know what time it is?' Sooze suddenly exclaimed. 'We need to head back to the house for lunch. And by the time we've eaten, we'll need to get ready before our visitors land on us.'

She hustled Millie back to the house.

Lunch, with Johnny and Sam present, was light and pleasant.

'Let's go up and get ready, now, Millie,' urged Sooze, as soon as it was over. 'Will you be there, Sam?'

Chapter Five

'Sorry, darling,' drawled Sam O'Leary. 'I'm going to Catriona's for one of our bridge afternoons today. But I'm sure you'll enjoy yourselves without me.'

Millie was sure of that, too. She was relieved to know that Sam's eye wouldn't be on every move she made on Johnny.

Millie showered, and slipped into her new shorts and a scoop necked T-shirt which, being Sooze's, was slightly too big for her. At first she tried to hide this by tucking it into her waistband. Then she decided, instead, to pull it out and tie it under her breasts. Yes, it looked good that way.

This time, she went to knock on Sooze's door instead of venturing down by herself. Sooze wasn't quite ready, but she called out, 'Is that you, Millie? Come on in! I won't be a tick!'

Millie opened the door, and was immediately stricken with envy. Sooze was standing in the middle of the room, examining herself in the full length mirror, and tying up her hair with a blue ribbon. She was wearing a tennis dress which was clearly a designer model. As she twirled round to show it off to Millie, the very short skirt flew up to reveal the all-in-one panties attached to it. It was, of course, white, and cut to flatter Sooze's fuller figure.

'Oh, Sooze, you look lovely!' Millie exclaimed quickly. 'Josh will fall head over heels for you all over again when he sees it!'

'Do you really think so?' Sooze asked. 'Does it really look okay? I made Mum order it for me – she's pretty good about letting me have nice things.'

'It's amazing!' Millie assured her.

'Great. Well, we'd better go on down,' Sooze said.

She must be quite nervous, Millie realised, for she hadn't thought of saying anything about how well Millie looked. But Millie, although envious of Sooze's tennis dress, was quite satisfied with her own appearance. Certainly her legs beat Sooze's hollow, she knew.

Johnny was hanging around downstairs, obviously waiting for them. He was wearing tennis gear which looked as if he'd never had it on before. Millie remembered, with an inward giggle, that Sooze had said he didn't usually play.

They went out into the sunshine, but hung around at the front of the house so that they could see people arriving.

Liam and Moira Bannon, brother and sister, arrived first, dashing up to the door in a very flashy looking convertible Mini with its roof down, and running over to embrace Sooze straightaway. They looked very like each other. Liam was obviously older by a year or two, but both were light haired, thoroughly tanned, and a little smaller than average. They were bright and lively and overflowing with enthusiasm.

'Marvellous to see you back, Sooze!' they both exclaimed, one after the other, and Sooze laughed, hugged them each in turn, and introduced Millie. Then the three who knew each other well sat down on the terrace at the side of the house and began to chatter like mad, exchanging news and gossip, while Millie smiled, did her best to be friendly, and felt rather out of it. This was her opportunity to follow up with Johnny, of course, but it seemed rather a boring thing to do, when the others were so much more interesting. However.

'Johnny, I don't seem to have seen anything of you for ages,' she began with her best shy smile. 'I'm so glad you're playing today. I'll be relying on you to help me out – I'm not very good, as I told you. But I'm sure you're really expert. You're so good at everything.'

Johnny looked pleased. 'Except bridge, according to my mother!' he joked nervously.

'Oh, that was such a shame!' Millie sighed. 'I really expected that you would have played, and you could have kept me right. I didn't want to refuse your mother when she invited me to play, but you would have been much better than Sooze as a partner.'

'I hope you'll partner me today, Millie?' Johnny asked. And Millie, although she would rather have partnered anyone else, agreed with all the apparent enthusiasm she could muster. After all, Johnny was still a rich man's son, who could give her the lifestyle she really wanted.

Stevie Thompson, a lanky, sandy haired boy, full of life and vigour, arrived next, followed shortly by Katie Morrison, a tall, dark haired beauty, so much quieter than the rest that she seemed hardly to speak at all.

Still no sign of Josh Gillespie. Millie could tell that Sooze was starting to get upset, although she was concealing it well.

Chapter Six

The chatter continued, and Millie admired how well Sooze kept up her share of it, and how naturally she kept a pleasant smile on her face. Then, in the middle of the chatter, Sooze's phone announced a text message. She read it, and at once looked brighter and happier.

'Josh,' she announced. 'Running late. So what's new? Let's move on down to the tennis courts, guys. He'll know where to find us. I'll get Zofia to brings us along some cool drinks.'

She vanished indoors, and Millie guessed that as well as speaking to Zofia, she meant to text Josh back in private.

When she reappeared shortly, they moved on down to the courts and Sooze began to arrange the first matches. There were seven people so far, so two games of mixed doubles weren't possible until Josh arrived.

'Suppose Millie and Johnny play against Liam and Katie?' she suggested. 'And Stevie and Moira can have a single on the other court.'

'It would be better to have you against Moira, Sooze,' objected Stevie. 'A ladies' single, okay?'

'No, no, as the hostess I can't have one of my guests sitting down while I play!' laughed Sooze. 'I'll wait on the sidelines for the late comer, so I can give him a good telling off!'

So you can talk to him until one of the games is over, Millie reflected shrewdly. *And so you can play with him next time round.*

There were no further objections, and the games proceeded.

Millie was a good tennis player, by the standards of St Bernadette's. It didn't take her long to see that she was quite a lot better than either Liam Bannon or Katie Morrison, and better by a mile than Johnny. But she found the game tricky enough. Her aim was to win easily, while making it seem as if Johnny's skill had been the cause of this. She needed to make sure that her own skill wasn't too obvious.

With some difficulty, she succeeded in winning the first few games, leaving easy balls for Johnny to return, and making her own most skilful returns seem like flukes. When Johnny's service was, unusually, inside the lines, but giving an easy return for either Liam or Katie, she managed to smash the return beyond their opponents' reach, before turning to Johnny and congratulating him warmly on his wonderful serve. Her own service she managed to make clumsy, while not quite a fault – except occasionally, when she made her first service a glaring fault, and her second just within the lines.

'Oh, Johnny, what a fluke that was!' she would whisper to him as they changed sides. 'You're such an inspiration. I'm watching what you do, and trying to copy it.'

Johnny glowed with satisfaction. Millie wasn't sure that she was fooling Liam or Katie, but she didn't really care. All she needed to do was to fool Johnny.

At Love-Thirty in the final game of the set, Johnny's service, things were looking dicey. Johnny and Millie were leading five games to four. But Millie wasn't sure how long she could continue to keep covering Johnny's mistakes. If they could only win this game, all would be well. But with Johnny's service, there was little real hope. Johnny kept serving double faults, serving far too fast for his abilities in the hope of getting aces. But at last, in the third serve, he managed to get his second service inside the lines, and Liam was so surprised that he somehow missed it.

The next two serves were to Katie, and again the first was a fault. But the second service once more went safely inside the lines. Katie returned it easily, and Millie, throwing caution to the winds, caught it with a smashing return which whistled down the court between Liam and Katie, too fast for either of them to reach it.

'Oh, Johnny, what did I do? I should have let you take that!' Millie cried in a pretence of despair. 'Is it out? I'm sure it's out!'

'No way,' Liam assured her gloomily. 'Well in. Thirty all, now.'

'You've been serving so well, Johnny,' Millie whispered as they changed sides. 'I'm sure we'll win. Those last slow serves were great! If you keep serving slowly like that, they'll be lost, for sure.'

She hoped by this flattery to stop Johnny from trying to serve would be aces which turned into double faults. And Johnny, not understanding fully, but seeing that his slower service had worked twice now (at least it hadn't been outside the court) served slowly and carefully again, setting up an easy return for Liam, who sent it back way out of Johnny's reach to just inside the back line. Millie, making full use of her long agile legs, raced for it, got it, and smashed it back, aiming it this time at Katie's backhand. She had noted earlier that backhand was something Katie was particularly weak in.

'Forty-Thirty!' she exclaimed joyfully, as Katie failed to get her racquet to the flying ball. 'Johnny, you've really hit a winning streak with that slow service!' She hoped that he would be sensible enough to repeat his previous slow style. And sure enough, again Johnny's serve was well within the lines, a really easy return for Katie. Millie had only to catch Katie's not too skilful return and send it once more to her backhand. And so, Millie and Johnny had won their set.

'Johnny, you played so well!' she exclaimed admiringly. 'And do you know, your skill must have rubbed off on me. I think I made some good strokes there at the end – or do you think I did?'

'Sure, you were brilliant, Mil!' Liam said dryly. Clearly Millie's pretence of being a weak player, carried by Johnny's skill, hadn't fooled him in the least. But as long as Johnny believed it, Millie didn't care. And believe it he certainly did, his face covered in a huge beam.

'You're really learning, Millie!' he told her. 'Keep trying, and you'll soon be quite good.'

Millie laughed quietly to herself, turning her face away out of his sight.

'And now I'm going to make you sit down with a cool drink, Millie,' Johnny said, not mentioning his own extreme need for rest and refreshment. 'Come on!'

He led her over to the outdoor tables and chairs beside the court.

That strenuous last game had left Millie no time to notice that the long waited for Josh Gillespie had at last arrived. When they came off the court, Sooze was sitting talking to a tall, good looking guy with fair hair, a slim, muscular body, very blue eyes, and a dazzling smile. Sadly for Sooze, Stevie and Moira, who had finished their set before the mixed double was over, were talking to him too.

'Millie, congratulations!' Sooze said warmly. 'I want you to meet Josh. Josh, this is my friend Millie.'

'Hi,' drawled Josh, turning away almost at once. 'Sooze, I brought a friend, too. Where's he got to? Horse, come over here!'

Josh's friend, nicknamed Horse, was hovering bashfully on the edge of the group. He was a tall, thickset youngster, strong looking, and with a red, pleasantly ugly face which the kindest observer could only have described as friendly, open and honest. His expression, as he looked at Sooze, told Millie all she wanted to know about his feelings for her friend. He was clearly hopelessly in love with Sooze, who, however, saw him only as a nuisance.

'Let's sit down for a minute and have a cool drink, before we arrange the next sets,' suggested Sooze cheerfully. And she took care to sit next to Josh Gillespie.

Roundabout – *Gerry McCullough*

Chapter Seven

'Okay, guys,' Sooze said eventually, setting her glass of lemonade down on the white painted iron table beside her. 'Time for another couple of sets. After all, that's what we're here for, to play tennis, right? We have enough for two mixed doubles sets this time round. The odd man out can act as umpire. Maybe you, Horse?'

Horse, although he would much have preferred to play – his tennis was one of his many physical skills – nodded eagerly. Anything to please Sooze.

'Certainly, Sooze,' he gulped. 'If it helps, I'd be glad to.'

'So, Millie and Johnny against me and Josh, okay? And Liam and Katie against Stevie and Moira? Right, guys?'

Nobody objected. Millie thought that Stevie and Moira were glad not to have to play against each other, this time. Stevie had won their single, but neither had seemed all that happy about it, to Millie's eye. She rather thought that there was something between them.

She took her place with Johnny across the net from Sooze and Josh. The sun continued to beat down strongly, and Millie was glad of the cool lemonade, squeezed from fresh lemons, which she had drunk. She was determined to beat Josh Gillespie, an unpleasant guy, to her mind – after all, he had practically ignored her! – and to allow Johnny a further triumph.

She had been angry at Josh's attitude to her. He had hardly glanced at her, and as his blue eyes flickered briefly over her, she had been aware of an icy coldness in them. She'd be very happy to give him a beating, quite apart from continuing her work with Johnny.

This time, she reckoned, there was less need to pretend. She had convinced Johnny that his style and ability at tennis had won their first contest against Liam and Katie and that his serves should be slow to give them a chance of being accurate – if only he would remember that! And that she was improving because of his inspiration. She could let herself go a little more.

She knew from school that she was much better than Sooze. Whether Josh was any good or not remained to be seen.

His first serve told her that he was. Millie, drawing on all her skill, sprang round the court, covering Johnny's failure to get anywhere near Josh's fast serve, and sent it back to Sooze, the weaker player. Sooze failed to get to it. Millie noted the angry frown on Josh's face, and prepared hopefully to take Josh's next serve herself. Some people improved with anger, but most of them didn't. She intended to annoy Josh as much as possible by playing at the peak of her form.

The first service came hurtling down the court towards her. Millie, standing well up to the net, picked it up neatly and again sent it straight to Sooze. But this time she was frustrated by Josh, who crashed across the court, coming in front of Sooze in time to return the ball swiftly towards Johnny.

Millie darted across, got to the ball and again sent it straight to Sooze. The battle was on.

When Millie sent the ball back for the fifth time, she aimed it high, well beyond Josh's reach, towards the back of the court, and by extreme skill, or maybe luck, managed to land it just inside the line, and far from either Sooze or Josh.

'Out!' shouted Josh triumphantly.

'Er – no, I'm afraid not, Josh,' said Horse, in his role as umpire. 'The ball was well inside the line. Love fifteen.'

Josh scowled. He was clearly unused to losing his service game, and determined not to let that happen.

His next serve, to Johnny, was an ace. Even Millie, springing round the court with all her skill, was unable to reach it. But the next, to Millie, was less successful. Millie managed with some difficulty to return it, once again towards Sooze, and this time Josh, trying to get to it, bumped into Sooze and almost sent her flying.

It took Josh some time and effort to comfort Sooze and to apologise to her. Millie was surprised to see that he actually seemed concerned about her and about how she felt.

It was the end of the game. Sooze, with a painful, although not broken, shoulder, caused by Josh crashing into her, felt unable to play any longer.

Josh led her off the court, weeping, and Millie hurried round to add her own consolations, followed by Johnny – who was determined not to let Millie out of his sight, by now.

'I hate tennis!' wept the unhappy Sooze. 'It's far too rough when people are determined to win. What does it matter who wins?' She glared at Josh, who, to Millie's surprise, seemed quite upset. He was clearly more attached to Sooze than she had guessed.

'Sooze, I'm so sorry!' he blurted out. 'I wouldn't have had that happen for anything. Let's forget about tennis for now. Tell you what, let's have a rest, and then go out tonight for a night out in Belfast – you'd like that, wouldn't you?'

Sooze's face cleared instantly.

'Josh, that would be great!' she breathed, beaming happily. 'You and me, and Millie and Johnny, and any of the others who'd like to come! I'd love that!'

'Great! We'll start at the *Limelight*, and move on from there.'

Sooze smiled at him.

Josh lowered his voice. But if he had intended that Millie, who had been hovering anxiously over Sooze, and had then rushed up to the house to fetch some brandy and arnica for her friend, should not be able to hear him, he should have waited for longer.

'Do we have to have this Millie character?' he asked, frowning. 'She's nothing but a vulgar slut. Millie by name, and Millie by nature, as far as I can see. Look at the way she has her T-shirt tied up to show her belly.'

'What on earth do you mean?' Sooze asked with a puzzled expression.

'Don't you know that in Belfast they call the sluts Millies?' Josh said.

Millie arrived back just in time to hear this. Ignoring it, pretending not to have heard, she began to fuss round Sooze, making her drink the brandy, and pulling down her dress from her shoulder in order to rub arnica into the hurt part.

'Oh, Sooze, I do hope you aren't hurt too badly!' she exclaimed.

Sooze, as always when Millie pulled out the sympathetic stop, was deeply touched. 'Oh, dear Millie, what would I do without you?' she sighed. 'Will you and Johnny come to the *Limelight* with me and Josh tonight? And Horse, too, of course,' she added kindly, seeing Josh's friend also hovering, an expression of extreme anxiety on his pleasant, ugly features.

'I'd love to, Sooze!' he blurted out, a beam covering his broad face.

'And any other of you guys who can come?' Sooze called.

But the others, for different reasons, were already booked up for that night.

Sooze didn't mind. As long as Josh was coming, she was happy.

'So, Horse and I will pick up you and Johnny – and Millie –' he added distastefully, 'around half eight or nine, okay? The music won't be starting until ten, of course.'

'Ten?' Sooze asked. After school hours, when lights were out in the dormitories at eleven, that seemed very late to start the evening. It did to Millie, too, but she remembered nights in her father's room when many of the guests – actors or singers for the most part, with a few painters – had reeled in after eleven or even midnight, and none of the others had been much earlier.

She wasn't all that happy at being stuck with Johnny for the evening. A spin with the gorgeous Tommy Kelly would have been so much nicer, she thought wistfully. But, on the other hand, what sort of lifestyle would she have with Tommy, even if things got serious? Whereas, with Johnny – !

She shrugged her shoulders, and looked on the bright side. This was a real opportunity to take things further with Johnny. She wondered if there would be a karaoke or an open mike? If so, Millie was determined to make the most of it. She knew she had a glorious voice – enough people had told her so, comparing her to her famous mother. She could sing something that would finally do the trick with Johnny.

A few more sets were played, and then people began gradually to drift off, with much hugging among the girls and, 'Great to see you back, Sooze,' from the boys. Some of them even remembered to say, 'Nice to meet you – er – um – Millie,' just before they left.

Last of all, Josh hugged Sooze enthusiastically, looked coolly at Millie, giving her a reluctant nod, and went, taking his friend Horse with him before Horse had a chance to do more than stammer out, 'See you later, girls!'

'Time they went!' Johnny muttered.

'I think I'll lie down for a while if we're having a late night,' Sooze announced. 'How about you, Mil?'

Millie, seeing that Johnny was looking at her hopefully, and obviously planning to get her to himself for a while before dinner, hastily agreed. But, in fact, she had other ideas. Would Tommy Kelly be free right now? He would hardly be driving John O'Leary anywhere a couple of hours before dinner? More likely washing and polishing the car after picking him up from work.

Chapter Eight

Millie headed upstairs with Sooze, but once she was sure her friend was safely in her room, came out again, still wearing her tennis gear, which she knew looked well on her, and slipped down the backstairs and round to the garage at the back of the house.

As she approached it, she could hear someone whistling sweetly.

Yes, sure, there he was, polishing away at the Mercedes. Millie tiptoed up, and put her hands over his eyes. 'Hi, Tommy!' she said softly into his ear.

Tommy whipped round in a flash and grabbed her in his arms. 'Hi, lovely!' he said, and before Millie was sure how she wanted to react, his lips were on hers, kissing her fervently. Then she was sure, and she kissed him back equally hard.

'Wow!' she said, as she surfaced for air.

'That's what you get for sneaking up on a guy,' Tommy said, his lips still close to her face.

'I must do it more often,' Millie murmured in reply. Then she drew back, and smiled cheekily up at him.

'How about that drive in the Merc, Tommy?' she asked.

'Right now?' Tommy sounded dubious. 'The thing is, Millie, I have to go out to collect yer man in a few more minutes. He's working later than usual at the office. By the time we get back, it'll be nearly dinner time, and if you missed it there'd be trouble, I reckon. Maybe later, after dinner, if you slip out?'

'No good. I have to go out with Sooze to the *Limelight* tonight. No chance of you turning up there, I suppose?' She gave him her best smile.

'Well, who knows,' Tommy said, grinning. 'Will you be there for long or will you be moving on?'

'Dunno.' Millie's face fell.

'Tell you what, if I'm not there by the time you move, ring me and tell me where you are, okay?'

Millie's face cleared. 'Okay!' She produced her phone. 'Give me your number – or better still I'll give you mine, and if you don't see me there, then you ring me! If you think it's worth it, that is?' she added teasingly.

'Oh, it might be. Let's see.' And at that, he took her in his arms again and began kissing her where he had left off.

Millie wriggled free eventually, and they exchanged numbers. 'Aren't you supposed to be away by now, Tommy?' she asked demurely.

'Yeah, you're not kidding!' Tommy leapt into the car, started up, and shot out of the garage, blowing Millie a kiss as he went. 'See you later, gorgeous!' he called back to her.

Millie, giggling happily, went back to her room to change out of her tennis kit and into something suitable both for family dinner and for a night out on the town. A very short green skirt, previously belonging to Sooze, and a matching glittery top, seemed appropriate for the *Limelight*, but she wasn't sure if it would do for dinner. However, she decided, with a shrug, to risk it, and was glad to see Sooze in a similar rig out when she knocked on her door presently.

Sooze was wearing an equally short skirt in her favourite blue, with a cream top covered in flowers and butterflies. Millie was pleased to notice once again that Sooze's legs, as revealed by the skirt, weren't a patch on hers.

She could see Johnny noticing that too, his eyes goggling as they fixed themselves on her thighs when she and Sooze came into the room. She felt she had made the right decision. It seemed her plans for a future with Johnny had every chance of working out.

Josh picked the three of them up at nine o'clock promptly, rather to Millie's surprise, for she had written him off as someone who wouldn't much care about keeping people waiting. But apparently he was out to impress Sooze's parents. When he came into the room, John O'Leary said approvingly, 'Hmm. Glad to see you're on time, Josh. Not like most people your age.'

Millie supposed that he wanted to keep in O'Leary's good books, with an eye to getting his financial blessing for Sooze. He must be serious about her, then – or about her prospective money.

Josh was driving a dashing Seat Ibiza, which was fine for himself and Sooze in the front, but turned out to be rather a squash for Millie and Johnny in the back with Horse, especially as Johnny's bulk took up most of the available room and Horse's took the rest. Millie ended up sitting unwillingly on Johnny's lap.

There was also a problem with parking. In front of the *Limelight* on Ormeau Avenue was impossible, but Josh managed to find a place a couple of streets away, helped by the small size of his car. He hurried Sooze through the dark streets, leaving Millie and Johnny, with Horse, to find their own way, until they came out into the well lit main road again.

The *Limelight* was packed, making it hard enough to find a table. Horse, who turned out to be good at that sort of thing, managed it eventually, and Josh went to buy the first round. Millie noticed that Johnny was drinking whiskey. She knew he had already had at least a couple before they left. It would be a pity if he passed out. She giggled at the thought of having to help him back to the car. Josh would have his work cut out.

She looked around cautiously for Tommy Kelly, but saw no sign of him so far.

She sipped her gin and tonic, planning on being careful not to overdo it herself. But a second round, purchased by Johnny, left her feeling a little reckless.

The band was setting up, and presently they began to play. Millie relaxed and began to enjoy herself. Johnny was mumbling in her ear, and Josh and Sooze seemed occupied with each other. Horse, to Millie, was of no importance, although she noticed his eyes fixed pathetically on Sooze.

She leaned back in her chair. The music was good enough to entertain her, and Johnny needed only the odd encouraging smile. A good night so far. It was Horse's round next, and Millie accepted a third Gin & Tonic from him. She was starting to float, but in a pleasant sort of way.

The band were announcing a guest singer.

'Hey, guys, guess who we have for you tonight!' The lead singer, a great looking boy with huge brown eyes and longish dark hair left loose and flying round his face, so that he was constantly shaking it back during his performance, was saying enthusiastically, 'You'll all remember this guy – you'll know his music, if you don't know him! Stevie Bones, who's going to sing you his greatest hit – recorded by the late great Cait Brennan! *You're the Only One.*'

'Wow!' Millie breathed. But she spoke only to herself. 'Cait Brennan. My mother.'

She knew the guest artist, too – Stevie Bones, aka Stevie Kilmartin, a good friend of her father's whom she had met often in her Dad's rooms when she lived there with him. Stevie, sandy haired with a cheeky, freckled face, was younger than her dad, although still a good bit older than Millie herself.

Stevie was starting to sing. His voice, although it was good enough, wasn't his strongest feature. But as a songwriter he was the best. Tears started to Millie's eyes as she listened to his rendering of her mother's greatest hit. He was good.

Sooze was speaking. 'My turn to buy a round, guys. Millie, the same again or what?'

'Whoa, whoa, Sweetie! You're buying no drinks tonight! This is on me and Horse – and Johnny, I suppose?' He turned inquiringly to Johnny, who nodded four times in rapid succession.

Millie, in the midst of her absorption in Stevie's singing, was conscious of relief. Spending money on a round would not have helped her budget.

The new drinks arrived, and Millie knocked hers back. She was beginning to soar happily above the clouds of earth.

The song came to an end. Millie jumped up clapping enthusiastically. 'Amazing, Stevie!' she called out in ringing tones. Stevie Bones heard her over the applause.

'Millie! Millie Brennan! Is it yourself, darlin'? Come on up here, girl!'

And as Millie recklessly made her way forward, she heard Stevie announcing into his still live mike, 'People, here's an even greater treat for you. This is Cait Brennan's daughter Millie, who has her mother's lovely voice in spades! I'm going to try to persuade her to sing for us, now. Come on up, Millie!'

Millie climbed gracefully onto the stage, wondering what she should sing. Cait had no more originals like that one of Stevie's but she had recorded some covers and been very successful with those, too. Millie wondered if she could remember the words of one. She had sung most of them for her Dad's guests, certainly. It shouldn't be too hard.

'What should she sing?' Stevie asked the audience, most of whom were a bit too young to remember Cait Brennan. But clearly there were some enthusiastic fans among the crowd. As Millie knew, a singer who died young from a drug overdose often became an icon, and she was aware that Cait had done this, in a minor way. A voice called from the back, 'Eternal Flame!' The rest of the crowd roared eager assent, and Stevie bowed to Millie and handed her the mike. 'Go for it, darling!' he said loudly, and then whispered to Millie, 'You'll be great!'

Millie certainly hoped so. But the drinks had given her confidence, and she began to sing, at first softly, and then with growing volume.

> *... Do you feel my heart beating*
> *Do you understand?*

Do you feel the same?
Am I only dreaming
Or is this burning an eternal flame?

Millie grew in confidence. The audience was still, hardly breathing as they listened to a magnificent voice which they had thought was gone forever.

As she reached the chorus again, Millie sought for and found Johnny's eyes, fixed on her. She deliberately directed her words towards him. His face lit up, and he looked at her with an intensity which made him seem suddenly more attractive and less of a fool.

Millie finished, received the thunderous applause modestly, and refused shouts of 'Encore!' with a shake of the head. 'You've come to hear these guys, not me,' she said with a smile. 'So I'm going to hand back to them now.'

She handed the mike back to the lead singer, mouthed her thanks to Stevie and the band, and turned to jump down from the platform. Stevie reached out a hand to help her.

'Give me your number, Mil. I'd like to keep in touch. Mind you, I'll be starting up in Derry in a pub called *The City Walls* soon.'

Millie gave him her mobile number, then hastily got herself back to her seat. Sitting down, she realised that Johnny was swaying dangerously. He leaned towards her and began to mumble. 'My little darlin' Millie!' she made out. Then, 'Eternal! 'Ternal! Burning, burning, wha' comes next?' And other such mutters.

He was obviously quite far gone. She wasn't sure she would get much further with him tonight. But maybe she had got far enough – if he remembered anything in the morning.

Meanwhile, she was getting worried about him. She couldn't cope on her own if he was going to collapse. She looked round helplessly. Josh and Sooze were in a world of their own. Horse would probably be useless. She looked round some more. Then her eye caught Tommy Kelly, leaning against the bar by the door. She didn't know if he had just come in, or if he had been there in time to hear her singing. She realised that she would quite like to know, and to hear what he had thought of her.

Tommy Kelly saw her looking at him, and once more smiled his devastating, sexy smile. Millie felt relief flood through her. If it came to that, she thought Tommy would be willing to help her by taking Johnny home in whatever car he had come by. She turned back to look at Johnny who was by now leaning against her shoulder. He felt uncomfortably heavy. Millie, in sudden anger, tried to push him off. She succeeded. Johnny swayed back into his own seat. Then he gave a gulp, was sick all over the table top, and collapsed forward into the mess.

Chapter Nine

Millie sprang back from the table in horror. Her movements alerted the others to what had happened, and they in turn got themselves away from the mess as quickly as possible.

'Oh, Johnny!' wailed Sooze. 'What are you doing? How are we going to get you home?'

'I'll help you, Sooze!' Horse said eagerly. 'I'll ring for a taxi.'

'No need for that,' said a voice in Millie's ear. It was Tommy Kelly. 'I have the Merc with me. I'll bring it round, if you guys can get him to the front door.'

'No problem,' Horse said thankfully.

'Thank you, Kelly,' Sooze added.

Millie felt annoyed. Why did Sooze persist in calling this man Kelly, as if she was an English aristocrat talking to a servant, instead of giving him his first name?

'You sound like someone out of PG Wodehouse, Sooze,' she said coldly. 'His name's Tommy.'

Sooze's mouth dropped open. Millie had never spoken to her like that before.

'Tommy, I'll come with you to help at the other end,' she went on, turning eagerly to Tommy Kelly.

'That would be good, Millie.' Tommy smiled at her.

Meanwhile, the management of the *Limelight* had not missed what was going on. Several of the younger bar staff had arrived in a hurry at the table, and were doing their best to clear up Johnny's vomit. It seemed there was less of it than Millie had at first thought.

Josh, who had previously kept well back, doing nothing to help, now decided he needed to show Sooze some concern. He and Horse between them hoisted Johnny out of his seat. Johnny was not really aware of what was happening, but he mumbled to himself as they tried their best to wipe him down with cloths provided by the bar staff.

Tommy Kelly had already left to fetch the car from its parking slot, and Millie and Sooze watched uneasily as Josh and Horse man-handled Johnny through the bar to the outside door. Tommy had wisely spread a sheet of polythene over the back seats, taking it from the boot where it was kept for covering the car if it had to be parked outside somewhere in cold weather.

'Will you really go with him, Millie dear?' asked Sooze. She seemed to have got over Millie's snappy remarks, and knew that she needed Millie's help if she was to avoid a gigantic row with her father, probably leading to him forbidding her to go into Belfast at night again.

'No problem, Sooze!' Millie responded. The two girls followed the unhappy procession to the door. By the time they made it there, the car had already drawn up ready for them. Between them they got the back door open and pushed and pulled Johnny inside. Millie slipped in beside Tommy in the front, and waved to the remaining three as they stood at the doorway, watching the car driving off. She wondered if they would have the nerve to go back in, or if they'd move on to some other nightspot.

'This is great of you, Tommy,' Millie said. 'I just hope the car doesn't get too messed up. I suppose if it does Sooze and Johnny will expect you to clean it before their Dad sees it?'

'I suppose so, Millie,' Tommy shrugged. 'After all, that's what I get paid for.'

'But you're not on duty now, and they've ruined your night.'

Tommy gave her a sideways glance. 'I wouldn't say that, beautiful.'

Millie smiled demurely. 'I'm sure some sort of reward could be arranged. Tell me something, Tommy, did you hear me singing?'

'Sure did, lovely. Great voice. Pity you were encouraging that eedjit Johnny, though.'

'Oh.' Millie felt flattened. 'I wasn't, really,' she said presently. 'Just – '

'Just, he's a rich man's son, right, Millie?'

'Oh, okay. I have to look out for myself, Tommy. You should know about that.'

'Sure, I understand, Millie. Poor little poor girl. Gotta take your chances.'

They were both silent.

The car purred on until at last they reached the O'Leary property.

'I'll drive to the garage, Millie,' Tommy Kelly said. 'You get out there. I'll get this guy upstairs to his room, stripped and into bed. His messy clothes will be his own problem in the morning.'

'I'm coming to help you, Tommy,' Millie said firmly.

The car stopped at the garage, and Tommy, with Millie's help, got the still comatose Johnny out from the back seat. He pulled out the sheet of polythene, rolled it into a ball, and chucked it into a corner, and squirted air freshener into the car, back and front.

'I'll dispose of that some other time,' he said. 'It seems to have done its job – the car seats are clean.'

Then he opened the garage's internal door, which led into the back of the house, and they hauled Johnny through it and up the stairs.

Millie admired Tommy's forethought. By going this way, he avoided the likelihood of John O'Leary seeing them.

'You've done this before, haven't you, Tommy?' she panted as they trudged up the stairs.

'Once or twice,' Tommy grinned. 'And for yer man, too.'

'John O'Leary?' Millie asked in surprise.

'Oh, yeah. Times when he didn't want his wife to know he'd been out boozing. They have separate rooms, you know,' he added, seeing Millie's look of surprise.

They reached Johnny's bedroom, and here Tommy took control and insisted that there was no need for Millie to help him undress Johnny. 'Wait out here,' he said. 'I won't be long. Then we'll go for that spin, right?'

'Right,' Millie agreed happily.

In a short time he rejoined her, and took her arm to lead her back downstairs and through the internal door to the garage. Once through the door, and with it safely shut behind them, he took her in his arms again. And kissed her thoroughly. Millie felt her legs tremble.

'Better get into the car,' she whispered when she could get her breath back. 'If you don't want me to collapse right here, that is.'

'Much more comfortable in the car,' Tommy Kelly said, and without more ado took her round to the passenger side of the Merc and opened the door for her. Millie got in, with an uneasy feeling of bridges being burnt. *How silly is this?* she wondered. But she had no intention of stopping now.

Tommy drove them to a turn off about five miles distant. It was little more than a lane, and ended up in a grove of thickly leaved trees which sheltered it in all directions. He pulled to a halt at one side of the lane onto a grassy verge, put his arms round Millie, and drew her to him. Millie yielded willingly.

Presently Tommy drew back and said, 'Let's get into the back – it'll be more comfortable, darlin'.'

'Okay,' Millie agreed. A certain amount of caution was creeping over her.

Tommy sprang out of the car, went round to the boot, and pulled out a thick rug and a couple of cushions. Opening the back door, he arranged them carefully over the seats.

'Come on, beautiful! Time to move!'

Millie opened the front passenger door and got out. She stood at the open back door for a moment inspecting Tommy's arrangements.

'Something tells me you've done this before, too, Mr Kelly,' she said.

'Once or twice,' smiled Tommy Kelly, parodying his words earlier. 'And for Her Nibs, too.'

Millie was slightly shocked. 'You can't mean Sooze's mum? Sam O'Leary?'

'Oh, yes. Definitely a keen lady. But you beat them all to flinders, Millie Brennan!'

Millie smiled and eased herself into the car. She was relieved to note that there was no lingering smell of sickness. That would definitely have been off putting. A moment later Tommy had climbed in after her and had started kissing her again.

The kisses grew fiercer and more passionate. Somehow or other, Millie found herself lying back against the cushions, with Tommy lying on top of her. His hands were moving all over her, and Millie couldn't help enjoying the sensation. But it was no part of her life plan to lose her virginity to a chauffeur, however bright, attractive and sexy. It would soon be time to stop him.

Chapter Ten

Time passed. Millie, enjoying herself and reluctant to stop, finally managed to say, 'Better call a halt now, Tommy. I've gone as far as I intend to.'

'Ah, now, Millie. Sure, you know you want to,' murmured Tommy softly into her hair. 'Come on, Babe, lie back and enjoy it.'

That reminded Millie of an old joke, and she giggled and tried to sit up. But Tommy's weight was hard upon her, and she found it too difficult.

'Tommy, let me up!' she demanded. 'Time to stop!'

But Tommy showed no signs of moving.

'Tommy, stop it!' Millie began to shove him hard.

'Aw, don't, darlin'. Relax,' Tommy said, continuing to nuzzle her ear.

'I've no intention of losing my virginity to a chauffeur in the back seat of a car, Tommy Kelly,' Millie said. 'Gentlemen always get off when they're pushed!' she added severely, and Tommy Kelly found he couldn't stop laughing.

'Sure, what makes you think I'm a gentleman?' Tommy asked her. But he was sitting back by now, smiling. 'All right, Millie. We'll call a halt for now, if that's what you really want,' he said. 'But there'll be other times, girl.'

'Maybe,' Millie said. But she said it to herself. As Tommy rolled off, she managed at last to sit up, and to scramble out of the car into the front. She leaned against Tommy's arm happily as he drove them slowly home.

Time to get out of the car, after one last enjoyable kiss. 'Bye, Tommy,' Millie said at last, climbing out. 'Don't think it hasn't been good.'

She pulled her top back into order and found her way to the inside door. Then she headed back to her room, the sound of Tommy's softly mocking laughter still in her ears.

She was about to enter the passage where her room and Sooze's were when she heard footsteps, and Sam O'Leary came round the corner, on her own way to bed, it seemed. Millie, acutely aware of her crumpled clothes, untidy hair and smeared lipstick, tried to avoid her, but it was no good.

'Good heavens, Millie, are you still out of your bed at this hour? I'm late myself – I got up to fetch some aspirin for my head. I certainly didn't expect to see you out and about still. I hope Sooze isn't still up?'

'Oh, no, Sam, Sooze went to bed ages ago. I found I couldn't sleep – I went for a wander about, to see if that would help,' Millie lied glibly. Then she saw Sam O'Leary looking at her clothes and realised that the lie had been a stupid one.

'You were trying to get to sleep, were you?' Sam asked coldly. 'Probably you would have found it easier if you had changed out of your clothes.'

She looked at Millie for another moment. 'I hope you don't think I haven't noticed you trying to get off with my son,' she said. 'You're mad if you think for a moment that Johnny would marry a slut like you. Just look at yourself!'

Millie became conscious again of her dishevelled appearance, out of her bedroom in the middle of the night with smeared lipstick and disarranged clothes. No wonder Sam was saying these things. She could think of nothing useful to answer. Sam glared at her for a minute longer, then said, 'Goodnight, Millie,' in frozen tones, and turned away.

Millie escaped thankfully into her room.

She showered quickly and tumbled into bed. It had been quite a day, she reflected. She only hoped she hadn't done for herself with Sam O'Leary, just when things were moving on so well with Johnny. She had been a fool to get into the back of the car with Tommy Kelly. But at least she'd managed to stop before going too far. That, she knew, would have been disastrous.

Suppose she'd got pregnant! Tommy had shown no signs of meaning to use any protection. Perhaps he assumed that she was on the pill. But so far Millie had had no opportunity to see about anything like that, coming as she had straight from St Bernadette's to the O'Learys' house. It would have been goodbye to any chance of getting Johnny to marry her. In spite of Sam O'Leary's comments, Millie still believed she was in with a good chance there.

She snuggled down under the duvet and yawned. In spite of the memories of the day which were still going round in her head, she was very ready to sleep. The last thoughts in her head were of Tommy Kelly's kisses. What a pity he was just a chauffeur, she thought drowsily. If only he had been the rich man's son, instead of Johnny. But Millie had learnt in her eighteen, nearly nineteen, years that life was never as easy as that. Stretching out her hand to turn out the bedside lamp, she drifted away into dreams.

Roundabout – *Gerry McCullough*

Chapter Eleven

There was no sign of Johnny at breakfast, not entirely to Millie's surprise. He must have the head to end all heads this morning. Sooze also put in a very late appearance, coming into the breakfast room only as Millie was about to rise from the table, yawning and looking rather shame faced.

'Oh, Millie, I didn't really thank you for being so helpful with Johnny last night,' she said, drifting over to the table and pouring herself some strong black coffee from the pot. 'Ugh! This coffee is lukewarm. I'll ask Zofia to get more. Zofia!' she yelled, going over to the door, then putting her hand to her head, she came over to the table and sat down again.

Millie was starting to say something deprecating when Zofia came in, not looking best pleased at being called at a time when breakfast should have been over. However she took the coffee pot and disappeared towards the kitchen.

'Did you get home OK, Mil?' Sooze asked, not, however, seeming all that interested.

'Oh, no problem!' Millie assured her. 'Tommy Kelly did everything necessary, actually.' (Well, almost everything, she giggled to herself, keeping her face turned away from Sooze to hide her amusement, as the double meaning of her words flashed through her head.) 'I left it to him to get Johnny up to bed.'

'Good,' Sooze said vaguely. 'Well, after all, it is his job.'

Millie was annoyed. It had been Tommy's night off, after all. But she thought it wiser to say nothing. She would need to keep Sooze's friendship and support, especially now Sooze's mother seemed to have turned against Millie.

'I thought we might have a restful morning, Millie,' Sooze went on. 'Would you like to take a nice book into the garden? I'm planning to have a long, relaxing bath. Then later we can see what we'd like to do.'

'Did you enjoy the rest of your evening with Josh?' Millie asked, trying to project a friendly interest rather than nosiness.

'Oh, yes!' Sooze breathed rapturously. 'Oh, Millie, isn't he a dream?'

Millie smiled, not wanting to say too much. 'Horse is nice, too,' she ventured.

'Horse!' Sooze looked annoyed. 'Just because he's been friends with Josh since school, he thinks it's okay for him to hang round all the time!' she burst out. 'It took us forever to shake him off, last night. Never mind – ' she giggled much as Millie had done a moment ago. 'We managed it in the end. Josh sent him for another round, and we slipped out while he was at the bar, and went on to *The Kitchen* pub. I wish I'd seen his face when he came back and found us gone.'

Millie was surprised. If she had cared more about Horse, she would have been angry with Sooze for her cruelty. However, Horse meant nothing but a nuisance in Millie's own life, so she didn't actually care. Just, it didn't seem like the usually soft hearted Sooze. She must have been really desperate to have Josh to herself, to behave like that.

'So, I'll go out into the garden, then,' she said peaceably.

'There are some lovely sheltered nooks with seats,' Sooze said. 'You should try the rose garden. Have you got anything to read? The library, next door along from here, has lots of choice.'

'Thanks,' Millie said. She wandered into the library, leaving Sooze to the fresh coffee which Zofia had now produced, and presently found the latest Jack Reacher mystery. Then she made her way to the rose garden.

The book was gripping, like all Lee Child's, but nevertheless Millie found her eyes closing before long. She'd been up late, and hadn't slept all that long. She came up to the surface again with a start much later, and saw from her watch that she'd slept for at least two hours. It must be nearly lunch time. Then she realised what it was that had woken her up.

'Oh, there you are, Millie,' said a voice which she automatically knew she disliked. It took her a moment to take it in that it was the voice of Sam O'Leary. Millie sat up straighter, her grasp on her book still firm.

'Hi, Sam,' she said. After all, the woman had told her to call her that.

'I've been looking for you, Millie,' said Sam in a would be pleasant manner.

'I've been resting in your beautiful garden,' Millie said politely. 'Sooze suggested that I come out here while she had a relaxing bath.'

'Yes, she had the bath some time ago. And since then she's been talking to Josh Gillepsie on her phone. Josh is a lovely guy. His parents are great friends of ours. We're expecting that Sooze and Josh will announce their engagement soon.'

'Yes, so am I,' Millie agreed politely. 'It's obvious how they feel about each other.'

Sam frowned. 'We have plans for Johnny, too. The daughter of another of our friends will be coming home from finishing school in Switzerland soon. Johnny has always admired her, and as for her, she's been crazy about him since they were no age.'

'That's nice,' said Millie deferentially.

'So you see, Millie,' Sam went on, abandoning all civility, 'you haven't got a chance, really. You should give up now.'

'I'm not sure what you mean, Sam,' Millie said.

Sam O'Leary suddenly lost control. 'I mean, you horrible slut, that you should stop chasing Johnny, and believe that there's no chance on God's earth that he'll ever marry you! He knows better! He knows that he's dependant on his father's money and that he'll never get any of it to finance a marriage to somebody like you!'

Millie drew herself up. 'You don't know anything about it, Sam!' she hissed. 'If Johnny wants me, I don't see how you can stop him from marrying me!'

'By refusing to give him any money, that's how. I don't see you marrying him if he's as poor as he would be then. You don't want to marry a poor man, do you, Millie?'

Millie halted in her tracks. Sam, curse her, was absolutely right. Johnny's only attraction for Millie was his father's money. If that was cut off, there was no way she would marry him.

'What's more,' added Sam, 'you'll be leaving here in a day or so. We agreed that Sooze could invite her school friend for a couple of days until she got herself settled – but if we'd known she meant to bring some-one like you, there's no way we'd have allowed it. When you've left, Johnny will forget you at once.'

She paused vindictively. 'Especially since he'll be in Dublin. He's packing now to drive down there to take up a senior position in the Dublin office of one of his father's friends. He's known for some time that that was what was planned for him. I spoke to John about it, and he agreed to speak to his friend and bring it forward to today. He'll leave immediately after lunch. If you can work out anything between now and then, I'll congratulate you, Miss Brennan!'

Millie hoped her face didn't reflect her anger and disappointment.

She knew that no matter what Johnny felt about her, he wasn't going to give up his future in his father's business for her. The most she could hope for was a promise from him to marry her at some point in the distant future when he had become independent. It wasn't what Millie wanted. She couldn't afford to hang about waiting, with no money except what she might be able to earn. She wouldn't let herself be tied down to something like that – even if she could persuade Johnny into it.

'What's more,' Sam went on triumphantly, well aware of Millie's feelings even though she hadn't spoken, 'as I've already said, you'll be out of here as soon as I can organise it. So you'd better go and pack – you'll just have time before lunch.'

'Just a minute.' Millie spoke coolly. 'I don't have a job or a place to go to. And I don't have much in the way of savings. In fact, practically nothing.'

'That's too bad,' said Sam, uncaringly.

'So, if you want me to leave without kicking up a fuss with Johnny – which I think you know very well I could do – you'll have to get me a decent job, and somewhere to stay, okay?'

'And why should I do that?' Sam snapped.

Millie pounced on the opening. 'Because, if you don't, I'm afraid I'll have to tell your husband, the great John O'Leary, that you've been sleeping with his chauffeur, the sexy Tommy Kelly. How about that, then, Sam?'

She watched Sam's face fall. Dismay showed in her eyes, in the droop of her mouth, in the fear she couldn't conceal.

It was a walkover.

'I'll see,' was all Sam said. Then she turned on her heel and stalked out of the rose garden. Millie couldn't help laughing.

Chapter Twelve

Millie went in to lunch feeling helpless. At least she had extorted the promise of a job and a place to stay from Sam O'Leary. But what would it be like? Oh well, it would have to do until she found something better.

Sooze was the only other person present at the lunch table. Sitting down opposite her, Millie asked, 'Where're the others, Sooze?'

'Well, Dad's at work, of course. Mum's in her room, nursing a headache. As for Johnny! All I know is that he's been bundled off to Dublin to work at some job down there. In one of Dad's offices, I suppose. He was driving, and I suppose he's left by now.'

Millie swallowed. She had expected to at least see Johnny before he left, and possibly arrange something for the future. A secret engagement, perhaps. Clearly Sam O'Leary had been taking no chances.

Millie said nothing. Presently, Sooze looked up from the melon which she'd been cutting industriously, and spoke. 'Mum says you've been offered a job in Derry, Millie. Are you going to accept it? I didn't even know you'd applied.'

'You know I need a job of some sort, Sooze, and the sooner the better. Yes, I'm taking it.'

'You must keep in touch,' Sooze said vaguely. 'Text me often. Maybe we could get together sometimes – I could drive up.'

'That would be lovely, Sooze!' Millie said, contriving to put as much warmth as possible into her voice. 'I'm afraid I'll be lonely there. I won't know anyone.'

'Mum said you should come and talk to her about it when you've finished lunch,' Sooze added. 'She said I could drive you to Belfast to get the train when you've finished packing.'

Sam O'Leary was lying down when Millie knocked on her door presently. 'Come in!' she called. 'Oh, it's you, Millie.'

Millie came in and stood beside the bed, looking at Sam resentfully. How dare this spoilt, rich woman, who wasn't even faithful to her husband, try to ruin Millie's life?

She waited for Sam to speak.

'I phoned my husband about a job for you,' Sam said at last. 'He's been looking into the possibilities. His business associate, Fergus Ryan, has a vacancy in his Derry office which he's willing to offer you on John's and my recommendation. Just basic office work. Filing, answering the phone, and so on. There's a possibility of promotion if you do well enough.'

'Okay,' Millie said. 'I don't know anyone in Derry, and haven't a clue how to find my way around it. Where am I going to stay? It needs to be somewhere I can afford, you realise.'

'Yes, I know that. Fergus Ryan's secretary shares a house with two other girls. One of them has left recently. You can take over the vacant room in the meantime.'

'That sounds all right,' Millie agreed. 'I'll need the address.'

'I have it here,' Sam told her. She sat up and picked up a notebook from the table beside her bed. Tearing off the top sheet she handed it to Millie. 'If you wait at the station Fergus's secretary will meet you there at five thirty or so. If your train gets there early, you can get yourself a cup of coffee or something – I suppose you can manage that without my help.'

'Just about,' said Millie, returning sarcasm with sarcasm. 'Her name would be useful.'

'Janice Hall.'

Sam seemed to have finished what she intended to say. Millie waited for a moment, but no goodbye or good wishes were forthcoming. She left the room, closing the door softly behind her, resisting the urge to slam it.

It didn't take her long to pack. The pretty things Sooze had given her made up most of her luggage. Slipping quietly along the corridor to Sooze's room, she found it empty, and took the opportunity to acquire a few more things which she was sure Sooze, with her crammed wardrobe, would never miss. Some dresses more suited to an office, she hoped, some pretty underwear and a handbag with a shoulder strap from a drawer crammed with bags in all shapes, sizes and colours. She got safely back to her own room and added these new things to her holdall, then carried it downstairs. Sooze was still sitting over her lunch, busily texting someone. Obviously the revolting Josh, Millie thought.

'I'm ready when you are, Sooze!' she said brightly. 'No need to say goodbye to anyone else. I'll just slip away quietly.'

'Well, who else is there?' Sooze asked, clearly puzzled. It was obvious that to her the staff didn't count as people. It was the thing about her that Millie liked least.

Millie would have liked to say goodbye to Tommy Kelly, but since there would be no chance of speaking to him privately, and anything else would be pointless, she abandoned the idea without much regret. If she had been staying on, it would have been nice to see something of him. But as things were, Millie could only put their brief relationship behind her.

'I've got my bag in the hall,' she said.

'Okay. I'll go and get the car and bring it round to the door,' Sooze said. 'Oh, Millie, I'm really going to miss you!' Her eyes filled with easy tears, and she gave Millie an impulsive hug before going outside.

For a few minutes, maybe, Millie thought. *When you're not texting Josh Gillespie or seeing him!*

She headed for the hall, picked up her bag, and went out into the sunshine to wait for Sooze.

'There's a train in an hour or so, I think,' Sooze said. 'We can check when we get to the station. Millie, I really will miss you.'

'I wonder how much the ticket costs?' Millie said, trying to make her question as casual as possible.

Sooze turned round to look at her. 'Oh, Mil!'

'Careful!' Millie exclaimed. 'Keep your eyes on the road, Sooze, or it won't matter to either of us how much it costs!'

Sooze obediently looked back, but her cheeks were red with embarrassment. 'Millie, I didn't think. Have you any money to get along on until you get paid?'

'Well, no, in fact,' Millie admitted in a low voice.

'Mil, you should have said! I don't have much on me, but when we get to the station I'll get plenty out of the hole-in-the-wall. You should have said!'

Well, she more or less had. Millie grinned to herself, and turned her face away to hide her amusement. Really, people like Sooze were so easy to manipulate. 'Sooze, I couldn't let you do that!' she started to say, but Sooze swiftly overbore her, and Millie was only too happy to let her.

Later, she was pleased to see Sooze withdrawing £500 on her debit card. 'That's as much as it allows me to take right now,' Sooze explained.

'But – are you leaving yourself broke or what?' Millie pretended concern.

'Oh, no, I'll ask Dad to transfer some more for me tonight!' laughed Sooze, with all the carefree lack of worry of the girl who had never been broke in her life. 'Here, take it!' She thrust the notes into Millie's hands, waited while they were carefully transferred to Millie's wallet, and then gave her friend another hug.

'You've just time to get your ticket before the train leaves, Mil.' She hugged her again. 'Keep in touch! I do hope all goes well for you!'

And as Millie, ticket in hand, went through the barrier, Sooze whirled off to the car park and out of Millie's life for the time being.

Millie found herself a seat, took out the magazine she'd lifted from the coffee table in the O'Leary's lounge, and settled down to enjoy her journey, with the comfortable feeling of wealth – or some wealth at least – in her pocket.

Chapter Thirteen

As she'd told Millie she would, Sooze spoke to her father that evening after dinner and asked him to transfer some more money to her account. But instead of the immediate agreement she had expected, she got instead a disbelieving grunt.

'Do you mean to tell me you've spent all the money I gave you last month already?' John O'Leary demanded irritably.

'Well, no, not exactly,' Sooze explained, still confident of her father's goodwill to her. 'Thing is, Dad, I had to give Millie some to buy her ticket to Derry and get through the first bit until she gets paid. She was flat broke, poor kid.'

John O'Leary frowned. 'No need for you to get involved, Susan,' he said severely. 'Her problems are hers, not yours. No need for you to invite her here in the first place either. However, it's done now. I suppose I'll have to transfer some more to you. You'll have to survive on a hundred until I can manage more.'

'But, Dad!' Sooze exclaimed tactlessly, 'don't you have it?'

John O'Leary frowned even more heavily. 'Money fluctuates, you know. There'll be plenty coming in when a certain stock I've invested in starts to rise. There's a takeover coming, and that always increases the value of the shares. But meanwhile, I need to be careful.'

It was the first indication Sooze had ever had that business might not always be so easy for her father as she had been used to believing.

However, she put the fleeting thought behind her and got on with her life. The evening at the *Limelight* with Josh Gillespie had been all she'd hoped for and more. Josh had been loving and affectionate, and had made it clear that he wanted to spend his life with her. Sooze was walking round in a dream for several days, until she began to wonder why he hadn't texted her to suggest getting together again soon. In the end, she texted him, which she'd rather not have had to do.

'How about meeting up soon?' she texted, and Josh replied at once.

'Great. Call for you tonight.'

'Time?'

'8.30.'

No love talk, but Sooze supposed that could wait until tonight. She floated through the day in bliss, and dressed with great care in a new pink skirt and silver top with lots of bling.

Dinner was only just over when the doorbell rang.

'Oh, that must be Josh!' Sooze exclaimed, jumping up in a hurry. 'Must dash, people! He's taking me out.'

John O'Leary smiled approvingly. 'Make sure you're back in good time,' was all he said.

'Be sensible, Sooze,' murmured her mother, coming to the door with her to greet Josh. Sooze agreed hastily, but wondered how she was supposed to be sensible, when Josh was so drop dead gorgeous.

'Where are we going, Josh?' she asked as she climbed into the Seat Ibiza, and arranged her skirt to show a little leg but not too much.

'Oh, I thought we'd go for a drive around and then maybe end up with a walk on the beach,' Josh said carelessly. 'Sound okay?'

'Fine,' Sooze agreed. 'Dad says be sure and bring me home in good time – just like he always does.'

'Your dad's a sensible man,' Josh said. He put one hand on her knee, driving with the other. 'You're looking very tasty tonight, Sooze.'

Sooze gave a sigh of contentment and snuggled down as close to him as she could get, while keeping out of the way of the gear stick and handbrake. Which wasn't, in fact, very close. She hoped the drive wouldn't take up too much of the evening.

It didn't. Josh must have had similar feelings about the difficulty of getting close in a moving car. He drove fast, heading for the sea. Presently he stopped, pulled onto the grass by the side of the road, and parked. They had reached the approach to Whitehead. The view down from the road above was breathtaking.

'If we walk down towards the sea by this track, Sooze, we should get to the beach. We can paddle if you like.' Sooze wasn't sure if he was joking or not, but the idea of walking on the beach was attractive. She scrambled out of the car.

Josh took her hand and led her carefully along the steep, rough track leading downwards from the road. Sooze wished she'd put on shoes which were easier to walk in. Still, she could kick them off when they got to the beach.

The moon was out by now and the sky was a soft dark blue. A mild summer breeze ran its fingers gently along Sooze's cheek. She shivered with happiness. The moon, the sea, and Josh – what could be more like heaven?

Well, a slightly less rough path to climb down in these shoes would have been, certainly. Sooze clung to Josh's hand and did her best. They reached the sand, and with a sigh of relief she kicked the shoes off, as planned, and carried them in her free hand. Josh led her down to the edge of the sea, turned her towards him, and kissed her, standing in the water. The waves splashed Sooze's legs, but she didn't mind, even when she felt a particularly large one come as high as her short pink skirt.

They strolled along the edge of the sea, staying in the water, stopping from time to time to kiss. Then Josh led her up the beach towards the sand hills. After a short while he found a pleasant recess where they could lie comfortably, close together.

Sooze was happier than she had ever been in her life.

'Sooze, you know I want to marry you, don't you?' Josh murmured in her ear. 'Think what it would be like to spend our lives like this.'

He moved his hands gently over her body, caressing her. 'I do love you, Sooze,' he said.

Sooze didn't know how to respond. This wasn't exactly being sensible, she knew. And she had promised Sam – well, sort of promised, anyway – that she would be sensible. She knew this was what Sam had been getting at. Perhaps she should sit up.

But Sooze didn't sit up.

She could hear the gentle waves lapping peacefully against the shore a short distance away. Above her, the stars shone with a steady confidence and the bright and beautiful moon smiled at her encouragingly. Also above her was Josh, who had now wriggled his body over until he was covering her. And yet somehow his hands were still able to touch her as she had never been touched before. Sooze thought that maybe she should have worn jeans and trainers. The short skirt made her only too accessible.

She had never known anything like this before. It was so wonderful, but so frightening, as well. Supposing she didn't stop Josh, and she got pregnant? Well, but he wanted to marry her. That would just hurry things along, wouldn't it?

The thoughts went through her mind, while her body responded more and more willingly to Josh's actions. His hands had found their way inside her pants now, and he was sliding them off.

It was no good. She daren't let this go on. She knew she had to stop him.

'Josh, we'd better stop,' she murmured. She took hold of his hands and imprisoned them in hers. 'You'd better take me home.'

Josh sat up resignedly.

'Okay, Sooze, if that's what you want.'

'It's just what we'd better do,' Sooze said.

Josh stood up and helped Sooze to her feet. She adjusted her clothes, especially her pants, pulling them back straight, and brushed off as much as she could of the sand. 'Please adjust your clothing before leaving the beach,' she joked, and was relieved to see Josh grin.

'Have you got your shoes?' he asked her. 'You don't want to climb that path barefoot.'

He took Sooze's hand again, and they headed back for the path and the car.

Sooze was feeling a strange mixture of disappointment and relief. Josh was thinking, *Well, there'll be a next time. And I'll make sure that's different.*

Chapter Fourteen

The following week, John O'Leary, sitting at his office desk, opened his morning newspaper and turned as always to the financial page and the listings of share prices. A heavy frown scurried across his forehead like a frightened mouse darting for the safety of its mouse hole. Amalgamated Shipping Ltd had lost even more overnight. So had Cross Border Transport Ltd. And, of course, O'Leary Goods and Services. He had expected that. But he had hoped for better things from the shipping and transport companies he had invested in last week.

For some time now, O'Leary had been juggling with his shares, buying and selling, always hoping to hit on a successful company or two with rising shares, which he could sell at a considerable profit, and so pull his financial position back up again to its previous level. He had been a rich man ever since he set up O'Leary Goods and Services and began to open shops and offices across the country. The depression of some years ago had hit him seriously, but he had managed to continue without having to close down any of his outlets so far. But it was becoming more and more difficult to struggle on.

Some of the shops, instead of being money makers, were simply a continual drain on his resources, as money was poured in to keep the business running, and returns grew smaller and smaller. He knew he should cut his losses and close some of the worst ones, but if he did that, it would soon become common knowledge that O'Leary was in trouble. The rumours would spread, and the shares in O'Leary Goods and Services would start to plummet as people hurried to offload theirs before they went to rock bottom. John O'Leary wasn't sure how wise he was being, but he was still trying to hold on to his outlets rather than close any down.

He considered again a possible way out which he had had in mind for some time. His good friend and business associate, Stephen Gillespie, the father of Josh, ran a business called Gillespie and Son which was similar to O'Leary's. If he could persuade Gillespie into a merger, it should work to the advantage of both companies. Share prices should go up, and he himself could close down the least profitable of his outlets without starting those dreaded rumours – it would look like just being the result of the merger.

Stephen had been a close friend for many years now, since their business college days. John had hopes of being able to talk him into it, of making him see a merger as something to the advantage of Gillespie and Son as well as O'Leary's. The only problem was that he was very aware of Stephen Gillespie's hard business streak. He wouldn't take any action that seemed to him bad for business. Would he see a merger as bad or good?

There were some things going for it which might make him more likely to agree. Apart from their long term friendship, there was always the fact that their children, Susan and Josh, were very attracted to each other. Stephen, like John, had seemed delighted to see their relationship grow over the last few years. Would that influence him in favour of the merger?

John O'Leary shrugged his shoulders. He didn't know. But as he glanced again at today's share prices, he made up his mind to call up Gillespie and arrange a meeting. He would give it a go and see what the outcome was. He decided that he would ring Gillespie from his office.

Sam O'Leary had no idea that things were so bad for her husband. Her life centred round her bridge club, her children – or rather, her son in particular – and her relationship with the very attractive Tommy Kelly. Sam had no intention of taking Tommy too seriously. He was a bit of rough trade, a bit of fun. Or so she thought, until the suspicion that Millie Brennan could only have found out about it from Tommy himself made her wince.

The thought that Millie had had something going with Tommy Kelly, who was Sam's property, made her angry. In fact, she realised, she was jealous. Surely there was no need for her to be jealous about such a casual relationship as hers with Tommy? And yet it seemed she was. Sam felt worried. Was she letting this get too serious?

She strolled casually down to the garage, on the morning that her husband had once again read bad news in the financial pages of his newspaper. As she came nearer, she heard musical whistling.

That meant that Tommy Kelly was there, probably cleaning the car after dropping John off at his office and driving back.

Sam put her head round the open garage door, and smiled.

'Hi, Tommy,' she said softly. 'I hope you're free this afternoon? I feel like a breath of fresh air, if you can drive me somewhere nice?'

'Hi, Sam,' Tommy replied. In public he gave her her title and addressed her as Mrs O'Leary, but in private it was quite another matter. 'I thought this was one of your bridge afternoons?'

'Oh, I can't be bothered with bridge today,' Sam said pettishly. 'It's far too nice a day to be indoors.'

'Well, if you'd like a drive out after lunch, I'll be delighted to oblige,' Tommy Kelly said. He winked at her, and Sam's cheeks reddened.

'Bring the car up to the front door at about two,' she said, and retreated hastily.

Meanwhile, John O'Leary had lifted his phone and entered Stephen Gillespie's number.

'Hi, Steve,' he said easily. 'Would you be up for a working lunch? Some ideas I'd like to run past you.'

Stephen seemed hesitant. 'I'm not sure there's much point, John,' he said, after hm'ing and ha'ing a bit. 'Well, okay, then.'

They agreed to meet at *The Merchant* at one thirty, and John, ringing off, instructed his secretary to book a table for two. It was short notice, but O'Leary was a good customer who came often and tipped well, so the hotel fitted him in.

John O'Leary arrived at the hotel with high hopes. He waited for a short while in the bar area, recruiting his spirits with a scotch and soda, but as the minutes passed and there was no sign of Gillespie, he decided to go to his table, after a couple of hints from the Maitre d'.

He glanced through the menu, trying to remain calm, and sipped carefully at a second scotch. At last, half an hour late, Stephen Gillespie arrived.

Making no apology, he slid into a seat opposite O'Leary, saying only, 'Can't stay long, John. Better order straight away, right? Make it a steak sandwich for me.'

O'Leary beckoned the waiter over and ordered. 'And a scotch?' he asked.

'Not for me. I'll have Ballygowan water, thanks. Can't get through the working day successfully if you drink at lunch time, John.' He ostentatiously removed his eyes from O'Leary's glass.

'I don't find it a problem,' O'Leary said defiantly. He ordered Stephen's water and steak sandwich.

'How's the family?' Gillespie asked. The two friends chatted for a few moments about their respective wives and children, and Gillespie broke the news that he was finally getting a divorce. 'Long overdue,' he added. 'How I've put up with Lynda's promiscuity for so long, I don't know. My solicitor's drawing up the papers as we speak. It'll be a shock to her, and to Joshua and my daughter Elaine, when I tell them, but things can't go on this way, man.'

'Sorry to hear that, Steve,' John O'Leary said.

'So, what was it you wanted to talk to me about?' Gillespie asked. Just then the waiter arrived with his water, his steak sandwich and O'Leary's BLT.

John O'Leary waited until they were alone again. He would have liked to ask for another scotch, but decided against it. No point in making a bad impression on Stephen. Although this was the first time he'd known the man to refuse a drink, working day or not.

O'Leary tried to be casual. The last thing he wanted was to give Gillespie the impression that he was desperate for help.

'Oh, I've been turning over a few ideas in my mind, Steve,' he said. 'It seems to me that both our companies have reached the stage where a merger might work well for us. There are several rival companies springing up, going for the same market – Andy Thompson, and young Jimmy Scott, for instance. If we got together, we'd be way too strong for any of them, right? What d'ye think? Idea?'

'Dunno, John. As far as I'm concerned, Gillespie and Son are doing fine. No real need of a merger from our end. Now that I have young Joshua coming on board, I'll have enough to think about, getting him trained up.'

'Oh, I'm sure he'll be a real asset to your company, Steve. A great wee fella – I've always said so. And I know our Susan thinks the same.' He winked, and smiled knowingly. To his dismay, Stephen, instead of giving him the warm agreement he was used to when the subject of their children came up, stammered and looked unhappy.

'Oh – oh, S-S-Susan. Yes, well. They're both a bit young yet for anything serious, John.'

John O'Leary looked as taken aback as he felt. This was a real change of attitude by Stephen Gillespie.

Gillespie recovered his casual manner, wiped his mouth with his napkin, and pushed his chair back.

'Well, if that's all you wanted to say,' he began, showing every sign of going.

'But we haven't talked about the advantages of a merger at all yet, Stephen! There's so much going for it!'

'Maybe for you, John, but not for me,' Gillespie said firmly. 'I'll have to run on, here. I'll be late for a meeting if I'm not quick. Thanks for the lunch. I've always said they do a great steak sandwich here. See you again soon.'

He stood up, gave O'Leary a casual wave and was gone before any more words could be exchanged. He'd been aware for some time that John O'Leary's business was going downhill. This talk of a merger simply confirmed it. O'Leary's remarks about Susan and Joshua had reminded Gillespie that he should warn Joshua off. No point in Joshua getting tied up with a girl whose father was a loser. There'd be very little money coming with Susan if he was any judge.

Stephen Gillespie made his way out of *The Merchant Hotel* wishing he hadn't agreed to go to lunch there with John O'Leary in the first place. It did him no good, businesswise, to be seen with someone whose business was in trouble.

From John O'Leary's point of view, the only good thing about the disastrous meeting was that O'Leary could have another scotch now without Gillespie's critical eye on him. He ordered it.

Roundabout – *Gerry McCullough*

Chapter Fifteen

Millie's arrival in Derry was very low key.

At the station in the Waterside she picked up her holdall, got out of the train, and made her way through the ticket barrier, looking around her for a stern middle aged woman in glasses – her mental picture of Ryan's secretary. Setting her bag at her feet, she stood there, feeling lost.

A glamorous young woman, only a few years older than Millie herself, came over to her.

'Millie Brennan?' she asked.

'Yes. Are you Janice Hall?'

'Yip, that's me. Well, Jan, not Janice, okay? I don't like Janice, see? C'mon, I'll take you to the house.'

Millie picked up her bag and followed Jan out of the station.

'Hardly worth getting a taxi,' Jan said. 'My house is quite near, in Robert Street. And you don't have much to carry, do you?'

'No,' Millie said, feeling small.

'Very wise,' Jan said approvingly. 'Always travel light.' Which made Millie feel okay again.

'I own the house,' Jan went on as they crossed the A5 and threaded their way along a number of small streets and up a very steep hill towards Robert Street. 'It's a three bedroom house, and until recently there were three of us – you'll make it three again – with a bedroom each, right. You'll pay £100 a week, and you just pay me directly, either in cash or by direct debit.'

It sounded like a lot to Millie, who still didn't know how much she would be earning, but Jan didn't seem the type to argue with.

Jan's home was a tall, neat looking terrace house on Robert Street, not too great looking to Millie, coming as she was from the O'Learys' mansion, but a lot better than the dump she had lived in with her father. There was a small Corsa parked outside.

'This is my car,' Jan told her, 'but it wasn't worth taking it just to go down to the station.'

Inside, the house was a lot better. Jan had clearly rehabbed it, or possibly the previous owner had done that in order to sell it for a higher price. There was a state of the art kitchen. 'We all use this,' Jan said. 'You make your own meals. Anything you want to keep in the fridge or the cupboards, you need to label it, right?'

Beside the kitchen was a communal living room furnished comfortably and with a TV on one wall. There was also a downstairs toilet and shower room. But no landline, Millie noticed. How did they phone anyone? Mobiles, of course. She was glad she had one, even if it wasn't the latest model.

Upstairs, the bedroom Millie was shown into was minimal, with a large bed and a built in wardrobe across the opposite wall.

'You can add anything you want,' Jan said, 'obviously. Katy took her pictures and bookcases and so on when she left, of course. She had some great stuff.'

Millie wondered if she herself would ever be in a position to add any 'great stuff' to the rather empty room.

'I'm afraid we don't run to en suite bathrooms,' Jan said, 'but the bathroom is just beside your room, and you have the use of it when it's free. If you want it at any special time, talk to us and we'll try to arrange it.'

'It all looks great,' Millie said politely. 'Is the other girl here? I'd like to meet her, of course, whenever it suits.'

'Anytime. But it's not a girl, it's a guy. Danny O'Hanlon. I think he's out at the moment.'

Millie, with her convent school background, was slightly shocked, but quickly recovered.

'Here's the key to the front door, and the one to your room,' Jan continued, handing over a key ring with two keys. 'You'll want to go out and get some groceries, maybe. There's a supermarket right around the corner. Or maybe you just want to order a takeaway tonight. There's a list of phone numbers on the notice board in the kitchen for takeaways, taxis, and so on.'

Millie had thought of going out to eat, possibly with the other people in the house, or else alone. But she didn't know her way round Derry yet, and it would involve getting a taxi, probably.

'Thanks for picking me up, Jan. And for filling me in. I might just unpack and have a rest, right now. Maybe go out later.'

'Okay,' Jan said carelessly. 'See you around. Oh – I'll show you how to get to Ryan's in the morning. You need to be there by nine, so we'll leave here about half eight.'

'Right, thanks,' Millie agreed.

It had been a long day. Her head was spinning with the information Jan had poured out. She was glad to be alone when the other girl went. She lay down on the bed, and found herself asleep.

When Millie woke it was dark. Her watch told her it was eleven o'clock. Too late now to bother about a meal. She supposed she could have ordered a takeaway, maybe pizza, but it was a bit late for eating now, she thought. She'd often envied Sooze for her possession of the latest *iPhone*. Well, when she knew what sort of salary she'd be getting, she would certainly think about updating her simpler model.

Meanwhile, she made her way to the bathroom, showered, and headed back to her room to get ready for bed and, she expected, to sleep. She just hoped she's be up in time for Jan in the morning.

She need not have worried. Checking to see if the bathroom was available at seven o'clock the next morning, she found that it was free, and was able to go in and enjoy a long, luxurious shower. As she came out again, hoping to slip quietly into her room without being seen, she almost bumped into a tall, lanky young man, probably not much older than herself, wearing only a towel wrapped round his waist. His fair hair was a mess, and his eyes half shut with sleep, although he was awake enough to give her a lop sided grin.

'You'd be Millie, right?'

'Yeah. And you'd be Danny?'

'That's me. Finished in here?'

'Yip, finished.'

Millie withdrew to her room as Danny sauntered casually past her into the bathroom. She hoped she wasn't blushing. She wasn't used to seeing half naked males at such close quarters, especially when she was wearing only a short nightie herself. Top of her shopping list, she resolved, would be a dressing gown. Well, second to the updated mobile phone.

She dressed in the most formal clothes she possessed, a dark blue dress acquired on the last of her private trips to Sooze's wardrobe, which she had thought might do for working in an office. Downstairs in the kitchen she found that no one else was there as yet.

Millie would have liked to get herself some breakfast. It seemed a long time since she had last eaten, at lunch yesterday at the O'Leary's. But she remembered what Jan had said about everyone supplying their own food. Surely they wouldn't grudge her a slice of bread for toast, and some coffee? She would buy her own stuff today at the first opportunity. She hesitated, wondering if she should go ahead, or wait until Jan appeared so that she could ask her.

To her relief, Jan came grumbling and sleepy eyed into the kitchen before very long.

'I suppose you haven't anything for breakfast?' she asked. 'Help yourself to my stuff – but you'd be best not to touch any of Danny's health foods. Apart from being revolting, he'll go ape if he finds you at it. He hit the stratosphere when I tried out one of his special yoghurts a while ago.'

'If you have any bread, I'd love to make myself a slice of toast?'

'No problem. Bread in cupboard, toaster on the work top over there. Fancy a cup of coffee? I'm making some for myself.'

'Great, thanks!'

This was better than Millie had feared. Jan was okay, she decided. Not as hard as she'd thought yesterday.

'Will I put on a slice for you?'

'Cool, thanks.' Jan was busy at the coffee machine. Presently she and Millie were sitting at the kitchen table eating toast and sipping the freshly made coffee.

'You'll need a lift into work this morning,' Jan said. 'I'm happy to take you this time, but you might want to arrange something for yourself after this. Will you be buying a car?'

'A car?'

Millie hadn't even thought of such a thing. 'Is it a long way?' she ventured.

'Across the Foyle. In the city centre. Your best bet is a taxi, unless you feel like walking the whole way. It's a bit far for that, I should warn you.'

'Oh. Thanks.' Millie said no more. Surely there would be a better way, once she got settled in?

'I give Danny a lift regularly, but often we go out together for the evening, so you'd have to have some way of getting back here yourself. That's why it wouldn't work for me to take you regularly. Into work, yes. But since you'll have to find a way to get back, you might as well go the same way, once you decide on it.'

So, was Danny Jan's boyfriend? Millie didn't like to ask, but it seemed like it.

Their conversation was interrupted by the arrival of Danny, who drifted into the kitchen, took a strange looking yoghurt from the fridge and a small spoon from a drawer, and propped himself against the nearest worktop to consume it in slow spoonfuls.

'Nearly time to go, Danny,' Jan said crisply. She pushed back her chair and stood up. 'I'll just fetch my handbag. Have you got everything you need, Millie?'

'I hope so.' Millie had brought her own handbag – another last minute 'gift' from Sooze, again without Sooze's knowledge – down with her. She picked it up from the floor beside her and stood up.

'You get a lift with Jan, Danny?' she asked.

'Be a bit daft if I didn't, seeing we're all going to the same place,' Danny drawled.

'Oh, you work in Ryan's, then?'

'Yeah. Only because yer man Fergus is the brother of my dear departed mother. She insisted he gave me a job in the old firm when I left school. Don't think I'm planning to stay, though! I'll be off to America to make my fortune before long, see?'

So Danny was her new boss's nephew? Millie looked at him thought-fully, as Jan reappeared and shepherded them out to her small car. That was something worth knowing.

Chapter Sixteen

Jan drove them over the bridge across the River Foyle, and through the streets, until they reached Bishop Street Within. Fergus Ryan's office was at the top of the street, guarded by iron gates.

'Fergus is a blurt,' Danny said. 'Don't let him faze you, Millie. Stand up to him.'

Jan frowned. 'Fergus is all right,' she said. 'I've never had any problems with him. No reason why you should, Millie.'

'Oh, yeah?' from Danny.

'Yes, yeah,' Jan told Danny. 'You have problems because he's your uncle and you expect too much from him. Family fights, Millie. Ignore Danny.'

She opened her car window down fully, leaned out, and pressed a remote control gadget which she had apparently been carrying with her in the car glove compartment. She swung the car expertly through the now open gates, high and impressive with decorated scrolls of iron work, into one of the parking spaces provided inside for Ryan employees, and they all got out.

'I'll take you along and introduce you,' she said. 'Then you're on your own, right?'

Millie gulped and produced a weak smile. 'Thanks for the lift, Jan, and everything. See you guys later.' She followed Jan and Danny into the impressive modern building.

They took a lift to the second floor. Fergus Ryan had his office at the corner of a long corridor, which allowed him to have windows on two sides and an impressive view across the city.

Jan pushed open the door without knocking.

'Hi, Fergus,' she said briskly. 'Here's Millie Brennan, okay? I'll be at my desk when you want me.'

Fergus Ryan was a middle sized, middle weight, middle aged man with nothing spectacular about him. He had brown hair which wasn't as plentiful as it had been ten years ago, and which was sprinkled with gray. His small bright nondescript eyes, which were shrewd and clever, were the most interesting thing about him. They blinked at Jan and Millie from behind John Lennon type glasses, presumably meant to be cool. There was a man with him, a stocky fair haired man some years younger than Ryan, with a round red face and hard eyes.

Fergus Ryan stood up and came round from behind his desk to greet Millie with an outstretched hand.

'Well, hullo, Millie!' he said in an enthusiastic voice. 'Welcome on board. Jan, thanks for looking after Millie and bringing her along. I'll need you presently, but first I want to fill Millie in about the company and her job.' He nodded a goodbye to Jan, as she left. 'This is Calum McKenzie, my assistant manager,' Ryan told Millie. Polite greetings were exchanged and Calum shook Millie's hand. 'All right, Calum, I'll see you later,' Ryan said, and Calum left in turn.

Fergus Ryan led Millie across the room to two comfortable chairs placed away from his desk, beside one of the huge windows.

The view out of the window, which included the river and the surrounding hills as well as some of the city walls, was magnificent. Millie found her eyes straying to it from Fergus Ryan.

She pulled herself together, sat down hastily in the chair he was indicating, and crossed her legs. She noticed that her skirt had ridden up rather far, in a too revealing way, and saw that Fergus Ryan was noticing it too. She adjusted her skirt quickly and smiled at her new boss, waiting for him to speak first. He cleared his throat and smiled some more.

'So, Millie, I was very happy to take you on at John and Sam O'Leary's recommendation. Sam's such a lovely lady, I'm always glad to hear from her and to do her a favour.' He coughed and looked smug.

The subtext, Millie thought, *is that Sam has often done him one in return. 'A lovely lady,' indeed!* Millie wondered if John O'Leary had any idea about his wife's contacts and activities. None or very little, would probably be the answer.

'Sam didn't give me much idea about your abilities, Millie. Perhaps you'd like to fill me in?'

Millie, having come straight from school with no experience in any office skills, tried to gather up her ideas hastily. 'I have GCSEs in English language and literature, and certificates in shorthand and typing,' she began. 'The A level results aren't out yet, of course, but I'm expected to get good grades in English, French and Computer Studies. I don't have any experience yet, I'm afraid, but I'd be very happy to learn. What exactly would you want me to do?'

'That all sounds good, Millie. As you know, I'm what's called a broker.' (Millie hadn't known, and was glad of the information. So far, she had only heard Ryan described as a businessman.) 'In other words, this office deals in stocks and shares, buying and selling for our clients, and of course on our own behalf. I'll start you off with some filing, but later on I'll get one of the guys who works on the computer with the various stock markets to give you some idea of the type of thing he does. Maybe you could take on some basic stuff there tomorrow.'

Millie gulped. It sounded a bit high powered. She felt as if she was being thrown in at the deep end.

'We'll put you in the main office to start with,' Fergus finished. 'Come on and I'll take you along there.'

'Okay, Mr Ryan.'

'Oh, none of your 'Mr Ryan,' Millie. We're all friends in this office. Call me Fergus, like everybody else does.'

He stood up, and Millie followed suit. At the door of his office, he stood back to allow Millie to go out first, and she felt him coming rather too closely after her and rubbing against her as he followed her out. She'd heard stories of bosses like that, but hadn't expected to run into one her first day at work. She pulled back as they came into the corridor and allowed him to go ahead of her, making sure she kept well out of his way.

However, as they reached the door of the general office, he turned to pat her arm and opened the door for her to go first again. He managed, in doing so, to partly block the doorway, so that she had to squeeze past him, leaving plenty of opportunity for further closeness and rubbings up against her. Millie was partly amused and partly angry. The up side was that he ought to be an easy boss to handle.

The room they entered was full of people, both male and female, sitting at desks and manipulating computers. At her first glance Millie guessed it at a hundred people, but later realised that it wasn't much more than twenty. One of them, she saw, was Danny, Fergus Ryan's nephew. *Funny*, she thought, *surely he should have a room of his own?* Then she remembered that Danny had complained about his uncle's attitude. Fergus didn't like him, it appeared.

Fergus led her over to a desk where a woman, rather older than the average age of the other people in the office, sat, like everyone else there, working at a computer.

'Lorraine,' he began. Lorraine stopped whatever she was doing and looked up at him in an annoyed way. 'Lorraine, this is Millie Brennan. She'll be working here from now on. I'd like you to fill her in a bit on what we do, and start her off with some filing or whatever's needed. She can have Lila's desk, now Lila's gone. You could help her find her way round the building, too – cafeteria, etc. She's new to Derry, so maybe you could give her a bit of advice on shops, buses, and so on, as well. All right?

'Millie, this is Lorraine Gusset, who sort of runs the general office for me. Anything you need to ask that Lorraine can't explain, just come and ask me, sweetie pie.' He gave Millie a final beam and bustled out.

'Sort of?' Lorraine snorted. 'Without me, this place would collapse. Hi, Millie. Good to meet you. Pull up that chair and sit down beside the desk for a minute and I'll explain things. '

Millie obediently dragged over a vacant chair from nearby, and sat. This time she didn't cross her legs, but kept them planted demurely together.

'Right, first things first,' Lorraine Gusset began briskly. 'The toilets are on down the corridor, turn left, and you'll see the sign, okay? The cafeteria is on the next floor up. Go up the stairs or in the lift and you can't miss it. I don't know what the great man means by filing – he must be thinking of his early days in some other office. He doesn't have much to do with engaging staff usually. I do all that as a general rule.

I take it you were recommended by a friend? That happens from time to time. It's okay as long as you can work. This is a paperless office. We communicate by email, and use the filing system on the computer, not paper files. Do you know anything about computers?'

'I've been working for my A Level in Computer Studies for the last two years,' Millie began anxiously. 'The results aren't out yet, but I've been forecast an A or a B.'

'That sounds hopeful,' Lorraine nodded. 'There's a spare desk just over there. The girl who had it got fed up and left to go to London. The computer is linked in to the network. I'll take you over and give you a couple of things to do, and we'll see how you get on. The important thing in this office is to understand the various stock exchanges and be able to deal with them. But we won't throw you in there yet. Danny can explain them to you, when I'm happy that you can do basic stuff.'

'Oh, that would be good. I know Danny. He's nice.'

'Oh?'

Millie said no more, but followed Lorraine over to the vacant desk she had mentioned. As she crossed the room, she caught Danny's eye, and found that he was grinning at her in a very friendly way. She felt herself cheering up. If she was going to work with Danny, things might not be too bad.

Roundabout – *Gerry McCullough*

Chapter Seventeen

The day passed in a haze for Millie. She entered data about new clients on the Ryan database, looking up some things as necessary on sites Lorraine pointed her to. At lunchtime Danny came over and asked her if she'd like to join him or if she'd made other arrangements. Millie was only too pleased to be taken under Danny's wing. They ate in the cafeteria, and in the afternoon Lorraine put her beside Danny to watch him working with the stock markets, making notes on price rises and falls.

'Tomorrow you can have a go at this sort of thing yourself, Millie,' Lorraine promised her, although to Millie it sounded more like a threat.

At five o'clock she realised with a surge of relief that people all round her were packing up to go.

'I suppose Jan will be giving you a lift home,' Danny said. 'If you're ready, we'll go down and meet her at the car.'

Millie was too exhausted by her first day, trying to concentrate on the new work, to do more than murmur that she wasn't sure if Jan intended to give her a lift, but Danny said, 'Aw, she's hardly going to make you walk when we're all going the same way. Come on.' And she followed him meekly down to the car park.

It wasn't like Millie to be meek. But keeping on top of the things Lorraine had expected of her had left her more limp and drained than she had expected. It was important to try to do well. If she lost this job, at least before she'd had a chance to look round for something else, she'd be in big trouble. So she had concentrated and worked hard.

As she had known would happen, Jan was annoyed to see her there waiting with Danny for a lift.

But Danny cheerfully broke into her initial comments that Millie would have to work out her travel arrangements for herself, 'Aw, com'on, Jan, don't be a pain,' – and Jan grumpily allowed her to climb into the back.

'I thought we might be going out tonight, Danny?' Millie heard her whisper to Danny before they both got into the front, and heard Danny's answer, 'Later, Jan, okay? The poor kid's tired out after her first day. Don't you remember yours? I remember mine, anyway.'

Danny was very kind, Millie decided.

'We'll be stopping at the pizza takeaway, Mil,' Danny told her, twisting round to speak to her over the back of his seat. 'I bet you'll want to get something there for yourself, right?'

'Right,' Millie agreed thankfully. Lunch seemed a long time ago. She hadn't been looking forward to another hungry night like the previous one, but hadn't felt much like struggling out later to find an open super-market or something.

They sat together in the dining area of the house in Robert Street, eating pizza, and Millie was amazed at how hungry she was.

When they had finished, Jan put her own rubbish and Danny's into the bin, and indicated it to Millie, who followed suit. 'Well, Millie,' she said briskly, 'I expect you're in need of a rest, now. The first day any-where is always tiring. So, see you at breakfast tomorrow. I hope you've got a mobile phone, by the way – you'll need it to check bus time tables or taxis, whichever you want in the future.'

Millie took the hint – if it could be called that – as pleasantly as possible. After all, why should Jan ferry her around. 'Yeah, I have one, Jan,' she said. 'But I'm hoping to update it tomorrow.'

She decided that tomorrow morning she would walk to work – it hadn't seemed all that far, and the exercise would be good for her – and that she would buy a better mobile with an internet connection at the first opportunity. Maybe during the lunch break? She would ask Lorraine for advice on the nearest phone shop. But before that, there was something else she was planning.

She went up to her room, and presently heard Jan and Danny, after trips to the bathroom and time to change and get ready for a night out, leave the house.

She got out her phone and looked up her contacts. Stevie Bones had given her his number, that night in the *Limelight*, before she had gone back to her table.

'Hullo, is that *The City Walls?*' she asked.

'Yeah.'

'Could I speak to Stevie Bones? This is Millie Brennan.'

'I'll see.'

A moment later, there was Stevie's voice.

'Millie? Wow! Where are you?'

'Here in Derry, Stevie. Could we meet up sometime?'

'Nothing I'd like better, Mil. But I'm on here in ten minutes. Tomorrow?'

'Thing is, I'm working, Stevie. Probably not for a couple of days – like, Saturday, right?'

'Right, darlin'. I'll give you a ring when I can make it. I have your number, right?'

'Yeah, I gave you it, Stevie. But I'll be buying a better phone tomorrow. I'll ring you then, okay?'

'Great! Got to run now, darlin'. See you soon! Love and kisses!'

Stevie rang off, leaving Millie feeling rather breathless, but happier than she had felt since Sam O'Leary had turfed her out of the O'Leary mansion. Things were moving in the right direction again.

It was good that Stevie Bones, as he had told her at the *Limelight*, was starting a season in Derry, singing and playing at one of its popular pubs. If all went well, Millie hoped to coax him into getting her an interview with the manager, and that might lead to a paid job for herself.

She didn't intend to give up her day job, as the saying went, just yet, of course. But it might be a start on another road for her future. Singing for a living was something she would much prefer to sitting at a computer, possibly making serious mistakes about the stocks and shares she was reporting on.

Well, she would see how it worked out.

She went out, found an open supermarket not too far away, and bought bread, coffee and milk for breakfast the next day. Back at the house in Robert Street, it didn't take her long to shower and get ready for bed. She read for a short while, opening the Jack Reacher book borrowed from the O'Leary's library – which she had kept, packing it with her other acquisitions – then felt herself dropping off to sleep.

Her dreams were vivid and complicated, and it seemed like years later when she was jerked violently awake by the sound of her door opening.

Millie sat up in bed, clutching the cover around her, and cried out, 'Who's that?'

'Shush!' came Danny's reproving voice in a low whisper. 'It's only me.' He came over to sit on the edge of the bed, rather near to her, his fair hair drooping over his thin pleasant face. 'Don't want to wake up Jan, she'll be asleep by now, I should think.'

'And why aren't you?' Millie retorted, nevertheless keeping her voice down. The thought of Jan waking, coming in, and finding Danny in Millie's room was enough to make her shudder.

'Thing is, I can't seem to get to sleep. I've got a tiger of a headache. I know, I know, I shouldn't have overdone it on a weeknight. Do you have any aspirin or paracetamol, Millie? I've run out of them.'

'Why didn't you ask Jan?'

'Oh, Jan's against anything like that. Uses natural medicines. But I never find the stuff she's given me in the past does anything for a head like mine. So, have you any, Millie? I'll bless you forever if you have.'

'Well, I should have something. Let me have a look in my bag.' Millie scrambled out of bed, aware of her very skimpy nightie, a relic of her time at St Bernadette's when all her clothes were second hand and either too big or too small. This nightie was very much on the small side. She knelt at the holdall, still not completely unpacked, and fumbled in its depths. Yes, there was her packet of paracetamol.

'How many do you want, Danny?'

'Can you spare three? Nothing less will be much use, I'm afraid.'

Millie reluctantly detached three tablets from their wrapping and handed them over, and Danny nonchalantly swallowed them without the aid of water, a thing Millie knew she could never have done in a million years.

'Thanks, angel – you've saved my life,' he said.

Millie, pulling her nightie down around her as she stood up, would have liked to get back into bed under the concealing covers, but Danny was in the way, still sitting on the edge. As Millie approached the bed cautiously, his hand shot out and took hold of her. Then both arms were round her.

'You deserve a reward for this, sweetheart,' he said, grinning, and began to pull Millie onto the bed beside him. Millie struggled uselessly. If only she hadn't been barefoot, she could have kicked him or stamped on one of his feet.

She resorted to tactics. Seeming to relax in Danny's arms for a moment, she allowed him to kiss her in the hope that it would end there. Then, as it became obvious that Danny had much more in mind, she bent her right arm and thrust the crooked elbow into his gut, as hard as she could. Danny, the breath knocked temporarily out of him, released his hold for long enough for Millie to spring away and seize the lamp from her bed-side table.

Chapter Seventeen

'Do you want me to hit you with this, Danny O'Hanlon?' she demanded. 'Or would you rather I started screaming and woke Jan?'

Danny, his breath recovered, rose hastily to his feet. 'Now, Millie, don't do anything rash!' he begged. 'I didn't mean any harm – I thought you were enjoying it. Sorry, I'm still half zonked – don't know what I'm doing.'

It was no excuse, but he looked so sheepish and crestfallen that Millie found herself laughing.

'Well, have more sense another time,' she said severely. 'And get out of my room. Buy your own painkillers another time.'

Still mumbling apologies, Danny headed for the door. About to open it, he leant his tall, lanky form against the frame, and turned to grin at her again. 'You shouldn't look so sexy in that wee nightie, Mil,' he said. 'Please let's still be friends, okay?'

And Millie, by now safely in bed with the covers pulled high around her, couldn't help grinning back. 'We'll see,' was all she said, but she was smiling as Danny crept quietly out of the room, and she lay down to resume her disturbed sleep.

Roundabout – *Gerry McCullough*

Chapter Eighteen

The next morning Millie left a note on the kitchen table, telling Jan that she was making her own way to Ryan's today, and left a lot earlier than they had done travelling in Jan's car.

She enjoyed walking, and the day was fine enough to make it a pleasure. She crossed the bridge by the passenger walkway, found her way up Ferrygate Street to the Diamond, and then climbed Bishop Street Within. It took her half an hour, as she checked by looking at her watch both as she left Robert Street and as she reached the huge wrought iron gates of McLaughlin & Ryan's office building.

To her dismay they were shut, but as she stood in front of them wondering how to get in, a car rolled to a stop and its driver clicked the gates open, just as Jan had done. Millie hurriedly got herself inside before the gates automatically shut again, and saw that the driver was Fergus Ryan. He parked, got out and stood waiting for her, a smile on his face, until she reached his car.

'Morning, Millie Brennan!' he said cheerfully. 'But what's this? Didn't you get a lift with Jan?'

'No, I didn't want to be a nuisance,' Millie said. 'I walked. It was very pleasant.'

Fergus Ryan frowned. 'Maybe today, but not if it's bucketing with rain, girl. I'll have a word with Jan about this. I assumed she would bring you in with Danny. Hardly a problem.'

'Oh, please don't, Mr Ryan!' Millie exclaimed. 'We agreed it would be better if I made my own arrangements. If it's wet I can always get a taxi.'

'I suppose so. Well, okay, it's between you and Jan. But you'll need a gizmo for opening the gate then. I'll get Jan or Lorraine to organise you one.'

Millie smiled her thanks.

'Oh, and while I have you here, Millie,' Ryan went on, 'I have what I think is a pleasant little habit of inviting new staff to my house for a meal, and to meet my wife. Are you free this Saturday evening?'

Millie supposed she was. She was to ring Stevie Bones about meeting up, but that needn't be in the evening, after all. In fact, better not the evening, when he was working. And she could hardly refuse an invitation from her boss without a good reason.

'Yes, that sounds lovely, Mr Ryan,' she said. 'What time should I get there? And can you give me the address?'

'Oh, about seven thirty for eight, I suppose, Millie. But what's with this 'Mr Ryan'? I told you – Fergus!'

'Well – Fergus, then,' Millie murmured.

'As for the address, it's out along the Letterkenny Road, but I'll invite Jan as well, and make sure she knows I expect her to bring you, this time at least, if not every morning to work. No, no, not another word.' For Millie was starting to protest. 'I'll invite that young scallywag Danny as well. Sure, his auntie Fran – my wife – would like to see him, I guess. Jan can bring him, too.' He began to walk into the building, Millie following at his side. 'Mustn't keep you late for work, eh? See you later.'

It was another busy day, though not quite so confusing as Millie's first day. The 'thank goodness it's Friday' feeling began to run round the office quite early. At lunch time, Millie asked Lorraine where she could buy a mobile phone, and was directed to a shop on down Bishop Street Within.

With the money Sooze had given her – Millie still had most of it left – she had no problem getting herself a good phone. It was an *iPhone*, and like most good phones had a built in camera and could link to the Internet. Millie was pleased with it. She felt that at last she had entered the twenty first century. On the way back to the office she amused herself by taking a number of pics of Derry with the river and the hills, and even attempted a selfie, which, she thought, came out okay.

She nipped off to the ladies during the afternoon and texted Stevie her new number. Then she worried in case he phoned her at work. But it was okay. Instead, he texted her back, not long after she'd returned to her desk. 'Hi, Millie. Meet you tomorrow afternoon in the Diamond? Three thirty?'

'Great. See you.' She texted back, carefully keeping her phone beneath the desk. So that was organised. She was delighted at how simple it had been.

'Millie,' said Lorraine Gusset, coming up quietly. 'I see you got the phone.'

'Oh – yes. Thanks for directing me to the shop,' Millie said, blushing. She knew Lorraine must have seen her texting.

'Glad you got it. It'll be very handy. Just, don't use it in work, okay?' Lorraine smiled to soften the rebuke, but Millie was unhappy about it for the next hour or so. That wasn't the way to do well and keep her job.

The day didn't seem so long as her first one. She sat with Danny again and began to get the hang of the work. Then Lorraine gave her a few simple shares to manage, and she found no difficulty in looking after them.

At half four, people began to pack up, the girls to drift off to the Ladies to repair their make up, the guys to stretch out their legs and share jokes and plans for the weekend. Jan came over to Millie and said, 'Fergus tells me he's invited you, me and Danny to a meal tomorrow at seven thirty. He suggests that I should bring you two. Okay?'

'Thanks,' Millie said, and Danny added lazily, 'I suppose we can't very well get out of it.'

'No, I suppose your aunt wants to see you occasionally, Danny,' Jan said sharply. Then she turned to Millie. 'Are you okay to get home tonight, yourself, Millie? Danny and I have tickets for a gig and we're eating out first.'

'No problem,' Millie said. After all, she couldn't expect Jan to change her plans just to suit Millie. She wondered what she should do herself. Then it occurred to her that she might surprise Stevie Bones by turning up to see his performance tonight, instead of waiting to see him tomorrow afternoon.

In the Ladies at going home time she asked Lorraine for a recommendation of a decent restaurant, not too expensive, somewhere nearby, and Lorraine obligingly gave her a list of several.

Millie strolled happily out into the pleasant summer evening, and spent half an hour or so exploring the centre of Derry. Presently she made her way to one of the restaurants recommended by Lorraine, Gino's Grill and Bar, where she ate a chicken dish which she greatly enjoyed, while reading her Jack Reacher book for company. She had tucked it into her shoulder bag that morning just in case she needed it.

Paying at the desk, she asked the man there whose name wasn't Gino, but Micky, 'How do I get to *The City Walls?*'

'Och, it depends which part of the walls you want,' he answered. 'If you go back up Bishop's Street Within, you'll come to the nearest way of climbing up.'

'Oh!' Millie laughed. 'Sorry. I didn't mean the actual walls. It's a pub called that, with live music.'

Micky laughed in turn. 'Ah, now, that's a different matter. *The City Walls* is in Waterloo Street. Your best plan is to go down Shipquay Street, turn left into Castle Street and that'll take you to Waterloo Street. Turn right and keep going till you see it. Have a good night!'

'Thanks!' Millie told him. She was turning away when Micky called after her, 'You'll be all right walking there now, in daylight, but if you're coming back after dark, be sure you get a taxi. Do you have a number for one on your phone?'

'No, I haven't,' Millie realised.

'Here, I'll give you this card with a few reliable companies on it, okay?'

Millie smiled gratefully at him. 'I'm going to hear my friend Stevie Bones,' she confided to him.

'Ah, you'll enjoy that,' Micky said. 'He's a great turn.'

It was quite a long walk down Shipquay Street and up Castle Street, but Millie enjoyed it. When she eventually reached Waterloo Street, *The City Walls* wasn't hard to see, its name shining out in neon lighting. She paid the admission charge, had her hand stamped in purple, much to her surprise, and headed in, looking for a seat.

The bar was packed, and the lighting was so dim that Millie found it hard enough to see anywhere free. Finally she managed to get a stool beside one of the tables where several other people were already sitting, three fellas and two girls, she saw.

'Anyone using this seat?' she asked, and one of the girls said, 'No, go ahead.'

'Coming to make up the number, cutie?' one of the guys asked her, and Millie wondered if she ought to move and find somewhere else, but they all seemed pleasant enough.

'That's right,' she grinned at him, and just then the band started playing, and a moment later she saw Stevie moving over to the mike. She'd arrived just in time.

She had half wondered if Steve would see her and invite her up onto the stage again, but he didn't seem to notice her, and Millie was quite glad. She wasn't sure what she wanted to do about her future, stay in her current job or start a new, much less secure, career as a singer, potentially much more profitable but at the same time dangerous. A singer could fail in so many ways, few of which had anything to do with his or her voice.

She was listening so hard to Stevie that it was some time before she noticed that the spare man who had welcomed her to the table was edging closer and closer to her, and it was only when his hand crept over to her leg that she jumped and drew rapidly back.

'Aw, don't be like that!' he whispered, far too close by now to her ear. 'Let's you and me be friends. I'll buy you another drink. What are you having?'

'No, thanks,' Millie said coldly. 'I'll be going soon.' She looked round for somewhere else to sit, but the place was jam packed. Stevie's act was over. She might as well go. She'd see him tomorrow as they'd planned. She pushed her chair back and stood up.

'Aw, don't go, sweetie!' The man, who was clearly far more drunk than Millie had realised, tried to pull her back down again, to roars of amusement from his friends. Millie lost her temper. She was wearing shoes with not much of a heel – stilettos would have been a lot better – but there was enough heel for the purpose. Pulling furiously away from him, she brought her foot down sharply on his instep. Then as his mouth opened to howl, she took the opportunity to get well out of his way, and out of the bar.

It would be as well, she thought, to get as far as possible from *The City Walls* as quickly as she could in case he came after her. She took off down the street the way she had come earlier, sprinting at a good pace, and had gone some distance before she noticed that the streets were now quite dark.

Remembering the warning given to her by Micky, the waiter in the restaurant where she'd eaten, she stopped to take out her mobile phone and the card he'd given her with taxi numbers on it. But alas, at some point in the evening she must have pulled it out of her shoulder bag, possibly when paying for her drink, and it seemed to be irretrievably lost. It was probably being kicked around and walked on in the pub.

Well, there was no way she was going back to look for it. She'd just have to walk. It couldn't be that dangerous. And soon she would be back in the city centre among the bright lights.

With a heart beating rather too fast, Millie set out to walk as quickly as possible back along the way she had come so recently in the sunshine.

Chapter Nineteen

There were far more dark alleys and turns off than she remembered. Millie hurried past each one, singing softly to herself to keep her spirits up. She gave a gasp of fear as something bounded out at her from one dark entrance, then relaxed, laughing at herself, as she saw that it was only a large dog, not far past the puppy stage, but of some breed, or probably a mixture of breeds, which grew to be outsize. She patted it on its head, and walked on.

The darkness was thicker now, but the streets were lined with overhead lights, and she could see the numerous lights of the city centre in the distance. Soon be there.

Then something else jumped out at her from an alley as she passed it, and this time it was no friendly dog. Instead it was a tall, thickset man, smelling of drink and unwashed clothing. Millie gave a shriek of fear and began to run again, but she could hear his feet pounding after her, coming closer all the time, his hands reaching out to grab her. She was pushing herself as hard as she could, but she knew she was getting out of breath.

'Help me! Help me!' she shouted, wondering if she was foolishly wasting valuable breath doing so. Was there anyone to hear her, and would they bother to help her if they did?

Unbelievably, she heard a voice answer her, a voice which she recognised.

'Millie Brennan? It's yourself, isn't it?'

'Tommy! Oh, Tommy!' Millie had breath for nothing else as she collapsed into the strong arms of Tommy Kelly.

She hardly noticed that the man who had been following her had melted away at Tommy's appearance.

Gasping, recovering her breath, Millie finally managed to say, 'Tommy, I'm so glad to see you. You saved my life – or something like that, anyway. But what on earth are you doing here?'

'Ah, well, that's a long story,' Tommy said. 'Would you fancy a drink to calm you down? There's a nice quiet wee pub along the next street. And then I'll drive you home. I'm parked down by the Diamond.'

'That would be great, Tommy.'

Taking her hand, Tommy led her to a small, friendly bar, found them a table in one corner, and fetched her a gin and tonic. Then he gave her his sexy smile, and Millie felt herself succumbing to him as she'd done before.

'So, Millie, what were you doing out by yourself in the dark in that part of town? Someone should have warned you.'

'Well, the waiter in the place where I had dinner did tell me to be sure and get a taxi once it got dark,' Millie confessed. 'But I must have lost the card he gave me with taxi numbers on it.'

Tommy laughed. 'And here's me thinking you were a girl who could look after herself, Millie Brennan.'

'Usually I am,' Millie said. 'This was exceptional. But you haven't told me what you're doing up here, Tommy. If it's such a long story, you'd better begin it.'

'Ah, maybe it's not so long as all that if I don't go into every detail,' Tommy said. 'The fact of the matter is, your friend John O'Leary has dropped a lot of money, his business has been doing badly for some time. So he's cutting back. No helicopter, only one car, which he drives himself. So, no Tommy Kelly, either. I heard of a job up here with a guy who has the sort of money O'Leary used to have, so here I am.'

'Who is he?' Millie asked curiously.

'It was O'Leary who put me in touch with him, as a matter of fact,' Tommy said. 'He's a business friend or acquaintance or something. Name's Brendan Cassidy. Friend of your boss Fergus Ryan, too, I'm told. All these fat cats hang around with each other. Until one of them runs into trouble, that is.'

Millie wasn't really interested in John O'Leary running into trouble with his business, except to feel thankful for a fleeting moment that she hadn't got any further with his boring son. Fancy being lumbered with someone like that, and no money to sweeten the deal. She barely thought about Sooze and how this might have affected her.

'John O'Leary is a selfish pig and his wife's a selfish cow,' she said. 'Serves them right.'

Tommy burst out laughing. 'Millie Brennan, you kill me! Quite a farmyard you have there. And how about yourself, how do you fit into the roll call?'

'Me?' Millie was surprised. 'I'm not particularly selfish. But I've no one else to look out for me – I have to do it myself, that's all.' She smiled winningly. 'So, tell me more about yourself, Tommy? You seem a bit of a loner. Have you any family? You've never talked about them.'

'You've never asked,' Tommy said. 'But, no, I haven't anyone living, except for my brother and his family out in Australia. I don't mind. I have a good life.'

'But don't you want to make money – to be more successful, not to spend your time driving the fat cats around? Living in someone else's house?'

'And sleeping with their wives, don't forget, or occasionally their daughters,' Tommy added slyly, grinning at her.

Millie in turn laughed.

'No, I'm not interested in making a fortune right now,' Tommy said. 'Someday I guess I'll want to settle down with my first million in a flashy apartment somewhere, with the yachts moored in the Mediterranean and the Caribbean, and a handy casino to pop into, but for now I've a life that suits me.' He didn't add that he'd managed to pick up quite a few useful tips on the Stock Exchange and had a steadily building bank account. He didn't want to put ideas into Millie's head – at least not just yet.

They had finished their drinks.

'Come on,' Tommy said. 'Time to shift.'

A short walk took them to the car park. And then a short drive back to Robert Street.

Tommy smiled his seductive smile again. 'Are you inviting me to come in?'

'Maybe not. My house mates might not be happy.'

'Okay. Come over here a minute.' His hand reached out to pull her towards him. His face came nearer to hers, and a moment later they were kissing fiercely.

Millie came to her senses after quite a while. What was it she'd thought the last time this had happened? She didn't plan to lose her virginity in the back seat of someone else's car to a chauffeur? Time to call a halt.

'Stop, Tommy!'

Tommy stopped at once this time. 'Same old Millie. Start/stop. You could get a good job as a traffic light.'

'I don't need to say sorry!' Millie flashed. 'It's up to me how far I want to go.'

'Yeah, but you shouldn't act as if there were no limits, and then there are.' He leaned over to open the door for her, and sat back.

'Will I see you again?' Millie couldn't help asking as she got out of the car.

'Depends if I'm free. Give me your number.'

And so goodnight.

Chapter Twenty

Next morning Millie got a message from Stevie Bones reminding her that they were meeting up at three thirty in the Diamond, and suggesting that they actually met at a coffee shop in Shipquay Street around the corner. She duly made her way there on foot. She was getting used to walking around Derry and was finding it interesting.

Stevie, untidy sandy hair, freckles and all, was there waiting for her at a corner table, with a gigantic mug of black coffee in front of him. When he saw Millie approaching his face lit up in a friendly grin.

'Hullo, darlin'!' he said enthusiastically. 'Come and sit down. What can I get you?'

'Something about a quarter the size of that, Stevie,' Millie shuddered. 'Just coffee with milk, no sugar.'

Stevie disappeared up to the counter, and Millie sat back and looked around her. The coffee bar was clearly used by musicians. The walls were covered in posters of the famous, from Jimi Hendrix to Mariah Carey. She was really pleased to see her mother, Cait Brennan, on the far wall, looking as beautiful as Millie had ever seen her. There were guitars, banjos, and tin whistles hung all around as well.

Stevie came back with the coffee just as she was getting orientated, and set it down in front of her, smiling. 'Great to see you, Mil,' he said. 'But what are you doing in Derry?'

'Well, like I told you, Stevie, I'm working. Have to do something to bring in the pennies, right?'

'Right.'

'I've got a job working a computer with a company. Stocks and shares stuff. But, hey, I'm not sure I want to spend my life like that. Any openings you could direct me to in the music business, pal?'

'Wish there were, Mil. It's as much as I can do to hold on to my own job.'

'Oh.' Millie dropped her eyelashes over her eyes, and put a huge amount of wistfulness into her voice, allowing it to quiver.

Stevie squirmed unhappily. 'Well. Maybe I could put in a word for you with the big guy.'

'The big guy?'

'The manager of *City Walls,* Declan Byrne. He might be able to pull something out of the hat.'

'Stevie, you're wonderful!' Millie breathed, looking up at him with big eyes.

'Tell you what, if you come along tonight, I could invite you up on the stage for a guest number, like I did at the *Limelight.* You'd go down a bomb for sure – give you a head start with the big guy.'

'Ah, Stevie, you're so kind. But I can't come tonight – I'm supposed to be going to my boss's for dinner, to meet his wife. I can't duck out of that and expect to keep my job, right?'

'Yeah, see what you mean. Well, how about Wednesday night? I'm on then, and it's a slower night, so an easier time to invite you up.'

'Great, Stevie! Thanks so much! I'll be there, no problem!'

Fergus Ryan's house out along the Letterkenny Road was big and impressive, if not quite as big and impressive as John O'Leary's. As Millie got out of Jan's car that evening, she looked around her with pleasure. This was more like the sort of surroundings she hoped to live in.

Jan had been pleasant enough about the lift, and had even given Millie some advice about what to wear.

'Not office type clothes – and not club type either. A pretty dress of a reasonable length if you have one. It needn't be an evening dress or anything like that.'

Fortunately among the many things Millie had taken from Sooze's wardrobe there were several which seemed to fit Jan's description. Millie picked out the prettiest, a waisted light green silk which came to mid calf and which like most green shades flattered her eyes, and felt happy with her appearance. Danny's 'Wow!' when she came down to the kitchen, her coat over her arm, assured her that the choice had been a good one. Even Jan smiled approvingly and said, 'Good. That's cool, Millie. Now, time we were away.'

Fergus Ryan opened the door to them himself, smiled welcomingly, and ushered them into the larger front room. 'Great! You made it, then. Come away in. My wife – Danny's Auntie Fran, Millie – is in here.'

A sweet faced woman who looked much older than Ryan rose to greet them. She hugged Danny, smiled warmly at Jan and Millie, and sat down again. 'Forgive me, but I find it difficult to stand for long these days. It's lovely to see you again, Danny and Jan. And I'm so glad to meet our new recruit – Millie, isn't it?' She reached up for Millie's hand and patted it. 'Now, come and sit down, all of you, and Fergus will get you a drink. Dinner will be ready shortly.'

Looking at her again, Millie realised that she was not really older than her husband, but that ill health had drawn too many lines on her face.

'It's lovely to meet you, Mrs Ryan,' Millie said.

'Oh, but you must call me Fran, Millie. I'm sure you call my husband Fergus.'

'Well, he asked me to,' Millie admitted, smiling, 'but to tell you the truth, I haven't dared to, so far.'

Fran Ryan laughed. 'You mustn't be shy, Millie. We're all friends here. The company wants to keep a family atmosphere. It's always been like that, right back to the days when my father owned it and ran it, in the early eighties. Well, well, those days are past, my father's gone to his blessed rest, and Fergus runs it now, but the family atmosphere is still present, I think.'

Fergus Ryan said, 'Well, we'll have to get you relaxed tonight, Millie. A drink should help. What'll it be, guys? Gin & tonic or what? We've got the lot.'

'Gin & tonic,' Jan said, and Millie agreed. Danny preferred whisky.

'And lime juice with soda for you, dear,' Fergus said to his wife.

'Doctor's orders, alas,' smiled Fran Ryan. 'I'm not allowed many of the pleasures of life any more.'

In a remarkably short time, Fergus was handing round the drinks. Millie was careful to sip hers slowly. She didn't want to make a bad impression on her boss and his wife, family atmosphere or not.

She wondered vaguely what was wrong with Fran. Some health problem. No one had mentioned it. Maybe they didn't like talking about it. Or maybe, like Millie herself, they found chat about illnesses boring and to be avoided.

'So, Millie, what do you think of Derry so far?' asked Fergus Ryan jovially. 'No complaints, I hope?'

'None – except for being assaulted on my way back from *The City Walls* pub the other night.'

'Millie! You should never walk around Derry away from the main streets in the dark by yourself!'

Millie considered saying that neither Jan nor Danny had volunteered to go with her, but contented herself with a brave smile. 'Oh, well – I got away safely, in the end. I went to hear my friend Stevie Bones singing. He's a great performer.'

'You like listening to music, Millie?' interposed Fran Ryan. Millie thought she was trying to save Millie embarrassment by changing the subject, but was sorry. She would have been quite happy to go on talking about her dangerous experience for a little longer. However. There were other things.

'Oh, I love it,' she answered enthusiastically. 'I love listening to other singers, and I love singing myself. Stevie has insisted on bringing me up to sing with him on stage before now.'

'You sing, Millie? You'll have to give us a song after dinner,' Fergus said. 'But I think the meal must be about ready, so I won't ask you to start right now.' And indeed, just then a woman put her head round the door and said, 'Food's about to go onto the table, Mr Ryan, if youse could all come through?'

'Bernie, our invaluable daily help,' whispered Fergus in Millie's ear as he took her arm to steer her into the dining room. 'Now Fran isn't up to cleaning and cooking any more, I don't know what we'd do without her.'

Millie smiled and followed his guiding arm obediently. Out of the corner of her eye, she noticed Danny giving his aunt Fran a helping arm, while Jan came behind them carrying Fran's handbag.

The meal was certainly the equal of those Millie had had at John O'Leary's house – indeed rather better, she decided. Bernie was an excellent cook, even if her manners were a bit unpolished. They started with a clear brown French onion soup, and followed it with pheasant, potatoes boiled, sliced and browned in the pan, and a selection of fresh garden peas, beans and carrots which must have been picked from the Ryan's garden, judging by their real carrotty taste. Millie ate ravenously, and praised everything to Fergus who was sitting beside her. The Eton Mess which came next was perfect.

'Bernie is a real treasure,' she said as she scooped up the last of the meringue, raspberries and cream mixture. 'You're really lucky.'

'The Lord has certainly blessed us.' Fran, across the table, smiled at her.

'But you should have tasted Auntie Fran's cooking, Millie,' Danny said. 'No comparison, right, Uncle Fergus?'

'Oh, no comparison, boy,' agreed Fergus. 'Fran's cooking was always a dream of bliss. Still she taught Bernie a lot, and the woman isn't bad at all, I'll say.'

'We'll have coffee in the other room and let Bernie clear away,' Fergus added, standing up. 'She likes to get away promptly as soon as she has everything in the dishwasher. Danny will put the coffee cups into it later on.'

Millie wondered whether to make any remark about Bernie going home on her own in the dark, but decided not to, and was glad a moment later, when Jan, who had been very quiet, said, 'It's just as well she has her own wee car. Otherwise, Fran, you'd be insisting on either Fergus or Danny dropping her home, wouldn't you?'

'Of course I would,' laughed Fran, 'but she's happily independent, tells me she loves driving in the dark, always keeps her doors locked and never gets out of the car for any reason until she's safely home with her husband.'

They sat around in the room where they had been before dinner, sipping the excellent coffee and chatting about nothing much.

Presently, when the coffee was finished, Fran Ryan showed that she hadn't forgotten that their new guest was a singer.

'So, what sort of music do you sing, Millie? And can you sing unaccompanied?'

'Yes, I've often sung without accompaniment,' Millie answered, 'I sing mostly popular stuff, but I can do a lot of traditional Irish folk tunes if the company wants them.'

'Just what Fran and I love!' Fergus said. 'Okay, Jan and Danny, I know you younger people want the popular things, but tonight I intend to pamper Fran. Give us a choice, darling,' he beamed at his wife.

'Well, but Millie might not know my favourites,' Fran protested.

'If she doesn't, she can say so. Come on, what would you like?'

'Do you know Raglan Road, Millie? Or The Parting Glass?'

Millie was glad that she knew them both. 'I'll start with Raglan Road, then.' She took a breath and began.

> *On Raglan Road, of an autumn day,*
> *I saw her first, and knew*
> *That her dark hair would weave a snare*
> *That I might one day rue.*

Her eyes roved round the room as she sang, her glorious voice adding to the magic of Patrick Kavanagh's words and the sad beauty of the traditional tune. Fran had tears in her eyes. Jan was looking rather bored. Both Fergus and Danny were riveted. She sang on.

> *I saw the danger, yet I passed*
> *Along the enchanted way*
> *And I said, let grief*
> *Be a falling leaf,*
> *At the dawning of the day.*

There was not a sound in the room except Millie's voice. As she sang on, she knew that the impact she was having on both Fergus and Danny was one that would last. She had seen men react to her singing, and therefore to her, many times before, most recently with Johnny. If things went on as she hoped they would, she should be able to do anything she liked with either of them.

Yet, after the applause and the warm comments, as Millie, flushed and smiling, began on *The Parting Glass*, she sensed a difference in the air. There was sorrow, distress. Even the previously bored Jan seemed moved. Danny had tears in his eyes, and Fergus, moving over to sit by his wife, was holding her hand. As the words moved on, it became more obvious that intense feeling was in the room.

> *... So fill to me the parting glass*
> *Good night and joy be with you all.*

> *Oh, all the comrades that e'er I had*
> *They're sorry for my going away*
> *And all the sweethearts that e'er I had*
> *They'd wish me one more day to stay.*
> *But since it falls unto my lot*
> *That I should rise and you should not*
> *I'll gently rise and softly call*
> *Good night and joy be with you all.*

Only Fran seemed less moved. When the last echoes of Millie's voice died about the room, she sat up, and said in a cheerful voice, 'Millie, that was so beautiful! I can't thank you enough!'

Fergus stood up, rubbed his hands together, and said in a deliberately cheerful voice, 'Hey, that was lovely, Millie. But we're all getting a bit melancholy, right? Let's play some games, now, cheer our-selves up.'

'Good idea, Uncle Fergus,' Danny said. 'What'll it be?'

So the cards came out, and Millie was able to show her skill at bridge once again. They cut for the odd man out, and Fergus was the first loser. The rubber passed quickly. Millie partnered Danny against Jan and Fran, and was a triumphant winner. Next time Jan cut out, and Millie played with Fergus against Danny and Fran. Again, she was winning easily when she noticed that her partner seemed to be making some unnecessary mistakes. In the end, chiefly due to this bad play on Fergus's part, Fran and her partner came out on top.

Millie made a point of seeming happy about the result and congratulated Fran and Jan warmly, hiding her annoyance. She smiled at Fergus. 'You had some rotten luck there, partner. A few better hands and you'd have aced them.'

'Oh, Fran's always been able to rooky me at bridge,' smiled Fergus. 'She has all the luck.'

'Not luck, Fergus – you know I don't believe in that,' Fran told him lightly. 'It's just a matter of skill.'

'Auntie Fran has always got us all beat at bridge,' Danny said.

'Yes, a good thing for me that I was her partner,' Jan added.

Millie was annoyed, although she took care not to show it, that no one commented on her own skill, which she knew was considerable. However, she said lightly, 'If I'd known how much skill I was up against in you, Fran, I'd have backed out of playing.'

She was rewarded by seeing how pleased everyone else seemed to be by her comment, but couldn't help thinking that rich people always had it their own way. If Fran Ryan was poor, like Millie, would everyone have praised her so much?

Not long afterwards, Jan said, 'Goodness, is that the time? Thanks for a marvellous evening, Fran and Fergus, but I'd better be getting these guys back to bed now, okay, everyone?' and people began to stand up and say goodnight.

It had been a good evening, Millie agreed later as she cuddled down into bed, and she'd made, she hoped, a good impression on Danny and Fergus. That could be very valuable in the future.

When their guests had gone, Fergus Ryan sat down beside his wife, took her frail hand in his and raised it to his lips.

'Fran, darlin' Fran, what am I going to do without you?'

'Hush, pet, hush.' His wife stroked his hair gently with her other hand.

'I can't bear to think of you going so soon. Oh, Fran!'

'I'm going to be with my loving Lord, Fergus. With my Heavenly Father. And I hope that when it's your turn, a long time from now, I'll see you there as well.'

'I don't know, Fran. I'm not such a faithful Christian as you. Maybe I'll never see you again.'

'Fergus, I know you will. Sure, I'm praying for you every day.'

Fergus bowed his head over his wife's hand and wept.

Fran let him cry for a while, stroking his head. Then, with a deliberately cheerful air, she said, 'Time you were getting me ready for bed, sweetheart. Help me up, now. I need my rest, don't I?'

Fergus helped her to her feet, and together they struggled across the room, to where Fran slept in a bed that had been placed for her in a side room downstairs, now that she could no longer manage the stairs.

Chapter Twenty One

Sooze was having rather a bewildering time in the weeks after Millie's departure for Derry. Not only her father, but Josh also, were behaving strangely. At first Josh continued to take her out and they got closer every time. Sooze's reactions to this were mixed. She loved Josh more and more, but she was getting worried by the demands he made on her. She tried to hold back, but found herself yielding further and further.

One particular warm summer night they lay on the sand, sheltered by sandhills, on a lonely beach out of sight of the world, and Josh whispered in her ear, as he drew her ever closer,

'Don't worry about a thing, darling Sooze. Before very long we'll be married, so what's the problem?' And he stroked her and held her close, unfastening her blouse and pushing up her short skirt, caressing her body until resistance became impossible. With a sigh which was mostly pleasure, and only partly anxiety, Sooze yielded to him.

Once it had happened, there seemed no reason to draw back next time they met, or the next, or the next. Josh's enthusiasm for her knew no bounds, and Sooze was very happy to yield to him repeatedly, as the July days and the long, soft July nights continued.

Then, strangely, Josh seemed to have less and less time for her. Their dates, from being almost nightly, dwindled down to once a week or even not so often. Yet when they did meet he was as tender and loving as before, as eager to make love to her. She brought herself to ask him why they weren't seeing so much of each other, but he only muttered something about getting involved in his father's business and having hardly any free time.

'In the evenings, too?' Sooze laughed at him. 'Really keeping your nose to the grindstone, is he?'

'You don't understand, Sooze. He's planning to take me into partnership – but he expects me to prove myself first. It's my whole future, Sooze. If he kicks me out of his business, what'll I do?'

'He wouldn't do that, Josh. And anyway, surely you could get another job if he did?'

'Oh, yeah, something that pays a couple of quid a week, I suppose. You don't understand, Sooze. Just let me make my own decisions, and keep out of it.'

In his mind, he played over to himself his father's words when he had called Josh into his study for a few words in private – as he had described them – just over a week ago.

'I don't want you to go on seeing that O'Leary girl, Joshua.'

'You mean Sooze, Dad?' Josh had asked in disbelief.

'Yeah, Susan, – Sooze – whatever you like to call her. Drop her, see? I have better plans for you than John O'Leary's brat. You can never trust Fenians. I should never have had the business dealings I've had with him, let alone getting mixed up with his family – and letting you! Anyway, I'm telling you to put a stop to it right now, see?'

Josh found it hard to believe he was hearing straight. As far back as he could remember, his father had happily encouraged him to be friends, and then more than friends with Sooze. What had gone wrong?

John O'Leary could have told him, but just yet he was aiming not to tell anyone.

When Sooze asked John for a further top up of her account, after the hundred quid he had put in when she had given Millie five times that, he had stammered and stuttered and then got angry. 'You need to learn not to spend what you haven't earned, Susan. The same goes for your mother. Johnny's the only one of the family who's earning his keep in his job down in Dublin.'

'I thought Johnny was just learning the ropes in one of your Dublin offices, Daddy?' asked Sooze innocently, and had her head bitten off in a bellow of rage.

'What use would that be? I'm paying enough useless staff as it is, without adding Johnny to the list. No, I got Johnny a position with a business guy I know, and he's pulling down a decent wage, thank goodness, with prospects of promotion. Wish I could say the same for the rest of the family. When your results come out shortly, you'll need to look around for something.'

Sooze had never heard her father talk like that before. She wondered if he was developing an ulcer. She'd heard that ulcers made people unreasonably cross.

She also heard her parents frequently shouting at each other, and Sam looked utterly miserable most of the time, when she wasn't snapping

Sooze's head off, and forbidding her to buy any new clothes for the next while until they saw where they were.

'You needn't look at me like that, either,' she added, less angrily. 'Oh, I know it's not your fault. It's all your dad and his stupidity. I don't know how he expects me to manage. You know he turned off Tommy Kelly and sold the Merc. Drives around in the Mini. And what am I supposed to use, tell me? And now he says Maria and Zofia will have to go, too. Does he expect me to do the cooking, and to clean this enormous house?'

Sooze saw with amazement that there were tears in her mother's eyes. She didn't think she'd ever seen such a thing before.

'It'll be okay, Mum,' she said, attempting to give her mother a hug. 'Things will get better soon. I know Dad says the market's down, but it's bound to pick up again, isn't it?'

Sam looked at her hopelessly. 'You don't understand, Sooze. You just don't understand.'

No, Sooze didn't understand. And no one was telling her. She wished they would. But although her parents were certainly a cause for worry right now, her main concern was Josh. How soon would she see him again? The gaps seemed to get longer and longer between their dates.

Then came the day when she acknowledged that the symptoms she'd been experiencing, the regular sick feeling morning and evening, the swollen, tender breasts, worst of all the fact that her period had shown no signs of appearing although it had been due several weeks ago, could only mean one thing. She drove to the nearest chemist's and got herself a pregnancy testing kit.

In the privacy of her bathroom, with the doors carefully locked, she tried it out.

To her horror, it was positive.

It didn't occur to Sooze to talk to her mother or her father about it. Her dad had always been concerned mainly with business and had had little time for her. Now he was even more withdrawn. As for her mum, her relationship with Sam had always been distant, to say the least of it. She didn't want to hear Sam's angry reproaches, or her hard hearted advice to, 'Get rid of it.' There was no 'It.' What there was was Josh's baby and her own baby. A little bit frightening, but very exciting as well.

To Sooze, the natural thing was to let Josh know. She fully expected that he would be as excited as she was. It would only be a matter of bringing their wedding forward a bit. Josh had assured her so many times that he was longing to marry her, and she hadn't doubted him for a minute.

She texted him as soon as she was sure the result from the pregnancy test was positive. She waited for a full day for his answer, telling herself that he was probably too tied up in work to have a chance to read his messages.

Then she texted him again.

When there was still no answer, she decided to ring. But the phone rang in vain. When Josh's answering machine came on and told her, 'I'm not here right now. Leave a message and your number after the tone, and I'll get back to you,' she cut off without bothering with a message. Josh knew her number. He'd had two texts now, and the record of an unanswered call. Sooze was beginning to be afraid.

Chapter Twenty Two

John O'Leary was still desperately trying to find someone to come into partnership with him and give his dying company the boost it needed. But no one was interested. Perhaps they were afraid he would bring their companies down with him? He didn't know. Everyone was very polite, but completely unhelpful.

His bank manager, until recently courteous almost to the point of being servile, had changed into someone who had no time for him and certainly no extra money to lend him. On the contrary, he was pressing continually for O'Leary to pay back the amount by which he had been allowed to go over his agreed overdraft. He spoke of pressure from headquarters, and O'Leary got the impression that he himself had been rebuked for allowing the extra money to be used.

He had done everything he could to reduce the amount he owed. He had sold the helicopter and the Merc, got rid of his houseful of servants. But no sooner had he managed to pay off the unauthorised spending than the manager began to talk of the need for him to reduce his agreed overdraft. He couldn't do it.

John O'Leary was very near to panic. The only thing left for him to sell, apart from his actual business, was the house itself. He dreaded telling Sam that this would have to be done, and yet he knew he would have to speak to her about it. John O'Leary was no longer the confident, dominant husband and father he had been for years. He had lost all his arrogance.

It was with a sinking heart that he sat down with Sam after dinner one evening, when Sooze had retired to her room to wait for a text or a call from Josh, and tried to explain to his wife what had been happening.

'So I'm afraid we have no option. We have to put the house on the market,' he ended. He sat looking at her.

Samantha O'Leary couldn't at first take in what her husband was saying. She had never thought John perfect. The list she could make of his faults would fill a book. But in one thing she had always thought him okay. He was a great provider. From the moment she had married him, twenty five years ago, she had never lacked for anything. Whatever she wanted, she could go out and buy. Suddenly that was no longer true. She found it impossible to believe.

'Can't we take out a loan on the house, instead of selling?' she asked at last.

'No. I wouldn't be given one. I already have a second mortgage. As it is, we'll not get a huge amount when we've paid off the mortgage – but the lump sum will let me make a new start. I'll put it into the business, sell off as many outlets as I think's wise, and begin to move up again. I've made a fortune once, Sam. I can make another one, if I can start free of debt. It's our only chance.'

Sam stood up slowly. She turned away from him and looked out of the window at the spreading view which she had almost stopped appreciating, she had grown so used to it over the years she had lived here. The gardens rolled down in front of her, bright and lovely. In the distance the low green hills spread out, and between them, far off, was a brief glimpse of the water of Lough Neagh, blue in the summer sun. Was all this lost forever?

'When do you intend to do this?' she asked at last.

'Straightaway. The bank manager is pushing me. If he sees the house on the market, he'll give me a couple of months' grace until it sells. Thank goodness house prices are high at the moment. We shouldn't do too badly. I've been in touch with the agent. He'll be coming out tomorrow to value it and take pics. It'll be up as soon as that's organised.'

'When do we have to move out?'

'Oh, not until the sale goes through. We'd better be looking for something else – something cheap. In fact, we'd better rent. I'll need all my spare cash to make a fresh start with my business. But we don't want to leave the house sitting empty. That always puts buyers off. You'll need to start clearing out as much rubbish as you can. Sort out the bedrooms and the cupboards – dump as much as possible. We can auction the furniture separately, unless anyone wants to include it in the sale of the house at a good enough price.'

'I think you mean *we'll* have to sort out stuff – you needn't think I'm doing it all on my own!' Sam flashed. John O'Leary was almost glad to see her more like her old self, instead of the dumbfounded, shocked person she had become since his first words to her.

'All right, all right, I'll help as much as I can. But I'll have a lot of business things to deal with. Shops and offices to close down, redundancies to settle, premises to sell or let, except where I've been renting them – which is most of them, in fact. If I had enough in the way of business premises to sell, I might not need to sell the house as well.' He grinned ruefully, but won no answering smile from Sam, who had lapsed back into her first reaction of shock.

'I'll make a start tomorrow,' was all she said.

'Can't you start now? Get something done before the valuer comes?'

'No. I'm unutterably tired. I'm going up to bed.' She left him sitting in the comfortable chair which would be going to the auction so soon. 'You'll have to tell Susan. I can't,' were her last words as she went upstairs.

The next morning after breakfast Sooze listened as John O'Leary told her, with considerable difficulty, how things had been getting steadily worse for him in business, and how they would be moving out of the house 'for the time being' as he put it. Her mind wandered and she found it hard to concentrate on what he was saying. It seemed to her to be just a repetition of the things she had heard from him before – 'Business is bad, Susan. The markets are down. We must cut back our spending for a while.'

She had been very sick before breakfast, and had managed only a slice of toast and some orange juice. Coffee had become something undrinkable these days. She realised vaguely that they were moving out of the house, but it was only when the man from the estate agent arrived to carry out a valuation and later still when the 'For Sale' sign went up at the front door, that she really took it in that the house was being sold. There was a sign down by the roadside as well. She saw it when she wandered aimlessly down through the gardens until she reached the entrance, looking for an escape from other people. She carried her phone, as always, hoping for a response from Josh. But the phone remained silent.

Later the same day, her mother told her, speaking in a quiet voice unlike her usual tones, that she must sort out her things, and decide what she wanted to keep and what could go to the charity shops.

'You mean my clothes, Sam?' she asked, trying to take an interest.

'Yes, I suppose so. The other stuff, TV, computer, *iPod*, and so on, will be sold in the auction with the rest of the household furniture.'

'My *iPod*? But what about my music? How can I listen to stuff? I need it, Sam.'

'We all need the things we've been used to, Sooze. But we have to learn to do without them, I'm afraid.'

Sooze lay awake for hours that night, weeping. Not for her *iPod*, although that was a shock. The tears were for Josh, and for the baby whose father didn't seem to want him. Or her, she reminded herself regularly. But she found herself thinking of her baby as a boy. She believed firmly he would look like Josh, fair haired and blue eyed, and, later, tall and strong.

Sometimes she could persuade herself that for some unknown reason Josh hadn't got her messages. Maybe he had lost his phone? It happened. And Josh was notorious for losing things. But he would have got himself a new one, in that case. He would have texted or rung to check if she was okay, to arrange to meet again. The gap since she had seen him seemed unbelievably long.

The valuer put a high price on the property. John O'Leary was pleased. Someone else came to value the furniture, in case the new buyer wanted to pay extra and take it over with the house. Sooze found it very hard to see him going into her own room to value her belongings. Bed, armchairs, desk, as well as the hardware. After the first moment she ran downstairs away from him, out into the garden.

But there the first thing to meet her eye was the 'For Sale' sign, and when she ran down through the garden, there was the other sign at the entrance.

She swerved off towards the tennis courts, and sat there in the sun remembering the last time she and Josh had played tennis there with their friends. It had been two months ago, but it seemed like yesterday. It was well over a month since she had first allowed Josh to make love to her. Sooze found herself crying again.

Chapter Twenty Three

Josh had not lost his phone. He had got all Sooze's texts, and knew that he had had an unanswered call from her. He didn't know what to do, what to say to her.

His father had been grumbling more and more about John O'Leary and his family.

'I'm just glad you aren't still tied up with that Susan girl. Nothing good could come of mixing with an O'Leary. He's a walking disaster.'

Josh knew that he'd been telling all his business friends and acquaintances to keep well away from the man, warning them over the phone and at meals to which they'd been invited that John O'Leary had no business sense and would drag anyone down who worked with him.

Josh knew, too, for Stephen Gillespie had spelt it out, that if he continued to see Susan, his father would refuse to support him any more. He would be thrown out of the house which had been his home all his life, he would find his allowance cut off, and he would have to get himself some sort of job, probably one which wasn't well enough paid. On the other hand, supposing Sooze really was pregnant – !

He hoped fervently that it was all a mistake. Probably she'd been irregular, and would presently have her period again, and all would be well. Josh wouldn't have to go on seeing her against his father's insistence, in that case. But he didn't want to let her down, either. If she was pregnant – his thoughts stopped there. She couldn't be.

Josh felt an urge to talk to someone about all this. Someone sympathetic, who would tell him it would all work out, that probably Sooze wasn't really pregnant, that there was nothing he could do in any case. As always when he wanted something done for him, his thoughts flew to Horse.

He had known Horse since his first year at school, when some boys from second year had started a systematic bullying of him at lunch time. They were bigger than Josh, and there were five or six of them. He hadn't had a hope. At first they wanted his pocket money, which they had noticed was always plentiful. Stephen Gillespie had always given generously to his only son.

Then it increased into punches and worse. Josh was in despair, when one day Horse happened to come round the corner of the gym building where the bullies usually took him. Horse was a first year boy, too, but unlike Josh at that time he was very well grown for his age. His anger stirred by the sight of several boys laying into one smaller boy, he advanced with a roar, knocked two heads together, kicked two other boys, and laid the remaining one out with a scientific punch. It didn't take the bullies long to decide to run for it.

Horse turned to Josh. 'Are you okay?' he asked kindly.

'Yeah, I am now. Hey, thanks.' Josh spoke in a muffled voice, being occupied in stemming the flow of blood from his nose, which one of the bullies had been punching when Horse arrived.

'Sit down and lean your head back for a few minutes,' Horse advised him. Josh sat, and leaned weakly against the gym wall. Meanwhile Horse, realising that the boy he had helped was one of the most popular in their year – for Josh had always been generous, in his turn, with his lavish pocket money – was overcome by shyness, and began to stammer.

'D - don't w - worry. I'll look out for you. I'll m – make s - sure they d - don't hit you again.'

And Josh, in his turn, had realised that his rescuer was a boy very much looked down on and despised by the rest of his year, partly for his stammer and partly for his clumsiness. He decided magnanimously to over-look all that and to let Horse hang round with him and his friends from then on. After all, as a bodyguard he would be hard to beat.

The relationship continued as it had begun, with Horse overwhelmed with gratitude that Gillespie should bother to be his friend, and Josh treating Horse with a mixture of disdain and a little kindness, while expecting him to be ready to do anything Josh wanted. And Horse was always willing to do what Josh asked of him.

So in his current situation, it was second nature for Josh to text Horse and instruct him to meet for a pint at the Deer's Head, a quiet bar where they could talk without being heard, or, conversely, having their words drowned out by loud music and noisy chatter. And Horse happily cancelled his judo session and went round to the bar.

But to Josh's dismay, he found Horse, for once, unsympathetic. All his concern seemed to be for Sooze. And Josh remembered that Horse had always been keen on her. It had been a joke between Sooze and him-self. But it was no joke now.

'She must be very worried and unhappy,' Horse said, when Josh had finished pouring out his woes. 'Her father's put the house on the market, you know, and I'm told it's been snapped up straightaway. The furniture and household goods are going to auction tomorrow.'

'Oh?' Josh said miserably. He couldn't care less about John O'Leary's troubles, except as it impacted on Sooze and therefore on his own father's reaction, and its effect on Josh himself.

'And then, to have this worry about her pregnancy on top of it!' Horse went on. 'I know you want to do what's right, Josh. I've always admired you, and always expected you to do the right thing.'

'But how can I, Horse?' Josh burst out. 'My father – '

'Your father is a wicked old man, Josh,' said Horse sternly. 'I've never said so before, because I didn't want to hurt your feelings, but I've thought it since I first met him. It's time you got out from under his thumb. You're not a kid any more, Josh. Time to start behaving like a man.'

Josh stared at him in astonishment. Horse had never spoken to him like this before. It was a long time since he had stopped stammering, but when he was talking to Josh he had always been slow, hesitant, uncertain of himself, wanting to please. If Josh had known it, the change was because his feelings for Sooze had by now grown stronger than his admiration for Josh.

'You shouldn't be coming to me to talk about all this, Josh,' Horse added after a moment's silence. 'It's Sooze you should be talking to. Ring her now, and arrange to meet and discuss things.'

Josh lifted his mobile and texted Sooze's number. *Need to meet and talk. Pick you up in half an hour.* Then it occurred to him to wonder if she was still at the same house. Horse had told him it had been sold.

'Do you know if she's still in O'Leary Towers?' he asked.

Horse reassured him.

'They aren't moving out until after the auction tomorrow.'

'How come you know all this?'

'I made it my business to find out, to ask around.'

'Oh.' It occurred to Josh that he could have done the same. But he was distracted from this line of thought by the sound on his phone of a text arriving. It was Soooze. *Okay. Love you.*

He hadn't thought to put 'Love you' on his own text, although it was something he had always done previously. He hesitated, then before giving himself time to change his mind, he texted back *Love you,* and stood up to go.

'Better get moving,' he said to Horse.

Horse hesitated. He would have liked to say something on the lines of, 'Be kind to her,' but he knew how much Josh hated being told what to do. Something, Horse knew intuitively, to do with always being told what to do by his father. He didn't want it from anyone else. So Horse remained silent, and hoped.

Josh picked Sooze up at the entrance to the gardens. He was surprised at how shocked he felt when he saw the house agent's sign with the 'For Sale' notice now covered with a large, triumphant, 'Sold.'

He was even more shocked at Sooze's appearance. She had lost weight, and looked ill.

Sooze would have been annoyed to know this. She had done her best to look as good as ever for Josh. But he hadn't given her much time, and she wanted to get down and meet him at the road. Somehow she didn't want him to come to the house and meet her parents. They were likely to be embarrassing, whether they were angry with Josh for staying away for so long – for she knew they'd noticed it – or whether they were over pleased at his reappearance. She did her best, and hoped it was enough.

They climbed into Josh's car, and drove down a quiet path which led to the woods, where they had often parked and made love.

Chapter Twenty Four

The wood was quiet except for the sound of birdsong. The scent of wild roses and honeysuckle drifted towards Josh and Sooze from the bushes, bringing with it, to Sooze at least, a vague feeling of comfort. Josh, acting on instinct, put his arms round Sooze and kissed her, as he had so often done before. But his anxiety wouldn't allow him to take long about it. After a moment, he stopped the kissing and blurted out, 'Sooze, are you sure?'

'I'm sure, Josh. I took a home pregnancy test.'

'But maybe you did it wrong, Sooze.'

'No, Josh, listen. I went to the doctor after that. He confirmed it. I'm definitely pregnant.'

Josh groaned. 'So now your parents know all about it.'

'Why should you think that? The last thing I want to do is to tell them, until I can tell them the date of the wedding.'

'But your doctor will let them know for sure.'

'No, he's bound by patient confidentiality. Besides, I made him promise me. I've known him all my life. I can trust him. If I'd been under age, he might have felt obliged to tell my parents, but I'm eighteen, Josh. I'll be nineteen in another two months.'

'And I'm twenty two. We're far too young to be getting married just yet, Sooze.'

'That's not what you said when you were persuading me to go all the way.'

'I know, I know.' Josh groaned again. 'If it wasn't for your father going broke – my father wants me to drop you. He doesn't know you're pregnant, of course – but I think that would only make it worse. He's threatened to kick me out of the house and stop my allowance if I see you again.'

Sooze's eyes opened wide. She stared at Josh. 'And are you going to let him rule your life, Josh?'

'It's not like that, Sooze,' Josh protested, while knowing that, in fact, it was exactly like that. 'But what sort of job could I get that would support you and a baby as well as me? It's just not possible.'

'Maybe some of your friends would help you. There must be jobs going.'

Josh hesitated to say how much he hated the idea of working at any sort of job. 'Sooze, couldn't you just get rid of it? I'd pay. You'd have to go over to England. But I still have my allowance. I could manage it.'

'No, Josh!'

'Why not? It's what girls do now.' Josh's lip curled. 'Your friend Millie wouldn't hesitate, for instance.'

'She wouldn't do it any more than I would,' Sooze exclaimed, although a question mark in her head asked how she could be so sure. 'Josh, you say, "it." But there's no "it." There's our son – or our daughter,' she added conscientiously. 'Your son, Josh – don't you care about him? Don't you feel even a little bit pleased? And proud?'

And to his astonishment, Josh realised that that he did feel something like pride. Even, if he were honest, a little whiff of pleasure. His son. Wow!

'Sooze, we can't decide now. Let me think what's best to do, okay? We can meet again in a few days.'

'You can text me – I'm being allowed to keep the phone.' In spite of herself a note of bitterness crept into Sooze's voice. 'But we're moving out very soon. The auction's tomorrow. Then we'll be packing up what's left and moving to cheap lodgings in Belfast. I'll text you the address when I'm sure what it is.'

He put his arms round her again and kissed her. It felt so right to hold her. But he mustn't let his emotions run away with him.

Sitting back, he put the car back into gear and drove Sooze home.

He left Sooze feeling almost as depressed as she had been before he texted her and arranged to meet. It seemed as if he no longer wanted to marry her. He was allowing his father to rule. Sooze had always thought Stephen Gillespie liked her, but apparently his liking was dependant on the fact that her father was well off. Now that he was broke – temporarily, Sooze continued to think – the liking had vanished like a soap bubble in the sink under the blast of the cold water tap when it was turned on.

Josh drove home. Like Sooze, he felt more depressed than ever. The meeting with Sooze which Horse had pushed on him had done no good. He had hoped that he would find she had made a mistake. But if her doctor had confirmed it, that was out. Failing that, he had hoped to get her to agree to travel to England for an abortion. But she had been so firm in her resistance to that idea. His feeling of pride in his possible son had trickled away. She ought to have agreed to the abortion. If she hadn't been a Catholic, probably she would have. That's what his dad would say, if he knew. If he knew. Josh shuddered at the idea.

Arriving home, he showered, changed and went down to dinner. His much older sister Elaine was there already, and presently Stephen came in. They ate in even more than the usual virtual silence, broken only by an occasional comment from his sister about someone she had met while out shopping that afternoon. Stephen said very little. Josh, who normally tried to make some conversation from time to time, had nothing to say.

When he came home, he had contemplated telling his father about Sooze's pregnancy. After all, it would be his grandson. You never knew. He might be pleased.

But seeing his stern face as they sat round the dinner table, Josh shuddered. His courage froze over, like a shallow lake high in the hills in the coldest part of winter. No way. His only hope was to keep silent about it and find some other way out.

After the meal, he went up to his room and texted Horse. *Need to speak to you. Now.*

They met up in the same quiet bar.

'I talked to my dad about you,' Horse said.

'You what? You told him – ?'

'No, of course not!' Horse interrupted him angrily. 'I told him you were looking for a job. I said you wanted to stand on your own two feet, instead of just relying on your own dad.'

'Oh?'

'He seemed pleased. He said he'd always liked you. He said he'd take you on as a trainee accountant, and see how it went.'

'Accountant? Horse, you know I don't do maths!'

'It's not just maths,' Horse said. 'And I'd be there. You know I've been with the firm since I left school, and by now I've worked my way up to Senior Accountant. I could have joined as a partner, but I didn't want to do that, and my dad was pleased that I didn't. He says he's glad to see that you're made of the same stuff as me.'

Josh said nothing. To him, it wasn't a compliment to be made of the same stuff as Horse. He'd always considered Horse to be very inferior to himself. He knew Horse's father was CEO of a very prestigious accounting firm, McBride & Buchanan, with branches in the USA, but he'd always looked down on Horse because he worked for his living instead of depending on an allowance from his dad.

'I'd be around and I'd be happy to help you out with anything you found difficult,' Horse said.

Josh said nothing.

'I'm guessing that Sooze isn't willing to have an abortion,' Horse said.

'No. She doesn't want to.'

'Well, I suppose you're going to marry her then?'

Josh gulped. There was a steely look in Horse's eyes that told him it wouldn't be wise to deny it.

'I don't see how I can,' he said.

'You'll have a decent enough pay even as a trainee,' Horse said. 'And I'd be very happy to help you out.'

Josh looked at him. It was hard to meet his eyes.

'Let me think about it,' he said.

Chapter Twenty Five

The auction of the O'Leary household goods went off smoothly. Sooze took herself to the far end of the garden with her phone. She didn't think she could bear to watch and listen as the auctioneer worked his way through one thing after another which she had thought would always be part of her home. So she wasn't there to see Horse buy her *iPod*, leaving instructions with the auctioneer to send it to an address he would give him in the next day or two.

John O'Leary had kept back a minimum of the less expensive things to take to their new rented apartment, and on the day after the auction, a van rolled up and two burly men came in and hoisted the pieces of furniture, one after another, into it.

This time Sooze watched. A box containing bedclothes and clothes belonging to herself and her parents. Another box holding some cutlery and crockery, mostly unmatched and not worth selling. A couple of worn, elderly armchairs. A small table and a few unmatching hard chairs. A double and a single bed, although not the ones where the O'Learys had slept. These were probably ones which had been used by the staff, Sooze thought. It didn't occur to her to wonder how the staff, turned out of their jobs at the shortest possible legal notice, were getting on now. Her thoughts were concentrated on herself – the move, the baby, Josh.

Presently the van drove off. 'All right, get your personal belongings, Susan, Sam,' O'Leary said. He picked up the case he used to carry his laptop computer. He hadn't sold that, Susan noticed. But then, he would probably need it if he were ever to get his business up and running again. She bitterly regretted her own *iPod*. At least she had her phone, and the necklace Josh had given her last Christmas. Sam, who had had to sell all her own valuable jewellery, had been quite kind about the necklace, and had told John O'Leary that to take it would be an unnecessarily cruel sacrifice to demand of Sooze.

'She's losing everything else,' Sam told him. 'Let her hang onto that, at least. It's not even as if it's worth much,' she had added, to Sooze's annoyance. But Sooze didn't care if the necklace was valuable or not. It was a token of Josh's love for her. Every time she looked at it, she was encouraged to believe that he still loved her, that he wouldn't let her down.

John O'Leary packed them both and any belongings they still had into his dark blue Mini, then got into the driving seat and drove off. They were heading for a small rented house, cheaper than any apartment he'd been able to find, off the Newtownards Road.

It was a dismal looking place with no garden, not quite two up and two down, but not much more than that. At least it had indoor sanitation, John O'Leary told his wife and daughter. 'So it could have been worse, right? Don't let's start grumbling, just get the things out of the car.'

The removal van pulled up ten minutes later and the men dumped the furniture in the appropriate rooms. Sam, with what help Sooze felt able to give her, began to unpack the boxes of crockery and cutlery and to find cupboard space for them in the small kitchen. When the beds had been taken upstairs she carried the bedclothes up after them, and ordered Sooze to help her to make the beds.

Sooze realised that it was only fair for her to do her share, but found it hard to concentrate. Her head was spinning and her stomach kept heaving. *So much for morning sickness,* she thought. *It seems to be morning, noon and night sickness.* When the beds were both made, she staggered to the minute bathroom which was squeezed in between the two bedrooms, and threw up copiously.

When she had recovered, she went into her bedroom, leaving her parents to do any more sorting out necessary, and texted Josh her new address.

Josh was with Horse when he got the message. 'Sooze's new address,' he said grumpily when he'd read it. 'Look – a real dump. Does she expect me to call for her there, or what?'

Horse refrained from comment. He knew that Josh could only be pushed so far before he reacted, and he was still hoping to get Josh's agreement to taking the offered job and arranging to marry Sooze before much longer.

'You should ask your dad to let you move out – have a place of your own,' he suggested instead. 'Most guys your age don't live with their parents. I don't, myself.'

Horse had a new apartment in an upmarket block on the Ormeau Road.

'I might just do that,' Josh agreed. 'He'd have to be willing to pay for it, mind you. Still, I think he could be persuaded, especially if I tell him all my friends have their own place.'

Horse left it at that. If Josh had his own apartment, he and Sooze would have somewhere to live in together when they married. It would make it a lot easier to persuade him.

A few mornings later, as Sooze was sitting listlessly over breakfast with her parents, wondering if she could eat anything or not, they heard the postman knocking.

'Must be a parcel. Probably for me,' said John O'Leary, getting up briskly. 'If it was just letters, he'd have put it through the letterbox without knocking.'

A moment later he was back with a parcel and a puzzled look. 'Turns out it's for you, Susan,' he said, handing it to her.

Susan opened it, trying to work up some interest. Could it possibly be from Josh? Her face brightened at once. 'It's my *iPod!*' she exclaimed. 'There's a note with it, from the auctioneers. They say that this item was to be held until they could be notified of the address to send it to! They've just received information that it was to be sent to this address!'

'Someone bought it back for you, Sooze,' Sam said. 'What a nice thought.'

Sooze looked and felt happier than she had done for weeks. She was immediately sure it came from Josh. 'How kind! How thoughtful!' she said. 'Whoever it was knew how much I would miss my music.'

Forgetting to help with the breakfast dishes, she ran up to her room, lay on the bed, and plugged in her earphones. The joy of being able to listen to her own playlists again was only exceeded by the happiness of knowing that Josh did really care about her. Only someone who loved her could have thought of doing such a lovely thing.

'Isn't Susan going to help you clear up?' asked John O'Leary with a frown.

'She's helping quite a lot,' Sam said. 'Let her enjoy having her *iPod* back, for a while. She can help later with the washing and ironing. I can manage the dishes – or perhaps you could help me!'

'I need to check out these prospectuses I've just got in the post,' O'Leary said hastily. 'Got to get some business ideas up and running, you know.'

Sam smiled to herself as she gathered up the plates. She hoped John would be able to make a go of getting back on his feet. But she had her doubts about it.

Roundabout – *Gerry McCullough*

Chapter Twenty Six

Meanwhile, Millie had settled down well into her new life in Londonderry. She was doing well at work, picking up the instructions given to her by Danny quite easily, and beginning to feel well on top of things. Fergus Ryan took a fair bit of notice of her, and several times invited her to lunch with him, on the pretence of checking on how she was getting on. But very little of their conversation was about work.

Danny, also, was showing himself very friendly. He was, as Millie well knew, Jan's boyfriend. But that didn't seem to stop him from flirting with Millie, taking every opportunity to talk to her out of sight of Jan. Millie liked him. Moreover, she had by now learned that his aunt, whose name had been Fran McLoughlin before her marriage to Fergus Ryan, owned most of the shares in the company which had been her father's, and was now McLoughlin & Ryan.

Jan had told Millie that his Aunt Fran had left 70% of her shares to Danny, and the rest to her husband, in her will. Danny's mother, Fran's older sister, had had a half share, but after her death her feckless husband had sold her shares back to Fran and gambled the proceeds away. So Danny was currently dependent on his job, but wouldn't be forever. Millie had received a strong impression on her visit to the Ryan's house that Fran Ryan, whatever was wrong with her, wasn't expected to live much longer. Jan filled her in on this, too.

'Cancer of the liver,' she said. 'Only diagnosed a few weeks ago. It's one of the serious ones. I suppose you know that.'

Jan's eyes filled with tears as she spoke. 'Don't talk to Danny about it. He's very attached to her – easily upset on the subject.'

Millie promised readily. The last thing she wanted to talk to anyone about was someone else's illness and expected death. She shuddered away from the thought, and focussed in on the thought that Danny was far more worth cultivating than she had realised at first. Much more than his uncle, in fact. As well as being much more attractive, with the fair hair which fell regularly over his face, and his pleasant lop sided grin.

On the Wednesday after her meal with the Ryans, Millie was due to sing, on Stevie Bones's 'impromptu' invitation, at *The City Walls* pub. She had no desire to repeat her experience there, coming home on foot in the dark. It seemed a good excuse to ask Danny to go with her. Jan, too, she supposed, if she couldn't get out of it.

But fortunately, from Millie's point of view, Jan had a pottery class that night, so she was forced to refuse the invitation. Millie was happy to set off by taxi with Danny alone.

The bar wasn't quite so busy as it had been on the Friday night she had first been there, and they managed to get a table quite near to the band. Stevie, at the front setting up his equipment, saw Millie come in, and gave her a quick salute and a smile. Danny went up to order drinks for them both at the bar, and Millie looked round happily while she waited for him to come back.

It was dark inside the bar, but flickering neon lights created an atmosphere of excitement. The two musicians who were playing with Stevie Bones were tuning up. She and Danny had come early enough to catch the whole set. The place was gradually filling up. It was busy enough by the time they had finished their second drinks, which Millie had insisted on paying for.

'It was my invitation, Danny. I don't expect you to pay for the whole evening – we'll share.' If it occurred to Danny that, since it had indeed been Millie's invitation and that he had come along as a sort of body-guard, it might be more appropriate for her to pay for all the drinks, and for the taxi, too, which he had paid for, he didn't say so.

The time came when Stevie Bones, having finished a number of songs to enthusiastic applause, began to introduce Millie. 'You've all heard of the late, great Cait Brennan, folks, the girl with the golden voice? Well, I'm delighted to say that we have her daughter here tonight, Millie Brennan, a daughter who has inherited that same great voice, and who has agreed to sing something for us now. Come on up, Millie – and let's hear the applause for this babe, you guys!'

Millie stood and made her way to the front. *The City Walls* had no stage, just an area reserved for the live music, and Millie was a little worried that the audience wouldn't be able to see her easily, but she was determined to do her best. Looking out at the listening crowd, she saw that there was a clear space round the musicians, and that most people were sitting at the little tables with a good view of the performers. Further back, it was true, they were standing round the bar in the sort of pack which would make it difficult for a good many of them to see her, but Millie decided not to let that faze her.

119

'What are you giving us, Millie?' asked Stevie.

Remembering her success at the *Limelight*, Millie was planning to sing *Eternal Flame*. Stevie played the appropriate chords, and she began.

At the first notes, the little hum of talk which had pervaded the bar until then died away. There was silence, except for Millie's voice echoing around the room. Millie was enjoying the experience. She put her whole heart into the performance, but wasn't too occupied to notice the expression on Danny's face. He was clearly deeply enthralled, his eyes fixed on her. Millie sang directly to him, just as she had done in the *Limelight* for Johnny,

> *Do you feel the same?*
> *Am I only dreaming*
> *Or is this burning an eternal flame?*

The look in her eyes told her that she was winning.

The applause which burst out at the final note delighted her. 'More! More!' the listeners shouted. But Millie was not to be persuaded. As she had done before, she laughed and said, 'No, no, you've come here to listen to the wonderful Stevie Bones, not to me! Stevie, take it away!' She hurried over to her seat, doing her best to blush. Danny seized her hand. 'That was so beautiful, Millie.'

Millie smiled at him, trying to look shy and modest. 'Did you really like it, Danny?' she murmured. 'I'm so glad.'

Danny continued to hold her hand during the rest of the evening, only letting go when Stevie Bones came up to them during the break to tell Millie he'd got the manager, Declan Byrne, to stand at the back during Millie's number and see for himself how good she was. He hadn't spoken to him yet, but fully expected that he'd be well impressed.

'Dec's got a lot of business sense. He'll probably want to fix you up with a gig some evening soon, and if that goes well, he'll offer you a regular evening. Not Friday, Saturday, or Wednesday, cause those are mine – still leaves plenty,' Stevie finished with a grin. 'Got to go outside for a smoke now before the break's over.'

He ambled off through the open door to the street.

'Let's you and me go outside, too, Millie,' Danny said.

'I don't smoke, Danny.'

'I wasn't thinking of smoking.'

Millie gave him an innocent look.

'Millie, you're so beautiful. You nearly made me cry with your singing. I want to hold you.'

'Danny, you're seeing Jan, aren't you?'

'That doesn't mean you can't be kind to me.'

Millie looked at him. She thought about her best options. She didn't want to lose whatever chance she had with Danny. He was clearly in the melting mood right now. Should she go for it while he was hot, like the iron? But nice as she thought Danny was, what she really wanted from him was his money, and she wouldn't get that unless she could bring him to the point of proposing marriage.

She knew from her experience of him on her first night at the Robert Street house that Danny would take everything he could from her, with no thought of marriage, if she was a big enough fool to let him. On the other hand, if she gave nothing, or nothing much, would he be driven to suggesting marriage or would he just give up? She made up her mind. Nothing right now, but maybe next time a little, not too much.

'Danny, I'm not that kind of girl. For me, it's all or nothing. I want to marry the right guy when he comes along, not just sleep around with any one who grabs me.' She opened her eyes wide and gazed at him earnestly, doing her best to look sweet and serious. She reckoned that in his present mood, Danny would believe her.

And clearly he did. 'Millie, I know. You're a very special babe. I only want to show you that I love you.' He took a deep breath. 'I didn't mean to say that – never said it to anyone before.'

Millie said, quoting from the advice column in a women's magazine she'd read some years ago in her dentist's waiting room, 'Danny, if you mean that, you'll show it by giving me time. It's far too soon for either of us to be sure.'

'Okay.' Danny was relieved. He'd had no plan to commit himself, but the words had come out before he could stop them. Time, that would be good. Time to think.

'Hush, they're coming back in.'

Stevie Bones and his support musicians trooped back to their places and the music began again.

Millie settled back to enjoy it. Later, in the taxi home, she might let him kiss her, but only a couple of times, briefly.

Chapter Twenty Seven

John O'Leary was spending his time sending off for more and more free prospectuses. He would get excited about a particular company, and then decide that the shares were too dear for him to risk buying into it. They'd be unlikely to go up much more – might even go down if the recession developed further. What he wanted was something where the shares were currently reasonably low, but would go shooting up quite soon. Something, he often thought wistfully, like his own company if he'd been able to persuade Stephen Gillespie to go in with him.

There was an expanding oilfield in South America – that had possibilities. He decided, after considerable thought, to try it. He'd never had much to do with oil, but it was something that could hardly fail. So he invested some of the money he'd put in the bank when he sold his house and everything else, instead of – as he'd originally intended – ploughing it back into his own business, to get it back on its feet.

As he arranged to buy the oil shares, he decided that if it seemed worthwhile, he might invest more. But maybe it would be better to find something else as well. Pity to buy shares when they were already dear. It would be good to sit back and watch his newly acquired shares go up on a rising market, as he'd been able to do at the start of the last boom, when he and Sam were not long married and the kids were still babies.

He sat sometimes in the small front room which he used as a study, to work on his computer, leaving the even smaller kitchen or their respective bedrooms for Sam and Sooze, and remembered nostalgically how happy he had been in those days.

Curiously enough, he didn't remember being so happy during the twenty odd years since. He'd had plenty of money, a good looking wife, and two kids to be proud of. But somehow he hadn't taken the time to enjoy these. It had all been work, work, work. He wasn't sure what Sam had felt about that. She'd enjoyed having the money, that was for sure. But they hadn't had much of a relationship for most of that time.

Maybe he could make it up to her, they could spend more time together.

As soon as he'd got his business up and running again.

Sam, to her surprise when she stopped to think about it, was finding that she was happier than she'd been for years. She had plenty to keep her occupied, without feeling over stretched. But she was worried about Sooze, who looked so miserable, and who was probably crying herself to sleep every night.

Sooze hardly noticed that her father spent most of his time these days on the computer. She knew, vaguely, that he was working out business deals. She helped her mother in the house, although not very much. Her mind was occupied with Josh. Did he still love her? Was he planning to marry her? Or had he dumped her?

The delivery of the *iPod* had given her hope for more than a week. But then, as the days went past with no texts from Josh, she began to worry again. After a few more weeks, she was once more in despair. If only he would say something.

Josh had started his new job and was hating it. To his surprise, Horse was looked up to by Josh's fellow workers as a clever, even brilliant, man, one who knew what he was doing and would be able to take over with great ease when his father retired. They referred to him as Horace, and Josh, who had despised Horse and treated him as someone wildly inferior since they had first met, and had almost forgotten that he had a name other than the belittling nickname Josh himself had bestowed on him, was taken by surprise the first time he heard the real name used. He remembered the day Horse had rescued him from the school bullies.

'What's your name?' Josh had asked in a condescending way, and when the reply was Horace Buchanan, he had laughed unpleasantly and said, 'Horace? What sort of a name is that? Sounds like Horse. And that would suit you better, Horse, because a horse is just what you look like!'

Now he found himself, to his astonishment, beginning to respect Horse almost as much as the rest of the work force obviously did. True to his promise, Horse helped him with his training, explaining technicalities in a simple way which Josh could manage to follow, and spending time with him out of the office going through Josh's assignments and correcting them.

'You're doing fine, Josh,' he would say. 'You should be able to pass easily enough. Then you'll start really earning.'

He was anxious to see Josh and Sooze safely married before her pregnancy became too obvious. It would need to be soon, now.

'Have you spoken to your dad about letting you have an apartment of your own, yet, Josh?' he asked one day.

Josh, who had been miserably typing in Horse's suggested corrections to his latest assignment, brightened up. 'Yeah, he's come round to it. I told him all my friends had their own place, and it was making me look stupid, and like someone really hard up, to be still living at home. He didn't want that – he's always wanted to outdo my friends and their parents. I found a great place down by the Lagan. He's going to pay the first year's rent, and increase my allowance to cover my new living expenses. I'm hoping to move in next week, when all the paperwork's signed.'

'Brilliant!' Horse exclaimed. 'Then you and Sooze can get married straight after that.' His enthusiasm wasn't matched by anything Josh felt. He supposed he owed it to Sooze to carry out Horse's suggestion. But maybe not quite yet.

Down in Dublin, Johnny had been working too hard to really take in what had been happening to his family. To his surprise, he was enjoying the job as he'd never expected to enjoy any job. He'd been sent down by his family under pressure, and had gone along with it unwillingly. But he found during the first week that he liked being on his own, having his own place, earning his own money and finding that he was good at the job he'd been thrown into.

He was assistant marketing manager for a huge chain selling every-thing from clothes, jewellery, and perfume to food, household goods and electrical products. On his first day, shown into the office of the CEO, he had sat as invited in front of the huge shining mahogany desk and listened as his boss spoke to him seriously.

'You have a chance in a million here, Johnny. You're getting it because I owe your father a favour, but if you don't make good, make no mistake about it, you'll be out. I'm starting you as Assistant Marketing Manager which is already bringing you in over the heads of people who've worked here for some time and who know the job. In six months the Marketing Manager, Phil Murphy, intends to retire. That means you'll be in with a chance of getting his job. It depends on how well you learn the job as assistant and how good you are at it. You understand?'

Johnny, who was impressed by the CEO, Michael Byrne, a tall, strong looking man with smooth dark hair and piercing blue eyes, said, 'Yes, sir,' eagerly. 'I'll do my best.'

'No one can do more,' Byrne said. He smiled at Johnny, who felt him-self glow with pleasure. Byrne pressed a bell, and his secretary, a tall sophisticated girl in a green suit with a short skirt and with long, straight red hair, came in.

'Isobel, take Johnny O'Leary down to Phil's office and introduce him. Phil's expecting him. Phil will start you off, show you the ropes,' Byrne said to Johnny.

That was the start of it. Every day Johnny became more and more engrossed in his work. It was only when his mother's letters began to talk about moving house, and, finally, when she told him that his father's business had collapsed and that they were selling everything, including the house, that Johnny woke up to the truth.

He asked for a couple of days off – citing 'trouble at home,' without giving more detail – and took the train up to Belfast late on Friday afternoon, with the intention of returning late on the Tuesday. That gave him four days to find out what was going on.

Coming out of Lanyon Station, Johnny followed the sign for taxis and gave the new address his mother had sent him. The taxi driver seemed surprised. When they reached the street, Johnny was surprised too. He knew things weren't good for his family, but he had never expected that it would be as bad as this. Paying the taxi and seizing his suitcase, he went to the door and rang the bell. The reddish paintwork badly needed redoing. The whole place looked as if it was about to fall down. When his mother answered the door – no Zofia any longer, he realised – she looked tired and somehow older. Her face lit up when she saw her son.

'Johnny! How lovely to see you.' She gave him a clumsy hug. It had been a long time, since his childhood, in fact, since Johnny had been hugged by his mother.

Chapter Twenty Eight

Millie had lunch with Fergus Ryan the day after her performance at *The City Walls*. It wasn't the first time. Fergus was clearly falling for her in a big way. Now that she knew on Jan's authority that before long Danny would be the owner of McLoughlin & Ryan, and Fergus Ryan would be much less well off, Millie was less worried about keeping his good opinion, but since it was second nature to her to encourage anyone who admired her, she smiled and flirted in her best manner.

'How's your wife, Fergus?' she eventually asked him sweetly when it seemed necessary to calm him down and call a halt to his advances.

Fergus's face fell immediately. 'As well as can be expected, Millie,' he said. 'Which is, of course, far from well. You know how serious matters are?'

'Yes, Jan explained to me.'

'I can't expect to have her for much longer,' Fergus said. He was silent for a moment, then pulled himself together with an effort. 'Now, Millie, can't I tempt you to a glass of wine?'

'I don't think I'd get much work done this afternoon if I took it, Fergus,' Millie laughed.

Fergus smiled. 'Well, what would that matter? The sparkle of your presence lighting up our dull old office is enough, without adding your brilliant work.'

Millie smiled teasingly. 'You might not think that, if I sell shares in a rising company for half their value, and buy rubbish at top price!'

'That might not be the best idea. But worth it to see your smile.'

Clearly, Millie felt, she had Fergus just where she wanted him. But did she want him? Not when Danny was set to inherit his aunt's shares.

She continued to see a lot of Danny. It was clear to everyone that the relationship between Danny and Jan could be considered over. Danny hadn't exactly dumped her, but he had stopped asking her out or spending time with her. Millie was well aware that Jan was murderously jealous of her.

It was the weekend after that that Danny and Millie went down to Belfast.

'It would be great to get away and spend some time together without Jan glaring at us, or Uncle Fergus for that matter,' Danny said, and Millie couldn't help agreeing with that.

They took the express bus and reached Belfast not much more than two hours later. Danny seemed to know his way around Belfast.

'I've booked us into the *Hilton*,' he announced as they left the bus station. 'It's not far from here – we could stroll over easily enough.'

'That would be nice, Danny.'

They crossed the road and walked along by the Lagan, passing the *Big Fish*, the mosaic sculpture by John Kindness – of the Salmon of Knowledge from the Finn McCool legend – down and past the *Belfast Barge*, and then up again to cross the plaza in front of the Waterfront Hall.

'It's just round the corner here,' Danny said. 'We can get settled in and then later on, when we're organised, we can have something to eat, either in the hotel or somewhere else. Plenty of choice. Then I thought you might like to go and have a drink and listen to some music. Celebrate, sort of.'

'Sounds perfect, Danny.'

Sometime later they ate at *Home*, a good restaurant a short walk up from the hotel and across past the City Hall. Millie was enjoying the Belfast ambiance. She was also enjoying the fact that Danny seemed to have money to burn. When she'd lived here with her father, and later when she was at school, there had never been any money to explore the more up-market side of Belfast. The night out at the *Limelight* with Sooze and her friends had been Millie's first experience of anything like that.

Later, when Danny asked her if there was anywhere in particular that she would like to go, she suggested the *Limelight* for want of anywhere else that she knew of.

As always, the *Limelight* was buzzing. Danny managed to find seats for them both at one of the tables, and fetched them drinks from the bar. By now he was familiar with Millie's tastes, but instead of going straight up for a gin & tonic, he hesitated.

'Special occasion, Mil,' he said. 'How about a cocktail? They do some great ones here.' He looked at Millie in her white dress, a diaphanous top layer over an underdress of satin, coming in tight at the waist and then flowing in a wide swirl to mid calf.

Millie had lashed out on it, spending a lot of the money Sooze had given her, secure in the knowledge that she'd by now received her first month's pay. The dress was embroidered throughout with silver thread in a pattern of lilies and stars. With it she wore a white enamel spray, fastening her red hair back on one side behind her ear. 'I think,' Danny said, feasting his eyes on her, 'that a *White Lady* might be appropriate.'

'Anything you suggest, darlin',' Millie murmured. 'I'm not very well up on cocktails.' This was true, although not for the reason Millie intended to suggest, of modest innocence, but rather because the drinking she had done with her father's friends had been mainly straight spirits.

'To us,' Danny said on his return from the bar, lifting his own Scotch and soda to Millie and clicking it against her *White Lady*.

'To us.' Millie smiled back at him and took a cautious sip. To her surprise, she loved it.

The band was starting up. Millie looked round the room. Her attention was caught by a party arriving at a table not far from their own. A pretty dark girl, a tall, fair man, with a more muscular build than Danny, and another man, big and dark haired with a red face. It was Sooze, with Josh and Horse.

'Sooze!' Millie exclaimed.

At the same time, Danny said, 'Hey, it's old Josh! And Horse!'

Their voices must have carried to the new arrivals in spite of the background racket. The band was still tuning up, getting ready to start, but there was a noisy babble of chatter and laughing people. Sooze looked round. Then she sprang back to her feet and hurried over.

'Millie! How lovely to see you!'

Her arms went round her friend, and Millie, standing up, returned the hug with the appearance of equal enthusiasm. Meanwhile, Danny was waving at Josh and Horse, who came over in their turn.

'Hey, haven't seen you since school, Josh, boy!' Danny said. 'Great to run into each other like this. Both of you, I mean,' he added at once, realising he was cutting Horse out.

'Come and join us,' Horse invited. 'There's room for two more at our table.' Josh was not so keen, but could say nothing. Sooze, hearing what Horse was saying, added her own enthusiastic invitation. Danny could do little but agree. He had hoped to have Millie to himself that evening, but it was his own fault for greeting his old school friends so extravagantly.

By the time they were all seated together, the band had started. It wasn't until the break, when Sooze and Millie went off to the Ladies together, that the three men were able to talk.

'Have you known Millie Brennan for long, Danny?' Josh asked after they had run out of memories of their schooldays and inquiries as to what each was doing now.

'Just since she came to work for my uncle's company in Derry.'

'Oh. Well, let me give you a word of warning,' Josh said. 'I'd keep away from her, if I were you. She's a conniving little bitch. She landed herself on Sooze when they left school, and Sooze has such a kind heart that she let her get away with it. She made a dead set at Sooze's brother Johnny, but the family caught on and bundled her off to Derry – '

'Shut up, stupid,' murmured Horse in Josh's ear, seeing Millie and Sooze approaching the table. He just hoped neither of them had heard.

But Millie had sharp ears, and although she showed no sign of it, she had heard clearly everything that Josh had said. She had never liked him much, but now she hated him. If there was ever an opportunity to get back at him, Millie knew she would take it.

Chapter Twenty Nine

A few days after she had finally mourned the death of her relationship with Danny, which had now become so clear to her, the same weekend that Danny and Millie spent in Belfast, Jan drove out to visit Fran Ryan, bringing a bunch of flowers.

Fran was looking very thin and ill. She was lying on a couch, with pillows supporting her and thick woolly shawls around her, in spite of the warmth of the central heating which was turned to high, and the additional heat of the sun shining in through the windows.

'Fran, I really wanted to see you,' Jan said. 'Here.' She thrust the flowers forward. 'I thought you might like these. I know you like flowers that have a real scent, not like the cultivated ones which smell of nothing.' She had brought Fran stock, late blossoming freesia, and sweet pea. Their mingled scents filled the room, and Fran smiled in delight as she held them to her nose. Jan fetched three large vases, filled them with water, and arranged the flowers carefully. 'There!' she said as she placed the vases around Fran where she could both see and smell them.

'Jan, you're so kind. I'm really sorry that I won't be around to see you happily married to Danny.'

Jan sat down beside the couch where Fran lay. 'I'm afraid no one will be around for that, Fran,' she said. A tear, and then another, trickled down from her eyes. 'Danny's dumped me. He's seeing a gold digging slut who only wants him because he's going to inherit your money.' She was careful not to mention Millie's name, knowing that Fran had liked her on the evening they had spent together, and was unlikely to think of her as 'a gold digging slut' on Jan's say so alone.

Fran struggled to sit up, realised she was too weak to manage, and lay back on her pillows looking horrified. 'But, Jan, surely he wouldn't do anything so stupid.'

'I'm afraid he has.'

'Jan, dear, I'm sorry. If only there was something I could do.'

'It's Danny I'm worried about as much as myself,' Jan said. 'I know if he marries this bitch he'll be miserable. She'll ruin him and when she's got all his money she'll probably leave him for someone richer.'

Fran looked at her, tears in her eyes. She had always loved Danny. She and Fergus had no children of their own. Danny, her sister's son, had been like her own child to Fran.

'There must be something I can do,' she murmured, half to herself. 'Maybe if I could talk to him –'

Jan sat and watched her, saying nothing. Presently she got up to go, and Fran hugged her again. 'Don't worry, Jan,' she said. 'I'm in your corner!'

Meanwhile Millie had been dividing her time between Danny and Fergus. She worked hard, getting on top of the job and earning praise from Lorraine, but at the end of each day she left with Danny and they ate together, went for long walks together, went to the movies. At weekends, and some-times at lunch time, she saw Fergus, and kept to her policy of allowing him to go so far and no further.

To both Fergus and Danny she had spelled it out long ago at the very start of each relationship. 'I wouldn't feel happy about making love to someone unless I was going to marry him.' Then she had looked up with her big green eyes, and a serious expression.

On Tuesday nights she was singing regularly at *The City Walls*, wowing the crowd, and drawing in more and more people as the word was spread by customers who loved her voice. Danny came every week, taking her there by taxi and bringing her back again afterwards. Millie knew that the repeated impact of her singing had had more and more effect on him.

And of course, the money on top of the salary from her day job was a very pleasant addition. Millie opened an account and began to save, as things advanced rapidly with Danny.

The day came, a couple of weeks after Millie's weekend in Belfast with Danny, when Fergus arrived at work wearing a black tie, then left after the first hour. He told a few people, Jan and Lorraine and Colum, his assistant manager, that Fran had died over the weekend. He had left it to them tell the rest of the work force.

Danny didn't appear at all. Millie hadn't seen much of him over the weekend, or indeed for some days before that. Fran had been moved to hospital earlier in the week, and Danny, together with Fergus, had been spending a lot of time there.

And so Fran Ryan slipped quietly off the Roundabout, happy to leave this world and its sadness behind, and to go into a new world and into the fullness of joy.

Danny still hadn't come back to Robert Street when Millie got back from work, but she got a text from him shortly afterwards, asking her to meet him at *Henry's*, their favourite low key restaurant, in about an hour.

Millie walked over. She was glad of the exercise, and it gave her time to think. She badly wanted to know about Fran's will, but she knew that Danny would still be feeling very upset by her death. He had really loved Fran, his only close blood relative. Fergus was the next closest relation he had, but Fergus was only an uncle by marriage. Millie didn't think either was very fond of the other. It probably wasn't a good time to inquire about the will. She would just have to be patient.

When she reached *Henry's*, Danny was waiting for her. They sat in a corner table for two, as far as possible from other customers, and Millie put her hand over Danny's as it lay on the table. 'I'm so sorry about Fran, dear,' she said softly. 'She was a lovely woman.'

Danny smiled at her, not far from tears. 'You're a lovely person yourself, Millie,' he said. 'Thanks.' Then he pulled himself resolutely together. 'Let's not be miserable tonight,' he said. 'It's really good to see you again, Mil. I've missed you this week. So, what would you like to drink – I see the waiter approaching?'

Millie continued to see Fergus for lunch sometimes. He was back at work, and clearly eager to see Millie as much as possible. So far, neither Fergus nor Danny had told Millie anything about Fran's will.

It was Jan who mentioned it casually to Millie, one day when the funeral was long over, when they were sharing a mirror in the ladies' cloakroom at work, repairing their makeup and tidying their hair before leaving for the day. 'I suppose you know that Danny's Auntie Fran didn't leave a will, after all?'

Millie froze. After a moment, she pulled herself together. 'Sorry?' she murmured, attending closely to her lipstick. 'I missed that. Something about Fran? So sad – such a lovely lady, everyone says.'

'She didn't leave a will,' Jan repeated impatiently. 'She told Danny that she was leaving a lot of her stock in the company to him, but she didn't, it turns out. So her husband, her next of kin legally, gets the lot.'

'But – are they sure? Maybe her solicitor has it?'

'Fergus checked with him, naturally, a week or so after the funeral. Didn't want to ask about it any sooner. Apparently Fran made a will, all right, leaving two thirds of her stock to Danny and one third to Fergus. She'd explained to Danny that half of her stocks had belonged to her sister, Danny's mother, and she only had them because Danny's Da, a no good guy, sold them to Fran when he needed the cash.

So Fran was leaving them to Danny, with some of her own original inheritance, because she felt he'd been hard done by. Then, only two weeks before she died, she phoned the solicitor and asked him to bring the will to her, because she wanted to destroy it and draw up another one. She still meant to leave Danny something, but nothing like as much.

There was a half finished letter to Danny, telling him what she was doing, and asking him to let his girlfriend know. I think she expected that the girlfriend – that would be you, Millie – would drop him like a hot potato when she heard. But Danny never got the letter, of course. Fran had time to burn the will – the solicitor was there when she did it – and to give him instructions for drafting a new one. But she got a lot worse just after that. She wasn't able to finish her letter or sign her will. So poor Danny gets nothing. What a shame, isn't it, Millie?'

Millie could see Jan's face in the mirror laughing at her unpleasantly. 'Someone must have been telling her bad things about Danny's new girl, I suppose, Millie. I wonder who that could have been, Millie, don't you?'

'It hardly matters to me enough to start wondering, Jan,' Millie said carelessly. 'Goodness, I must dash!' And she got herself out of the cloak-room as quickly as possible.

Chapter Thirty

Josh had finally got round to asking Sooze to marry him. Their meeting, in the company of Horse, at the *Limelight*, had settled it for him. Seeing her again, he felt a stirring of the old passion. He wanted this girl. It seemed the only way to get her was by marriage. Before he could change his mind he had blurted out to her, during Horse's absence to fetch his car from where it was parked round the corner, 'Sooze, I really do love you. Can we get married very soon?'

'Josh, that's what I want, too,' Sooze said, as he leaned forward to kiss her.

The return of Horse and the car was the only thing that ended the long passionate kiss.

But when they were driving home, Sooze said, 'I don't know what my father will say. He blames your dad for the collapse of his business. It doesn't make a lot of sense to me, but he does.'

'Don't tell him until it's over,' Josh said promptly. 'I certainly won't be telling mine.'

Sooze looked unhappy. 'I'd like to tell my mum. I think she'd be pleased. And I think she might have guessed about the baby. I haven't said anything, but she knows I'm being sick quite a lot.'

'If you tell her, will she tell your dad?'

'Maybe not, if I ask her to promise.'

'Even if she does, there's nothing he can do, Sooze,' Horse said sensibly. 'You're an adult, officially. You can get married without anyone's permission.'

'I suppose so. But I'd sort of like to tell them both, anyway. It feels bad, not to.'

'How about getting Johnny to come back up for a few days and support you?' Horse suggested. 'Now he's doing so well, they have a lot more respect for him. Your dad might listen to his opinion.'

Johnny had gone back down to Dublin, but he had arranged for some money to be paid regularly into his father's account, and had suggested that they use it to get themselves a better house or apartment to rent. John O'Leary, although humiliated at having to depend on his son – temporarily, he insisted – was glad to move from the dump they had lived in to a rather better place, an apartment further out from the city centre.

'That's a good idea, Horse,' Josh agreed.

'So, you should book to get married at the registry office,' Horse further suggested. Josh, not quite sure how to go about this, decided to ask Horse about it as soon as they had left Sooze home.

'I'll do that,' he agreed. 'Sooze, it's going to be great! We can live in my new apartment, and I'll have plenty of money to support us when I get my promotion.'

Arrived at the O'Learys' new home, Josh and Sooze both got out of the car and indulged in a prolonged goodnight, while Horse tactfully and painfully looked the other way. He wished that it could have been he who was arranging to marry Sooze, but he knew, and had known since he first met her, that Sooze had no interest in him. Against Josh he didn't stand a chance. Sooze was deeply in love with his friend and probably always would be.

When Sooze had gone in, Josh turned to Horse. 'Horse, how do you go about booking to get married in a registry office? And how soon can we do it?'

'For Belfast, it's in the City Hall,' Horse said. 'I suppose you ring or call in or book online. I think it has to be booked a week beforehand, but I'll check it for you, if you like.'

'Horse, you're a real friend,' Josh said, feeling emotional from the long kiss with Sooze and the drinks he had had in the *Limelight*. 'Horse, I want you to promise me that when Sooze and I are married, if anything ever happens to me, you'll look after that wee girl. And the baby, too, of course.'

'What's going to happen to you, you great fool?' Horse said, grinning. 'You're sloshed. But, yes, I promise, if you really want me to. I'll always look after Sooze and your kid, okay?'

And Josh, feeling even more emotional, hugged Horse before collapsing against him, and had to be pushed into the car, and driven back to his new apartment.

Johnny, contacted by Sooze on his mobile the next day, was delighted that she and Josh were getting married, and texted back that he would be happy to come up and support her when she told their parents, and more-over to give her away if their father refused to. 'Just let me know the date when it's sorted,' he finished.

The date would be another week away. Horse had checked the details for Josh and together they had gone to the City Hall to make arrangements. Two days before the date, Sooze spoke to her mother in the kitchen, while her father sat at his computer in the front room, hoping to discover some company whose stocks, if he bought them, would earn him another fortune like the one he had lost.

'Mum, Josh Gillespie wants to marry me, and I've said yes. Will you come to my wedding? It's arranged for the day after tomorrow, at the City Hall Registry Office.'

'Oh, Sooze! That's wonderful!' Sam O'Leary threw her arms round her daughter and hugged her. She became aware as she did so that Sooze was already showing signs of the pregnancy which she'd guessed at some time ago, but said nothing about it. There was no need to worry about it any more. Sam felt thankful.

'Johnny is coming up. In fact, I'm expecting him any time now. He said he'd help me tell Dad.'

'That's probably wise, Sooze,' Sam agreed. 'I don't think he'll take it well, even so, but he'll take it better from Johnny than from anyone else.'

Johnny arrived an hour or so later. First, Sam insisted he had to be fed, and Johnny himself insisted on a shower and a change of clothing while she prepared the meal.

Then they sought out John O'Leary in the room he called his office. The new flat had more space, and more rooms, than the back-street house they had lived in before Johnny's money made the move possible. It had three bedrooms as well as kitchen, bathroom, and reception room. That meant there was a room for Johnny to sleep in, but still no room for Sooze and her mum to sit in to relax except the kitchen, since O'Leary had annexed the reception room for himself to work in. But they didn't mind. The kitchen was roomy enough for comfort, with two soft chairs as well as the hard dining set.

They all three trooped into John O'Leary's office.

'John,' Sam began brightly, 'Sooze has some good news for you. She's getting married the day after tomorrow.'

'Married?' John O'Leary pushed his chair back from the computer and looked round at his family. 'Who to?'

'To Josh Gillespie, Dad.'

O'Leary's mouth fell open. But before he could say anything, Johnny spoke.

'Stephen Gillespie has ordered Josh to dump her, Dad. I think Josh is doing something really good in refusing to do that. We should all support him.'

John O'Leary looked at him. 'I suppose the lad's doing right. But I still hate to have a son of Gillespie coming into my family.' He turned his back on them and began to fidget with his computer again. 'Well? What are you waiting for?' he said presently in an irritated voice. 'If it's my blessing you're waiting for, Susan, you won't get it. But I suppose you'll do what you want, no matter what I think.'

'Come on,' Johnny murmured to his sister and his mother, and he hustled them out of the room and back to the kitchen.

'It's as much as we could have expected, Sooze,' he said when they were sitting down again. 'He couldn't bear to say anything good about you marrying a Gillespie. But he won't oppose it.'

Sooze looked at him, tears brimming from her eyes. 'Oh Johnny!' was all she could say.

'So both of you plan your wedding gear, and I'll hire a car and collect you. I'll come and give the bride away, or whatever they do in registry offices,' Johnny said. 'Cheer up, Sooze. This time the day after tomorrow you'll be a married woman.'

When Johnny's hired car pulled up in front of the new apartment on Sooze's wedding day, John O'Leary took care to be well out of the way. Sooze was sad not to have her father's blessing, but her mother and Johnny did their best to encourage her, and the knowledge that in a few more hours she and Josh would be together for ever was enough to bring a fluttering smile to her face.

She hadn't been able to buy anything special to wear, but her favourite blue dress, now showing signs of considerable tightness round the waist, nevertheless looked well. As for Sam, she had enough left in the way of smart clothes to be sure of finding something to suit the occasion.

They parked behind the City Hall and went in. Josh and Horse were waiting for them inside the courtyard. Josh looked nervous. Horse was holding a bouquet of red roses carefully arranged by a florist with fern, a few white lilies, and a trailing red ribbon. Waiting until Josh and Sooze had exchanged greetings and hugs, he came forward shyly and presented it to Sooze, mumbling, 'For the beautiful bride.'

Sooze was touched, and impulsively hugged Horse as well, something she'd never bothered to do before. Horse went a bright red. Then they all went in and found the registrar's office.

Chapter Thirty

There were plenty of seats, arranged in rows, for guests, but only Sam and Horse occupied them. Josh and Sooze stood before the registrar's desk, with Johnny beside Sooze in his role as the person who was giving away the bride.

The promises were made, and Joshua Stephen Gillespie and Susan Mary O'Leary took each other for better or worse. They signed the registry, followed by their two witnesses, Samantha Bernadette O'Leary and Horace Nathaniel Buchanan. Then it was over, as surprisingly quickly as all weddings for such a momentous, life-changing event, and they found themselves outside the registrar's again. Sam hugged her daughter, her eyes misty.

'We need to take some photos,' Johnny said.

'Good idea,' enthused Sam, who wanted her smart lilac wedding suit to be recorded for posterity. 'Let's find our way to the stairway and take some there.'

'Great,' everyone agreed. They made their way to the impressive marble staircase which ran down to the front entrance hall, and took a few appropriate snaps posing on the steps.

'Right!' said Horse, no longer seeming embarrassed. 'I've booked a wedding lunch for us all on the *Belfast Barge*, so let's get the cars and drive round there now. And we can drink the health of the bride and groom in champagne. As long as no one expects me to make a speech.'

A lovely meal, more photos taken with the *Belfast Barge* in the background, and it was time for Johnny, Sam, and Horse to leave the happy couple on their own. They were heading back to Josh's new apartment, and hoped to have a brief honeymoon at the weekend.

Roundabout – *Gerry McCullough*

Chapter Thirty One

Millie had been more shaken by Jan's news about the will than she had shown. The next few weeks were difficult for her. Fergus appeared back at work, and resumed his attentions to her almost at once. Millie was reluctant to do anything to offend him. After all, he had the money now. But she didn't want to annoy Danny either.

'Let's go for a day out, this weekend, Millie,' Fergus suggested one Friday. 'We can go up the coast and see Malin Head – the most northerly part of Ireland, you know. We can climb up and look out over the Atlantic Ocean. I always love looking out at the sea. Time you saw more of the local sights, girl. We can have a snack lunch, drive back round the coast, and then we can have a slap-up meal later on.'

Millie was unsure what to do. Danny would be expecting to spend Saturday with her. It had become a habit. Maybe if she explained to him that she was just trying to keep in with his uncle and persuade him to give Danny some shares, as Fran would certainly have done if she'd had time to write the new will? She hadn't meant to cut Danny right out, according to the solicitor. Just to reduce what he got. Fergus had a moral obligation, and she thought she could persuade him to see it that way.

Danny sounded doubtful when she explained this to him later on. 'I don't think Fergus means to give me anything, Mil,' he said ruefully. 'It may be a moral obligation as you say, but Fergus isn't strong on morals, at least as far as business is concerned. Still, go, if you think it may help.'

So the following morning Fergus pulled up in front of the house in Robert Street and dooted his horn. He stayed in the car, to Millie's relief.

She had been on the lookout for him, and ran out straightaway, in order to catch him before he became impatient and came to the door. Fergus swung the car door open for her.

'Lookin' good, Millie. Climb in, and we'll get going.'

He drove back down to the bridge, crossed it, and drove out along the quay to the Moville Road. It was a lovely day, sunshine sparkling on the river, and Millie felt bright and hopeful. She exerted herself to be amusing and pleasant to Fergus.

Moville, when they passed through it, was tiny. They got out of the car and wandered down to the small pier, and Fergus took Millie's hand to help her over some of the rougher ground. She moved away from him as soon as she could without causing him offence, and sighed deeply in enjoyment. 'I love the sea, Fergus. It seems ages since I was so close to it. The river is beautiful, but the actual sea is something else.'

They drove on, gradually getting higher as they approached the cliffs.

Malin Head, when they finally reached it, was everything Fergus had told her it would be. As they drove along he had boasted happily about its beauties as if the country belonged to him. They climbed the hill from the car park and stood side by side looking out at the broad sweep of the Atlantic. Millie noticed presently that Fergus had taken her hand again.

'Amazing, isn't it?' he said.

'Wonderful,' Millie agreed, gently releasing her hand. 'I'm really glad to have seen it.'

'The old tower is pretty interesting, too. The place where it's built is called Banba's Crown. The tower itself is only about a couple of hundred years old, but the place is the most northerly point of Ireland, and was mentioned by ancient historians. Banba was the patron Goddess of Ireland before St Patrick came, and I suppose this is called Banba's Crown because it's the furthest north of her country, or something.'

Millie allowed herself to look fascinated. 'Wow, Fergus, you know such a lot of stuff.'

Fergus looked pleased. 'Oh, I wouldn't say that. I like to take an interest in things, I suppose. Fran wouldn't like me talking about heathen goddesses, mind you. She was such a keen Christian. She loved Irish things, but mostly not the old religions. But I shouldn't talk about Fran when I'm with you, Millie.'

'You can't forget her all at once, Fergus,' Millie said softly. 'She must have been a wonderful person. I only met her the once, but she struck me as someone special.'

Fergus dashed a tear from his eye. 'You're right, Millie. I shouldn't forget her all at once. But I should move on as soon as I can, right? It's left me very lonely, you see. And I'm a man who needs companionship. You're helping me a lot, these days, Millie.' He smiled, and Millie smiled back.

Fergus pulled himself together. 'Well, Millie, time we got back to the car and started to look for some lunch, right?'

'Right, Fergus.'

They drove on round the coast, going west, and found a snack bar where there were tables outside, overlooking a beach.

'This seems like a good place, Millie, seeing how fond you are of the sea. I don't think it's too cold today, even though it's the end of September,' Fergus said. He led her up to a small table and pulled back a chair for her. 'Now, I'm going to insist that you have something to drink – you don't have to go back to work today.'

So Millie had a glass of white wine, and ordered a chicken salad sandwich, and Fergus had a glass of Guinness and a cheeseburger.

'I think I'll skip the chips – got to look after my figure, or the girls won't!' joked Fergus, and Millie groaned, and then hoped he would take the groan as a back-handed compliment. He must know that no one actually laughed at a joke like that. A groan was as much of a good response as could be expected.

Over the meal Fergus kept off the subject of his late wife. Instead he talked about himself, and his plans for expanding the company, opening up branches in Belfast and even Dublin now that he had sole charge. Millie listened, hoping for an opportunity to ask if he planned to give Danny at least some shares, even if not as many as he should have got, if Jan hadn't been a manipulating bitch. But as Fergus talked on, it got more and more difficult.

At last she managed to cut in, in desperation, 'And what about Danny? Have you any plans for him?'

'Danny? Oh, yes, I'm planning to promote him – put him in charge of the Belfast branch, maybe. He's a good worker, I'll give him that, knows his way round the business. Not that he has the drive and ability I had at his age – ' Fergus talked on, and at last Millie despaired of saying anything more direct.

Lunch over, Fergus suggested a stroll on the beach. 'Pity we haven't brought swimming things,' he added.

'I think it might be a bit cold for me,' Millie said. Heated swimming pools were one thing. The Atlantic Ocean was quite another. 'But I wouldn't mind a paddle.'

They walked on the beach for some time, while Fergus talked happily about himself. Millie finally kicked off her shoes and ran down to the water's edge, where she paddled and laughed, and splashed Fergus playfully, until her feet began to freeze.

Back in the car, Fergus drove her along the *Wild Atlantic Way*, on what Millie considered fearsome cliffs with amazing, but frightening, views of the sea down steep bending narrow roads.

Back on more level ground again, he drove her on around with occasional stops to see somewhere of interest, arriving finally, much later, as the sun was going down the sky, at O'Doherty's Keep, built in 1333, Fergus told her, on the north bank of the river Crana where it enters Lough Swilly.

The Keep was just outside Buncrana, and when they drove on into the town Fergus said, 'There's a great wee restaurant here that you'll love, Millie, called *Ubiquitous*. It's right on Main Street. They do a Salmon Hollandaise to die for. And a great champ. We can take our time, it's not late yet, and we've come round in a sort of circle, so we'll not take too long driving home.'

Millie, whose usual healthy appetite had been sharpened by the fresh air, was happy to agree. They parked the car and went in.

Chapter Thirty Two

It turned out that Fergus had rung to book a table in advance, which was just as well, for the place was hiving. The food was everything Fergus had promised it would be, and Millie, noticing a cocktail list, and remembering how much she had enjoyed the *White Lady* Danny had bought her, allowed herself to be persuaded to try a Daiquiri, since there was no *White Lady* on the menu. It seemed quite similar, with Barcardi instead of gin, according to the description.

When it came, she sipped it cautiously at first, then with more enthusiasm. She realised that she would have to be careful. It would be a bad thing to drink too much, get carried away, and end up giving Fergus the wrong idea. Fergus was okay, she could probably enjoy herself getting off with him, especially if she had a few more drinks, but sex wasn't what she'd come out with him for.

The food arrived, a chicken dish for Millie and the salmon hollandaise he'd mentioned for Fergus, with a bottle of white wine, and Fergus, as he had done all day, began to talk profusely. This time, however, it was not about himself, but about Millie. He paid her extravagant compliments, and encouraged her to tell him about her life.

Millie, while enjoying the compliments, never enjoyed talking about her life. There were too many things she had to be careful to leave out. Descriptions of the boozy parties at her dad's were definitely out. She herself had been a child, but she had been allowed to drink anything that was going, to sing and dance and show off, to flirt with her dad's friends, and generally speaking to behave in a way which, Millie knew, would shock most of her recent acquaintances, and would demolish the picture she wanted to present of herself as a demure, respectable girl.

'My parents both died when I was still quite young,' she began. 'I still miss them a lot.' She allowed her eyes to blink away a few imaginary tears, looking down and producing a handkerchief to pretend to wipe them. 'I was sent to St Bernadette's School, and that was where I met Sooze O'Leary.

The O'Learys knew what good friends Sooze and I were, so they invited me to stay with them when we both left school. But I told them I could only stay for a short while, until I found a job, and could earn my own living. That was why Mrs O'Leary – she told me to call her Sam – got me the job with you, Fergus. I'll never forget how kind it was of her.'

'Sam's a lovely lady,' Fergus agreed, and Millie hid a smile as she remembered Sam's real attitude to her. 'But you're even lovelier. We're two sad people, Millie. We should comfort each other.' He poured Millie another glass of wine. 'I'd better not have any more myself,' he said as he poured her a generous glassful. 'I have to drive us home, remember. But you can enjoy the rest, Millie.'

Fergus had had only one glass, and Millie hoped she could resist her instinct, born of her youthful poverty, not to waste food and drink. She accepted the second glass, and listened to Fergus's continued compliments while finishing her chicken. Somehow or other, by the time they had both finished their main courses and were deciding on the *Ubiq's Wild Berry Mess* for desert, the bottle was nearly empty, as Millie noticed, with a tinge of anxiety. She somehow failed to prevent Fergus, a few minutes later, from tipping the remains into her now empty glass.

The Wild Berry Mess was delicious, and when it was finished Fergus said, 'Now, you'll have to have a liqueur coffee to finish up with, Millie. Come on, don't spoil the day for me by refusing. I want to make sure you have a really good time today, right?'

So Millie, against her better judgement, accepted an Irish Coffee.

'*As rich as an Irish brogue,*

As strong as a friendly hand,

As sweet as the tongue of a rogue,

As smooth as the wit of the land,' quoted Fergus, ' and I'll just have a black coffee, myself. Counteract the Guinness at lunch time and the glass of wine tonight.'

Millie was glad to hear it. She didn't trust Fergus to drive her safely home if he drank any more. She had to admit that he'd had very little, but the hair raising cliff top drive of earlier that afternoon hadn't give her a lot of confidence in him.

They lingered over their coffee, and at last Fergus called for the bill. 'I think a little walk by the river in the moonlight might be a nice end to the day, Millie, what do you say?' he asked her.

'That sounds good, Fergus.'

Presently they strolled outside and found their way down to the path beside the river Crana. The moon was high by now and shone upon the water, presenting it with a decoration of little trickles of silver. Millie was feeling the effects of the cocktail, the wine, and the whiskey in her Irish coffee. She made no demur when Fergus took her hand, saying, 'I'd better help you along here, Millie. The path's a bit on the rough side.'

Millie giggled.

'Would you sing to me, Millie?' Fergus asked her suddenly. 'You have such a beautiful voice. You give pleasure to everyone who hears it. Give pleasure to me now, Millie.'

'What do you want me to sing, Fergus?' Millie asked, unsure whether this singing was a good idea or not. Men usually felt the effect of her singing. She didn't want to stir up Fergus any more. She had been wondering to herself if it would be possible to bring up Danny's name, and his future, without annoying Fergus, which would be a great pity. She had her own future to think of. The last thing she wanted was to turn Fergus against her. Or against Danny.

Besides, far from encouraging him to give Danny some of the company shares, suggesting it might possibly put him off doing anything for Danny at all. If she sang for him, it would probably turn his mind towards making love to her, and this was something Millie was determined not to allow. She had made up her mind long ago not to sleep with anyone without a firm offer of marriage, and from a wealthy man, at that.

'Oh, anything, Millie. You choose, you know your own repertoire best.'

So Millie, after a moment's thought, began to sing *The Salley Gardens.*

Down by the Salley Gardens my love and I did meet;
She passed the Salley Gardens on little snow-white feet.
She bid me take love easy, as the leaves grow on the tree;
But I, being young and foolish, with her would not agree.

In a field by the river my love and I did stand,
And on my leaning shoulder she laid her snow-white hand.
She bid me take life easy, as the grass grows on the weirs;
But I was young and foolish, and now am full of tears.

It was only when she was halfway through the first verse that she realised how unhelpful this song would be.

Fergus stood still, obliging Millie to stop also, and hung onto her hand as if it was the only thing that was keeping him alive.

'Oh, Millie, Millie! You're so beautiful! I want you so much!'

'Fergus, you know I won't sleep with someone unless we're married. I wasn't brought up that way. I've explained that to you before.' Millie tried to speak gently.

'Then marry me! Oh, not just yet – people would be shocked. It's too soon after Fran's death. But promise me that you'll marry me in another six months, Millie. I need you! I'm so unhappy. You could make me happy again. I've been happy today, just because I'm with you.'

Millie pulled her hands away and in her confusion almost tripped into the river. The shock had been too much for her. The last thing she had expected was that Fergus would propose. She had thought he just wanted to get her into bed with him. The foremost thought in her mind was that she had made a real mess of things. It was Fergus who had the money now, and she could have married him and shared it with him.

'Oh, Fergus,' she wailed. 'I'm so sorry! I can't. I'm married already!'

Chapter Thirty Three

Sooze's first few weeks of married life were deliriously happy. She and Josh made love tenderly, and while Josh was out working she also worked hard, trying to keep the house clean and tidy, and preparing meals which she knew were Josh's favourites. She had learned more than she had ever known about running a house, during the last few months of helping her mother when they had lost their servants.

But it must be confessed that Sooze wasn't a very good cook. At first Josh said nothing, but after the first couple of weeks he began to get irritated at being served up hard, undercooked potatoes, or apple tart with not nearly enough sugar, and at having to wait for more than an hour for the meat to be ready, while everything else cooled down or got burnt.

'You should buy a cookery book, Sooze, and practice getting recipes right,' he lectured her. Sooze, who wasn't used to being told off or criticised, and especially hadn't expected it from Josh, found herself weeping. At first this made Josh sorry for what he had said, but after a while he got used to it, and it began to make him even more annoyed.

Horse, coming round by invitation for a meal with the happy couple, found it hard to keep from punching Josh when he heard his remarks to Sooze about what, it must be said, had been a disastrous meal.

'I suppose you're planning to go away for a week or two for your honeymoon?' he asked, hoping that some time together when Sooze didn't have to cook might help them to get on better. 'You should go before the baby comes. Babies in hotels can be a problem, I've heard.'

'Why, where did you hear that, Horse?' exclaimed Josh.

'I read it in a woman's magazine in my doctor's waiting room last year when I had flu,' confessed Horse, grinning. 'Don't laugh, there was nothing else to read. And it sounds right to me. Babies apparently wake up the other guests by crying during the night, they need special food, and they can't be left alone if you want to go out for the evening.'

Then he noticed that the faces of both his listeners had fallen.

'Wow! What a future!' Josh groaned. 'I suppose it would be the same at home, not just in a hotel.'

'It wouldn't be so bad, Josh.' Sooze tried to mend things hastily. 'At home, we would have all the baby food we needed on the premises, and if he cried, I could get up and soothe him – you could sleep on, and there'd be no one else to be annoyed. And if we wanted to go out at night, my Mum or one of my friends would babysit, I'm sure. All Horse means is that we wouldn't know anyone to get to babysit, in a hotel.'

'I suppose so,' Josh said grudgingly. 'As long as I don't have to get up at night.'

Horse's face was growing more and more black. 'I hope you intend to help Sooze with this baby,' he said severely. 'It's your son we're talking about, dude.'

'Oh, yeah, yeah, course I'll be helping her,' Josh muttered. He had begun to have a lot more respect for Horse, even to be slightly in awe of him occasionally, since working in McBride & Buchanan's. 'Just, I can't get up and go to work if I don't get my sleep.'

'So, a honeymoon soon would be great, Josh,' Sooze said enthusiastically, hoping to guide Josh's thoughts onto a happier path. 'Where shall we go?'

'Well, it'll have to be somewhere fairly cheap,' Josh said. He hadn't quite recovered his spirits, in the light of the horrendous future Horse had sketched out for him.

'How about Portrush? Or Newcastle?' Sooze suggested.

'Well, it certainly can't be anywhere abroad. Portrush might do, if the weather stays good.'

'The forecast for the rest of September and the start of October is fine and sunny,' Horse said.

Sooze stood up and began to clear the plates away. When she had gone into the kitchen, Horse resumed.

'I know a very nice guest house in Portrush, I can give you the name and website if you like. Then you can book online. Or I don't mind booking for you.'

'Would you mind, mate? You'd have to use your card, but I'd pay you back at the end of the month.'

Horse, who had already lent Josh quite a lot of money which he had never seen again, knew that his chances of being repaid were slim, but he didn't mind. He wanted Sooze to have a good break, to be able to relax and rest, and to be free from the cooking which she did so badly. She would learn in time, he supposed, but meanwhile the last thing she needed was Josh shouting at her.

'I'll have to ask for leave from work for a couple of weeks,' Josh added. 'It's very short notice. Could you put in a word for me, do you think?'

'A honeymoon is a pretty good excuse, mate. I'll explain to my dad. He won't mind.'

So the holiday was booked, and Sooze ran around packing and getting ready. She managed to get everything they wanted into one case. She didn't think she could carry one of her own. This way, Josh would be carrying her stuff as well as his own in the one case, without having to be asked to help. Sooze was already learning some things about managing her selfish, if attractive, husband.

She explained to her doctor that she would be away for two weeks, and changed her next appointment with him until she and Josh got back. The doctor was friendly and helpful. He had known Sooze since she was born, and when she had first gone to him for the more formal pregnancy test which had confirmed the result from the home test, he had promised not to tell her parents until Sooze had a chance to do that herself.

Sooze had told her family about the coming baby soon after her wedding, calling to see Sam and talking to her on her own. Sam had been unexpectedly relaxed and pleasant about it.

'I certainly didn't expect to be a grandmother at my age,' she joked. 'Even worse, I'll be sleeping with a grandfather! Make sure you look after yourself, Sooze. No heavy lifting or anything silly like that. And make sure you see Dr. Morrison regularly and do whatever he tells you. He's a good doctor, he'll look after you.'

'Now I'll have to tell Dad,' Sooze said. But she looked so woebegone at the prospect that Sam laughed, and said, 'I think you'd better leave that to me, sweetie.'

Johnny was no trouble. Sooze rang him in Dublin and told him he was about to become an uncle, and he seemed pleased and unquestioning.

At the end of the week, they travelled up to Portrush in the train, since by then they had had to sell Josh's car. Arrived there, they found that the place which Horse had booked for them was not just a guest house. It was a pretty good hotel.

'Wow!' Sooze said as they drew up in front of it. 'This must be costing us a bomb, Josh.'

'Oh, Horse insisted on booking it for us as an extra wedding present,' Josh said carelessly.

'But he's already given us that dining room set, the lovely table and chairs,' Sooze wailed. 'Josh, you shouldn't have let him.'

'Oh, old Horse isn't short of a bob or two. His dad owns the place where I work, McBride & Buchanan. He can pay for this without missing it.'

Josh knew very well that this wasn't strictly true, since Horse lived on his own salary, but he didn't want Sooze to know that he'd been sponging off Horse and intended to go on doing so for as long as he could. After all, Horse had more or less pushed him into this marriage, so it was up to him to support them. Or so Josh thought.

Their room was everything they could have wanted, with an ensuite bathroom, huge double bed, comfortable armchairs and desk, and colour television. Josh set the suitcase down on the rack provided, expecting Sooze to unpack it, but she was over at the window, staring down with delight at the sea view.

'Isn't it lovely, Josh! We can see one of the beaches, look. It's enormous, isn't it?'

'Let's have a look.'

Josh came over beside her, and slipped an arm round her waist. They looked out together over the blue sea, tossed with small white ruffles, and the wide expanse of beach with its golden sand.

'This looks like a good bed, too, Sooze,' he whispered in her ear. His mouth found hers. 'Let's see how good it is, okay?' He drew her to the bed and they lay down together.

Much later, showered and changed, they went out to stroll about and enjoy the ambience of the seaside town.

'I always loved coming here as a child, Josh,' Sooze sighed in contentment as they strolled hand in hand.

'I don't think I came as a child, Sooze. We mostly went abroad.'

'Well, so did we, but we came here sometimes as well.'

Her eye caught sight of someone – two someones – walking towards her.

'Josh! Isn't that Millie Brennan?'

'So it is,' Josh agreed. 'And that's Danny O'Hanlon with her!'

Chapter Thirty Four

Millie's and Danny's presence in Portrush was easily explained. Like Sooze and Josh, they were taking a late honeymoon. Millie had found it impossible to keep her husband's name a secret for long, after she had blurted out to Fergus the truth that she was married.

She wished afterwards that she had held her tongue. The amount of alcohol she had drunk must have had more effect on her than she had known.

Fergus's first reaction was to assume that she and her husband were separated, since he had seen no sign of a husband who was living with her. 'Poor little girl,' he said, tenderly. 'You're better off without him, Millie. Why don't you get a divorce?'

Millie stared at him, unsure what to reply. Finally, she said, 'Oh, Fergus, I can't talk about it right now. We should go home.'

'Don't worry, little girl. I won't push you. Take your time and think about it. I'll take you home now, since that's what you want.'

Much to Millie's relief he allowed the subject to drop on the drive home, which, as he had said, was a lot shorter than the drive out had been. She was very glad to say goodnight to him when he dropped her at the house in Robert Street where she was still living.

Danny was waiting there for her, lounging on her bed with his feet up and the door safely shut. When she pushed open the door he swung himself off the bed and took her in his arms, kissing her enthusiastically. 'You're later back than I expected,' he said. 'So, Mil, did the trip do any good? Did you get my uncle to say he'd give me a reasonable number of shares?'

'Sorry, darlin', it didn't work out like that. But he says he's going to expand the company to Belfast and put you in charge of the new office there.'

Danny's dismay was ludicrous. 'But, Mil, you know I don't want to spend my life working for this company! The idea was to get enough cash from the shares to be able to look around for something that really suited me, instead of a nine-to-five life.'

'I know, Danny – but I did my best.'

'I know you did, Mil. You're a real smart cookie, as they say on the movies. If anyone could have swung it, you could. But, hey, we might as well tell people that we're married, now. No point in this secrecy if it's not going to get us anywhere. I never quite followed why you thought it was important to keep it from Fergus, anyway. Not his business, right? And I don't see why he would disapprove. He likes you, Mil.'

'Oh, Danny – I know he does,' Millie confessed. 'Too much! He's just finished proposing to me.'

Danny scowled. 'The dirty old man! You're less than half his age! Well, that settles it. We'll tell people straightaway. And then we'll be able to get somewhere of our own, instead of trying to avoid Jan all the time. You've got to admit that's been pretty embarrassing.'

Millie wasn't convinced, but agreed in the end that since her tactics hadn't got them anywhere, they might as well forget the secrecy.

'But I really hope he won't chuck you out of the business, Danny,' she said anxiously. 'He thinks I'm separated from my husband, wants me to get a divorce.'

'What put that into his head, Millie? You didn't say anything to make him think it?'

'No, of course I didn't, silly.' Millie laughed up at him. 'How could you think I'd say anything like that about my darling Danny, when I'm so happy?'

'He can't really chuck me out,' Danny said. 'After all, he's my uncle by marriage. And it was my grandfather who set up the business. He'd be afraid of what people would say.'

Millie wasn't so sure, but she said nothing more that night, and comforted both Danny and herself by allowing him draw her back down onto the bed, and to make fervent love to her.

The next day, however, when Danny arranged an interview with his uncle and told him that he and Millie were married, it was obvious right away that Millie's prediction of Fergus's reaction had been more accurate than Danny's. His face darkened, and he sprang to his feet, bellowing out, 'You deceitful brat!' Then he rushed to his door and into the main office. 'Millie! Millie!' he roared. 'Come in here. I want to speak to you.'

Millie took her time, and came into Fergus's office looking calm and composed. 'I see Danny's told you about us, Fergus,' she said.

'Yes, he has! And what I don't understand is why you didn't tell me yourself, Millie. Why did you lead me to believe that you weren't happily married – might be thinking of divorce?'

'I was very unhappy when I had to tell you I was married, Fergus, because I knew I was ruining your hopes.' Millie looked at him with big eyes, and contrived to produce a few tears, mostly from worry at what would happen next. 'It broke my heart to hurt you, Fergus – we've been so close. I've looked on you as a true friend.'

'And it broke my heart, too, Millie. I don't think I'll ever get over it.' He turned his face away from them.

'You know, I don't think I'll be able to bear working in the same office as you from now on, either of you,' he said at last. 'I'm going to move you down to Belfast, Danny. I've plans already set up for an office there. And you'd better go with him, Millie. And I'd like you both to take a couple of weeks leave of absence in the meantime. I'll get Lorraine to arrange for your work to be covered until we can get some new people in. I don't want to talk any more about it now. Just go away, both of you. I'll email details to you, Danny.'

Millie and Danny collected their things and made an unobtrusive exit. They didn't know whether to feel relieved or shattered.

Fergus emailed Danny details about the office premises they had bought in Belfast, and when they would be available to occupy. It would be Danny's job to recruit a few staff – maybe only a few to start with, were Fergus's instructions – and to get things moving.

'Doesn't tell me much,' Danny complained. 'Get things moving how?'

'Well, you can recruit me for a start,' Millie said.

'Of course.'

'Let's not worry about it just yet. Time we had a honeymoon, boy.'

They decided to find an apartment in Belfast and move their belongings in there as soon as possible. Meanwhile, Danny suggested, they might spend a week or so at Portrush. It wasn't Millie's idea of a honeymoon, but she realised that they would have to keep expense to a minimum for the time being. Later, when business was booming, would be the time for seeking the sun.

Jan, who had been avoiding them both for weeks, was only too delighted to hear that they were moving out. The news of their marriage, broken to her by Millie – Danny was very reluctant to do it himself – came as a shock, but a day or so's thought showed her that she was well out of her relationship with a weak person like Danny, swayed by anyone who bothered to try. She told herself, and before long meant it, that she was glad to see the back of him.

Danny contacted a few Estate Agents in Belfast, rented an apartment sight unseen, and arranged for their heavy belongings to be delivered there.

Millie explained to Stevie Bones and to Declan Byrne, that she was now married, and was moving to Belfast, so that Tuesday must be her last at *The City Walls*. It took all Millie's charm to persuade Declan out of his annoyance, and to separate on good terms, so that he wouldn't blacklist her to other managers, as she had been afraid he might do.

Stevie was another matter. 'Another one gone,' he said philosophically. 'Ah, well, Millie, I never thought I had a chance with you anyway.'

'You never showed any signs of wanting to have!' Millie retorted, smiling. 'You're such a flirt, Stevie Bones!'

'All the best for your future, Millie,' Stevie said, hugging her. 'With your voice, you can get gigs anywhere. I'll expect to run into you in Belfast, when I'm next down there.'

And so they parted.

Danny and Millie set off happily for Portrush. The sun was shining, their future held at least some promise, and they were glad to be leaving quite a few problems behind.

Chapter Thirty Five

Portrush is a beautifully positioned seaside town on the north coast of County Antrim, next door to Portstewart, which is just across the border in County Londonderry. For years it was a popular holiday resort for families, until the cheap package holidays cut out the risk of rainy weather and a huge number of Portrush's previously regular holiday makers disappeared abroad every year instead of going there.

It remained a popular place for young people to visit, especially over the Easter break, and its golf course, the Royal Portrush, attracted thousands when the big competitions were played there, and hundreds at other times.

The town is situated at the end of a green grassy peninsula which has beaches along both sides, so that the visitor can walk across the small resort from one stretch of golden sand to the other. The encircling sea, stretching far and wide, deepest blue on a sunny summer day, and heaving with exciting waves for surfers when the wind is right, still attracts enthusiastic swimmers to both beaches.

It was towards the western beach that the two newly married couples strolled after their accidental meeting. Sooze had not been slow to notice Millie's wedding ring, although of course she had been full of the news of her own marriage first.

'I'm so glad for you, dear Sooze,' Millie said, with renewed hugs. 'And, Josh, huge congratulations.' Her words to Josh were noticeably cooler than those to Sooze.

'But, Millie,' Sooze asked, when she had finished enthusiastically telling Millie all about her wedding, Josh's job, and their apartment, 'is that a wedding ring you're wearing? Are you and Danny …?'

'We are, Sooze! In fact, we were just married when we met you that time in the *Limelight*. We got married in Derry. Easier there, because we both had residential qualifications, but we wanted to get away by ourselves for a weekend, so we slipped down to Belfast.'

'And the first thing you did was bump into me and Josh. And Horse,' she added after a moment's thought. Horse was so easy to forget, but he'd been very helpful to her and Josh. She should really be more grateful.

'Oh, but you're different, Sooze. My best friend! I didn't want to get away from you.' Millie carefully omitted Josh's name. She was glad to see from his face that he was regretting what he had said to Danny about her, realising suddenly that he'd been talking to a newly married man about his wife.

They walked along by the side of the beach, the girls chattering happily, while Danny and Josh tried to pretend to be glad to have their honeymoon interrupted, and reminisced rather stiltedly about their schooldays. Presently the 'So, do you see old so-and-so these days?' 'Do you remember how we used to fool about in Science?' and 'Do you remember?' in general, dried up.

Neither Sooze nor Josh had cared to mention the anger of Josh's father, and the probable cutting off of Josh's allowance when his father found out about his marriage. So, when the reminisces were over, Millie, who had decided that Josh must be forgiven in the light of his wealth, and his prospective usefulness to the O'Hanlons in their present hard up state, and knowing nothing of Josh's actual financial position, smiled graciously on him. There was more than one way of making Josh sorry for his spiteful words, after all.

She said, 'Marriage is treating you well, Josh. You and Sooze are both looking great. And so happy!' And she gave Josh the sort of smile which had been working so well for her with various men for years now.

Josh was relieved that Millie apparently didn't seem to be holding a grudge. 'Marriage to Sooze would make anyone happy,' he replied, and found himself returning Millie's smile.

'Where are you staying?' Millie asked.

'The *Imperial*,' Sooze answered.

'So are we!' Millie exclaimed. 'We must have dinner together tonight. And afterwards we might see what the night life in the Port is like now, or if there's not much else doing, maybe you might come and see our room, and we could have a game of poker together.'

The last thing Sooze wanted to do was spend a precious evening of her belated honeymoon playing poker, which she wasn't very good at. But Josh was responding eagerly, 'Hey, that sounds like an idea!'

There was no point in spoiling his evening for him. Sooze said nothing. Later, in their hotel room, tidying up before dinner, Josh called laughingly from the shower, 'So, don't you think I'm being a good boy, agreeing to spend time with your friend Millie, darlin' Sooze?'

'Yes, very good,' Sooze replied unwillingly. 'I thought you didn't like her?'

'Oh, maybe she's not as bad as I thought,' Josh said carelessly, stepping out of the shower naked and hugging Sooze as she approached to take her turn. 'She can't be all bad if you like her, babe.' He kissed Sooze's neck and his hands caressed her.

'Josh – later, boy! I need to get washed.' Sooze disappeared into the shower.

Later still, after a pleasant enough meal and a short walk which didn't reveal much in the way of options for entertainment – several attractive pubs, the cinema, and Kelly's, – which Millie ruled out as, 'Much too far to go. Maybe another night' – they returned to the hotel and went to the O'Hanlons' room.

Here two packs of cards were produced and the four people settled down for an evening's play, three of them eager to gamble and the third more than reluctant. Sooze knew that she and Josh could not afford to lose, especially to lose heavily.

'Let's just play for matchsticks,' she suggested lightly. 'It's just as much fun.'

But she was sternly overruled, Josh in particular scoffing at the idea, and saying, 'If you aren't risking anything, it's no fun.'

For the first part of the evening, Josh did quite well. Sooze was careful not to risk much, so, although she didn't win and in fact was an overall loser, her losses were small. She regularly folded unless she was sure her hand was good enough to win. But Josh, although he lost some, on the whole was winning by the time Danny said, 'I vote we have a break, and order a few drinks on Room Service. And after that, Millie might sing to us, if we ask her nicely, before we go back to the game.'

Everyone agreed, Sooze hoping fervently that by the time Millie had finished singing it would be late enough for Josh and herself to call it a night and go back to their room.

The drinks were ordered, and came reasonably quickly. A bottle of Scotch for the guys, a bottle of gin for the girls, a few suitable mixers, and four glasses. Sooze looked at the order for bottles with some misgiving. When Danny was phoning it down, she had been in the bathroom, and hadn't heard him. There were supplies there in sufficient quantity to keep them playing cards through until the next decade, she thought in her innocence.

The drinks were poured, they settled down to enjoy them, and then Danny repeated his suggestion that Millie should sing.

'Oh, Danny,' Millie said modestly, 'I'll sing for you some other time, but I'm sure these two don't want to hear me.'

Sooze felt obliged to say, 'We'd love to hear you, Millie.' Anyway, it would stop them playing cards for a while. She was more than surprised to hear Josh saying, 'Yeah, please sing for us Millie. You've got a really cool voice.'

But Josh, to his own surprise, had found himself responding more and more to Millie's flattery and smiles during the course of the evening, from her praise of his choice of wine with their meal, to his card play. 'That's really clever, Josh,' she had said after one hand. 'You should turn professional, if you can handle your cards like that.'

'Oh, mostly luck,' Josh said.

'No, there's real skill in playing a hand of poker as it should be played,' Millie insisted. The smile that went with the words, and the look in her eyes, reinforced her admiration of him. Josh glowed, and didn't really mind when he lost heavily on the next deal.

'See, what did I tell you? The luck of the cards,' he said, smiling at Millie in his turn. She was a really fascinating woman when you got to know her, he had decided.

So now he added his voice to Danny's and Sooze's requests. 'Please sing, Millie.'

'All right,' Millie smiled. 'What shall I sing?'

And she sang several songs, before firmly stopping, pleading with a laugh that her voice would soon be giving up on her.

'I know everyone's dying to get back to the card table,' she said with a modest smile.

Sooze wasn't. She wanted nothing less.

And as she watched with a sinking heart as Josh lost hand after hand, ending up the evening as a consistent loser, she wondered how much he had left of their spending money for the rest of their holiday.

She was even more upset when Josh, who had drunk more than his share of the room service bottle of Scotch, staggered to bed more than half cut, and immediately dropped into a heavy sleep marked by a series of loud, unsexy snores. For the first time, Sooze wondered just what she had married.

The pattern of that first night, once established, was followed regularly. Sooze spoke of her worries to Josh the next morning, but allowed herself to be solaced and comforted by Josh's evident desire to make love and his tenderness as they did so.

'Don't worry, Sooze,' was his final word on the subject. 'Remember, old Horse is joining us next week for the last few days. If we're short, he'll be sure to help us out. Anyway, I'll probably get back to my winning streak tonight. I was doing all right the first part of the evening, wasn't I?'

Chapter Thirty Six

Horse had been wondering how wise it was of him to plan to join the happy couple and possibly spoil their honeymoon, even though Josh had encouraged him seriously to come.

'Well, I'll see,' was the most he had said.

'Meantime,' Josh said, 'there's something you could be doing for me. I still haven't told my dad that Sooze and I are married. I thought you could tell my sister Elaine, and get her to break it to him. Maybe when he knows he's going to have a grandson, it will make a difference. I'm sure you could persuade Elaine to put it as well as possible. She fancies you, you know,' he added slyly.

Horse blushed. He was well aware that Josh's sister Elaine was keen on him, but since he hadn't the slightest interest in her, he was reluctant to give her the wrong impression. On the other hand, he was only too willing to do anything he could, not only for his old friend Josh, but for Sooze, who had reigned in his own heart since the day Josh introduced him to her.

'Well, I'll see,' he said again.

So on the day that Sooze and Josh met up with Millie and Danny, Horse called at the Gillespie's house and had a cup of coffee with Elaine.

Elaine, a wispy fair haired girl several years older than Josh, a pale washed out copy of her brother in colouring but without his good looks or charm, was excited and almost overcome to have Horse arrive to see her. Brushing a strand of thin flying hair back from her face, she invited him to sit down on a comfortable couch in the room the Gillespies kept for visitors, and bustled off to make the coffee.

Returning shortly with a tray holding two mugs of coffee and a cake which had been intended for her father, she drew up a low table by hooking it dexterously with one foot, plonked the tray down on it, and settled herself beside Horse on the sofa, far too close for Horse's comfort.

'It's lovely to see you, Horace,' she said invitingly. 'We've seen nothing of you since Josh went to work for your dad's company and moved out to his own place.'

'Yes,' said Horse heavily. This gave him an opening to talk about Josh, but instead of taking it, he said nothing, reached for a slice of the rich fruit cake, and took the opportunity to move farther away from Elaine as unobtrusively as possible.

Elaine chattered gaily away, about this and that. Presently she raised the subject of a friend of hers who had just got engaged to be married. 'It seems more and more people are getting married now, rather than just living together. I think it's so much better, don't you?'

At last, an opportunity. 'Yes, I think if two people love each other, they should certainly get married. Actually, Elaine, that's sort of what I wanted to talk to you about.'

Elaine's eyes opened wide. With a snuggling movement she brought herself back closer to Horse, to his annoyance. He didn't dare move away again, in case she noticed and was offended.

'Oh?' she breathed, and waited eagerly.

'Yes, I want to tell you about two people – you and I both know them well.' Horse struggled for words. This was the crucial bit. So far Elaine seemed sympathetic, but when he mentioned Josh's name, and still more when he mentioned Sooze, would the sympathy remain?

He tried again.

'I know you have a kind, loving heart, Elaine – I know you wouldn't be cruel to anyone who was in love and just wanted to be happy.'

'Oh, I wouldn't, Horace, I wouldn't! You know that! Just ask me what you want to ask, and see!' Elaine spoke rapturously, and Horse suddenly woke up and realised that she was reading quite another meaning into his words. Did she really think he was proposing to her? It seemed like it.

Horse stood up hurriedly and began to stride about the room. He needed to put things in a much more straightforward way before she misunderstood him completely.

'I'm talking about Josh, my friend and your brother,' he blurted out. 'Josh and Sooze love each other. You've known that for years. And they've got married, because, as you and I have just agreed, that's the only thing for two people in love to do.' He stopped, horrified, as Elaine's face grew blacker and blacker. 'So I thought you might be the best person to break the news to your dad, Elaine, because you could put it sympathetically. You have such a nice nature – such a kind heart.'

Elaine's lips quivered. Horse saw to his utter dismay that she was on the verge of tears. What had he done? He certainly hadn't intended to mislead her. But there was no way he was going to marry Elaine Gillespie just to stop her crying.

Elaine pulled herself together. 'I'm afraid you've misunderstood my nature, Horace. Yes, I have a kind heart. But if I try to be kind to Josh, I'll end up being cruel to my dad. What has Daddy ever done to be hurt like this? Josh just doesn't care about him at all. All he's ever wanted was to take, take, take, whatever Daddy would give him. I couldn't possibly be the one to deal him this blow. Josh should take his own responsibility for his actions and tell him himself.'

Horse, while aware that Elaine's quite correct moral attitude arose mostly from jealousy and spite – for he knew, had known for some time, that the way her father had spoiled Josh at the expense of his daughter had, not unreasonably, made Elaine jealous for years – also acknowledged to himself that Josh wasn't very good at admitting his own responsibility for what he did. Horse himself knew that Josh had used him to cover for him since they'd first met. He got away with it somehow because he had so much charm, when he wanted to exert it.

So, he would have to go back to Josh and say that Elaine wasn't going to tell his father, and that he would have to do it himself. But Josh wouldn't do that. He was more likely to try to persuade Horse to do it. He made one last effort.

'You're right, Elaine. Josh should really do it himself. But he's afraid of the row it would cause, and the effect of that on your father's heart. Josh tells me he's got a bad heart, isn't that right? I thought if you broke it to him gently, as I know you could do so well, it would be the kindest thing for him. Wouldn't it, don't you think so?'

'Well, Horace, I see what you mean.' Horse was smiling pleadingly at her, and Elaine found this hard to resist. Maybe he did care, after all? Maybe he just needed more encouragement? Maybe if she let herself be persuaded to help him in this way – ?

Horse continued to smile, waiting for her response.

'I can't make up my mind all at once,' Elaine said. 'I'll have to think about it. Maybe you're right and it would be best for him to hear it from me, broken gently. If you come back tomorrow, I'll know by then what I should do, dear Horace.'

Horse, much relieved, pressed the hand she reached out to him, and made his clumsy departure, saying, 'That's great, Elaine. I'll look forward to seeing you tomorrow, then.'

He was afraid he might have left Elaine with a false impression of his feelings for her, but he didn't want to make her so angry by telling her the truth bluntly that she would be completely resistant to helping Josh. After tomorrow, he decided, he needn't ever see her again.

Chapter Thirty Seven

As it turned out, Horse need not have worried about seeing Elaine again. The same evening, her feelings of resentment against Josh, and her conviction that there was no point in expecting Horse to care for her, since he clearly didn't, got the better of her.

'Daddy,' she said to Stephen Gillespie as they were sitting drinking their after dinner coffee by the fire, before Gillespie took himself off to his study to work on his computer, 'there's something I think you should know.'

'Oh?'

'He should really have told you himself, but since he hasn't, I think I should, now that I know.'

'Goodness, Elaine, what on earth are you talking about?' Gillespie had never allowed himself to use strong language before his daughter, but he felt tempted to now and his tone was sharp. 'Why can't you come right out and tell me whatever you think I should know – if it's anything worth hearing, that is.'

'It's about Josh.'

'Oh?' Gillespie said again. To tell the truth, he wouldn't be displeased to hear something about how Josh was getting on. He'd been worried about him since he insisted on moving out, to the new apartment Gillespie had provided. His pride had kept him from asking questions, even of Elaine, but if she was about to volunteer some information, that pleased him considerably.

'I don't want to hurt and upset you, Daddy,' Elaine said untruthfully.

'You won't. I'm not that soft. Get on, get on.'

Thus rudely adjured, Elaine began. 'Well, Horace Buchanan called round yesterday – '

'Horace? Josh's friend? Why can't you call him Horse like everybody else? Have you fallen for him or what? Much good that'll do you!'

Elaine flushed indignantly. 'No, of course I haven't Daddy. What a silly thing to say.'

'Don't call your father silly, girl.'

Instead of replying, 'I will if you act like it!' Elaine, whose spirit had been crushed years ago by her father's attitude to her, said, 'No, Daddy. He was talking to me about Josh.'

Gillespie's ears pricked up. He couldn't help asking, in as neutral a tone as he could manage, 'Why? Has the boy got some sense at last and wants to come home? Did he send Horse to tell me that?'

'Oh, Daddy, I'm afraid it's nothing like that.'

'Well, what is it, then?' Gillespie, disappointed in his unreasonable hope, was even angrier with his daughter. Elaine had always been a fool, he considered, and she was behaving even more foolishly than usual. He wished she would come out with whatever it was she was trying to tell him. So he barked at her, and made it harder than ever for Elaine to deliver her message.

'Horace asked me to b - b - break it to you gently,' she stammered.

'What, has something happened to him? He's had an accident?' Gillespie sprang to his feet and his tone sharpened with sudden anxiety. 'Tell me, for pity's sake!'

Seeing that he was really shaken, Elaine said at once, 'No, no, nothing like that. Josh isn't hurt, Daddy.'

'No? Then for Heaven's sake, why did you worry me like that? If he isn't hurt, what is it?'

'Oh, Daddy – he's not hurt. He's married!'

Stephen Gillespie stared at her for a long moment, giving her time to add, 'To Susan O'Leary!'

'What!' Gillespie bellowed. Like a bull in the ring whose dangerous charge is halted and his life threatened by an unexpected knife thrust to the heart, he staggered, then collapsed into the nearest chair. 'Brandy! Brandy!' he gasped. Elaine hurried to supply it, pouring out a full glass. Gillespie grasped the glass like a drowning man reaching for a straw and gulped the brandy rapaciously. He thrust the empty glass at Elaine, croaking out, 'More.'

Elaine, carrying out his request, was torn between horror and satisfaction at what she had done. *But it wasn't me, it was Josh. I just told him the truth*, she thought.

Gillespie dragged himself upright after a few more minutes. 'He's no son of mine, if this is true!' he howled. 'I'll change my will. I'll cut him right out of everything! He'll never see another penny of my money!' His face had flushed an alarmingly strong puce colour. After a moment, he calmed down enough to add, 'But I want to hear it from his own mouth before I believe my son Joshua would do a thing like this to me.

'Tell your friend Horse that I want to see my son. I want him to tell me himself, to my face, not send messengers – if it's even true that that's what he did. I don't believe it. I don't think it's like him. He's too brave a boy to go behind my back and get someone else to tell me about it. I'm going to my study, now. There's something I want to do. And I don't want to be disturbed again this night, d'ye hear?'

Elaine, who would never have dreamt of disturbing her father in his study at the best of times, was only too thankful to see him make his way there without further signs of collapse.

She sat down straightaway, and sent Horse a text, in which she tried to explain that she had done as he asked her, and broken the news of Josh's marriage gently, but that their father had been angry. 'He wants to see Josh to ask about it,' she finished up. 'Can you tell him?'

She didn't pause to reflect on the reason why she wasn't texting Josh himself instead of going through Horse. She knew very well why. In the first place, she wanted to convince Horse that she had done her best to do as he'd asked her. And in the second place, she had never got on well with Josh, and was sure that if she told him herself how angry their father was, he would immediately jump to blame her.

And it hadn't really been her fault, she told herself again. Josh should have told their father himself what he'd done. And since he'd been silly enough to marry that pain Sooze O'Leary, with her airs and graces and her crowd of boys who were after her, then it wasn't Elaine's job to get him out of the mess he'd jumped into. He could try to get himself out of it, without expecting her to help him.

So Elaine went to bed, persuading herself that her conscience was clear. It was a strange thing that in spite of this she slept very uneasily that night, dosing fitfully and waking every few minutes, until the dawn chorus eventually sang her to sleep.

Horse was upset by Elaine's text. He wished he hadn't tried to use her to break the news. Clearly she had made bad worse. He should have done it himself, or insisted that Josh should speak directly to his father.

Using his sister as a go between had been Josh's own idea, but Horse couldn't excuse himself on those grounds. He should have known better. He had known better.

He was glad he hadn't mentioned the coming grandchild. Josh could do that himself, now. It might give him a chance of melting his father's heart. Or maybe not, Horse realised gloomily.

Meanwhile, his own course was clear. Reluctant as he was to interrupt the honeymoon, he must go up to Portrush straightaway, and tell Josh that his father, although very angry, wanted to see him. Horse had been invited by Josh to go up anyway, to visit his friends, although he hadn't promised to go and hadn't, in fact, intended to. But he couldn't deal with Josh on this matter by phone.

Josh and Sooze had gone down to the beach, he was told at the hotel when he arrived there. No, the receptionist wasn't sure which beach, but he was sure Josh could find them easily. She booked him in to the hotel as she chattered, and suggested that he should take his suitcase up to his room before going out again, an idea which Horse accepted. He was feeling hot, cross, and grubby after his train journey. A shower would help, he considered.

Not long after, feeling clean again, he set off for the western strand. But although he walked along its length, he saw no sign of his friends. Okay, he needed to try the eastern strand now. Before he had gone more than a short distance along it, he saw Josh, and to his amazement he saw him walking close beside Millie Brennan. Horse looked again, doubting his eyes.

And where was Sooze? Then he saw her, some distance away further up the beach, being helped over some rocks which lay in their path by Danny O'Hanlon, of all people. Sooze looked tired and unhappy. Her pregnancy was beginning to show. As he watched, Sooze stumbled in spite of Danny's helping hand and almost fell.

But why was a stranger – a stranger to her, anyway – helping her instead of Josh? And why was Josh leaving her so far behind, while he flirted, as Horse could clearly see he was doing, with another girl?

'Josh!' he called in a loud angry voice, and strode towards them.

169

Chapter Thirty Eight

Josh couldn't be said to look pleased to see Horse. Maybe his friend's presence brought home to him the feeling of guilt which he had been pushing down since he started to get so close to Millie.

He and Millie were walking at the edge of the sea where the huge Atlantic rollers of further out had dwindled to small frilly white wavelets, and Millie had kicked off her sandals and was paddling, her legs in their short shorts brown and beautiful in the bright sun, so unusually hot for the beginning of October. She seemed to be trying to drag Josh in with her, splashing water over his legs and laughing. Josh was laughing back, and as Horse watched, he pulled off his own socks and shoes, rolled up his jeans, and made for Millie, kicking up the foam as he did so.

As Horse strode forward, calling his name, he started guiltily and backed away from Millie, back onto the beach.

'Horse! Good to see you, dude! We weren't expecting you just yet.'

'You invited me to come today, in fact,' Horse said coldly. 'I didn't say definitely I would come, but as you see, I decided I'd better. Why aren't you looking after Sooze, Josh? She almost fell just now.'

To do him justice, Josh looked horrified. 'I thought Danny had her safely. Millie wanted to paddle, so I – ' His voice trailed off. 'Sooze!' he called, turning away from both Millie and Josh. 'Sooze, are you okay?'

'I'm fine, Josh,' Sooze said, but she didn't sound fine, Horse noticed.

Josh, however, appeared to notice nothing wrong. 'Great!' he called back. Then he turned again to Horse. 'We got quite a surprise, bumping into Millie and Danny the other day,' he said conversationally. 'And guess what? They're married, too!'

'Congratulations, Millie,' Horse said.

Millie smiled cheekily. 'You're supposed to congratulate the groom, not the bride, Horse,' she said. 'You wish the bride happiness.'

'Oh?' was all Horse said.

Millie flushed angrily. Horse was another one of Sooze's friends who had never seemed to like her. But it wasn't worth while taking the time to make him change his mind. As far as she knew, he wasn't particularly well off, unlike Josh. For Millie knew nothing about Josh's present circumstances.

Neither did Josh, as yet. Horse caught his eye, and muttered, 'Need to speak privately, Josh.'

Josh looked surprised. 'Later, then.' He wanted to speak to Horse privately, too, as it happened. He had lost more to Millie and Danny at their now nightly games of poker than he could pay. He needed a bit of financial help from Horse as soon as possible, but he wasn't worried. He felt confident of getting it.

It was after dinner before they were able to slip away from the other three and talk.

'Mustn't be too long,' Josh said. 'Millie's expecting me round to their room for poker in another hour.'

Horse had plenty to say to Josh already, but this added another subject. 'You mean you're playing poker with those two? Josh, I thought you had more sense. Don't you remember that at school, Danny had a reputation for never losing? Nobody ever proved that he was a sharper, but it's like the old saying, if you see the cat with cream on its whiskers, you can be pretty sure it's been stealing the milk.'

Josh had nothing to say on that subject. 'Er – as a matter of fact, dude, I've lost quite a lot to Danny. When I sat down and added it up last night, I couldn't believe it. I was wondering – ' He paused delicately.

'Yes?' Horse wasn't going to help him to say it.

'Could you lend me a bit to cover it?' Josh said in a rush. 'You've always been so decent, that way, and I've spent my salary for this month. I'll get paid again just after we get home, you know, but until then – well, it'll be tough.'

Horse gave him a look that Josh had never experienced from his old friend before. 'Josh, grow up,' he said. 'You have Sooze to look after now, as well as this baby when it arrives. Your salary ought to be enough for that. But not if you're going to act the eedjit and gamble it away! And what are you playing at, flirting with that girl Millie and leaving Sooze to struggle along behind you, in her condition?'

'I was just being pleasant, Horse!' Josh protested. 'I can't afford to annoy the pair of them right now. Millie likes me, so I'm taking advantage of that to make sure Danny gives me a bit of leeway with the cash. Anyway, Danny was looking after her.'

There was a pause. They stood looking at each other. Then Josh spoke again. 'So are you going to turn me down, about the money?'

'No. You can have it. I'll write you out a cheque and you can endorse it to Danny. But never again, boyo!' Horse had so much else to say to Josh that he wanted to move on from the gambling debts issue. But he intended to say a lot more to Josh about it some other time.

'Thanks.' Josh wasn't effusive. He had expected Horse to be much more friendly and willing about it.

'That wasn't why I came up here to talk to you, Josh,' Horse said abruptly after a moment. 'It's about your dad. I did as you suggested and got your sister Elaine to break it to him about the marriage. I don't know if she made a mess of it, or if it was always going to happen, but he nearly had a heart attack, or so Elaine says. He insists on you coming to see him, to tell you himself face to face. It's what you should have done in the first place.'

'Oh, yes, you told me so, of course! Horse always knows best.'

'I didn't say that. But I think if you go to him in an open, straight-forward way, and tell him about marrying Sooze, you might be able to calm him down. Especially if you tell him about his prospective grandchild. So far he doesn't know about that.'

'And that's supposed to soften him, to melt his heart? He hasn't got one. It'll only make him madder than ever, to have a grandchild who's half O'Leary.' Josh spoke bitterly.

'Well, you won't know if you're right this time, or if I am, until you try it,' Horse said bracingly. He had said nothing to Josh about Gillespie's threat to cut his son out of his will. He was hoping that that was only something said in the first heat of anger, which could be forgotten in the pleasure of seeing his son again, and hearing he was to have a grand-child. Stephen Gillespie had always loved his son, spoiling him continuously. At least, that might not have been love, but only pride in the Gillespie name. Horse wasn't sure. He could only hope for the best.

Josh took some time to be persuaded, but at last Horse got him to agree. They were due to leave the hotel in another day, and Horse also wrung a promise from Josh that he would refrain from playing cards with the O'Hanlons that last night.

'You should make it a special night for just you and Sooze,' Horse said. 'Take her out somewhere – here, I'll pay for it. Take a taxi.' He gave Josh a wad of notes from his inside pocket. 'And go for a romantic walk along the beach or somewhere, afterwards. Sure, I don't have to tell you how to give a girl a good time, mate! And I'll make your excuses to Millie and Danny, and give them that cheque, when you've endorsed it.'

As he spoke, Horse was taking out his cheque book and writing in it. 'There, endorse the back of it for Danny, and go and tell Sooze you're taking her out. Go on, get on with it!'

'Okay, I suppose you're the boss,' grumbled Josh as he signed Danny's name on the back of the cheque. 'But you're wrong about my dad. He's not going to accept this, you'll see.' Though even as he said this, Josh hoped fervently that he was wrong. He had always been able to charm his dad up until now. Why not this time, too?

'Oh, I don't know,' Horse replied. 'What's the betting he'll be so chuffed about the baby, his own grandchild, that he'll overlook the fact that Sooze is its mother?'

He was reasonably hopeful that he might be right.

But it turned out that Josh was the one who was right, this time.

Chapter Thirty Nine

Josh took Sooze by taxi out to Kelly's, and they danced there until late. Sooze didn't want to drink much, because of the baby, and Josh, who had never been a heavy drinker if left to his own inclinations, was happy to go along with her, so after one round they spent the rest of the evening dancing.

Sooze was inclined to think her body too clumsy for dancing now, but Josh told her not to be daft, and she found to her pleasure that once up on the dance floor, she was as agile as ever. Their steps suited each other just as they had always done, whether clinging close together in the slow dances or letting their excitement go in the faster ones. By the time they had to leave, Josh was feeling glad he hadn't wasted the last night of their belated honeymoon with other people. He loved Sooze, of course he did. He'd always loved her.

Afterwards they went for the moonlight walk along the beach that Horse had suggested, and found a secluded nook among the dunes where Josh pulled Sooze down beside him and made love to her tenderly on the soft sand, with the moon shining down on them and turning Sooze's dark hair to bright silver, and the waves creeping nearer to play them a soothing and peaceful lullaby.

'Brings back good memories, darlin', right?' Josh whispered into her hair, and Sooze giggled happily.

She was as happy as she could ever remember being, and Josh was feeling good, too. They staggered back to the hotel, drunk more with happiness than with the limited amount of liquids they had consumed, and fell onto the bed, leaving all thought of packing until the next day.

Horse was to travel down to Belfast with them. They all three caught the train by the skin of their teeth, although the station was only a few minutes walk away. This was mainly because of the time – unnecessarily long, both Horse and Sooze thought – taken up in saying goodbye to Danny and Millie.

Josh was full of excuses for not meeting up with them the previous night, and plans to get together once they were all back in Belfast. Josh was aware of a fleeting regret that he had missed the previous evening, and even a brief, fleeting moment of wonder, which he guiltily dismissed immediately, as to what Millie's red hair would have looked like in the moonlight, lying under him on the beach as Sooze had lain.

They hustled out of the hotel and with moments only to spare settled themselves in a comfortable half empty carriage, their luggage stowed safely around them.

'I think you should ring your dad as soon as you get home, Josh,' Horse began when they had travelled the first few miles, 'and arrange to see him as soon as possible. You'll want to get home and shower, etc, first, I suppose. You don't want him to see you looking – well – '

'A mess?' inquired Josh over politely. Horse had rescued him with a very timely cheque, but that didn't mean he could run his life. Josh was beginning to resent it.

'You said it, mate, not me!' Horse grinned, and Josh couldn't help grinning back.

'What's all this?' inquired Sooze. 'I didn't know you were going to see your dad, Josh. Why? Is it to tell him about us?'

'Josh, do you mean to tell me you said nothing to Sooze about this?' Horse demanded.

'I didn't want to upset her,' Josh said sulkily. 'It's okay, Sooze. Just my dad wants to see me to ask if it's true we're married. Horse got Elaine to tell him.'

Horse didn't bother to say that it had been Josh's idea. Instead, he concentrated on soothing Sooze.

'It'll be all right, Sooze. Mr Gillespie just wants to hear it from Josh, naturally, right?'

'Yeah, I suppose so.' Sooze sounded doubtful. 'Then, sure, you'd better go, Josh. I hope he isn't too angry.' She shuddered at the thought. Sooze had never liked angry men, although she'd seen very few. Her own father's anger had never been directed against her, but she'd seen him angry with others and would have shrivelled up if a similar blast had been sent her way.

The two men hastened to reassure her, lying in a good cause.

'No reason why he should be, Sooze,' Horse said.

'He'll not be too bad, I'm sure, sweetheart. I can always talk him round,' Josh added, conveniently forgetting that Stephen Gillespie had already made his feelings about Josh's relationship with Sooze very clear, and had shown no signs then of being easy to talk round on that subject.

If only Sooze wasn't a Catholic, it might have been different. But then there was the whole business of O'Leary's financial collapse, and the belief which Stephen Gillespie had come up with so unreasonably that O'Leary had tried to involve him in the collapse, and to drag Gillespie down with him. Gillespie had poured out so much scorn and derision on Sooze's dad. The last thing he wanted was a family connection with this man whom he despised. Josh, knowing this, was not looking forward to the interview.

However, on the following morning he walked confidently into his father's study at ten o'clock, the time they had arranged on the phone, and greeted his father with a cheery smile. Stephen Gillespie rose from the chair behind his desk and came forward to greet his son.

'Good to see you, Dad. I've missed you, what with living away from home these days.' Josh attempted to give his father a hug, but was repulsed.

'You needn't try to get round me with hugs!' Stephen Gillespie growled. 'First I want to hear the truth of this nonsense Elaine told me. Joshua, son, tell me you haven't ruined your life by marrying that O'Leary bitch.'

He looked torn between tears and anger, but Josh's only feeling in response to his words was anger.

'Don't talk about Sooze like that, Dad!' he yelled. All thought of conciliating his father had fled. 'She's worth a hundred of you.'

'And don't you talk to your father like that, boy!' yelled Gillespie back. 'Tell me the truth – have you married this girl or not? Or are you ashamed to tell me? If you're regretting it – I hope you are – we can get you out of it.'

'Ashamed?' Josh said hotly. 'No – the only person I'm ashamed of is you. The only reason I could have for regretting marrying Sooze is that I've given her a father-in-law like you! You don't deserve to have a daughter-in-law like Sooze, but you have her. When you learn to appreciate her properly, perhaps you'll let me know. I don't want to stay for another minute with someone like you!'

He was so angry that he completely forgot to tell his father about the coming baby. Instead, he flung himself round and dived out of the house without hesitation.

Stephen Gillespie stared after him. He was as angry as he'd ever been in his life. He was so angry that he was speechless. Joshua, his only son, the boy he had pampered for years, the boy he had given everything to. The boy he had expected to take over his business, and who had refused to do that. The boy who had married a Catholic, and one who was the daughter of his bitterest enemy.

After five speechless, motionless minutes, spent in listing and piling up his grievances against Josh, Gillespie made his way to the chair behind his desk.

'Elaine!' he called out at the top of his voice, 'get me a glass of whiskey!'

Elaine came at a run. 'Dad, what is it?' she gasped out.

'That brother of yours! Joshua!'

'Why, what has he done?'

'He's married O'Leary's daughter! And he refuses to consider divorcing her!'

Elaine refrained from saying that she had already told him about the marriage. And that he could hardly expect Josh to consider a divorce when he was so newly married. But her usual dread of her father made her hold her tongue. Instead, she fetched him the whiskey as requested, although the thought passed through her mind that Gillespie could easily have got it for himself. The decanter and glasses were in the cupboard just across the room. But Stephen Gillespie was a man who, even in this day and age, was used to being waited on by the women in his family. Now that he had divorced his wife, the burden fell automatically on Elaine.

Elaine placed the decanter and two glasses on a tray on the desk, poured him a generous amount into one of the glasses, and asked nervously, 'Is there anything else I can do, Dad?'

'Ring my solicitor for me. I'll speak to him myself as soon as you get hold of him.' Gillespie gulped down his whiskey and poured himself another glass while Elaine got the number, spoke to a secretary, and waited patiently for Gillespie's solicitor to get on the line.

Presently she was able to say, 'Here he is, Dad,' and hand over the phone to her father. She waited for a moment, then, as he waved her irritably away, she left the room. As she went, she could hear her father saying, 'Is that you, Wilkinson? It's about my will. I want to cut that young scoundrel Joshua out of it – yes, completely. Not a penny will he get from me. How soon can you draw up something for me to sign? Yes, yes, I understand I'll need to nominate someone else to get what would have been his share. Better make it my daughter – there's no one else. Best of a bad job.'

Elaine closed the door softly behind her.

When he had finished his business with the solicitor, and arranged for him to bring the new will round for signing on the following day, Stephen Gillespie leaned back in the chair at his desk for a comfortable minute while he drained a third glass of whiskey. Something had been achieved.

Then his face hardened again. He had someone else to punish for the disaster which had landed on him.

Leaning forward again, he picked up the phone and dialled the number for his broker.

'Milligan and Martin? Yes, it's Stephen Gillespie. Is that you, Patrick? I want you to find out for me what John O'Leary's doing these days – what shares he holds in what companies, and how they're doing. Okay, get back to me.'

He sat back again, an expression of grim determination on his face. He was going to put the finishing touches to John O'Leary's ruin, if it was the last thing he did.

Roundabout – *Gerry McCullough*

Chapter Forty

Millie and Danny were pleased to get Josh's cheque, although disappointed that they hadn't had one more night of continuing to skin him. Millie felt that he deserved anything she could do in that line for his previous attitude to her, while Danny said, 'Well, Mil, I never liked him. A conceited, bumptious showoff, he always was at school, and I don't see that he's changed any. Horse is a nice fella, but Josh is just a pain. It'll do him good to lose a bit – he's always had far too much cash!'

Neither of them were aware that Josh was currently hard up, and might soon be even more short of money, so they made plans to follow up on him when they went back to Belfast, and meanwhile felt pleased with the large cheque which he had paid them, courtesy of Horse.

Their return to Belfast was to be soon rather than later. Their spending money was rapidly running out, and Millie put her foot down firmly on Danny's suggestion that they cash the cheque and use some of it to stay a few more days.

'We need to save this, boy, she said. 'Who knows when we may urgently need it? It's been a great wee honeymoon, darlin' boy,' she added caressingly, 'But it's time we got back, started setting up the new business, and began to make a bit of money ourselves.'

'Easier said than done,' Danny replied ruefully. 'I haven't a lot of ideas about how to go about that, Mil. You're the bright one – you'll have to help me.'

Another day saw them back in Belfast, settling in to their new flat, and sitting down together to their first meal in their own home, a dinner cooked expertly by Millie, who had done a lot of cooking for her father in the past, and had picked up tips from the cook at St Bernadette's, with whom she had been on friendly terms, in accordance with her habit of always making friends with the staff wherever she was living.

'Chicken in red wine – one of my all time favourites!' Danny exclaimed enthusiastically. 'Mil, you're a treasure!'

He enjoyed his meal, second helpings included, but when they sat down afterwards to discuss the setting up of the new business, he had less to say than ever. Millie, seeing that he was getting upset at the very idea of it, said presently, 'Well, Danny, let's leave it for now. We can go round and inspect the premises tomorrow and maybe by then we'll have more ideas. Meanwhile – ' she smiled sexily and nuzzled closer to him – 'we can probably think of some other way of spending tonight?'

'No question!' grinned Danny. He swept her into his arms, and headed for the bedroom, ignoring, as he was meant to, Millie's laughing protests.

The new office, when they came to inspect it, was in an attractive part of town, part of a large purpose built block of offices not all of which, by any means, were occupied – possibly that was why Fergus Ryan had been able to get this one at a reasonable rate.

And when they rode up in the lift and went inside the third floor office space, they saw at once that it was on the small side. It might, in fact, have been originally part of a larger office, cut in two in order to reduce the price and encourage a quick letting.

'We needn't worry too much about hiring staff, Danny,' was Millie's first comment. 'There's just about room here for an office for you, one for me, and a reception room for customers.'

'True.'

'And I suppose, in fact, that we'll be able to deal with all our customers between us, for the first while, until we built up a client base. I had meant to suggest putting in an ad for experienced assistant brokers, but we may let that go for now.'

'Yeah.' Danny was aware that he wasn't contributing much to the planning session, but he didn't mind. He knew that Millie was much brighter than he was, and could probably do the whole job by herself. He didn't mind. When it came to actually dealing with the clients' stocks and shares, he knew his way around, and could begin to pull his weight.

But then Millie raised what was, he realised, the main question. 'So – where do we find these clients? Any thoughts, darlin'?'

'Ah. No.'

'I suppose we could start with an ad for the company. We might pick up a few that way,' Millie said thoughtfully.

Danny brightened. 'Yes, of course – why not?'

'And then,' Millie went on, 'we should probably try some of our friends – well, your friends mostly, love. See if they can suggest us to their dads. Maybe I could try some of my own school mates, too, but the thing is, they're obviously all girls. And Northern Irish men still haven't come into the twentieth century, let alone the twenty first, in thinking girls' opinions are worth having about business. Especially their daughters. But your friends, being male, might well have a pull with their dads.'

'Certainly worth trying,' agreed Danny.

'Meanwhile, you might invite some of them along for a poker game. Including Josh and Horse. See if we can pick up a bit that way while the business is still just starting to take off, okay?'

'You got it, babe!' agreed Danny with much more enthusiasm. 'I'll text a few of them right now.'

'Yeah,' Millie agreed happily. 'Then, when we've got some of them relaxed and enjoying themselves, that would be the time to talk about the new business setup, and encourage them to tell their dads about it, what d'ye think?'

'Right! That's what we'll do, then.' Danny produced his mobile and began to check through suitable contacts immediately, fired with enthusiasm for his clever wife's idea.

And I'll follow up on a few of those contacts Stevie Bones gave me, and hope for a few gigs, Millie thought to herself. But she said nothing, knowing that Danny was less than keen on seeing her performing in public now that they were married, and waited until he was fully involved on his mobile to slip away into the next room and do some texting on her own account.

Not every one Danny texted was free that night, but several were. A group of five, plus Danny and Millie, gathered that same evening in the comfortable front room of the O'Hanlon's apartment, among them, to Millie's satisfaction, Josh – although not Horse.

Horse, in fact, had tried hard, but unsuccessfully, to persuade Josh not to go. But the more he tried, the more stubbornly determined Josh became. He was going, and that was all there was about it. Sooze, when he stood up after dinner and told her that he was going out, and where he was going, was even more alarmed than Horse, but said little, well aware that nothing she could say would make any difference. Josh's stubbornness was well known to her, and the days when he would allow himself to be talked out of something by Sooze were now definitely gone. The difference, Sooze realised wryly, was between a girl friend who needed to be persuaded into sleeping with him, and a wife who would automatically be willing.

As well as Josh and the host and hostess, there were Mike, a tough looking red haired boy who was a poker addict and also a poker expert; the good looking, dark haired Bugsy who knew little about the game but was inclined to be lucky; thin, mousy Hughie who was the easy going, easily influenced sort; and Big Geordie, sandy haired and solid muscle from the neck down, who was always ready to go anywhere for any reason, but who had to be watched around the alcohol, since he was liable to start a fight after too many glasses.

Millie looked round them in satisfaction. This looked like a good start to her campaign. Danny produced a pack of cards. 'I'll deal for the first hand, will I?' he asked easily, and was beginning to shuffle when Mike interrupted him.

'Hold on there, Daniel my boyo! Not so fast! This may be only a friendly game, but let's do it right all the same, okay? We begin by cutting for dealer. Highest card deals.'

'Aw, Mike, no problem. We'll certainly do it that way if you want.' Danny laughed, and offered the cards to Millie. 'Ladies first,' he said.

Millie drew a card. It was the four of diamonds. Josh, who had contrived to be sitting next to her on her right, drew next. A seven of clubs. Then came Hughie, who drew a Jack of clubs, Danny, who drew the ten of hearts, Big Geordie whose card was a three of spades, Mike who drew ten of clubs, and finally Bugsy who, lucky as usual, drew the Queen of diamonds.

'Bugsy deals,' Danny said, handing the pack to Bugsy to be shuffled when the cut cards had been returned to it. 'Okay, Mike?'

'Okay, Dan.'

The play began. Bugsy won easily. Next time, however, Danny won after a long drawn out series of raises, until finally everyone but himself and Josh had folded. Danny called Josh, who showed three diamonds, which Danny topped with his four spades.

After the first hour there was a break, drinks were topped up, and Millie, at Josh's request, sang two songs for the company, but laughingly refused to sing more. Instead, she deftly turned the conversation to what everyone was doing these days, and told them that Danny was setting up a local broker's business. 'On the spot info – can't beat it,' she said. 'If you guys have any shares you couldn't do better than let our new business handle them for you. Or if you know anyone who has,' she ended, laughing again.

The listeners, melted by Millie's voice and by the moving words of her songs, listened readily. But when Danny followed up her comments, they seemed less impressed.

'I suppose your old man has plenty of stocks and shares, Hughie,' Danny began. 'And likely, all the rest of you have dads with shares, too. You should put yourselves in good with them by giving them the tip. Here.' He produced some newly printed business cards and handed them out. His friends took them, glanced at them casually, and stuck them in their pockets. He was ready to go on, and to answer questions, but none came. It didn't look to either Millie or Danny as if much good was going to come of their plan of campaign.

'Talking of cards, let's get back to the game,' growled Big Geordie, who had had some luck in the last hand and was hoping for a run of it, so they did.

It was late by the time a halt was called. By this time, Josh, once again, had lost heavily. Danny had won, and Bugsy had won. Mike had broken even, and so had Millie. The other two, Hughie and Big Geordie, had lost almost as heavily as Josh. They finished with another round of drinks, but most of them, in spite of that, left in a rather depressed mood.

Roundabout – *Gerry McCullough*

Chapter Forty One

Stephen Gillespie had not forgotten his determination to complete the ruin of John O'Leary. He had given it some thought, and had decided that the best way to do this was, after his broker had discovered which shares O'Leary was investing in most heavily, to plan some way of bringing them down. Buying in bulk, and then selling, would be the obvious way.

He knew, however, that his own stock brokers, Milligan and Martin, were too reputable a firm to take such action on his behalf. He would need to find another company for that. But meanwhile, Patrick Milligan, the member of the firm who usually conducted his business, had been willing enough to look into the matter and provide him with the information he needed about John O'Leary's shares, as long as no further action was required of him. Milligan's involvement would have to stop there.

And he had noticed an ad in the local papers for a new company, who would, he supposed, be struggling to get established, and who might, therefore, be less scrupulous about the actions he intended to take. The name of this new company was McLoughlin & O'Hanlon. He had no idea that it was under the management of friends of his son.

Patrick Milligan, although sounding wary on the phone when Gillespie explained his request, had agreed to get the information required.

'But I still don't quite follow why you want it, Stephen,' he said.

Gillespie was careful to make his voice pleasant. 'Och, well, I thought if John O'Leary thinks well of a company, it would be worth finding out more about it. I understand he's investing in some small businesses, rather than in the more established companies, looking for a bigger and better return as their stock goes up.'

'And is my opinion not good enough for you, Stephen?' asked his broker, making a joke of it but with an underlying serious inquiry in his voice.

'Och, of course it is, Patrick. I'll be wanting your opinion on the companies John O'Leary's backing, as soon as you've found out which ones they are.'

'Oh, I see. Well, Stephen, I'll ask around among my broker mates and get back to you in a day or two, right?'

'Right. Thanks,' Gillespie had said. He had put the phone down with a feeling of satisfaction. The ball was rolling.

Millie had drawn up the ad which had caught Stephen Gillespie's attention. It read, in part, in a large, bold font:

Need a broker? For on the spot knowledge

and experienced know how, you need

McLaughlin & O'Hanlon

Followed by the address and phone number.

So far the response had been scanty. However, they had had a few phone calls, and had booked appointments with the callers, and they were hoping these would become actual clients as soon as they came and were impressed. Danny had rehearsed a few things to say about himself, mentioning his years of experience with the well known and established Londonderry firm, McLaughlin & Ryan, of whom they were a branch, and offering a special introductory package of various skills for a very cheap cost, for the first month.

Millie's was the hand that had been instrumental in drawing up the words for him to say, as well as the words of the ad, but she was firm in insisting that Danny would be the one to meet the new prospective clients. His name was in the company's title, and he was the one with several years, rather than several months like herself, of first class experience. He was to continue by reeling off remarks about the world's stock exchanges and how important it was to be informed about what was happening all across the globe in the world of stocks and shares.

Danny knew he could do this, given Millie's introductory remarks, so he wasn't too nervous in the end. A slug of whiskey would probably have helped, but Millie firmly prohibited that. She didn't want him breathing whiskey fumes over prospective clients. It wasn't as if Danny was ever a heavy drinker.

Meanwhile, she'd had some enthusiastic responses to her texts to Stevie Bones's contacts, a couple of new clubs on the outskirts of the city centre, ready to take on new singers. It was clear that Stevie, if they had got in touch with him as she'd suggested, must have spoken really well about her.

She was due to meet the manager of *Rafferty's* that afternoon, and someone from *The Striped Tiger* the following day. She had no qualms about making a good impression. She felt confident, too, that she could persuade Danny that it was only sensible to make use of her gifts while the business was getting on its feet and they needed the money. The poker parties were to continue, too. Not every night, but at least once a week, maybe twice if everyone was keen.

Her meetings with the two managers both went well. She was to have a trial with one on the following Thursday, and with the other on the next Monday. If these went well, she would have regular, well paid spots every week for as long as she wanted. Millie skipped back from her second interview, and set about the job of winning Danny round to being as pleased about it as she was herself.

'I hate to think of you having to sing for those crowds of bluithered fellas, Mil,' was his first reaction, as she had known it would be.

'But, Danny, they won't all be drunk – only a few. Sure, if you come and keep an eye on me, there'll be no trouble. We really need a steady income until the business takes off, and the poker doesn't always work our way, does it?'

For Mike had been the overall winner for two sessions in a row lately, leaving Danny and Millie to just about break even. True, the other players, including Josh, had lost heavily, but it was Mike, not Danny, who had reaped the reward.

Danny was at last persuaded to agree to the truth of what she said. 'Well, okay, we'll give it a go. I'll come with you and see nobody annoys you, darlin'. They'd better not try anything on!'

Millie didn't say, 'Sure, I can look after myself, boy,' although she felt very like doing so. Danny had become very protective of her lately, since their marriage, in fact. Instead, she said, 'I know you'll look after me, darlin'. With a big strong man like you around, I'll be fine.'

'So, poker tonight,' Millie reminded him. 'Better get some beer in.'

'We should make it a Bring Your Own evening from now on,' Danny said. 'The drinks are eating up too much of the profits lately.'

'Sure, that'd be a good idea, Danny. We'll tell them tonight, for next time.'

The same five people had been turning up regularly for the poker nights, although Danny wondered privately why on earth Josh, Hughie, and Big Geordie, who practically never won, kept coming. He could understand Mike coming, with his skill, and even Bugsy, who won less often but every now and then had a really lucky evening.

Millie, aware that all three of the regular losers were falling for her in a big way, didn't wonder. She was just happy to keep them attracted enough to keep coming and losing their money, and had been wondering if there was any way of getting rid of the clever player Mike, and even the too lucky Bugsy. But so far, nothing had occurred to her.

Millie's two tryouts went well. Her voice was in fine tune, the audience roared their appreciation, nothing happened to upset Danny, and both managers enthusiastically signed her up to sing in a regular spot, one on

Thursdays, the other on Wednesdays. The money was good. Millie was delighted. She would have to work out a set of suitable songs. Just a matter of scrolling through lists on the Internet, making a note of the ones she thought best, and then practicing them.

She spent a lot of time around the apartment singing, which Danny enjoyed, and also tried out a few on the poker players, who mostly loved them. The only exception was Mike, who was tone deaf and considered it a waste of good poker playing time.

Mike was also showing general signs of disgruntlement. He was used to winning much more often than he managed in Danny's company. The thought had gone through his brain more than once that the games might be rigged. But in that case, probably Danny would win a lot more often than he did.

Unless – the thought occurred to him – Danny was deliberately holding off, winning less often than he'd like to, in order to disarm suspicion? Would Danny have the sort of mind that would plan for that? Mike didn't think he would. But he wouldn't put it past that scheming little wife of his.

Millie had been deliberately cold to Mike lately, hoping to discourage him from coming, and the contrast between her attitude to him and the warm, flirty way in which she treated the other players had had the effect of turning Mike against her. At first he had been attracted. But now, he wouldn't put anything past her. In fact he found himself disliking her quite a lot.

Chapter Forty Two

Josh's frequent absences these evenings were upsetting Sooze considerably. She knew, by now, that he was attracted to Millie. She just hoped it wasn't very serious. She could deal with it, she thought, if it was a fleeting fancy which would soon pass.

But as the weeks went past, and there was no sign of Josh stopping his regular attendance, at least twice a week and sometimes more often, at the O'Hanlon's poker parties, Sooze became more and more desperate. It wasn't just the question of Millie. There was also the matter of the money she knew he was losing. He had taken out two credit cards and Sooze knew that both of them were fast approaching their limit. It was as much as they could do to pay the monthly interest and have enough left to feed and clothe themselves from Josh's wages.

His father had long since stopped his allowance. The rent of the apartment had been paid for a year in advance by Stephen Gillespie when he took the place for Josh, so that was all right. But what would happen when the year was up and they couldn't afford to take on the rent on top of their other expenses? And they would have a baby to feed and clothe by then.

If Sooze had been able to take on a job herself she would gladly have done it, but she had had no success in her previous efforts to find one. Her A level results had been pretty bad. And apart from that, her obvious pregnancy made her an unwelcome choice to most employers, legally or not. And once the baby was born, it would be even more difficult. Sooze didn't want to leave him or her with someone else, not even her mother, whose maternal instincts she didn't really trust. They couldn't afford to pay a child minder, even if she had been prepared to trust one.

She had been trying with great difficulty to squeeze out enough money, from the amount Josh gave her from his salary for housekeeping, to build up a store of baby clothes, for the birth was coming so close, now. Once Christmas was over, it would be only three more months. Sooze was alternately thrilled at the idea and in dread of it.

Christmas came and went. Sooze managed enough from her scanty savings to buy Josh some of the expensive aftershave he loved, and which he had run short of not long before. Josh hadn't really planned a present for Sooze until the last moment, when a lucky evening at the poker table allowed him to buy her a box of chocolates. Sooze, who was trying not to put on more weight than she could help during this pregnancy, managed with difficulty to seem pleased and delighted.

She had bought her mum a scented candle and her dad a box of cheap small cigars, not his usual brand, but it was the best she could do. Sam had given her, on behalf of them both, some clothes for the baby, which Sooze really appreciated. Her only personal gift came from Horse, who bought her a bunch of flowers and a pretty top to wear after the baby was born, and who gave Josh two new shirts to wear to work, which Josh was glad of, now that his own were getting a bit the worse for wear.

Sooze was ashamed to realise that she had forgotten to put aside any money for a gift for Horse. Instead, she gave him a never read copy of a book of poetry one of her admirers had given her last summer, and which still looked brand new, as well it might, and had nothing written on it, diving out of the room to wrap it hastily in her bedroom before presenting it with her best smile. Horse treasured that book for years, but to tell the truth Sooze's smile meant even more to him. He thought she was beginning to like him.

Her mother was a great help to Sooze at this time. But when, one day, Sam dared to criticise Josh for his neglect of Sooze at a time when she needed him so badly, Sooze flew off the handle, and shouted at her in defence of her still dearly loved husband.

'Josh is doing everything he can for me and the baby!' she shouted at Sam. 'He loves us both. Don't you dare to say such critical things about him ever again!'

She stormed out of Sam's apartment, caught a bus back to her own place, and once safely inside flung herself down on the bed and burst into tears, crying in a heartbroken way until a long time later she fell asleep, only to wake guiltily an hour later and jump up to make Josh's tea. It was badly cooked, and Josh was angry.

The row with her mother was patched up. Sooze so badly needed her support. But she was aware of an undercurrent of coldness from Sam, however much her mother tried to hide it.

And Josh wouldn't stop going to the poker nights. 'You just wait, Sooze,' he told her, grinning. 'The luck's bound to change. Any day now, I'll be making our fortune. Then you'll be glad I kept on.'

Sooze knew how unlikely that was. But she didn't want another row. Presently, Josh left her once more to go round to the O'Hanlon's, taking with him a pack of beer whose cost left Sooze hard up for housekeeping money for the rest of the month.

Josh really believed he was bound to win in a big way some time soon. But also, he was finding more and more that he couldn't keep away from Millie. He sent her texts which expressed his fervent love, and her replies, if still not too serious, were always encouraging. Millie had a light hand at flirtation by now. She was getting plenty more experience.

It was that night that the fight broke out.

It wasn't a physical fight. No one was injured or even hit. But after the first few games, Mike looked at his hand, threw down his cards and stood up, thrusting his chair back with so much force that it fell over.

'This isn't just bad luck!' he shouted. 'Every time you deal, Danny O'Hanlon, I end up with a hand that isn't worth peanuts, and the cards I draw are even worse. Someone's rigging the deck, and I don't need three guesses to tell you guys who it is.'

'Are you accusing me of cheating, Mike Kennedy?' Danny asked, his lean face, with the fair hair drooping over it, looking amused. 'Can't you take a bit of bad luck?'

'I can take bad luck. What I can't take is someone who's supposed to be a mate deliberately taking me for all my cash. And you'd better take that smirk off your face or I'll take it off for you.'

Danny's lop sided grin disappeared. He stood up in turn and pushed back his chair, stepping away from the table into the clear space beside it. His face no longer looked even faintly amused. In fact Millie had never seen him look so grim. He was clearly about to land a punch on Mike's jaw as soon as he could get near enough to him.

But Millie didn't relish seeing her pretty living room broken up, or her husband laid out, as she expected would be the result of any fight. The red haired Mike was stronger and tougher than Danny and probably more used to violence. Springing up from her own seat, she darted round to get between Danny and Mike.

'Fellas, sit down again and be sensible!' she ordered them. 'Mike, you know fine well Danny would never cheat. Danny, be sensible. Mike must have drunk too much.'

Mike breathed hard. 'Hiding behind a girl, O'Hanlon?' he sneered. 'You don't seriously expect me to sit down again to play with someone who's cheating me? No way!'

'Then you'd better leave, now,' Millie said coldly. 'Don't forget your jacket.'

'Don't worry, I'm on my way.' Mike grabbed his jacket, for the weather had recently turned as cold as it usually did in January. 'And I'll take the rest of my beer with me. No, I'm not drunk, Millie O'Hanlon. It'd be hard to get drunk on what you offer your guests, exactly nothing.' And with that parting shot, he marched out of the apartment.

'Sit down, Danny,' Millie ordered him, and Danny meekly seated himself again. 'I'm so sorry, fellas, for that exhibition,' she said to the other players.

There were embarrassed murmurs. 'No need for you to apologise, Millie,' Josh said earnestly. 'I would never have expected behaviour like that from Mike Kennedy. He's always been a good lad.'

'Yeah,' Hughie agreed. 'Musta been drinking, like you said, Millie.'

'Been topping himself up before he got here,' Big Geordie contributed.

Bugsy nodded in agreement. He wasn't entirely sure that Mike had been wrong, mind you, he told himself. His own hands had been suspiciously bad for some time now, whenever Danny was dealing. His luck usually saw him through poker games better than it had been doing at Danny's.

'Let's have a song, Millie,' suggested Josh, and to murmurs of agreement Millie sang to them until they felt relaxed and happy again.

When Josh finally left the apartment, much later, and after the others, a shadowy figure loomed up in front of him. A breathe of whiskey in the air told Josh who it was. A moment later, the figure came nearer under the street light, and revealed itself beyond question as Mike.

'Mike! What the –?'

'Shut up. Don't make a row,' Mike urged. 'Want a word.' He led Danny further away from the entrance to the O'Hanlons' apartment block, and away from the street light, into the shadows.

'Okay, what?' Josh asked.

'Listen. Do you want to try somewhere else? I know a good, clean game we could join in. You've been losing as often as me, and probably a lot more in cash, because I'm a cautious player. I don't risk anything unless I have the right cards. Well?'

'You got Danny wrong, Mike. He wouldn't cheat.'

'I don't want to argue about that. You have your opinion. I have mine. Okay. I just want to know if you're interested in checking out this other game?'

'Sure am,' Josh agreed. He had no intention of stopping going to Danny's and Millie's, but another game, where he might win more money, sounded good to him. 'When would it be on?'

'I'll text you.' And the whiff of whiskey retreated from the corner, leaving Josh to make his own way home.

Roundabout – *Gerry McCullough*

Chapter Forty Three

John O'Leary was finding life puzzling and difficult.

He had been forced by now to cut his losses and to sell his business premises and goodwill, on top of his previous sale of his helicopter and his cars, his house and most of his household goods. His business had been going steadily downhill all winter. By the time he had paid off his business debts, bank loans, and everything else he owed, he had only a small sum left.

Now that his son Johnny was paying, by direct debit, the rent of the new apartment Johnny had arranged for his family, with a bit over for living expenses, John O'Leary was able to devote this small lump sum to more investments which, he hoped, would make his fortune for him the second time around. His earlier choices in this area had been sad failures, leaving him even harder up. But it didn't stop him trying again.

He had carefully picked out four small companies whose shares were currently at low prices, but which had every chance of rising steadily. He divided his money between them, and watched their prices daily. A small rise in one gave him great satisfaction, and he kept an eye out, studying the market, for anything which looked like a better deal, occasionally selling a few shares from a company which wasn't doing too well and investing in one which could show regular growth.

Then one day, a while after Christmas, he saw with delight that one of his companies had had a sudden growth spurt. As he watched, the price continued to rise. O'Leary made the obvious decision, sold out from his other companies, and invested everything in the shares of the rising business.

He had no way of knowing that the rise in prices was due to Stephen Gillespie, who was regularly buying, through his new brokers, enough of the shares to ensure a rise in prices. He had given instructions that as soon as the brokers were confident that the ceiling had been reached, they should sell out.

His former brokers, understanding was he was up to, would have refused to operate such trickery. But his new brokers, McLaughlin & O'Hanlon, seemed to have no such moral scruples.

Danny, in fact, had been reluctant to take on Stephen Gillespie. He knew he was Josh's dad, and he was fairly clear, after checking on the other owners of shares in the company in question, that his target was John O'Leary, Sooze's father.

'I think we should turn him down, Mil,' he said. 'And maybe warn Sooze, so she can tell her dad what's happening before he gets done.'

But Millie would have none of it. 'Nonsense, Danny, big business-men do that sort of thing all the time,' she said briskly. 'John O'Leary can take care of himself. He wasn't very kind to me, why should I go out of my way for him? We only have three other clients, so far. We can't afford to turn one away.'

So Danny had allowed himself, against his better judgment, to be persuaded.

In due course, the shares seemed to have reached their ceiling, and Danny, in accordance with his instructions, sold out Gillespie's holding, which by then was a huge percentage of the shares.

John O'Leary, gazing with unbelieving eyes at his computer screen the following day and seeing the plummeting price of his shares, did the only thing possible, and rushed to sell out in his turn. He would still make a small profit if he could unload his shares before the price sank lower still.

But, alas, he and his broker could find no takers. The falling price was putting off all possible buyers. With horror O'Leary watched his shares hit rock bottom. Once again, he had lost all his money and was penniless.

Several sleepless nights followed. John O'Leary couldn't make up his mind. Should he let go of everything, forget about making his fortune again, and live on the charity of his son?

Or should he try for a loan, and further investments?

If he chose the second option, there was only one way he could get a loan now. Only one thing he could offer as security. And that was the direct debit which Johnny had set up for him.

The risks were enormous. A bank wouldn't accept the direct debit as security, of course. But one of the other loan companies would, he was sure. He had seen their ads on the Internet. And if he was given a loan, and somehow his investments failed for a third time? What would happen then? He would lose the money from the direct debit, which would go to the loan company.

He would no longer be able to pay their rent. He and Sam would have to leave their home, and would have nothing to live on. He would have to apply for Social Security, and they would insist that he applied for any sort of job that was going, and took whatever was offered to him. The thought was unbearable. He, John O'Leary, a wealthy man so recently, having to work as a waiter or a shelf packer in a supermarket. He shuddered at the very thought.

But if he could make a go of his investments this time? Surely his luck couldn't continue to go on letting him down like this?

And so John O'Leary put his fears aside, arranged a loan, with Johnny's direct debit for security, and breathed a sigh of relief when it was signed and settled. He began at once to search for sensible investments. This time he wouldn't put all his eggs in one basket, however roomy and safe the basket might look.

He didn't know, of course, that Stephen Gillespie was waiting patiently like a vulture hovering over a thirsty, dying man in the desert, ready to pounce again at the right moment.

Neither Sam nor Sooze knew anything about O'Leary's problems or decisions. Sooze had her own worries to contend with. Josh was going out more than ever in the evenings, leaving Sooze, who was coming nearer and nearer to the due date for the birth of her baby, on her own. Josh seemed to have lost all interest in either her or the baby, and she was frightened of finding herself alone when the contractions started.

Sam, who was calling round with her frequently, reassured her. 'You've got your mobile, and the landline too. Ring me as soon as anything starts. I'll come right round. And ring your midwife. She'll advise you about how soon you should go to the Royal. You'll be okay, Sooze.' She gave her daughter an unaccustomed hug, and carefully refrained from criticising Josh for his regular absence at a time when he should be staying with Sooze and looking after her. It wouldn't help matters if Sooze reacted as she'd done before and flew off the handle with her mother.

'But suppose it's the middle of the night?' Sooze worried.

'Well, in that case I suppose Josh will be with you. And if he hasn't come home, ring me, late or not, and I'll come.'

Sooze, who knew her parents still hadn't managed to afford a car, wondered briefly how she would manage that. Would there be taxis available in the middle of the night? Then she put her worry aside and accepted her mother's assurances as she had done as a child.

She and Josh hadn't managed to keep his car either. They had sold it some months ago, finding the cost of repairs, MOT, insurance, and petrol becoming too much of a burden. Its sale had helped temporarily with money management, but as Josh's poker losses mounted, things got harder than ever. Josh was still waiting for the promotion he had been so confident of. But his late nights had led, too often, to late arrival at work, hung over and not very competent. Horse had covered for him as much as possible. But it wasn't always possible. He spoke to Josh about it one day.

'Josh, you're ruining your career chances, mate.' He paused to see how Josh was taking this. Was he about to blow up? Or was he listening? He seemed to be taking it seriously.

'If you don't catch yourself on, you'll be slung out,' said Horse bluntly. 'My dad's mentioned it to me several times, and I've done my best for you. Explained that Sooze is expecting and that you've had to do a lot of work at home, and had sleepless nights. He's a decent man and so far he's allowing you some rope. But it can't go on for ever.'

'Thanks, Horse. I know you'll always help,' mumbled Josh. 'But it won't be much longer. I need to make enough to clear myself, then I promise I'll stop.'

Horse had heard this sort of thing before, not just from Josh, but from other friends. The gambling fever seemed to have broken out on all sides lately.

He decided that he might have said as much as Josh would take right now, and wisely left it alone for the time being.

Chapter Forty Four

Josh was enjoying his evenings at the new poker night he had been introduced to by Mike. They met on the corner by Josh's apartment, and Mike picked him up in his car. The venue was in Glengormley, a suburb of Belfast to the north of the city, nestling under the Cave Hill, and one Josh had always thought of as highly respectable. And, indeed, the house to which Mike drove him was a big, pleasant one, set in large gardens, and as far as Josh could see on the dark winter nights when he visited it, well designed, in a Georgian style which he admired.

Inside it had wooden floors and bright rugs, minimalist furnishings, and for décor, pale creamy walls with a few striking pictures in bright colours, and a beautiful rock crystal figure of a scantily clad dancing woman set on a low table, an indication, if Josh had understood it, that there were no children in the house either as residents or visitors.

Mike introduced him to his host.

'Josh, this is Andy Patterson, otherwise Pat. You should keep your eye on him – he's mustard at the poker table. Pat, this is Josh, the guy I told you about.'

'Good to meet you, Josh,' murmured Andy Patterson, shaking Josh's hand in a languid way. He didn't look as if he was mustard, either at the poker table or anywhere else. He was tall and thin, with drooping mousy hair falling forward over his bony face and a pale complexion which matched the walls of his house. He was middle aged, to Josh's surprise. He had been expecting a much younger man. Josh wasn't sure that he liked the look of him, but greeted him pleasantly.

There were two other men, both quite a bit older than Josh or Mike, introduced as Taffy, a small, tubby Welshman with a cheerful grin, and Pete, red haired and strong looking. Josh thought he looked like Mike, and the likeness was explained in an aside from Mike a few minutes later, while everyone was greeting the last arrival. 'My cousin. It was him introduced me to Pat.'

The late arrival was a girl, and although she wasn't as attractive as Millie or even as pretty as Sooze, Josh found her interesting. She was tall and hefty with long, straight blonde hair and a face you couldn't call either plain or ugly, but – well, unusual. A clown's face – but definitely not ugly.

That was as far as Josh had got, when he found that he was being handed a glass of whiskey by Patterson, and invited to take his seat at the large table where everyone else was in process of sitting. He was settled between the girl, who seemed to be known as Blondie, and the friendly Welshman, Taffy, and Patterson had them cutting for deal almost at once.

For once Josh was lucky. He drew the ace of clubs, and was first dealer. He found he had given himself a good hand, with a pair of threes and another ace, diamonds this time, and when he drew another three he knew his luck was in. He went for it, staying in until only Pat, as he was now beginning to think of his host, was left, as one after another the remaining players threw in their hands. Pat had two Queens, but Josh's three threes won.

The pot wasn't too high, since most people had folded early. They were all experienced players, including Blondie, who Josh soon realised was amazingly good, and they'd been able to read Josh easily. Josh wasn't aware that his face had revealed that he expected to win. He had never had a good poker face, although he wouldn't have believed that himself.

Josh enjoyed his evening. It was late when Mike ran him home and dropped him off at the corner of the apartment block.

'So, do you think you'll come again?' he asked as Josh opened the car door to step out.

'Oh, wow, yeah!'

'Better than the O'Hanlons?'

'Aw, now, I wouldn't say that.'

'Does your wife not mind you being out like this so much?' asked Mike curiously. He had no wife himself, no experience of how one would react, but he thought that these days they would probably have firmer ideas of how their husband should behave than his mum had had. His mum, the downtrodden wife of a loud mouthed forceful bully, had put up with everything until finally she died, too young in Mike's opinion. He wouldn't have wanted a wife who followed her pattern, and would have been surprised to find out that Josh's wife did.

Josh blushed, but he had stepped into the darkness outside the car by now and it didn't show.

'She's okay with it. Means she can get to sleep early,' he lied, then with a quick, 'See you!' he dived through the apartment entrance.

Sure enough, Sooze was asleep when he reached their bedroom.

The next night it was the O'Hanlons' turn to have the pleasure of Josh's company at their poker table. He went early, gobbling down the meal Sooze, with some effort, had made for him on his return from work, barely thanking her for it, although her cooking had improved a lot with practice.

'Okay, love, gotta run.'

And he was out of the apartment in a flash.

Sooze sighed. If she wasn't so tired all the time now, she would have said something to Josh, maybe have asked him to stay with her more, now that the baby was due so soon. But it didn't seem worth the effort. She had already tried once, telling him that she was scared of being alone when the baby started to come, but Josh, although he had promised to stay home much more, had promptly broken his promise, going out the next night for his first visit to Andy Patterson's. And instead of improving, things had in fact got worse.

When Horse called round a few nights later, expecting to find Josh there, he was surprised and angry to find Sooze sitting on her own, trying with clumsy, unaccustomed fingers to knit a warm jacket for the baby.

'Why, Sooze, I didn't expect to find you on your own.'

Sooze smiled wanly. 'Oh, Josh is a busy man these days.'

'Busy? What could be important enough to keep him away from you at a time like this?'

'He's run up some debts,' Sooze confessed. 'He's hoping if he goes out to play poker, he'll make enough to clear them, and then some. It's for me and the baby, really, Horse.'

Horse's anger grew. He struggled to control it. He was quite sure that Josh's continued gambling wasn't for his wife and future child's sake. It was his own greed, and the pride which refused to accept defeat, which led him to continue.

'So, he goes to play poker at Millie and Danny's?' he asked slowly.

'Not just there,' Sooze said. It was unexpectedly comforting to pour out all her troubles to Horse. She hadn't wanted to tell her mother and give her even more ammunition against Josh. She had enough already. 'There's a new place he goes to now, as well. Up in Glengormley. Someone called Andy Patterson – Josh calls him Pat.'

She didn't notice how Horse stiffened at the name.

'Oh, Horse, I'm so worried. He's losing more and more. He took out a third credit card recently, and he's nearly up to his limit with that one, already, as well as the first two. Couldn't you say something to him – stop him somehow?'

'I'll speak to him tomorrow, Sooze.' Horse stood up abruptly, and paced around the room. 'What happens if the baby comes while he's not here?'

'Mum says to ring her and she'll come at once. And I've to ring the midwife, too. But, oh, Horse, I would so much like Josh to be here. I need him to comfort me.'

'Ring me, Sooze. I'll pick up your mother and come round and take you to the hospital in my car. Ring Josh as well, of course,' he added as an afterthought. 'He'll come as quickly as he can, I know. But maybe he'll be here when it happens.'

Sooze said no more. She was embarrassed to tell Horse how very seldom Josh was ever there, these days. If he wasn't at one or other of his poker parties, he would be watching Millie sing at her regular two nights a week gigs. He was probably her most faithful fan. Late nights, in any case.

Horse left soon, promising again to speak to Josh the next day, and Sooze went to bed, feeling vaguely comforted by Horse's kindness and reassurance.

Chapter Forty Five

She would have been less happy if she had been aware of Horse's thoughts.

The name Andy Patterson, 'Pat', had not been strange to him. He had heard it before, in a number of unpleasant contexts.

'Pat' Patterson had been a young activist in the more extreme of the Protestant paramilitaries, the UFF. When the peace agreement finally put an end to the actual fighting and bombing, Pat had been one of those released from prison under the Good Friday agreement. Like others, he had found it impossible to settle down to a peaceful life in a nine to five job, and had slipped easily and naturally into a life of crime.

Starting with drug dealing, he had moved on to other branches of organised crime, prostitution and people trafficking among them, laundering his money, as Horse happened to know, through one of the major banks, until more stringent controls had been introduced, and he had moved his business dealings down south and opened offshore accounts. He was one of the last people Josh should be mixing with.

He sketched out in his own mind a few things to say to his old friend at the first opportunity.

Josh was not, in fact, Millie's most faithful fan. She had built up an enthusiastic following, mainly men, although she had the admiration of some young girls as well. Most of her fans fell into the younger age bracket, but an exception was Malachi Charles, who had been impressed enough by Millie's voice, and also by her looks and personality, at one hearing, to give her a gig in his blooming city centre club bar, *Mal's*.

Mal was in his mid thirties, and had been a successful entrepreneur in the entertainment business since his early twenties. Leaving school at sixteen, a gangling, brown haired kid, he had quickly realised the opportunities newly awakening Belfast gave to anyone who had the skill and initiative to grab out for them. Belfast was ready again to go out and be entertained, and Mal was the man to give the people what they wanted.

He needed capital before he could take over an empty city centre building and refurbish it in the way he wanted. There was no shortage of ruined buildings, in need of a bit of work but in prime sites. He set to work to build up his capital. He worked hard at any job he could get, putting in long stints at a computer software factory, and adding to that as many hours as he could cram in as a part time waiter.

He bought and sold on the Internet, sitting up late and making a regular profit out of whatever came up. And he saved. Those were the days when he walked to his various jobs, rain, hail or snow, to save bus fares or taxis, and ate sparingly, getting free meals during his job as waiter and making that meal a good one which would last him for the next twenty four hours, living in one dingy room in the cheapest part of town and building up, ever building up, his savings, until he was ready. By now he had grown into a well built, confident looking man.

He had had his eye for some time on an empty building in the Cathedral Quarter, so called because of its proximity to St Anne's Cathedral, an area becoming known as a centre of music and the arts. As soon as he could, he took out a mortgage on it, putting down most of his money as a deposit, and using the rest for repair and décor. There was very little actually wrong with the building, in fact.

Mal threw in a gang of cleaners and scoured the place from top to bottom. Then he put in a set of unisex toilets, hung the stairways with bright gold gauze and red velvet curtains to cover the dismal walls, laid new bright multi striped stair carpet, and put up a horseshoe bar in the main room, with plenty of tables and chairs. He painted the walls cream with bright red, green and gold stencils of flowers, leaves and birds. He painted the front door in the same bright stripes as the carpet, shut off the other rooms until he could afford to decorate them, put up a neon sign saying *Mal's* in shrieking pink, and was ready for opening night.

People crowded in the first night out of curiosity and to drink the offers of cheap beer and wine which on that night only Mal gave them at cost. He had had his eye on several good local bands who were so eager for exposure that they were willing to play for very little, and the entertainment at *Mal's* soon got the reputation of being really cool. People came back, and others joined them. Before long, Mal was able to pay his musicians a more reasonable rate, to decorate and open the other rooms, to pay off his mortgage and to look around for other venues to take on. By the time he was in his thirties, he was a very rich man.

He had had many girl friends from the time when he could first afford to take a girl out, but none of them had meant a lot to him. Until the first time he saw and heard Millie Brennan.

Mal saw a beautiful, sexy girl with a golden voice whose smile seemed to be just for him. Millie saw a rich, reasonably young and reasonably good looking man who could further her career. Later in their relationship she saw a man who could change her life, if she handled things right.

She and Danny were getting along fine. But although they were both working hard, it would be a long time, if ever, before they were as rich as Millie felt she deserved to be. Christmas hadn't been too bad. Danny had spent his poker winnings on a necklace for her with real diamonds.

'You can thank yer man Josh for it, next time you see him,' Danny joked. 'He kindly donated most of the dosh for it.'

'Oh, Danny, it's beautiful,' sighed Millie rapturously. And indeed, she was well pleased. She reckoned she could sell the necklace for a pretty large amount, whenever she wanted to. She herself hadn't done quite so well by Danny, getting him two pairs of boxer shorts, and making up for it by murmured words about how much she was looking forward to seeing him wearing them, and then helping him to take them off. Danny had reacted with pleasure.

Millie could well have afforded to spend at least as much on Danny as he had spent on her, for the earnings from her gigs were growing rapidly. But they were going into Millie's private savings account, instead of into the joint account she and Danny had set up together. As well as her own earnings, Millie was regularly depositing, in her savings account, large amounts drawn by herself from their joint savings account, which was fed by Danny's earnings both from the poker games and from McLoughlin & O'Hanlon's.

Danny hadn't noticed Millie's regular withdrawals so far. Millie had handled their online banking from the start, including both their savings account and their joint current account, and he was content to leave it in her hands, together with all the general administration of the business, something which had never interested him.

Not long after this, she started singing at *Mal's*. She had been singing at the two lesser known bars for some months now, and it was only after she'd met Mal himself that she learned that these two bars also belonged to him. He had dropped in to see her at these bars shortly after Christmas, on the recommendations of both his managers, and had been so impressed that he'd offered her a gig at his most important bar, *Mal's* itself.

But it was not just her voice that had impressed him, as he soon made very clear to Millie. She didn't need telling that he had fallen for her like a ton of bricks. It was in his eyes every time he looked at her. This was just the sort of man she'd been looking for, for years. True, she was tied to Danny. But something could be done about that, if she could be sure about Mal.

Millie thought about it.

Slowly and carefully, she planned out her course of action.

She began by suggesting to Danny that he was overdoing things, exhausting himself.

'You don't need to come to my gigs all the time, darlin' boy,' she said, making her voice soft and loving. 'You're working all day, and you need to be on top of your form for the poker nights. Why not give yourself a break and take a few early nights?'

'I love coming to hear you, babe,' Danny protested at first.

'Darlin', I can sing for you any time – you know you just have to ask.' The smile she gave him was not only sweet but very sexy.

'But you need me with you, to get you home safely at that time of night.'

'You could drop me off, sure,' Millie said, for by this time she and Danny had bought a car, registered and insured in his name, cheap and second hand but running well. 'And you could go on home then, and get to bed. I can always get a lift back with someone else, or find a taxi.'

'I don't know that I want you getting a lift with any of those guys who come to see you all the time,' Danny grumbled. 'I wouldn't trust any of them within a mile of you, Mil.'

'Well, there's always Mal,' Millie suggested. 'You could trust him, sure. We have a good business relationship – he doesn't think of me as a woman to be mauled about. And he wouldn't dare lay a finger on me in case I walked out – he couldn't risk losing me. I'm a big draw at the club. Anyway, Mal's not that sorta guy.'

Danny agreed. He didn't think Mal was that sort of guy either. So, after several discussions along similar lines, he began finally make a habit of dropping Millie off at the club and then leaving her to get a lift home with Mal, or a taxi, while he had some much needed rest.

That was the first part of Millie's campaign. It was easy, during the rides home late at night in Mal's car, to further their relationship. She developed the habit of snuggling up to him as he drove, telling him it was because she was so tired. 'You feel so soft and cuddly to rest on,' was the reason she gave. Before long, it had become the custom for them to kiss goodnight.

After this had happened a few times, Millie said, leaning against Mal's shoulder, 'I suppose this makes it difficult for you to drive, Mal, darlin'. How about stopping for a little while until I feel a bit rested. You aren't in a hurry to get home, are you?'

Mal was no fool. He found it hard, at first, to be sure that this delicious girl was encouraging him, but it didn't take him long to know that she definitely was.

'It makes it hard for me to breathe, too, babe,' he said, grinning at her.

'Oh?' Millie asked innocently. 'Maybe I should move?'

'Don't do that, Millie. There's a nice little spot nearby where we can pull in for a few moments.'

A car, as Mal knew, wasn't an ideal place for more than a kiss and a cuddle. But that seemed to be all Millie wanted. He let it go at that, for several weeks. Stupid to spoil his chances by rushing her. And very likely being turned down.

'My apartment's not too far from *Mal's,* sweetie,' he told Millie one night when he felt it might work. 'How's about dropping off at mine for a drink or two before I take you on home? You aren't expected home at any special time, are you?'

'Oh, Danny'll be asleep,' Millie responded carelessly. 'And if he isn't, I can always say the crowd wouldn't let me go, I had to do lots of encores.'

'Okay, then?'

'Okay.' Millie hesitated, then added, in accordance with her previously tested system, 'But, Mal, I hope you don't think I'd do much more than kiss you? I couldn't let Danny down – it wouldn't be right, unless it was the sort of relationship that would be permanent. And I don't think you're looking for that, are you? Just a good time, then drop me. Well, I'm not on for that, not after a certain point, right?'

'Right, Millie.'

Mal wasn't sure enough yet that he was ready for a permanent relationship. But he wasn't ready to rule it out, either. He said no more, waiting to see how things would develop.

Roundabout – *Gerry McCullough*

Chapter Forty Six

Danny was finding his life busy enough, these days. The business seemed to be picking up, with several new clients. Danny was an experienced broker. He knew his way around the stock markets, and could pick out the best buys for his customers unfalteringly.

Word soon got around, as client after client found himself making a killing – sometimes small, sometimes large, but always an encouragement to trust young O'Hanlon's skill, and probably, in boasting about their success to other well off friends, to mention their clever young broker. 'New on the scene, locally, running his own company now, but very experienced in the place he worked for previously. You should try him!'

So the clients rolled in and Danny was busy. He needed his wits about him. Start giving bad advice and word would get round just as quickly about that. Millie was right, he realised after a few early nights and some sound sleep. He was waking up refreshed these days, ready to tackle everything brought to him. If the company went on growing like this, he would soon be able to cut out the poker nights. He was becoming aware that the two late nights he still put in took the edge off his alertness on the following morning. Maybe soon he could cut them down to one, and make that one a weekend night?

In a way, of course, he would miss the games. No need, he reflected, to cut them out altogether. He'd always enjoyed poker, and knew he had honed his skill there to a fine edge. It was rarely, now, that he lost a game unless the luck of the cards was really against him. When it was, he had enough sense to throw in his hand straightaway, cutting his losses.

He found it hard to understand Joss, for instance, who would continue to raise his stake even though his hand, when he finally exposed it, was one that had never had much chance of winning. Josh must surely have realised that, so why go on?

And he wasn't the only one. The dark haired Bugsy trusted too much in his luck. Certainly, it often brought him a big win, but at other times his losses were equally large. Big Geordie, like Josh, had very little poker skill, and a face that revealed too much, so that Danny could always tell if he was gambling in the hope of improving his hand, or if it was already a winner.

Danny was able, therefore, to fold and by doing that reduce both his own losses and Big Geordie's winnings.

He didn't need, with these players, to use any of the tricks he had practised in the past. At school, he had often won by cheating, as Horse had warned Josh a good while ago. To have a reputation for that had meant that presently, very few of his school mates would play with him. He didn't want to develop a similar reputation these days. So the games, as far as Danny was concerned, were straight.

He wasn't too sure about Josh, though. Several times he had thought Josh was using tricks he must have read in some book, or learned on the Internet where, Danny was aware, you could learn almost anything, including cardsharping. If Josh tried it too obviously, Danny was going to have to call him on it. He kept Josh behind one night, saying it was ages since they'd had a chat, and then talked, not accusing Josh outright, but hinting round the subject, about the tricks of cardsharpers.

'I'd hate to see anyone trying that at my table, Josh,' he said lightly. 'It's easy enough to tell. And then, I'd have to chuck them out of the game. We're all mates here – be bad to have to do that.'

Josh took the hint, and the cheating stopped. As a matter of fact, Josh was feeling relieved that Danny had wanted to talk to him about the cards, and not about Millie, as he had feared at first. His relationship with Millie had continued to develop to a dangerous level. He would have hated Danny to notice anything, and maybe pass the info on to Sooze, or pick a fight.

Not that Josh was afraid, but Danny, although no taller than him, and lean where Josh was well built, was a good fighter, or so he'd heard. The days when he'd been bullied at school until rescued by Horse had put Josh off fighting for life, and he'd regularly ducked out of any question of joining in a fight, if ever it had arisen.

But if he was going to have to give up winning by cheating at Danny's, then all the more reason to cheat at Pat's. He read up more on the subject, and polished up his technique in private before trying it out there.

It would be more dangerous, he knew. So far, he hadn't risked it. He remembered the things Horse had said to him about Pat and his history and reputation, which Horse had told him forcefully when he called him into his private office at work recently.

'Patterson is one of the last people you should hang around with, Josh,' Horse had said earnestly, after he had outlined Pat's history as a terrorist and his present involvement in crime. 'He has the bad reputation to beat them all. I don't know how many people he's killed but they say it's in the thirties or maybe higher. And I've heard that he's touchy. He'll fly off the handle in a moment, and then, look out! Keep away from him, Josh. Please. I wouldn't bother to tell you all this, but we've been friends for a long time. I'd hate to see anything happen to you.'

Josh knew this was true. He was touched by the earnestness of the expression on Horse's face.

'Thanks, mate. I appreciate it. I know you're telling me this because you care, right.'

'So, will you stay away from this character?'

Josh hesitated.

'You should be home with Sooze, looking after her,' Horse added. It wasn't the wisest thing to say. Josh stiffened.

'I know how to look after my own wife, Horse, thanks. You're taking too much on yourself.'

Before Horse could add more, he said, 'And are you sure you're not just mixing up this Andy Patterson, the one I play poker with, with the one you're talking about? The one I know is a quiet bloke, looks as if he's never been involved in a fight even at school. Quiet spoken. No sign of that temper you were talking about.'

'It's the same one.' Horse spoke flatly. He could see he wasn't going to persuade Josh to pull out of the poker game. 'The one I mean is tall, thin, with a sallow face and mousy hair drooping over his forehead. Lives out in Glengormley these days, I hear.'

'Well, then, maybe he's reformed.' Josh couldn't deny that the description Horse had given him bore a very strong resemblance to the Pat he knew. It was more than a strong resemblance. It was identical. But he really didn't want to pull out of the poker game.

Horse had shrugged and said no more, and Josh had been relieved.

But now, warned off cheating at Danny's poker table, he was seriously considering attempting it at Pat's. And he found Horse's warning reverberating in his ears again.

Roundabout – *Gerry McCullough*

Chapter Forty Seven

One of the clients who was keeping Danny busy was Stephen Gillespie. Stephen had been thinking about what else he could do to ruin John O'Leary. He blamed O'Leary bitterly for his break with his only son, denying any suggestion of his conscience that he had only himself and his prejudices and his appallingly bad temper to blame.

He knew he couldn't expect to play the same trick on O'Leary twice. Instead, he aimed to takeover any of the companies in which John O'Leary had invested, and run them into the ground. He estimated that if he bought shares steadily rather than in one big rush, until he owned everything except O'Leary's own shares, and then sold them all at once, the various companies were bound to collapse, leaving O'Leary, again, holding a bunch of worthless shares, this time in all his investments.

This stealthy approach would take longer, but it would ultimately be very satisfying. Moreover, it would be less likely to cause suspicion from his new broker. McLoughlin & O'Hanlon's had so far served him well, but he had a sneaking suspicion that the young man he worked with, young Danny O'Hanlon, wouldn't continue to allow him to victimise O'Leary. It would be as well that he would remain unsuspecting, this time round.

In this he underestimated Danny. Influenced by Millie and anxious to please her, Danny had gone along with Stephen Gillespie's actions the first time round, but he was keeping a sharp eye on him, determined not to allow him to repeat his performance. Danny, for all his happy-go-lucky life style, had an underlying reluctance to hurt or harm anyone, and a belief, implanted in him by his aunt Fran, who had taken over his upbringing when her sister, Danny's mother, died, that doing what was right, especially in how you treated other people, really mattered.

Like most of his generation, he was happy to sleep around, drink, and gamble, and generally enjoy himself without much thought. But there was a line which he drew and would not easily cross. He had a guilty feeling that he had crossed it when he allowed Millie to persuade him to act for Stephen Gillespie in what was obviously a campaign against a personal enemy, and he was determined not to cross that line again.

So when Stephen asked him to buy a few shares in several different companies, none of which, to Danny's experienced eye, were particularly promising, his suspicions were alerted. He checked. Yes, all of these companies were ones in which John O'Leary held some shares.

He bought a few shares, as requested. It seemed harmless enough. Even if Gillespie instructed him soon to sell out, the small number of shares could make little difference. But when Gillespie repeated the instructions a week or so later, his suspicions grew. He bought them, but with growing reluctance.

It wouldn't do, he realised, to discuss it with Millie. Millie's attitude to John O'Leary was, to give it an unpleasant name, vindictive. She considered that he and his wife had treated her badly, and she would be happy to see him ruined even further. She had said as much when they first discussed taking on Gillespie as a client. She would simply tell him to go ahead.

Danny didn't want to have a row with Millie. He was frightened of what her reaction might be. She would be very angry, and might even decide to leave him. She had a promising career ahead of her, and was earning enough without his contribution. No, it would be useless to talk to Millie about his reluctance to follow Stephen Gillespie's instructions. There was only one other person it would be any use to talk to.

Danny picked up his phone and rang his uncle by marriage, Fergus O'Ryan, in Derry.

He and Fergus had parted on not very good terms. And Fergus had treated him rather badly when Fran had died without leaving a will. Still, he was Danny's nearest relation, apart from a few very far out cousins. And he certainly knew his way around the stock exchange and the business world in general. His advice, if he was willing to give it, would be worth having.

In a minute or so, he heard Fergus's voice. 'Danny?'

'Yeah.'

'Danny, it's good to hear from you. I know we had a bit of a spat about you marrying Millie, but if you'd like to put that behind you, so would I. I took it too hard. I've been moving on. Millie's not the only girl in the world. I know several nice ones.' Fergus laughed nervously.

'Nothing I'd like better, Fergus. I'm glad you've moved on.'

'Yes.'

Danny hesitated, and then took the plunge. 'Fergus, I need your advice. It's about one of my clients.'

'Happy to help, Dan, as long as you realise you shouldn't break client confidentiality?'

'If I describe the problem without naming any names, how would that do?'

'That sounds okay, boy. Go for it. I'm listening.'

Danny outlined what Stephen Gillespie had previously got him to do, and then the current situation.

Fergus listened in silence. When he was sure Danny had finished, he said, 'That sounds to me like something you shouldn't get involved in, Dan. If people got to hear about it, you'd have done yourself no good as an honest broker. You'd have a reputation for dirty tricks. Neither you nor I want a reputation like that hanging round our business.'

'No,' said Danny thankfully. He was very happy to have Fergus Ryan's support in his own view of the matter. 'So, what do you advise me to do?'

'You need to speak bluntly to this client of yours, as soon as possible. Tell him you can't be involved in any further action against another share-holder. Make it clear you've caught on to what he was up to before, and that as far as you're concerned, that's the end of it. If he refuses to stop, tell him you can't continue to have him as a client.'

'That sounds right, Fergus.'

'I know it'll be hard on you, losing a client if it comes to that.'

'I wouldn't worry about that, uncle. I have enough in the way of other clients to keep me going.'

'Good boy! Glad to hear it.'

'Thanks, Fergus. I'm really glad to get your advice.'

'No problem, boy. How about you and me getting together soon? Not Millie, right? I'm moving on, but that might not help.' Fergus laughed nervously. 'Just you and me, eh, Danny? A friendly family chat, and maybe a bit about business matters if we want to.'

'Sounds good, Fergus.'

'Good! Give me a ring next week, then. Look after yourself, Danny. And ring me any time you need to, about any problems, right?'

Danny wondered if he should tell Millie about this conversation. As it happened, this was one of her gig nights, and she had told him Mal had asked her to come early for a chat about a possible record deal. He still hadn't made up his mind about telling her by the end of the working day, when they drove home, and rushed through tea. He dropped her off at the club as usual, then came home to a lonely evening with plenty of time to think, even with an early night.

In the end, he decided to say nothing to her about Stephen Gillespie, and the advice Fergus had given him. Instead, sitting across the breakfast table from her, he said casually, 'I gave Fergus a ring yesterday.'

'Fergus Ryan? Your uncle Fergus?'

'Yeah. Seems silly to keep up the coolness. After all, he's had time to get over it now.'

'I suppose so.' Millie wasn't sure if she should feel insulted or not by this suggestion.

'He said he'd like me to come up to see him some time. I'm to give him a ring next week and arrange a date.'

'Me, too?'

'No, Mil. He said he would find that a bit hard – and I suppose I can see that.'

Millie nodded, feeling less insulted now. 'Yes, he probably hasn't got over me just yet, actually, Danny. Well, I'd really much rather you went on your own. I'm still not very happy with him for not giving you the shares you should have got. Maybe if he wants to make it up with you, he's thinking of doing it now. Better late than never.'

'I wouldn't count on that, Mil. But I'll ring him.'

'What night were you thinking of, darlin'?'

'Well, not a poker night, right? And it might as well be one of your gig nights, since I don't see much of you then, anyway. I'd rather not make it one of our free nights. I like to see something of you now and then, you know, babe.'

Millie agreed. A gig night would suit her fine. She would be able to invite Mal back here, instead of going to his apartment. She felt that that would give her a freer hand. She needed to get a bit further with him, without just jumping into bed. Going to his own apartment with him, although she'd done it a few times already, was likely giving him the wrong idea.

Getting him to bring her home, then inviting him in to say hullo to Danny, would be good. Then she would be surprised and disappointed to find that Danny had gone out somewhere. And she could probably feed him a sob story about her husband's neglect, never being around, and who knows where that might take them?

Chapter Forty Seven

Her plan was to implant the idea firmly in his mind that she and Danny had not much going for them any longer, and that if Mal tried, he could persuade her to finish with Danny. A divorce, that was what she wanted Mal to hope for. Then, she was pretty confident, she could get Mal to propose. Mal was a very rich man. Visions of fast cars and diamonds danced in Millie's head.

Roundabout – *Gerry McCullough*

Chapter Forty Eight

Stephen Gillespie rang McLaughlin & O'Hanlon's the next day to speak to Danny about buying some more shares in the four minor companies he'd named. Danny was glad that Millie had gone out of the office to do some shopping for an hour, at the time the call came. It meant he could speak openly to Gillespie without Millie overhearing.

'Sorry, Mr Gillespie,' he said bluntly as soon as Stephen had finished his instructions. 'I've thought about this, and I'm afraid McLaughlin & O'Hanlon's can't continue to work for you in this matter, or in fact in anything similar.'

'What! Why not?' spluttered Gillespie, anger and astonishment tearing him in different directions.

'We at McLaughlin & O'Hanlon's believe in the importance of maintaining an ethical approach to business and in ensuring that in all our actions we hold to the honest and lawful course of conduct,' Danny read from the company's code of behaviour. He had planned to do this in advance, looking up the details of the code which he had recently noticed for the first time on the company's website.

He attempted to make his words sound natural. 'I'm afraid your instructions fell far short of the ethical, Mr Gillespie. If you wish to continue as our client, and have instructions for us which do not contravene normal ideas of correct procedures, we would of course be happy to act upon them.'

'I'll see you in hell first!' shrieked Stephen Gillespie, slamming his phone down. He was shaking with anger. There must be someone who would carry out his wishes, even if he had to work through every broker in the yellow pages.

And sure enough, there was. The broker he found had not the advantage of Danny's knowledge of Gillespie's previous actions. He accepted the instructions to buy shares in the four small companies which between them held all John O'Leary's worldly wealth. There was no reason why he should be suspicious of Gillespie's reasons, even when he was instructed, a few days later, to repeat the action by buying more.

And so, in spite of Danny's honesty, John O'Leary's ruin grew more certain.

A few weeks later, Stephen Gillespie, who by now had a sizeable holding in each of the companies, unloaded them all, and watched gleefully as the share prices tumbled helplessly into the murky depths of big business.

O'Leary also watched, with feelings of despair. This could not be happening to him again. He was now ruined beyond recovery, and the worst of it, he realised in profound misery, was that he would no longer have the money to pay interest at the end of this month to the loan company he had dealt with. So the direct debit which Johnny had set up for him to pay his rent and allow a bit over for living expenses, and which he had used as collateral, would now be seized by the company to cover his loan.

How was he going to tell Sam that they were now homeless? He sat at his computer and buried his face in his hands and wept. He felt old and helpless.

Sam's interest these days was too much focused on her daughter Sooze and the grandchild so soon to be born, to have noticed her husband's misery yet. Sooze was now past her due date by a few days. Sam assured her that this was normal enough.

'Babies have very little idea of the calendar,' she said. 'They tend to come when they're good and ready.'

Half of Sooze believed her, and the other half worried away about it. She was having regular check ups with her doctor, and the mid-wife called frequently. Both of them assured her that all was well. But the knowledge that she herself was actually going to have a baby, for the first time, terrified her when she let herself dwell on it. She remembered the stories she'd heard from girls at school, and tried to put them out of her mind as old wives' tales.

She wasn't sure that Josh had even taken in that the due date had passed. She had mentioned it to him at breakfast one morning – breakfast was one of the few occasions when she could be sure of seeing him – and he had replied casually, 'Oh, good,' and gone on reading his newspaper.

'Josh, are you listening? Did you hear what I said?'

Sooze spoke in a sharp voice which Josh never heard her use before. His head came up with a jerk, and he said hastily, 'Yes, of course I heard you, Sooze.' Then his mind replayed her words, and he took them in for the first time. A worried frown spread across his forehead and he exclaimed, 'You're late? But – is that okay? Isn't it dangerous?'

Sooze's mouth trembled, but she said stoutly, 'No, the doctor and the midwife and my mum all say it's quite normal. No need to do anything just yet, they say.'

Josh stood up and took Sooze in his arms for the first time in weeks. He kissed her gently. 'Just be careful, babe. I don't want anything to happen to you or wee Josh, okay? Keep in touch with the doctor and follow his advice.'

Sooze was touched. It seemed as if Josh did really care, after all.

'Yes, don't worry, Josh. I'll be careful,' she said, smiling lovingly at him. 'Better go, sweetheart. You'll be late.'

Josh, who had already made himself late by dawdling over his breakfast after sleeping in, dashed out of the house. As he went, he called back to Sooze, 'See you later, babe.' Then he corrected himself. 'No, sorry, Sooze, this is my night for poker at Pat's. See you after that, anyway.'

So he wasn't even planning to give up his poker for one night, to stay with her. When the door banged shut after him, Sooze, who had been hopeful after his loving behaviour that he would begin staying with her for the remaining few days, sat down among the breakfast dishes and, like her father John, wept.

But Josh wasn't prepared to give up this, of all nights, at Pat's poker table. He had been making plans for some time, and tonight, he hoped would see the successful culmination of them.

Cardsharping. Whenever Josh said the words to himself, he felt a pleasant quiver of romance. River boat gamblers. The Wild West. Saloons, with beautiful girls, and men wearing bootlace ties and fancy waistcoats. Josh shivered again, but this time with pure anticipation.

He had studied the books and the online information. He had practised over and over again, with the pack of cards he had bought for the purpose. He felt confident that when he finally tried it out for real tonight, he could carry it off. He didn't plan to win too much at first. That would be too suspicious. He intended to win a little the first night, then gradually build up his winnings over time.

All he wanted, he told himself virtuously, was to clear his debts. Once he'd done that, and given himself, Sooze and the baby a fair start, he wouldn't cheat again. In fact, he might even give up playing at Pat's. It would be quite enough to play at the O'Hanlons. He didn't want to give that up. He would miss his darling Millie too much.

He arranged with Mike to arrive early at Pat's this evening. That was part of his strategy. Position at the table could be helpful. He didn't really expect to get much help from the wall mirror which hung temptingly opposite him, behind two players across the table from him. Mike, Pete, Blondie, Taffy, and Pat were all experienced players, unlikely to reveal their hands, however fleetingly, to someone looking in the mirror. Still, it was always possible that he would get a little help that way.

No, the basis of his strategy lay in the pin he had concealed inside his shirt sleeve, easy to slip out, easy to use in marking the backs of his own cards whenever he had something worth marking. He had memorised the positions for the scratches he would make, according to whether the card in question was an ace, a court card, or whatever. Top left, top right, top centre, middle left, right or centre, and low on the left, right or centre.

Too far down would be impossible to see, and moreover the player holding the card would be able too easily to feel it and would know that the cards were marked. Even if that happened, Josh felt confident that he could bluff his way out of it. He would drop his pin immediately the suspicion arose, and kick it well away from him. The natural suspect would be Pat himself, the owner of the cards they were playing with.

Josh sighed in satisfaction, and positioned himself carefully to make marks as unobtrusively as possible.

Chapter Forty Nine

Danny rang Fergus and arranged to drive up to see him the following Wednesday, Millie's next gig night. Fergus was delighted.

'Get here early, and we can have dinner at Fitzroy's,' he said. 'I'll buy you a lamb shank – melts in the mouth. Or whatever you fancy. Can I persuade you to stay the night, even?'

'Aw, thanks, Fergus, but Millie would hate it if I didn't come home. So would I, actually.'

'So speaks the newly married man.' Fergus's voice over the wire sounded as if he was grinning. 'No problem, boy. But get here in time to eat, won't you?'

'Yeah, thanks. I'll cut out of work early. Should get there by six, okay?'

Millie was pleased when Danny told her he'd rung and settled a date. 'Good idea to get on his right side, darlin'. Never know what might come of it, right?'

Danny flushed. 'Look, Mil, I'm not going to ask him to give me some shares – get that straight. If he ever does decide to, that's up to him. No way I'm going to twist his arm.'

Millie said nothing, except, 'Well, have a nice time, sweetheart.' But inside she was angry. Clearly Danny would never be any use to her. It had been the mistake of her life to marry him. She would never have done it if she hadn't fully expected that he would be inheriting his auntie Fran's shares within a few weeks. And then that had been messed up.

'I'll miss you, babe.'

'I'll miss you, too, honey,' Millie lied. Secretly, she was making her plans. The gig would be over by around eleven, if all went well. With any luck, Danny wouldn't make it back until well after midnight or more likely one o'clock. Plenty of time to cry to Mal and persuade him that she was a poor little thing with a broken heart, who needed him to pick her up and mend her pain.

The gig went as well as always. Millie wore a short, green dress in a diaphanous material which was saved from indecency by an under dress of thin satin. There were imitation diamonds in the shape of birds and flowers embroidered over it, and with it Millie wore the real diamond and emerald bracelet and the matching diamond drop earrings Mal had given her recently.

She had been careful to keep these jewels hidden from Danny, who might not be too pleased if he knew Mal had given them to her. But she loved to wear them on safe occasions like the present. She could have gone on giving encores until much later, but she never gave more than two. Keep 'em hungry and wanting more, that was how it worked.

'Do you think you could drop me home soon, Mal?' she asked him with a special smile.

'No probs, Millie. Just let me sort out a coupla things, right. Get your coat and wait for me outside.' Mal turned towards his barman, and said, 'Okay, Billy, I'm heading off, now. You can manage, can't you? I'll leave you to lock up, as well. If Hughie comes looking for me, tell him I'll give him a ring and sort out his gig tomorrow. Keep truckin'!'

He hurried outside. He was really looking forward to this time with Millie. He'd been getting more and more keen on her for the past weeks. That wicked smile she had – did it mean anything or not? How far was she going to go?

He walked with her to where his car was, just round the corner in a little entry.

'So, do you want to come to mine, again, tonight, Millie, have a goodnight drink?'

'Aw, that would be lovely, Mal, but I thought for a change you could take me home tonight and call up to see my husband, Danny. You two ought to know each other better.'

Mal shot her a swift look. What was she getting at? Why should she think he'd want to get to know Danny? It was her, not her husband, he wanted to be with. He looked at her suspiciously, but her face showed nothing but innocent expectation.

'Okay.'

The big car moved quickly through the mostly empty streets until it came to Millie's apartment. There was a parking space just outside. Mal pulled in, and turned to Millie. He put his arm around her. 'How's about a thank you kiss for the lift, then, girl?'

Millie's smile this time was the wicked smile which lit him up. She leaned towards him and her lips found his.

Then, all too soon, she sat back up, and said, 'Let's go inside, Mal.'

They went upstairs and Millie unlocked the apartment door. Pushing it open, she called out, 'Look who's come to see you, Danny!'

There was no answer. Millie turned a bewildered face to Mal. 'That's funny. He must have popped out for something. Come on in, anyway, and I'll get you a drink.'

Mal followed her in, dropped his leather jacket on the nearest chair, and sat on the comfortable big sofa, while Millie mixed him a Scotch and soda.'

'I know what you like, by now, Mal,' she said. Handing him the glass, she took off her own coat and settled herself down beside him. 'I'm sure Danny won't be long. At least, I hope he won't.' She allowed her lips to tremble a little. 'I never really know where he goes, these days,' she confessed. 'I see so little of him. I didn't think this was what marriage would be like.'

'But, Millie – is he neglecting you, the so-and-so? He doesn't deserve a wife like you.'

As he spoke, Millie's phone rang. She looked at the caller ID and saw that it was Danny. Good. He was probably ringing to say he had left Derry and was heading home. She could make use of this. But it wouldn't do to let Mal hear the conversation.

'It's Danny, Mal. Probably ringing to say he'll be home in a minute.' She let her face brighten up. 'Oh, I do hope so!'

Standing up, she smiled an apology to Mal and took herself and her phone into the bedroom, shutting the door behind her.

'Danny?'

'Mil, this is really urgent! I need your help right away.'

'What is? Talk slower, Danny, I can hardly make you out.'

'It's my car insurance.'

'Yeah?'

'I was nearly home, just coming into Belfast, when the cops stopped me.'

'Why, were you speeding?'

'No. Mil, don't interrupt. This is important!'

Millie was silent.

'Mil, are you still there?'

'Of course I'm still here. You said not to interrupt, right?'

'Oh. Well, it was a broken tail light. Didn't even know I had one. You'd think they'd have more to do than worry about stuff like that. Well, that was okay, they just told me to get it fixed, and I promised to, but then they wanted to see my license and insurance before they let me drive on. The license was okay, but when they checked the insurance apparently it wasn't paid for this year. Millie, I thought you paid it? I know I asked you to pay it online, a few weeks ago when it was due?'

Millie thought quickly. She couldn't tell Danny that instead of paying the insurance she had put the money into her private account by online transfer.

'Danny, I told you! I paid it and it didn't go through! I told you!' She was remembering, as she spoke, that a summons had arrived in the post for Danny shortly after that, to attend court or pay, with the threat of a fine or imprisonment. She hadn't mentioned it to Danny, mostly because she'd genuinely forgotten, but partly, to be honest, because she'd thought it would do him no harm to get into a bit of trouble.

Danny was silent in turn. Could he really have forgotten something as important as that, if she'd told him? He'd had a lot on his mind, but even so.

He said, 'I don't remember that, Mil.'

'I don't know how you could have forgotten!'

'Well, I suppose I must have. But that's not the point. Millie, you need to get enough money to cover it – there should be something in the savings account. Draw it out from the hole in the wall, and take it – now! – to Donegal Pass police station.'

'But, Danny! We don't have anything left in the savings account. We used it to buy the car.'

Danny was stricken. 'What on earth can we do?' he asked helplessly.

'We can get it tomorrow. I'll beg, borrow or steal it in the morning. Can't go knocking people up now, at this time of night. But there must be someone who'd help.'

'Maybe.'

'They'll accept that, won't they? If you tell them you'll have it tomorrow?'

'Oh, I daresay. But meanwhile they'll keep me locked up, Mil. It's a serious offence, they say, not being insured.'

'Oh, Danny! Oh, babe, I'll get the money for you first thing! Hang on in there, darlin'!'

Danny rang off.

Millie went back to Malachi Charles. She was rather pleased at this development. Danny wouldn't be coming home until she chose to bring the money for his release. She had the rest of the night to work on Mal, or at least as much as she needed. Time to turn on the tears, or try to. At least to look really unhappy.

'So, is Danny coming home now?' Mal asked.

'Oh, Mal! No, he isn't! He's off gambling somewhere, and I don't suppose he'll be home until morning. I can't bear much more of this, Mal. He doesn't care about me any more. He doesn't want to be with me. Sure, sometimes I think no one does.' She collapsed onto the sofa beside Mal, and covered her eyes with her hands, producing some realistic sobs.

'Aw, don't say that, darling wee Millie!' Mal said. He was deeply moved by the sight of her crying. Coming closer to her he put his arms round her and leant her head against his shoulder. 'If you don't have Danny, you've still got me. I love you, Millie. I'll look after you, if you let me.'

'But I'm married to that rotten slob. I've always been against divorce. I wouldn't just live with you, Mal, I've told you that. And if I did divorce Danny, what then? Would you find out that you didn't really want me, after all? Not enough to marry me?' She gave a further heart rending sob.

'Never, darlin' – never!' Mal found himself saying much more than he had intended, in the heat of the moment babbling out words, promising a lifetime commitment of the type he had always flinched from.

'Millie, if you'll say you'll marry me, I'll be so unbelievably happy. I can't imagine anything better than being with you every day for the rest of my life!'

Millie looked up at him, allowing doubt to appear in her big green eyes, then smiling tremulously. 'Aw, Mal, if I thought you really meant that – !'

'I do, Millie, I do!' Even as he said the words, Mal wondered if he'd gone crazy. But the look of happiness in Millie's eyes assured him that he'd never said anything wiser.

'I'll get my solicitor on to it straightaway,' he said. 'We'll push that divorce through for you, Millie. I can't let you go on suffering like this any longer.'

Roundabout – *Gerry McCullough*

Chapter Fifty

Josh could hardly believe his luck when his first night of card-sharping at Pat's poker table worked successfully. He was careful not to do too much of it. Just enough to come out with a useful profit. He was looking forward to the next evening, when he planned to take things a bit further and win much more.

Mike, who had noticed what Josh was up to early on, was horrified. Patterson was not the man to mess around with like that. He just hoped that when, inevitably, Pat caught on, he wouldn't include Mike himself in the blame. After all, it was he who had introduced Josh into their game. Mike was quite relieved when he got a text from Pat postponing the next game until later in the week.

The other regular players got identical texts. Josh was the only exception. Instead, Pat rang him personally.

'Listen, big guy, Mike asked me to let you know he can't pick you up this Tuesday night,' he began easily. 'Poor kid's got a bad cold and he's lost his voice. Has to stay home. But as it happens, I'll be out your direction earlier, and I can pick you up at the corner where you usually meet Mike, if that suits?'

'Yeah, ta, that'd be great.' Josh was pleased that an important man like Pat was willing to go out of his way to be helpful. Particularly as it must mean that he had no suspicions. Well, Josh hadn't expected that he would have. He thought he'd been pretty clever about the whole thing. He didn't see how anyone could have seen anything.

'Same time as usual, then.' Pat rang off.

Josh didn't bother to tell Sooze any of these details. He wasn't too sure of being able to keep his cheating a secret from her if he told her anything. Sooze had known him a long time. She knew a lot about him. And he didn't want her to know about the cheating. He, equally, had known Sooze a long time, long enough to know that she would be horrified at the idea of such deliberate dishonesty, cheating in order to make money. Better if she just thought he'd had a run of luck.

'See ya, Sooze,' he said kissing her casually as he left the house after tea.

Sooze knew very well that something was wrong. Josh had had something on his mind recently, and it wasn't the baby. It was as if he had forgotten how near the birth must be, in the pressure of this something else, whatever it was.

Sooze was glad she had her mother and Horse to rely on in case anything happened. She had her case of necessary things ready packed, as the midwife had advised her to do a couple of weeks ago. She had been told that if the baby didn't come by itself in the next few days she would have to come in for an induction. Sooze didn't want things to come to that. She really hoped Josh junior would get a move on.

In fact, only an hour after Josh had left the house, she felt the first severe twinge.

Was she imagining it? Sooze had no previous experience to go by. She decided not to panic straightaway. But when another twinge, much more severe, came twenty minutes later, then another in another twenty minutes, she knew she needed to ring someone. It was no use ringing Josh. He had told her he needed to concentrate while playing and would have his phone switched off once the game started.

Well, first of all, the midwife. Then her mum, and finally Horse, who had promised to pick up her mum and then herself to go to the hospital. She was going to the Royal Victoria, said to have the best maternity wing of any of the local hospitals. Sooze stood up to reach for her phone. She felt something odd and heard a sound like the pop of a bursting balloon.

And realised that she was standing in a puddle of water.

She knew what this was. Her waters had broken. Trying hard not to panic, Sooze began her list of phone calls.

Josh stood at the corner shivering in the cold March wind, waiting for Andy Patterson to pick him up. When the big Mercedes finally flashed into view and pulled up beside him, the back nearside door swinging open, he was quick to scramble in. His main thought was to get into the warmth of the car out of the freezing cold outside.

'Thanks for the lift, Pat,' he said. He looked around him, and realised that he knew neither of the two other men in the car, one sitting beside Pat as he drove, the other in the back beside Josh.

'So, hi, guys,' he said, aiming for a light friendliness, which didn't come easily considering that the expressions on all three faces matched the hard wind which blew ferociously down the road towards them. 'I suppose you two are mates of Pat here? Are you joining us for a hand of poker tonight, then?'

'No.'

'Josh,' said Pat, 'shut your trap.'

He drove on, increasing his speed as they moved out from the city centre.

Josh was too nervous by now to heed this good advice. 'Hey, did you know you're going the wrong direction, mate?'

'It's the right direction for us, boy.' It was the man who sat in the back beside Josh, and who had already spoken. He was a paunchy man in his middle forties, similar in age to Pat, with not much of his dark hair left, and what he had spread over his head in a careful arrangement to make the most of it. His hard face was weather beaten, with the redness in his cheeks which comes not from health but from drinking too much.

Josh couldn't see much of the other man since he was sitting directly in front of Josh beside the driver, Pat, and had a woolly hat crammed down over most of his head, but he got occasional glimpses of a cruel looking hooked profile.

It seemed best to Josh to say no more. He sat looking out at the motorway which they had reached a few minutes ago, and wondering uneasily what was going on. The Motorway, the MI, ran first of all to Lisburn, then on as far as Dungannon. Surely they weren't going as far as that? There were green fields and leafless trees on both sides. It looked pretty in spite of the cold. Far too pretty for anything terrible to happen.

They passed the turnoff for Lisburn and kept going. About seven or more miles further down the motorway, Pat pulled off to the left, and after a few more turns brought the Merc out into a rugged lane, rutted and full of holes. To Josh it looked the type of thing which would lead up to a farm.

Pat followed it for another mile, then pulled in to park in a gateway which allowed him to leave the car just off the road.

'Okay, this is where we get out,' he said, swinging open his own door. Woolly Hat did the same at his side. Josh stared at them. 'Seriously?' he gulped.

'Get him out of there, Artie,' Pat snapped. The man who sat beside Josh, now identified to him as Artie, said, 'Out you go!' and prodded Josh in the ribs. Looking down, he saw unbelievingly that a gun was sticking into his side. Scrambling and tripping over his own feet in his haste, Josh flung open his door and almost fell out of the car.

As he recovered his balance, he saw that Woolly Hat was also pointing a gun at him. Josh was no expert in guns, but it looked like a big, powerful weapon.

Anyway, he thought in a wry amusement which he knew was completely inappropriate to the circumstances, *I suppose a small, not very powerful weapon would do whatever job they want it for just as well.* He swallowed hard, feeling suddenly sick.

Pat opened the gate and all four of them went through it into the field. A high, uncut hedge now hid them from the sight of anyone coming along the lane.

'I guess you know why we've brought you here?' Pat asked, in a flat tone which Josh found more worrying than any amount of anger. He carried no gun himself. *Leaving that to the henchmen,* Josh thought. *Horse warned me that Pat was pretty high up in the organisation.*

Meanwhile, Pat seemed to be waiting for an answer.

'Can't think,' he said, then wondered if Pat would think he was being flippant – which probably wouldn't help. 'I mean,' he added hastily, 'is there something I'm supposed to have done?'

'Not just "supposed,"' Pat said evenly. A pulse in his neck was beginning to throb. Josh realised that this must be a bad sign. 'No one tries to rip me off and gets away with it, Joshua.'

No one but his father had called Josh Joshua since he started secondary school. He had hated it on the rare occasions when the old man lost his temper with him. Oh, how he wished it was his father talking to him now. No matter how angry he was.

'Rip you off?' he said in a would be uncomprehending tone. 'Me? You've got me all wrong, mate. When did I ever rip you off? I wouldn't do such a thing to you!'

'No? So you didn't mark the cards in my pack, last poker night? Oh, sorry. It must have been your twin brother. But bringing outsiders, even a twin brother, to a game without asking first is against the rules, too, Joshua.'

The nasty, sneering tone in which he spoke sent unhappy shudders up and down Josh's spine.

'So I'm afraid,' Pat went on, 'it doesn't really matter if it was you or your twin. I'm afraid you have to bear the responsibility. And the punishment.' His voice changed, sharpened. 'Which knee would you like to keep? I wouldn't be too hard on you for a first offence. I wouldn't do both. So, right or left? Most people prefer to get it in the left.'

Josh panicked. He was going to be kneecapped. He'd heard of it. Heard that the agony was excruciating. Before the two hard faced men could take hold of him, he kicked Artie's shins, head butted Woolly Hat, and ran for his life across the field.

Chapter Fifty

He had covered less than a hundred yards when he heard a crack. Then there was a sharp pain in the middle of his back. He stumbled, tried to recover, and then fell off the Roundabout, only part way through his ride, into darkness. He had never enjoyed the ride very much. But now it was over.

Roundabout – *Gerry McCullough*

Chapter Fifty One

Pat and his two henchmen walked over to Josh's body where it lay helpless and vulnerable, exposed to the bright moonlight, spreadeagled in the rough grass and thistles. Pat knelt down and felt for a pulse. 'Gone,' he said. 'You're getting too trigger happy, Mush.' He stared at the big man in the woolly hat with the hard cruel face and the beaked nose. 'There was no need for that. I'd said it was to be a knee-capping. Are you trying to take over this outfit, or what?'

Mush looked worried and crestfallen. Josh, if he had been able any longer to see anything, would have been amazed to see such a hangdog expression on the cruel face.

'Sorry, boss,' he said. 'I didn't want him to get away with dissing you.'

'Okay.' Pat stood up. 'Another time, wait for instructions or you'll wish you had,' he said softly. He stood looking down at Josh for a moment, before turning to walk away. 'Search him, and take any identifiers,' he instructed his men. 'Wallet, mobile, that sort of stuff, right? Then get back to the car and we'll be on our way.'

There was nothing left to tell the police, when the body was reported to them the next morning, who Josh was. It was several days before they were able to identify him.

Danny took some minutes to recover from the blow of Millie's response to his call for help. Then he thought about it. The more he thought, the more he was convinced that he had checked, before asking Millie to make the payment for the car insurance, and there had been an adequate balance in their current account to more than cover it.

And surely there should be a few thousands in the savings account? He'd been adding a generous part of his salary to it every month, and although he had taken enough out for the car, it had, after all, been a fairly cheap second hand one. True, there had been the amount he had spent on Millie at Christmas. And, sure, if she was in doubt about getting enough money from friends to get him released, she could raise it on the expensive diamond necklace he had given her then?

It didn't seem to Danny to add up. Meanwhile, he decided that he must take further action himself tonight. He didn't want to spend the rest of the night in jail. A horrible thought.

'Sorry,' he said to the policeman standing by the car, 'that didn't work out. But if you give me a minute, this should.' The policeman nodded agreement. Danny lifted his phone again, and called his uncle Fergus.

Fergus answered at once. He was full of sympathy as Danny outlined the fix he found himself in.

'No problem, boy. I'll transfer the money.'

'But, Fergus, even if you transfer it to my account, I don't have access to use it myself tonight.'

'Never heard of online banking, Danny? And you the tech expert, I thought! I'll transfer it to wherever it should go. Let me speak to the cops and I'll get the details from them.'

Danny breathed a sigh of relief and handed over his phone to the nearest policeman. He listened as the policeman reeled off the details. Then he waited some more, until finally the money appeared to be through, for he was told that he could go. 'But be more careful another time, sir.'

Danny rang to thank Fergus fervently, and was told not to worry. 'Get on home now, before it gets any later, boy. Have a good night's sleep, and forget it.'

Danny drove with a light heart to his apartment, which wasn't too far away now. He was looking forward to seeing Millie and comforting her worries, probably wiping away her tears. Although, come to think of it, he didn't know when he had ever seen Millie cry.

As he stepped out of the lift in the apartment block at his own floor, he thought he could hear laughter from inside the door. No, impossible. He walked over, inserted his key, and pushed the door open. Then he stood very still, staring.

On the big sofa two figures were stretched out. Right now they were laughing at some joke he hadn't heard. Their arms were round each other, and as he watched, the man brought his mouth down hard onto the woman's lips, and they kissed passionately.

Danny dived across the room. He couldn't speak. He reached out and seized the man round his neck, hauling him to his feet. The man wasn't particularly small, but Danny's height and weight were superior enough to give him a powerful advantage. He shook the man whose neck he had in his hands as a terrier shakes a rat.

Millie began to shriek. Scrambling to her feet, she tried to undo Danny's grasp. 'Stop, Danny, stop! You'll strangle him!'

That was Danny's idea. He shook off Millie's clinging hands, almost without noticing them except as an unwelcome obstruction. Millie fell back against the sofa, breathing hard. Somehow, Mal recovered himself enough to begin kicking Danny's shins. At the third kick Danny came to his senses. He looked at the man he was strangling and saw that it was Malachi Charles. Stepping back, he released Mal from his clutches.

'What are you doing here with my wife, Mal? Talk quick, if you don't want me to finish strangling you.'

'He came back with me to talk about getting me a record deal,' Millie said, her words tumbling over each other in her haste to get her cover story out and across to Mal, so that he could pick it up and run with it. But to her annoyance, Mal seemed speechless.

'So? Was that why you were kissing her, lying down with her – ' Danny found himself unable to say anything more. Instead, he took a swing at Mal and knocked him down. Mal lay on the carpet, feeling his jaw with one hand.

'I don't see why you should care,' he croaked finally, through his dry mouth and aching throat. 'She's told me all about you. How you don't care about her any more, how you go out gambling every night and leave her, how you don't come home until all hours. I heard you ringing her tonight to tell her you wouldn't be coming home until dear knows when. The poor wee girl was crying because of your neglect – !'

'Is that what she told you?' Danny asked slowly. 'Is that what you said about my phone call, Millie? You didn't tell him I'd been stopped by the cops, and was going to be locked up if I didn't pay my car insurance? You didn't tell him you'd refused the money, although you're wearing diamonds that would have covered it twenty times over? Where did you get those diamonds, Mil? Did you take the money for them from our account?'

'No, no, I didn't, Danny!'

'I gave her the bracelet and the earrings,' Mal said. 'Is this true? Haven't you been going out, leaving her, neglecting her?'

'Other way round, dude. She's been going out, neglecting me, haven't you, Mil? Singing gigs. But I haven't seen much of the money in our account, have I, Mil?'

'But she told me – ' Mal looked suddenly grim. 'So, has she been lying to me?'

'And to me, right, Mil?' Danny's face, usually so pleasant, so relaxed and smiling, was unrecognisable.

Faced as she never remembered being before by two angry men, Millie thought of bursting into tears, but pride and a refusal to be humiliated by them came to her rescue.

'Yes, I've been lying to you both. A pair of wimps, aren't you? You let me twist you round my little finger, didn't you, Danny? And you did, too, didn't you, Mal? And now you can get out, both of you. I can make a better man than you two from two lumps of coal, some plasticine and a couple of lolly sticks. Go on, get out!'

Mal began to head towards the door, but Danny's hand on his sleeve stopped him. 'No one's going anywhere but you, Millie. This is my apartment. Sit down, Mal, you and me need to talk. You're the one who's going to get out, Millie. The only place I ever want to see you again is in the divorce court. Not even there – sure, my solicitor can handle it all without me appearing.

'Leave your printouts of the bank statements, I want to check how much you've stolen from me, you bitch. Go on, I'll give you ten minutes to get packed.' He stood, arms folded now, implacable, the glare on his face directed straight at her instead of Mal.

Millie knew it was no use trying to use her wiles on him any more. She went into the bedroom and packed her clothes hurriedly, concealing beneath them the jewellery box which held not only Danny's necklace but the valuable gifts of several other men, as well as a bank roll for emergencies, most of the money earned from her gigs and a considerable amount withdrawn from their joint account, which had been deposited from his salary by Danny. She eventually came back out with a smile on her lips directed at Mal. Going over to him, she slipped her arm through his.

'Let's go, darlin',' she murmured. 'We'll go to your apartment. Should have gone there earlier instead of here.'

Mal stood up, pushing her arm roughly away. His eyes had been opened and he'd been forced to see the 'poor wee girl' as she really was – selfish, scheming and conniving. His anger, at much at the fact that he had been so emotionally moved that he had asked her to marry him, while all the time she'd been lying to him, caring nothing for him, burst out.

'Go to my apartment? Stop dreaming, Millie! You're on your own, now. And don't think you've still got a singing deal at any of my clubs. Or anywhere else – I'll see to that. I'm like your husband. I never want to see you again.'

Chapter Fifty One

Millie flushed angrily. Then she walked steadily to the apartment door, went out, and slammed it behind her. Yes, she knew she was on her own now. But when had she ever been anything else?

Roundabout – *Gerry McCullough*

Chapter Fifty Two

For a first baby, young Josh came reasonably quickly. Not that it seemed like that to Sooze. After she had phoned Horse and her mum and the mid-wife, she had cleared up from the mess made when her waters had broken. She had put on the maternity pad she'd been directed to have on hand. She had changed into a nightie.

As she sat waiting for the response which she knew would come to her phone calls, she had never felt so alone. This was something she had to do herself. No one else could have this baby for her. She remembered a cartoon seen years ago, a pregnant woman on her way to the delivery suite, calling out, 'Hey! I've changed my mind!' Sooze would have laughed if she hadn't been nearer to crying.

She'd tried Josh a couple of times on his mobile, but found, as she'd expected, that it was switched off.

Then Horse arrived, bringing her mother, both of them offering com-forting words, and then her midwife, her own personal midwife who'd been allocated to her early on, and who had been visiting and checking up on her regularly. With her came a wave of confidence. Here was someone who really knew what to do.

She sat down beside Sooze and started by timing the contractions.

'Hmm. Every ten minutes, now,' she said. 'Better head on in to the maternity ward. No worries, we've got plenty of time, but no sense in leaving it until we're cutting it too fine.'

Sooze, with memories of films and true life stories from friends, of babies born in taxis on the way to the hospital, was very happy to agree.

After that it all became a bit blurred. She knew Horse had helped her down to his car and had driven carefully to the Royal Victoria Hospital, bringing Sam as well, and followed by the midwife in her own car. He had come in with her, but had been told to go to the waiting room while Sooze was taken to the ward and allocated a bed. Her mother was allowed to stay.

Then, what seemed like eons later to Horse, but much less to Sooze, floating in the cotton wool wrapping of pethidine, it was all over. She knew she'd been wheeled through to the delivery ward early in the proceedings. She knew her mother was holding her hand, and she was grateful for something to hold onto hard as the contractions grew stronger. Someone was telling her to push. She knew vaguely that it was her midwife. 'Okay, Sooze, you can push now. Come on, that's a great wee girl, push hard. Push!'

And then it was all over, and they were handing something to her. No, not something, someone. An incredibly tiny bundle was laid in her arms, wrapped up so that all she could really see was the small, wrinkled face and the fair hair. The eyes were shut. Then as she looked, they opened. Lovely blue eyes – Josh's eyes. Sooze gazed and gazed, looking at the child whom she would love more than anyone else for the rest of her life.

'Josh,' she murmured, so low that no one could hear her distinctly. 'Josh.'

Then the baby was taken from her to be washed, and Sooze closed her own eyes and drifted into a light sleep.

When she woke up, she was back in the maternity ward, and there was a baby in the cot by her bedside. Sooze looked at him, finding it hard to believe that she had produced this little creature by herself. *With a little help from Josh*, she grinned to herself. But Josh's part in it all seemed strangely distant. It was she, Sooze, who had pushed this baby out into the real world. She found it hard to believe. It was the most important thing she had ever done. *But not again.* The decision was firm, unyielding. *Never again.* The memory of the pain was still too vivid.

Presently a nurse came into the cubicle. Sooze noticed for the first time that there were curtains round her bed, giving her some privacy from the rest of the ward.

'Awake?' asked the nurse brightly. 'Good. Baby wants something to drink, Mummy.'

Sooze stared at her. Yes, she had ticked the box to breast feed. It would be so much easier than getting up in the night to make bottles, she had thought.

The nurse helped her to sit up, adjusted Sooze's nightie, and held the tiny shrimp to suck at her breast. First one breast, then the other. She seemed pleased.

'Good. That's fine. Some new mothers have a lot of difficulty getting the knack, and some babies are even worse, but both you and baby are real experts already. He's not getting milk yet, of course. This is colostrum, something your body supplies before the milk starts to flow. It's very good for baby, gives him immunity and stuff like that.'

She smiled at Sooze and sat contentedly beside her, supervising this first feed, until presently she glanced at her watch and said, 'Good. That'll be fine for now. I'll put baby back in his cot, and both of you should have a nice sleep. When you wake up, I'll help you to wash and tidy up. Would you like a drink of milk, yourself?'

'Yes, please.'

'And then you can have a visitor or two – but not for long.'

Sooze went back to sleep. It seemed to be the only thing she wanted to do, apart from feeding her baby – something which had given her such strange satisfaction and pleasure. Her last waking thought was that this little creature was hers, forever.

Josh's body was found the day after his shooting, by the farmer who owned the field where he lay. It took the police another couple of days to identify him. He had no wallet, no card case, no mobile. In the end, it was Mike who gave them the clue.

Mike's conscience had been eating at him since he got the text from Patterson postponing the poker session, and found, when he tried Josh's home number later, having got no response from his mobile, that according to Josh's wife he had gone out to his usual poker game.

Sooze sounded strange. She had just felt the first serious contraction, and was in no mood to talk to one of Josh's poker friends, whom she blamed for leading him astray. Mike had no idea of this, but was clear enough that she didn't want to talk.

He worried about it overnight, tried Josh's mobile the next day, and later again, and knew by then that something had happened to him.

The news that evening spoke of an unidentified body found in a field near Donaghacloney, a small country village which Mike had only heard of vaguely. Anyone who could help identify the man was asked to contact a number, which Mike made a note of. A sinking feeling in his stomach made him ring the number anonymously and suggest Josh's name.

He made no mention of Patterson. He would dearly have liked to. But the instinct of self preservation was strong enough in him to hold him back. Instead, he gave the name of Josh's employers, a red herring which, he hoped, would lead them to believe he was someone who worked with Josh. Then he tried to wait patiently for confirmation.

Horse's dad knew that his son's friendship with Josh was a close one, as well as being longstanding. For that reason, when he broke the news to him that the police thought the body that had been found might be Josh, he said, 'I'm sure the last thing you want to do is to go along to identify him, Horace. We'll ask Dave – he's been working closely enough with Josh to be able to tell if it's him.'

'No,' said Horse slowly. 'No, I'd rather go myself. If it is him,'– his voice trembled, then was strong again – 'if it is, then it's one last thing I can do for him. And for Sooze.'

As he stood an hour later in the city morgue, looking down at his dead friend's face, cold and still, he found tears coming. He couldn't remember when he had last wept. Not since childhood, probably. And at the thought of childhood, memories of his long friendship with Josh flooded over him, and his tears flowed more strongly.

Wiping his eyes, he turned away. 'Yes, it's him. Someone must tell his wife.'

'You might like to do that yourself, sir,' the policeman suggested. 'She might take it better from a friend.'

'No!' Horse said violently. Then he changed his mind. 'Yes, all right. I suppose it might be easier for her. She's been in the Royal, having a baby. But she's getting home today. I'm booked to give her a lift. I can do it then.'

The policeman, used though he was to tragic situations, looked horrified. 'I wouldn't do that, sir. Give her a chance to settle in first.'

'Okay,' Horse said listlessly. So he waited until he had Sooze settled with a cup of tea, the baby in his cot beside her, before he broke the news.

Sooze took it well. At first she almost seemed not to care, even to be relieved. It was only after the first few minutes, that she began to wail.

'Oh, Josh! Oh, Josh! There'll never be anyone like him for me. What will I do without him?'

'I'll be here, Sooze,' Horse said. 'I'll help you every way I can.'

Sooze turned on him in fury. 'You? What use are you to me? You aren't Josh!'

Horse stared at her. He was hurt as he had seldom been hurt before.

Sooze, her fury spent, gave him a look of scorn. 'You mean well, Horse, I'm sure, but how can you think for a moment that you could make it up to me for losing my Josh?'

Horse said nothing.

'My Mum said she'd come round and stay to help me for the first week,' Sooze said after a while. 'Could you pick her up, please?'

And Horse left to do the only job Sooze seemed to think he was fit for, to act as messenger boy.

Roundabout – *Gerry McCullough*

Chapter Fifty Three

When the door slammed behind Millie, Danny gave an explosive breath of relief.

'What're you drinking, dude?'

'Don't you want me to go?'

'Nah. She fooled you and me both. I've got nothing against you.'

The two men sat sipping whiskey in silence for some time. Then Mal spoke.

'You're talking about a divorce as if you could just whistle for one, mate. It's not that easy. It takes time. Two years separation for a no fault divorce. I know, I got divorced a year ago.'

'You, Mal? I never heard that. Didn't even know you'd been married.'

'Oh, aye. Not something I wanted to talk about.'

'But do I have to wait two years, then?'

'You can divorce her for other stuff much quicker. Like, adultery, or unreasonable behaviour. I think financial problems come into that. Stealing from you, like Millie's been doing, for instance.'

'If I go for adultery, would you give me some details?'

'Like a shot, dude. I'd be lying if I said she'd ever actually slept with me, mind you, but, hey, I'd be happy to lie about that slut.'

'Sounds possible.'

'Talk to your solicitor. He'll be able to advise you which way to go.'

'Right. Thanks, mate.'

Danny talked to his solicitor. He also talked to his uncle Fergus. Fergus was horrified when Danny told him about Millie's behaviour.

'She played tricks on me, too, boy,' he said, almost hoarse in his indignation as he thought back over Millie's deceptive behaviour to him. 'I let her come between you and me, what's more. Can't really blame her for that. My own stupid reaction.'

He paused for a moment and Danny at the other end of the phone waited for him to resume. After a minute he said, 'Are you okay, Uncle Fergus?'

His uncle's voice came. 'Yes, fine, boy. Listen, Danny, how'd you feel about coming back home? The idea of setting up a branch in Belfast wasn't good. We have more clients than we can handle up here, and the Belfast ones can always talk to us by phone or online. No need for a branch anywhere but here, in our business.'

'I'd like that, Fergus,' Danny said quietly.

'And there's another thing, Danny. I've been a real bastard to you about Fran's will – or rather, her not having left one. Fran meant you to have the shares your mother inherited. I'm going to turn them over to you, legally. Sure, even if you hadn't wanted to come home, I was going to do that.'

Danny felt himself choking, and was glad Fergus couldn't see the tears dripping down his face. 'There's no need to do that, Fergus.'

'Yeah, there is, boy. Don't give me any arguments about it, now.'

'Well, we can talk when I get back, then. See you as soon as I can settle things here.'

But while Danny was trying to settle things at the Belfast end, winding up the company, offering clients the option of continuing to work with him through the home branch in Derry, instead of leaving his company, arranging to give up his apartment, and giving his solicitor the go ahead to plan the divorce in whichever way was quickest, something happened which changed the circumstances for him radically.

When Millie walked out of the apartment and, she very much hoped, out of Danny's life, she felt momentarily helpless once her blazing anger had died down. True, she had plenty of money for the time being, but it wouldn't last forever.

She decided that she would go to a hotel that night, but certainly the money would soon be gone unless she found somewhere much cheaper very soon.

She was concerned above all at Mal's threat. He would never have her in one of his night spots again, and would see to it that no one else would, either. Mal was a powerful man in the music scene. Could he, or couldn't he, carry out that second part of his threat? If she could no longer get gigs, she was in real trouble.

She booked into the new hotel, the *Grand Central*, as an act of defiance, and when she had viewed her room and dumped her suitcase there, she went back down and ordered a vodka martini at the bar. She would have liked some food, but the kitchen was shut, and the only option was nuts, crisps, and olives, set out along the bar and on the little tables, in small dishes. Much better than nothing, Millie decided philosophically, settling herself at one of the tables, sipping her drink, and eating the snacks with gusto while she thought about her position.

She was no worse off than when she'd started out in her adult life with no clear ideas except to make whatever use she could of Sooze and her family. In fact, she was a lot better off. She had the money and jewels she'd acquired in the last year, as well as her experience both as a singer and as a broker. She had her excellent A level results. Sure, she should be able to get a job somewhere.

And could Mal really block her from all the night spots in Belfast? And further afield? She could always move out of Belfast and try her luck in one of the seaside towns or somewhere, and he surely couldn't pull any strings as far away as that? What's more, she remembered, there were several clubs in Belfast which weren't under Mal's thumb, and whose owners might be very happy to do Mal a bad turn by pinching her, if she could put it across to them like that.

Finishing her drink, and the rest of the nuts, crisps and olives, she made her way happily to bed, and to sleep soundly.

A couple of months or so later, Millie was feeling a lot less optimistic. She'd moved out of the hotel after one night and found herself a room in a run down guest house not far from the district where she and her father had lived in their poverty stricken days. It was depressing in itself to have come back to that, but she didn't want to spend more than she had to on a place to sleep until she was sure of a good income. Her savings were going down fast.

Alas, her efforts to secure a gig or two, let alone a residential booking, at any of the clubs whose owners were independent of Malachi Charles, had been failing dismally. They had all heard the gossip Mal was putting round about her. Unreliable, dishonest, rude to the customers – there seemed to be no end to the stories Mal had circulated about her. In vain Millie pleaded, cut her terms drastically, used all her wiles. No one was willing to even give her a try.

On the one occasion when she was allowed to sing at a very down market pub in West Belfast called *The Spider's Web*, a crowd of hecklers – employed, Millie knew, by Mal – had tried to boo her off the stage. Millie had refused to stop and had sung on over the uproar, putting out all the strength of her powerful voice, but they had continued their shouts and jeers until the end of her set.

The owner, Liam McCracken, had been regretful but firm.

'Sorry, Mil. I'd be happy enough to do Malachi Charles a bad turn by employing you, and you've certainly got a great voice, babe, but I can't afford this sort of carry on. The regular punters won't be back if it happens again. The place'll be getting a bad name for itself. Sorry, kid. I'll pay you for tonight, okay, but that's it.'

Millie stared at him, finding it unbearable to be forced to believe that Mal's hand could stretch so far. She collected her money, and turned to leave. It was as she reached the street, that she heard a familiar voice as a man came out of the bar behind her.

'Millie! Hey, it's yourself, Millie Brennan!'

Millie turned her head, dumbfounded. A tall dark haired man with a twinkle in his dark blue eyes and a sexy smile on his lips.

Was it? Could it be?

'Tommy Kelly!' she exclaimed. 'What on earth are you doing here?'

Chapter Fifty Four

'I've been looking for you, Millie. Someone told me you'd be singing here tonight. I couldn't believe it, mind you. You, Millie Brennan, singing in a grotty place like *The Spider's Web!* But never mind about that,' Tommy Kelly said. 'Let's get out of here. The car's just round the corner.'

The car was a Mercedes.

'So, still driving for the rich and thick, Tommy?' she asked as he showed her into the passenger seat, got in himself on the other side, and began to drive away.

'I don't want to talk about me, Millie. I want to hear about you. Last I heard, you were having a raving success in all Mal Charles's flash clubs. How come I find you in a grotty bar like this, Millie Brennan?'

'Well, for a start, it's not Millie Brennan, it's Millie O'Hanlon,' Millie told him. 'Although it won't be for much longer, if I have anything to do with it.'

'Oh? Tell me more.'

'Aw, Danny and I didn't make a go of it. Sure, he wants out of it just as much as I do. But I'm told it will take two years.'

'Quicker if you file for adultery. But I suppose Danny wouldn't have given you grounds? No, he's not that type, as far as I've ever heard. Listen, Millie, I want to know more than you're telling me. Why were you trying to get work at a pub like that? Why aren't you singing at Mal's? And I don't want any sob story – the truth, the whole truth, and nothing but the truth, right, girl? Remember it's me, Tommy Kelly, babe. I know you inside out. No way you can fool me.'

'Aw, Tommy, I'm glad!' Millie cried passionately. 'You have no idea how sick I get of lying and buttering up people. I can be myself with you. I'll tell you everything. I want to.'

The car had arrived at a large, prosperous looking house in the up market area of West Belfast, halfway up the Black Mountain.

'Come in and I'll get you a drink, and you can relax and tell me everything. Just pretend I'm your psychiatrist, or something.'

Although Tommy was his usual jokey self, Millie knew that she could trust him. 'Okay,' she said, and slid out of the car. 'But, Tommy, won't your boss mind you bringing a girl home and feeding her his drinks?'

'He won't mind. He's a very easy going fella. And we'll be in my private rooms. No one else ever comes in there.'

He led Millie into a comfortable small living room, obviously not the main one, settled her on a sofa with a glass of gin and cointreau in her hand, poured himself a whiskey, and sitting down beside her put one arm over her shoulder.

'Now, if you're sitting comfortably, let's begin.'

And Millie, sitting back happily against the warm arm and sipping occasionally at her glass, began.

'Well, Tommy, you know I intended to marry a rich man.'

'You made that clear enough, Millie. Not that I ever thought of marriage, mind you. But I did have other ideas. However, you made it clear to me that you didn't – how did it go? – plan "to lose your virginity to a chauffeur in the back seat of a car," wasn't that it?'

'That was exactly it, Tommy Kelly!' Millie retorted. 'Well, I thought I'd found a rich man. In fact, I had the option of two rich men. Only, I choose the wrong one – the one who ended up poor after all.'

The whole story came out. Millie pulled no punches, and Tommy grinned as she brought it up to date with her plans for Mal, which had failed so dismally.

'You're a rare wee hallion, Millie Brennan! But you've got something, all the same.' He set his glass down carefully on a low table at the end of the sofa. Then he bent round, took the glass from Millie's hand and, setting it aside, began to kiss her thoroughly.

Time passed. Millie sat up, suddenly aware that she was far away from her boarding house, and that it must be very late.

'Tommy, I'd better get home,' she gasped. 'You're lovely, but your boss won't be very pleased with you if he finds me here.'

'Aw, Millie, sure, like I said, my boss is a very easy going fella. He won't mind anything as long as it keeps me happy.'

'I suppose he's afraid to lose you,' said Millie shrewdly. 'Even so, Tommy, there must be limits on what he lets you get away with.'

'Oh, I don't know about that. I haven't found any, so far. But Millie,' Tommy grinned, 'if you really want me to, I can drop you back home. But I've got a better idea.'

Millie waited.

'The virginity's long gone, Millie, now you're a married woman. So why not move in with me? I've a lovely bedroom on offer, not just the back seat of a car, and the best of everything. Nobody need see you. You can keep to these rooms of mine, and go in and out by my private door when you feel like some fresh air. Then you can send O'Hanlon the info that you're living with me, and he can get his solicitor busy divorcing you for adultery. Why should you mind?

'I'd be happy to marry you myself, as soon as the divorce is through. Or maybe you'll find another rich man.' There was a sparkle in his eye, and Millie found herself falling for it all over again. There was something about Tommy Kelly which she had always found hard to resist. The last hour or so on the sofa had reminded her forcefully of how sexy and attractive he was.

She spoke fast, before she could change her mind. 'Right, Tommy, you're on. I'll move in, and let Danny know so's he can go ahead with the divorce. After that, we'll see.'

'That's my girl!' Tommy swooped down on her, gathered her, laughing and wriggling, into his arms. He carried her into the bedroom, and threw her onto the bed.

'Now, Millie Brennan!' he said, switching off the light, 'Now, I've finally got you.'

The next morning, Millie wrote to Danny, giving him details of her new address and the fact that she was living with a man called Tommy Kelly. When he had taken it in, Danny rushed to phone his solicitor, beaming with delight. The solicitor warned him that the facts would have to be checked, but promised to get that done as soon as possible.

The facts were checked and put before the court. The divorce went through quickly.

Millie was a free woman again.

She hadn't needed to go to the court, since she was admitting the adultery. The final papers came to her in the post, and she at once flourished them to Tommy.

'Great,' he said. Then he looked at her, an expression on his face which was unfamiliar to Millie. Looking at him carefully, she identified it as a mixture of nervousness and gravity. Millie couldn't remember ever having seen Tommy with anything but laughter at the back of his eyes.

'Well, Millie Brennan,' he said, standing in front of her and taking hold of her by each arm, holding her above the elbows and looking directly at her, 'it's decision time. You're back to being Millie Brennan again. Are you going to make it Millie Kelly? Wait, now. Don't be jumping to answer. You might find a millionaire out there yet. I'm not a millionaire, Millie. But I'd like to marry you, all the same. So. What's the answer? Will you?'

Millie looked at him. It was true that he wasn't the answer to her lifetime aim. But he was Tommy Kelly. Living with him had been fun. It reminded her of the times with her dad, when life had been lighthearted, before she'd gone to St Bernadette's, mixed with rich girls who looked down on her poverty, and grimly decided that she would be rich herself someday soon. Life with Tommy had been fun, with a lot of great sex thrown in. Millie made up her mind.

'Sure, how could I resist a romantic proposal like that, Tommy?' she said, grinning at him. 'You big eedjit, how do you think I could get on without you in my life? But you might have told me you loved me, while you were at it.'

Tommy gave a shout, put his arms properly round her and lifted her off her feet before kissing her thoroughly.

'Millie, Millie, sure you know I love you! Far too much. You'll be starting to twist me round your little finger, now you know that. But if you try it, you'll find I'll have something to say about it, babe. You'll not get away with it – I'm no wimp like O'Hanlon or Malachi Charles, girl!'

He kissed her again. 'We'll get married as soon as possible,' he said, and Millie was happy to agree. 'And after that, I've a few things to tell you. I've got a sorta secret wedding present for you.'

It was as they were leaving the registrar's, just over a week later, well and truly married, that Tommy explained something to her.

'I wasn't going to tell you this until you'd married me, thinking I was a poor working man, darlin',' he said. 'But to tell you the truth, though I'm no millionaire yet, I'm not too badly off. I don't work for anyone, I own that house we've been living in, and I own enough shares in solid, blue chip companies to keep us in style for the rest of our lives. Now, say you're pleased with your wedding present, and we'll go back home and move into the master bedroom.'

And the stars in her eyes told him that Millie was.

Chapter Fifty Five

Meanwhile, things had been going badly for Sooze, in her own opinion. Not only her mum, with the intention of helping her through the first week or so of being a new mother, but also her dad, had been collected and brought round to her apartment by Horse. Sooze didn't want to be unwelcoming, but didn't know what to say.

'So, Dad,' she said eventually, 'I suppose you wanted to see your new grandson?'

'Yes, yes, of course,' mumbled John O'Leary. He looked so much older and frailer suddenly that Sooze, although her attention was focused on her baby, had to realise that her father was in a bad way. Sam rushed in before anyone else could say more.

'Sooze, we need your help,' she said quickly. 'Yes, yes, we both wanted to see baby Josh, and I'm planning to give you as much help as I can in looking after you for as long as you need it, but the thing is, we've nowhere else to stay. Can you put us both up for a while?'

'But – what happened, Mum? Johnny's paying for your apartment and food, isn't he? Don't tell me he's stopped?'

'No. But your dad used Johnny's monthly money as security against a loan, and then wasn't able to keep up the repayments. So the loan company has taken all our money, we can't pay our rent, and we've been evicted.' She spoke bitterly. This double humiliation had landed heavily on Sam. She had stood by her husband when his business first went crashing. It was hard to summon up the guts to go on standing by him when he'd messed up again. Sam hadn't been a faithful wife, but she'd never let John down in any other way. She hoped she wouldn't do it this time either. But it was impossible not to feel some bitterness.

John O'Leary stood silently while his wife spoke, his eyes on the ground. His humiliation was complete, as he listened to his wife begging for help on his behalf.

'Johnny would help you again if you asked him to,' was Sooze's first response. She really didn't want to have to share her apartment with both her parents. Yes, she would be glad to have her mum for the first week or so, while she still felt weak from childbirth and knew so little about nappies and things. But not for longer – not for the foreseeable future.

'Your dad doesn't want to ask Johnny again, Sooze. We can ask you – we gave you a home for most of your life. And I've done my best to help you with this baby business, and I'm happy to go on helping now. We feel we can ask you for help more easily than Johnny, after wasting the money he's been giving us.'

Sooze knew there was nothing left for her to say, except, 'Yes, you'll have to share the spare room – it's not very big. I want to keep wee Josh in his cot beside my bed for a while yet, anyway. I couldn't put him in the spare room on his own. So, you'd better take your stuff in there.' She bent her head forward to kiss her mum coldly on one cheek, but made no move to kiss the father who'd been generous with money and gifts all her life, but had never shown her much in the way of physical closeness, hugs or kisses. It would have seemed strange to kiss him now.

John O'Leary smiled weakly. He would have liked to say, 'Thank you,' to his daughter, but didn't know how. Together, he and Sam moved silently to the spare room, and settled in.

Presently, Sam made a meal for the three of them, cleared up, washed the dishes, then helped Sooze to bath the baby, to put on a fresh nappy, and to breast feed the baby with the milk which had now come in and was flowing freely, before tucking them both up, Josh in his cot and Sooze in her lonely bed, for the night.

Horse didn't come in after collecting Sooze's parents and helping them up to the apartment door with their luggage. Sooze, when she came to open the door to let Sam and John in, didn't invite him, didn't even seem to notice him, and he didn't feel like inviting himself. The next morning he spoke to his dad about the possibility of being transferred, at least temporarily, to the company's Dublin office.

'It'll give me more experience,' he explained. 'I think I'd like a change, too, after what happened to Josh.'

'Fair enough, Horace, my boy. I'll arrange something for you.' His dad loved Horse and wanted to do what he could for him. Josh's death, especially such a death, had, he knew, upset Horace deeply. Maybe a change would help.

Horse didn't tell him that the real reason he wanted to get away was that he knew he needed to get his feelings for Sooze out of his system. Yes, Josh's death had hit him hard. But Sooze's attitude to him had hurt at least as badly, or more so. During the time since he had brought her the news of Josh's death, she had made it clear repeatedly that she not only didn't care for him, she actually disliked him.

Perhaps she was shooting the messenger, or blaming Horse for being a bad influence on Josh. Horse knew that he hadn't been, that on the contrary he done his best to stop Josh's wild behaviour, but he didn't know how he could make Sooze see this. He thought that maybe if he could get far enough away and never see her, he would be able to move on, meet another girl, form a permanent relationship, even marry.

It took a few weeks for his dad to sort out a senior enough position for Horse in the Dublin branch. When eventually it was time for him to go, Horse drove down the M1 from Belfast with a thankful heart.

There was another person who had been hard hit by Josh's death. Stephen Gillespie had felt his son's death as a near fatal blow. He had suffered a heart attack when he first heard the news, and it took him many months to recover.

The first thing to bring any sort of relief to his feelings was the information, brought to him nearly a year later by his daughter Elaine, that Josh had a son, Josh junior. Stephen found himself longing to see the boy.

Elaine, who had met Sooze by accident when she took her son out for a walk in his pushchair in the park, and continued to meet her by arrangement after that, brought her father the information that young Josh was the image of his father already.

'A fine, sturdy boy,' Elaine said. 'Strong looking, with lovely fair hair, just like his dad. Learning to walk already.'

'Hmm. His father was an early learner, too. Strong, clever. Able to learn anything from his babyhood on,' commented Gillespie.

From that time on, his burning desire was to see the boy for himself.

Elaine finally managed to arrange it, and Sooze took her son to Stephen Gillespie's house to visit his Granda. Stephen Gillespie still felt bitterly angry with Sooze, whom he blamed, illogically, for his son's death. He couldn't bear to see O'Leary's daughter. But the child was another matter.

So Sooze stayed in the kitchen drinking a cup of coffee while Elaine took wee Josh to the study. Stephen watched him toddle across the room with a heart bursting with pride, and admired Josh's courage when a tumble only made the boy chuckle. From that instant, he was determined to have wee Josh for his own.

He immediately made Sooze an offer. He would adopt Josh and do everything for him, and he would pay Sooze a regular sum for her own support.

Sooze refused angrily, and when she returned with the boy to her apartment, she told Sam about Gillespie's ridiculous offer, unable to resist sharing her anger.

Sam sympathised, but felt bound to say, 'It's very hard to bring the boy up with only benefits to live on, Sooze. You refuse to get a job and to let me look after him. Okay, you want to bring your own child up. But your father isn't fit to work or even to be left alone, his health has gone right downhill, so I can't get a job either. We're stuck if you won't leave the boy with me and go out to work yourself. Things are very tight, you know. I would at least think about this offer if I were you.'

Sooze couldn't bring herself to reply, anger with her mother adding itself to the anger she felt for Gillespie until it was as if a volcano of boiling lava were about to erupt from her stomach.

But Stephen Gillespie had not given up his plan at Sooze's refusal. He had renewed the lease on his son's apartment when it became due a while before Josh's death, but now another year had gone by, and the renewal reminder for the apartment's rent had come to him. He had learnt, moreover, that his old enemy, John O'Leary, was now living, and had been for some time, in the apartment he himself was paying for.

He wanted very much to throw the lot of them out, these people who between them, he still thought, had led his son astray and caused his death. But maybe there was a better way. He wrote to Sooze, and she got the letter while having breakfast with her parents.

'It's from that man Gillespie,' she said slowly. 'I can't believe anyone could be so evil.'

'What is it, Sooze?' That was Sam. John O'Leary felt crushed at the name of the man who had destroyed him, and sat silently, unable to bring himself to speak.

'He says that unless I agree to his offer to adopt Josh, he'll refuse to renew payment of this apartment's rent, and we'll all be evicted. But if I let him have Josh, he'll continue to pay.'

'Well,' said Sam presently, 'maybe now you'll realise you'll have to accept his offer. '

'What? Mum!' Sooze's anger flared out. Her mum couldn't really mean it, could she?

But Sam was serious. 'If we get chucked out of here, you'll have nowhere to bring the boy up yourself. Oh, I'm not pushing this for your dad's sake, or for mine – although heaven knows most children would think twice before letting their parents be thrown on the streets. But think about wee Josh. You can't look after him yourself any more.

You'll need to get a job if we have to leave here. A job that pays enough for us to get somewhere else to live. If you do that, I can look after him. But it'll be a miserable, poverty stricken life for us all, the child included. If you let him go to his granda, he'll be brought up in the lap of luxury like you were yourself. Don't you think you're being selfish, insisting on keeping him?'

Sooze had no answer. She was grimly determined to keep her child, but she acknowledged that what her mum had said had a lot of truth in it.

Only one way out occurred to her. 'I'm going to text Johnny and let him know what's happening,' she said. 'We can't go on considering Dad's pride when it's a choice of giving up my son or starving. Johnny will help us.'

'Johnny has already helped us as much as he can manage,' Sam said. 'We can't expect any more. He has to live, himself.'

'Johnny's been getting promotions and pay rises since the time he set up that direct debit for you,' was all Sooze said. 'He can probably manage a bit more by now.'

She picked up her phone and rang him. But there was no answer. Instead, she left a text, and waited.

When Johnny read Sooze's text, he was horrified. How could this stuff have been happening to his family and no one had told him? As it happened, he was having a drink with his friend Horace, whom he'd known as Horse until he met up with him in Dublin nearly a year ago.

Since Horace had moved to Dublin, he'd become very friendly with Johnny. Johnny had acquired a lot of respect for Horace, having seen him and heard people speak of him in his role as second-in-command at Buchanan's, Johnny's own company's auditors.

He was proud of his friendship with a man like Horace Buchanan. It was second nature to him, by now, to tell Horace about his family's situation. Horace, he knew, had been Josh's best friend, and cared a great deal for Sooze.

'I need to get something set up for them, Horace,' Johnny said.

'No, I think you should leave it to me,' Horace said. 'I once promised Josh I would always look after his widow and child. I should have been keeping more of an eye on them.'

It was over a year since he'd seen Sooze, but he hadn't succeeded in forgetting her.

'I'll drive up to Belfast tomorrow and see just what the situation is,' he told Johnny. 'Then I'll do whatever's necessary.'

'I'll come with you,' Johnny said.

They drove up together in Horace's car, a new BMW, and went straight round to Sooze's apartment. Johnny went in first, with Horace hovering in the background. As soon as she saw her son, Sam burst into tears and told him the whole story through her sobs.

Johnny was both angry and upset when he heard how his dad had used the direct debit Johnny had set up to support his whole family as security for a loan, and how he had lost it. But that was nothing to the anger Horace felt at Stephen Gillespie's behaviour. He blamed himself for not staying around to make sure all was well with Sooze and the baby.

'Don't worry, Mum,' Johnny said, hugging her. 'Tell Dad and Sooze it'll be all right. We'll get it sorted. I'm going round to the bank now to see what we can do.'

Horace slipped out of the apartment before Sooze could appear from her room, where she was dressing her son for his usual morning walk. Johnny followed him within minutes. Together they went first to the bank, to check the position with them. They found that John O'Leary no longer owed money there, which was one relief. Then they moved on to the house agents who handled the leasing of the apartment, and here Horace insisted on paying the rent for a long term lease.

'It's no use setting up another direct debit for your dad, Johnny. Who knows what he might do, another time. He's obsessed with making his fortune again,' Horace said, and Johnny acknowledged the truth of this.

'Don't tell Sooze it was me who paid this, Johnny,' Horace instructed him. 'You go back now and tell them it's okay, the rent's paid for five years ahead. I'll see you later.'

Then he went to speak to his father to arrange about moving back to Belfast. His father was only too glad to agree to this.

'In a very few years now, I'm wanting to retire, and I need you to take over the business, Horace my boy,' his dad said. 'I'd be really glad to have you around and involved again. But apart from all that, I've been missing you, boy.'

Stephen Gillespie found that the wind had been taken out of his sails. Sooze wrote back refusing his offer, and when, hoping to drive her to her knees, he told the house agents that he would not be renewing the lease, they told him, cheerfully, that that was all right, since another customer had renewed it on behalf of the current occupants. 'We understood that you were aware of that, sir. In any case, you'd left the renewal for too long. It was well past the due date when this other client came to us. A son of the current occupants, and a friend acting with him, I believe.'

There was nothing for Gillespie to do but swallow his anger.

When he moved back to Belfast, Horace Buchanan at first tried to keep away from Sooze. But hearing from Johnny that she was to be found in Ormeau Park on most fine days, taking wee Josh for his regular walk, he took to hanging around there, and was eventually rewarded by bumping into her, accidently as it seemed to Sooze.

'Why, Horse!' she exclaimed, and he thought she seemed pleased to see him. 'It's ages since we met. Come and sit down on the bench over there, and we can watch wee Josh on the swings.'

Horace was only too pleased. When he had asked after her health and the boy's, and her parents, he ventured to say, 'It feels really strange to be called Horse again. I've got used to everybody calling me by my real name, Horace, for several years now.'

'Horace? Is that your name? Well, I'd better try to remember to call you by it, then, I suppose.'

They chatted in a friendly way for a while, watching Josh playing happily on the swings and slides, and presently Horace felt emboldened to ask her to have dinner with him some evening.

'I'd like that – Horace,' Sooze said, managing to remember the name, so new to her. 'But what about wee Josh?'

'Can't you get a babysitter? Wouldn't your mum look after him, just for a few hours?'

'I suppose she could, if he's asleep first,' Sooze agreed rather reluctantly, and so it was arranged.

It became a regular thing that she and Horace went out together at least once a week. But when he tried to kiss her goodnight gently, she always managed to turn her face so that the kiss landed harmlessly on her cheek rather than on her mouth. And when, after a long time, he gathered up the courage to propose to her, she refused, saying there could never be anyone else for her but the man she had married, her dear Josh.

Horace was cast down. If it had been possible, he would have gone away again, but his dad's retirement was too near by now for him to do that. Moreover, he was aware that John O'Leary couldn't be trusted not to get his family into more trouble. He'd been talking lately about trying out a few shares again, and it had taken all the tact Sam and Sooze between them possessed to dissuade him from trying to float another loan.

Horace was glad that Sooze had passed on her worries about this to him, and that she had followed his advice to discourage her dad firmly. He had told her to keep him informed if there was any more talk of this, and that was another reason why he didn't feel that he could go away.

The time came when the rent needed to be renewed again. Sooze, in all innocence, sent the request to Johnny, only to be told by him that the person who was dealing with that was Horace Buchanan, and that she had better let him know it was due, as soon as possible.

Sooze was dismayed. But by this time, although she had turned him down some years ago, she was coming more and more to trust and rely on Horace, as she'd now got quite used to thinking of him. She didn't, some- how, want Horace to know that Johnny had told her of his generosity. Instead, she asked Johnny to pass the rent renewal request to Horace, without telling him she knew.

Johnny, who had remembered that he'd promised Horace never to let Sooze know, and who was dismayed to realise that he'd broken his word, was only too glad to oblige her. He sent the request to Horace, and a further instalment was promptly paid.

'Why don't you marry the man?' Johnny texted Sooze cheerfully. 'I know he's nuts about you, dear knows why.'

And Sooze realised that she could do much worse.

It was a month after this that Millie, walking in the park with her new little daughter, ran into Sooze. Things had been going wonderfully well for Millie. She was really happy with Tommy. It was a shame that Sooze still seemed to be carrying a torch for that useless fella Josh Gillespie, whom Millie had never liked for all her flirting with him.

She felt that for once she might do her former friend a good turn. She still had some of Josh's messages to her on her mobile, for at first she had deliberately kept them in case they came in useful to her some day, and then she had forgotten about them.

It was time Sooze knew how her wonderful Josh had been behaving behind her back.

'I think you should see these, Sooze,' she said. 'Time you stopped thinking of your dead hero, and got married to that nice rich man, Horace Buchanan, who loves you. Here, this is the sort of message your beloved Josh was sending me while you were expecting his baby.'

She held out the phone for Sooze to read. The first message ran, *My darling Millie, how I wish I was getting into bed with you tonight, instead of with Sooze. Tell me it can be soon, darling.*

Sooze read it, and then laughed and handed back the phone. 'There are lots more,' Millie said, pushing it back to her.

'I don't want to see them. I don't want to know this stuff,' Sooze said. 'That's all past history, Millie. Here, look.'

She held out her left hand for Millie to see the rings on her third finger, a gold wedding ring and an engagement ring with the traditional large solitaire diamond. 'You're a bit on the late side with your good deed, Millie,' she said. 'Maybe because you're not in practice with them. Horace and I were married three weeks ago.'

Sooze was at first quite sure that having her would be enough to make Horace really happy. She became pregnant again, in spite of her former resolutions, and when the baby, a little girl, was born, she found that she loved her as much as she still loved wee Josh – no longer so wee. As for Horace, it was obvious to her that he loved little Ellie even more than he loved Sooze herself.

She thought wistfully of how she had thrown away his love when it was fresh and strong, and how her treatment of him over the years must have finally worn it thin.

Horace had never said anything to let her think this. He was consistently kind and generous to her. But little Ellie was his only consolation for the mistake he had made in his persistence in thinking he still loved Sooze, and his foolishness in marrying her when he knew how little remained of the original feelings she had trampled on for so long.

So the music played, and the Roundabout continued to spin, taking the people seated on it round and then back round again, until the time came for them to get off. And who can say how many of them enjoyed the ride, or felt it was worth it?

Roundabout *– Gerry McCullough*

About the author

Gerry McCullough has been writing poems and stories since childhood. Brought up in north Belfast, she graduated in English and Philosophy from Queen's University, Belfast, then went on to gain an MA in English.

She lives in Northern Ireland, just outside Belfast,, has four grown up children and is married to author, media producer and broad-caster, Raymond McCullough, with whom she co-edited the Irish magazine, *Bread*, (originally published by *Kingdom Come Trust*), from 1990-96. In 1995 they also published a non-fiction book called, *Ireland – now the good news!*

Over the past few years Gerry has had around one hundred short stories published in UK, Irish and American magazines, anthologies and annuals – as well as broadcast on BBC Radio Ulster – plus poems and articles published in several Northern Ireland and UK magazines. She has also read from her novels, poems and short stories at many Irish literary events.

Gerry won the *Cúirt International Literary Award* for 2005 (Galway); was shortlisted for the 2008 *Brian Moore Award* (Belfast); shortlisted for the 2009 *Cúirt Award*; commended in the 2009 *Seán O'Faolain Short Story Competition*, (Cork) and shortlisted in the 2015 *Harmony House Poetry Competition*, Downpatrick. In 2016 she won the *Bangor Poetry Award* for her poem, *Summer Passing*.

Gerry currently has a total of sixteen books in publication –

Stand alone romantic suspense novels (4):

- *Belfast Girls* (November 2010, re-issued July 2012)

- *Danger Danger* (October 2011)

- *Johnny McClintock's War* (August 2014)

- *Roundabout* (July 2020)

The Angel Murphy thriller series (3):
- *Angel in Flight* (June 2012)
- *Angel in Belfast* (June 2013)
- *Angel in Paradise* (January 2017)

The Hel's Heroes romantic comedy series (2):
- *Hel's Heroes: a romantic comedy* (June 2015)
- *Hel's Heroes 2: Christie and the Pirate* (March 2019)

Short story collections (5):
- *The Seanachie: Tales of Old Seamus* (January 2012)
- *The Seanachie 2: Norah on the Beach & other stories* (September 2014)
- *The Seanachie 3: Seamus and the Shell & other stories* (August 2016)
- *The Seanachie 4: Paddy and the Snake & other stories* (June 2019)
- *Dreams, Visions, Nightmares* – a collection of eight literary and award-winning Irish short stories (January 2016)

Fantasy novels (2):
- *Not the End of the World* – a comic, futuristic fantasy novel (February 2016)
- *Lady Molly and the Snapper* – a young adult novel time travel adventure set in Dublin (August 2012)

Belfast Girls

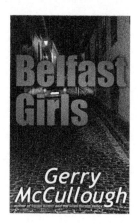

The story of three girls – Sheila, Phil and Mary – growing up into the new emerging post-conflict Belfast of money, drugs, high fashion and crime; and of their lives and loves.

Sheila, a supermodel, is kidnapped.

Phil is sent to prison.

Mary, surviving a drug overdose, has a spiritual awakening.

It is also the story of the men who matter to them –

John Branagh, former candidate for the priesthood, a modern Darcy, someone to love or hate. Will he and Sheila ever get together?

Davy Hagan, drug dealer, 'mad, bad and dangerous to know'. Is Phil also mad to have anything to do with him?

Although from different religious backgrounds, starting off as childhood friends, the girls manage to hold on to that friendship in spite of everything.

A book about contemporary Ireland and modern life. A book which both men and women can enjoy – thriller, romance, comedy, drama – and much more ...

"fascinating ... original ... multilayered ... expertly travels from one genre to the next"
Kellie Chambers, **Ulster Tatler** (Book of the Month)

"romance at the core ... enriched with breathtaking action, mystery, suspense and some tear-jerking moments of tragedy.
Sheila M. Belshaw, author

"What starts out as a crime thriller quickly evolves into a literary festival beyond the boundary of genres"
PD Allen, author
"a masterclass, and a vivid dissection of the human condition in all of its inglorious foibles"
WeeScottishLassie

Belfast Girls

Gerry McCullough

Published by

Chapter One

Jan 21, 2007

The street lights of Belfast glistened on the dark pavements where, even now, with the troubles officially over, few people cared to walk alone at night. John Branagh drove slowly, carefully, through the icy streets.

In the distance, he could see the lights of the *Magnifico Hotel*, a bright contrasting centre of noise, warmth and colour.

He felt again the excitement of the news he'd heard today.

Hey, he'd actually made the grade at last – full-time reporter for BBC TV, right there on the local news programme, not just a trainee, any longer. Unbelievable.

The back end shifted a little as he turned a corner. He gripped the wheel tighter and slowed down even more. There was black ice on the roads tonight. Gotta be careful.

So, he needed to work hard, show them he was keen. This interview, now, in this hotel? This guy Speers? If it turned out good enough, maybe he could go back to Fat Barney and twist his arm, get him to commission it for local TV, the Hearts and Minds programme maybe? Or even – he let his ambition soar – go national? Or how's about one of those specials everybody seemed to be into right now?

There were other thoughts in his mind but as usual he pushed them down out of sight. Sheila Doherty would be somewhere in the hotel tonight, but he had plenty of other stuff to think about to steer his attention away from past unhappiness. No need to focus on anything right now but his career and its hopeful prospects.

Montgomery Speers, better get the name right, new Member of the Legislative Assembly, wanted to give his personal views on the peace process and how it was working out. Yeah. Wanted some publicity, more like. Anti, of course, or who'd care? But that was just how people were.

John curled his lip. He had to follow it up. It could give his career the kick start it needed.

But he didn't have to like it.

* * *

Inside the *Magnifico Hotel*, in the centre of newly regenerated Belfast, all was bustle and chatter, especially in the crowded space behind the catwalk. The familiar fashion show smell, a mixture of cosmetics and hair dryers, was overwhelming.

Sheila Doherty sat before her mirror, and felt a cold wave of unhappiness surge over her. How ironic it was, that title the papers gave her, today's most super supermodel. She closed her eyes and put her hands to her ears, trying to shut everything out for just one snatched moment of peace and silence.

Every now and then it came again. The pain. The despair. A face hovered before her mind's eye, the white, angry face of John Branagh, dark hair falling forward over his furious grey eyes. She deliberately blocked the thought, opening her eyes again. She needed to slip on the mask, get ready to continue on the surface of things where her life was perfect.

"Comb that curl over more to the side, will you, Chrissie?" she asked, "so it shows in front of my ear. Yeah, that's right – if you just spray it there – thanks, pet."

The hairdresser obediently fixed the curl in place. Sheila's long red-gold hair gleamed in the reflection of three mirrors positioned to show every angle. Everything had to be perfect – as perfect as her life was supposed to be. The occasion was too important to allow for mistakes.

Her fine-boned face with its clear translucent skin, like ivory, and crowned with the startling contrast of her hair, looked back at her from the mirror, green eyes shining between thick black lashes – black only because of the mascara.

She examined herself critically, considering her appearance as if it were an artefact which had to be without flaw to pass a test.

She stood up.

"Brilliant, pet," she said. "Now the dress."

The woman held out the dress for Sheila to step into, then carefully

pulled the ivory satin shape up around the slim body and zipped it at the back. The dress flowed round her, taking and emphasising her long fluid lines, her body slight and fragile as a daydream. She walked over to the door, ready to emerge onto the catwalk. She

2

was very aware that this was the most important moment of one of the major fashion shows of her year.

The lights in the body of the hall were dimmed, those focussed on the catwalk went up, and music cut loudly through the sudden silence. Francis Delmara stepped forward and began to introduce his new spring line.

For Sheila, ready now for some minutes and waiting just out of sight, the tension revealed itself as a creeping feeling along her spine. She felt suddenly cold and her stomach fluttered.

It was time and, dead on cue, she stepped lightly out onto the catwalk and stood holding the pose for a long five seconds, as instructed, before swirling forward to allow possible buyers a fuller view.

She was greeted by gasps of admiration, then a burst of applause. Ignoring the reaction, she kept her head held high, her face calm and remote, as far above human passion as some elusive, intangible figure of Celtic myth, a Sidhe, a dweller in the hollow hills, distant beyond man's possessing – just as Delmara had taught her.

This was her own individual style, the style which had earned her the nickname 'Ice Maiden' from the American journalist Harrington Smith. She moved forward along the catwalk, turned this way and that, and finally swept a low curtsey to the audience before standing there, poised and motionless.

Delmara was silent at first to allow the sight of Sheila in one of his most beautiful creations its maximum impact. Then he began to draw attention to the various details of the dress.

It was time for Sheila to withdraw. Once out of sight, she began a swift, organised change to her next outfit, while Delmara's other models were in front.

No time yet for her to relax, but the show seemed set for success.

* * *

MLA, Montgomery Speers, sitting in the first row of seats, the celebrity seats, with his latest blonde girlfriend by his side, allowed himself to feel relieved.

Francis Delmara had persuaded him to put money into Delmara Fashions and particularly into financing Delmara's supermodel, Sheila Doherty, and he was present tonight in order to see for himself if his investment was safe. He thought, even so early in the show, that it was.

He was a broad shouldered man in his early forties, medium height, medium build, red-cheeked, and running slightly to fat. There was nothing particularly striking about his appearance except for the piercing dark eyes set beneath heavy, jutting eyebrows. His impressive presence stemmed from his personality, from the aura of power and aggression which surrounded him.

A businessman first and foremost, he had flirted with political involvement for several years. He had stood successfully for election to the local council, feeling the water cautiously with one toe while he made up his mind. Would he take the plunge and throw himself whole- heartedly into politics?

The new Assembly gave him his opportunity, if he wanted to take it. More than one of the constituencies offered him the chance to stand for a seat. He was a financial power in several different towns where his computer hardware companies provided much needed jobs. He was elected to the seat of his choice with no trouble. The next move was to build up his profile, grab an important post once things got going, and progress up the hierarchy.

In an hour or so, when the Fashion Show was over, he would meet this young TV reporter for some preliminary discussion of a possible interview or of an appearance on a discussion panel. He was slightly annoyed that someone so junior had been lined up to talk to him. John Branagh, that was the name, wasn't it? Never heard of him. Should have been someone better known, at least. Still, this was only the preliminary. They would roll out the big guns for him soon enough when he was more firmly established. Meanwhile his thoughts lingered on the beautiful Sheila Doherty.

If he wanted her, he could buy her, he was sure. And more and more as he watched her, he knew that, yes, he wanted her.

* * *

A fifteen minute break, while the audience drank the free wine and ate the free canapés. Behind the scenes again, Sheila checked hair and makeup. A small mascara smear needed to be removed, a touch more blusher applied. In a few minutes she was ready but something held her back.

4

Chapter 1

She stared at herself in the mirror and saw a cool, beautiful woman, the epitome of poise and grace. She knew that famous, rich, important men over two continents would give all their wealth and status to possess her, or so they said. She was an icon according to the papers. That meant, surely, something unreal, something artificial, painted or made of stone.

And what was the good? There was only one man she wanted. John Branagh. And he'd pushed her away. He believed she was a whore – a tart – someone not worth touching. What did she do to deserve that?

It wasn't fair! she told herself passionately. He went by rules that were medieval. No-one nowadays thought the odd kiss mattered that much. Oh, she was wrong. She'd hurt him, she knew she had. But if he'd given her half a chance, she'd have apologised – told him how sorry she was. Instead of that, he'd called her such names – how could she still love him after that? But she knew she did.

How did she get to this place, she wondered, the dream of romantic fiction, the dream of so many girls, a place she hated now, where men thought of her more and more as a thing, an object to be desired, not a person? When did her life go so badly wrong? She thought back to her childhood, to the skinny, ginger-haired girl she once was. Okay, she hated how she looked but otherwise, surely, she was happy. Or was that only a false memory?

"Sheila - where are you?"

The hairdresser poked her head round the door and saw Sheila with every sign of relief.

"Thank goodness! Come on, love, only got a couple of minutes! Delmara says I've to check your hair. Wants it tied back for this one."

* * *

The evening was almost at its climax. The show began with evening dress, and now it was to end with evening dress – but this time with Delmara's most beautiful and exotic lines. Sheila stood up and shook out her frock, a cloud of short ice-blue chiffon, sewn with glittering silver beads and feathers. She and Chrissie between them swept up her hair, allowing a few loose curls to hang down her back and one side of her face, fixed it swiftly into place with two combs, and clipped on more silver feathers.

She fastened on long white earrings with a pearly sheen and slipped her feet into the stiletto heeled silver shoes left ready and waiting. She moved over to the doorway for her cue. There was no time to think or to feel the usual butterflies. Chloe came off and she counted to three and went on.

There was an immediate burst of applause.

To the loud music of Snow Patrol, Sheila half floated, half danced along the catwalk, her arms raised ballerina fashion. When she had given sufficient time to allow the audience their fill of gasps and appreciation, she moved back and April and Chloe appeared in frocks with a similar effect of chiffon and feathers, but with differences in style and colour. It was Delmara's spring look for evening wear and she could tell at once that the audience loved it.

The three girls danced and circled each other, striking dramatic poses as the music died down sufficiently to allow Delmara to comment on the different features of the frocks.

With one part of her mind Sheila was aware of the audience, warm and relaxed now, full of good food and drink, their minds absorbed in beauty and fashion, ready to spend a lot of money. Dimly in the background she heard the sounds of voices shouting and feet running.

The door to the ballroom burst open.

People began to scream.

It was something Sheila had heard about for years now, the subject of local black humour, but had never before seen.

Three figures, black tights pulled over flattened faces as masks, uniformly terrifying in black leather jackets and jeans, surged into the room.

The three sub-machine guns cradled in their arms sent deafening bursts of gunfire upwards. Falling plaster dust and stifling clouds of gun smoke filled the air.

For one long second they stood just inside the entrance way, crouched over their weapons, looking round. One of them stepped forward and grabbed Montgomery Speers by the arm.

"Move it, mister!" he said. He dragged Speers forcefully to one side, the weapon poking him hard in the chest.

A second man gestured roughly with his gun in the general direction of Sheila.

"You!" he said harshly. "Yes, you with the red hair! Get over here!"

6

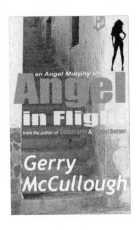

Angel in Flight:

the first Angel Murphy thriller

Gerry McCullough

Is it a bird? Is it a plane? No, it's a low-flying Angel!

You've heard of Lara Croft. You've heard of Modesty Blaise. Well, here comes Angel Murphy!

Angel, a 'feisty wee Belfast girl' on holiday in Greece, sorts out a villain who wants to make millions for his pharmaceutical company by preventing the use of a newly discovered malaria vaccine.

Angel has a broken marriage behind her and is wary of men, but perhaps her meeting with Josh Smith, who tells her he's with Interpol, may change her mind?

Fun, action, thrills, romance in a beautiful setting – so much to enjoy!

"it's a fast-paced read, ... exciting, and you can not put this book down"
Thomas Baker, Santiago, Chile

"I could not stop reading! ... a gripping thriller from beginning to the end"
SanMarie Lamprecht

"fast-paced, exciting read. From the moment I read the first line, I was hooked"
Cheryl Bradshaw, author, Wyoming, USA

"sassy bigger then life heroine in an action packed adventure thriller in Greece"
Book Review Buzz

Angel in Belfast:

the 2nd Angel Murphy thriller

Gerry McCullough

Angel Murphy is back, in true kick boxing form!

Alone in his cottage near a remote Irish village, Fitz, lead singer of the popular band *Raving*, hears the cries of the paparazzi outside and likens them in his own mind to wolves in a feeding frenzy. Next morning Fitz is found unconscious, seeming unlikely to survive, and is rushed to hospital. Has he been driven to OD? Or is someone else behind this?

His friends call in Angeline Murphy, 'Angel to her friends, devil to her enemies,' to find out the truth. But it takes all Angel's courage and skills to survive the many dangers she faces and to discover the real villain and deal with him.

"brings the city and its people ... to life with evocative description and scintillating dialogue"

Elinor Carlisle, Berkshire, UK

"I could not stop reading! ... a gripping thriller from beginning to the end"

SanMarie Lamprecht

"makes the troubled city of Belfast vibrant and appealing"

P A Lanstone, UK

"I felt like I had been transported to Belfast's often tough, gritty streets"

Bobbi Lerman, USA

"love the fact that we are reintroduced to characters from Belfast Girls"

Michele Young, UK

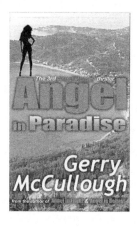

Angel in Paradise:

the 3rd Angel Murphy thriller

Angeline Murphy, 'Angel to her friends, devil to her enemies,' is on holiday in Corfu with her friend Josh Smith, hoping to relax and recharge her batteries, and perhaps develop her relationship with Josh. But Angel finds it impossible to sit back and do nothing when she learns of the assault and robbery carried out on her parents' old friend Sophie.

Before long Angel is fully involved in tracking down the brutal gang of jewel thieves who are terrorising many of the island's elderly but wealthy inhabitants. Her plan is, with Josh's help, to identify and arrest the gang's leader.

But soon Angel is in serious danger herself, from men who don't hesitate to kill to cover their tracks.

And meanwhile, the growing trust she has been feeling for Josh, as they build their relationship carefully after the disaster of Angel's first marriage, is threatened. When Angel finds Josh left for dead in an olive grove at midnight, it seems that this might be the end for them both…

Thrills, hairsbreadth escape after escape, danger, and a full helping of romance, all in the beautiful setting of Corfu, the Paradise island.

"in my opinion this is the best in this series so far."

Tom Elder, USA

"it even excelled its promotion hype. One off the best I have read"

Thea1710, USA

"a fast paced, brilliantly plotted and complex reading experience …

the plot twists and turns will have you on the edge of your seat"

Soooz Burke, Australia

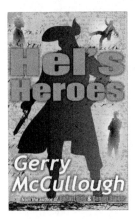

Hel's Heroes

Hel wants a hero like the ones she writes about, but does one exist?

A contemporary romance and an

historic romance in one book!

Helen McFadden – Hel for short – is a successful writer of Historic Romance for the eBook market. But one day she decides that she needs to get out and experience a bit of real life. She is soon clubbing, partying and generally having a good time – and men are springing up in her life from all directions.

There's Jason, the actor, Paddy the happy-go-lucky businessman, Jordie the footballer, Markie the pop star, even Pete, her old friend.

But do any of them measure up to the heroes she writes about – especially Jack, the highwayman in her current book?

Will Hel ever learn to relate to a real man and stop expecting to meet a clone of one of her heroes?

Hel's Heroes 2: Christie & The Pirate

A contemporary romance and an

historic romance in one book!

Christie McCafferty's simple life as a Librarian becomes suddenly complicated when she meets Steve Armstrong. Can she trust Steve or is he a crook?

Meanwhile, Christie is reading a book called *The Pirate* by Helen – Hel for short – McFadden on her *Kindle* at night. In it, Prue is shipwrecked and picked up by a ship flying the Jolly Roger. Prue finds the pirate chief, Black Nick Hawkeye, very attractive. But surely she isn't going to fall in love with a pirate, someone she could never trust?

Christie sees that her own situation, falling for someone who may be a crook, is only too similar to Prue's with 'Hel's Hero', Nick the Pirate. How will it work out for either girl?

A pleasure to read

What a lovely addition to this series. Christie works in the library and her life is pretty smooth and easy. In fact you could say boring, nothing exciting seems to happen.

Then one day she meets Steve and suddenly her life becomes complicated. To make matters even more confusing Christie is reading a book written by Helen (Hel) McFadden about Prue who gets involved with a pirate – Black Nick Hawkeye. While in the real world Christie is trying to figure out if Steve can be trusted, at the same time in the book Christie reads how Prue is also wondering if she can let herself fall in love with Nick.

We are taken on a delightful journey as we follow both Christie and the fictional Prue. Will both find happiness or heartbreak? Have an enjoyable time finding out how it turns out for them.

Ann Stanmore, *Amazon.com*

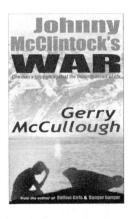

Johnny McClintock's War:
One man's struggle against the hammer blows of life

The story of one man's struggle to maintain his faith in spite of everything life throws at him.

As the outbreak of the First World War looms closer, John Henry McClintock, a Northern Irish Protestant by upbringing, meets Rose Flanagan, a Catholic, at a gospel tent mission – and falls in love with her.

When Johnny enlists and sets off to fight in the War he finds himself surrounded by death and tragedy, which pushes his trust in God to the limit.

After more than five years absence he returns home to a bitter, war torn Ireland, where both he and Rose are seen as traitors to their own sides.

John Henry and Rose overcome all opposition and, finally, marry. But a few years later comes the hardest blow of all. Can John Henry still hang on to his faith in God?

"brilliant .. this book had me captured from the start"

Tom Elder, Amazon.com

*"displays her insightful vision into the human condition ..
a gut-wrenching emotional ride .. a must read"*
Tom Winton, author, USA

*"Gerry McCullough's best book yet ..
a powerful tribute to those who died for their countries and what they believed"*
Juliet B Madison, author, UK

*"an emotional roller coaster ride .. an epiphany .. highly recommended
.. a book that will make you think about how wonderful life truly is"*
Thomas Baker, Amazon.com, Santiago, Chile

*"will hold you spellbound until the very last sentence ..
I breathed every heart-beat with the characters .. I love this book"*
Sheila Mary Belshaw, author, UK, Menorca, Cape Town

The Seanachie series:
Tales of Old Seamus

Gerry McCullough

Four collections of this humorous series of Irish stories – 12 stories in each – set in the fictional Donegal village of Ardnakil and featuring that lovable rogue, *'Old Seamus'* – the Séanachie.

All of these stories have previously been published in the popular Irish weekly magazine, *Ireland's Own*, based in Wexford, Ireland.

"heart warming tales ... beautifully told with subtle Irish humour"

Babs Morton (author)

"an irresistible old rogue, but he's the kind people love to sit and listen to for hours on end whenever the opportunity presents itself"

G. Polley (author and blogger – Sapporo, Japan)

"This magnificent storyteller has done it again. Each individual story has it's own Gaelic charm"

Teresa Geering (author – UK)

"evocative characterisation brings these stories to life in a delightful, absorbing way"

Elinor Carlisle (author – Reading, UK)

Lady Molly & The Snapper

A young adult time travel adventure, set in Ireland and on the high seas

Gerry McCullough

Brother and sister Jik and Nora are bored and angry. Why does their Dad spend so much time since their mother's death drinking and ignoring them? Why must he come home at all hours and fall downstairs like a fool?

Nora goes to church and lights a candle. The cross-looking sailor saint she particularly likes seems to grow enormous and come to life. Nora is too frightened to stay.

Nora and Jik go down secretly to their father's boat, the *Lady Molly*, at Howth Marina. There they meet The Snapper, the same cross-looking saint in a sailor's cap, who takes them back in time on the yacht, *Lady Molly,* to meet Cuchulain, the legendary Irish warrior, and others.

Jik and Nora plan to use their travels to find some way of stopping their father from drinking – but it's fun, too! Or is it? When they meet the Druid priest who follows them into modern times, teams up with school bully Marty Flanagan, and threatens them, things start getting out of hand.

Meanwhile, Nora is more than interested in Sean, the boy they keep bumping into in the past ...

Other books from:

A Wee Taste a' Craic:

All the Irish craic from the popular
Celtic Roots Radio shows, 2-25

Raymond McCullough

*I absolutely loved this! I found it to be very informative
about Irish life culture, language and traditions.*
Elinor Carlisle (author, Reading, UK)

*a unique insight into the Northern Irish people
& their self deprecating sense of humour*
Strawberry

Ireland – *now the good news!*

The best of *'Bread'* Vols. 1 & 2 –

personal testimonies and church/
fellowship profiles from around Ireland

**Edited by: Raymond & Gerry
McCullough**

"...fresh Bread – deals with the real issues facing the church in Ireland today"
Ken Newell, minster of Fitzroy Presbyterian Church, Belfast

The Whore and her Mother:

9/11, Babylon and the Return of the King

Raymond McCullough

Could the writings of the ancient Hebrew prophets be relevant to events taking place in the world today?

These Hebrew prophets – Isaiah, Jeremiah, Habbakuk and the apostle John, in *The Revelation* – wrote extensively about a latter day city and empire which would dominate, exploit and corrupt all the nations of the world. They referred to it as Babylon the Great, or Mega-Babylon, and they foretold that its fall – 'in one day' – would devastate the economies of the whole world.

Have these prophecies been fulfilled already?

Is Mega-Babylon:

- the Roman Catholic Church?
- A world super-church?
- Rebuilt ancient Babylon?
- Brussels, Jerusalem,
- or somewhere entirely different?

Should this city/nation have a large Jewish population?

Why all the talk about merchants, cargoes, commodities, trade?

Can we rely on the words of these ancient prophets?

If so, what else did they foretell that is still to be fulfilled?

Do they refer to other major nations – USA, Russia, China, Europe?

What about militant Islam?

"AMAZED when I read this book ... in awe of your extensive knowledge on so many levels: Christian, Jewish, and Muslim culture; the Jewish diaspora ... Greek & Hebrew; ... thought-provoking and troublesome ... many will be offended, but you consistently build your case instead of being sensationalistic."
James Revoir, author of **Priceless Stones**

Oh What Rapture!

Is a *'Secret Rapture'* going to spare believers from the tribulation to come?

Raymond McCullough

Many are convinced that very soon an event known as *'The Rapture'* will take place, where bible believers all over the world will suddenly dis-appear, leaving society at a loss to explain the disappearance of so many. Many non-fiction books, fiction thrillers and movies have capitalised on this theme, earning a fat revenue for their authors/producers.

- **But is this really what the bible teaches?**
- **Is *'The Rapture'* genuine, or a false hope?**
- **Are those who trust in it being duped, so that they don't prepare for what is coming?**
- **Are they being disobedient to the clear command of the Lord?**

Written by the author of Amazon best-selling book, *The Whore and her Mother* – also on the topic of bible prophecy – this volume focusses on the false teaching of a *'secret and separate Rapture'* – an event which is NOT supported by scripture!

The book investigates the scriptures used to back up the *'secret Rapture'* theory and clearly compares them to the other scriptures concerning the return of the Messiah, Jesus (Yeshua). The evident truth is revealed and the origins of the false *'secret Rapture'* doctrine are exposed.

Believers around the world are taught to expect persecution, some-times even death, for their faith. More have been killed in the past century than in previous centuries combined – in China, Cambodia, Nigeria, Iran, Egypt, Indonesia, Vietnam, etc. Yet many believers in the west confidently expect to avoid any persecution and be *'beamed up'* out of any coming tribulation!

If you thought believers were soon going to be lifted out of the worsening world situation, be prepared to meet the exciting challenge of scripture head on!

The **Six Hours** apocalyptic thriller series

Raymond McCullough

A friendship forged in war leads four young men on separate journeys to their final destiny – in a Middle East heading for meltdown.

As bitter enemies race towards nuclear conflict, only a miracle can save Israel from the hostile Islamic forces surrounding her. The USA, Russia and the western world are playing with fire in the Middle East, as Iran rushes towards a nuclear climax. In just six hours the face of the Middle East – and the world – will change forever!

While fighting the Taliban with the ISAF forces in 2012, four young men from very different backgrounds meet in Kabul, Afghanistan:

- Shaul *'Solly'* Levine, an Orthodox Jew from New York City;

- Micky *'Dev'* Devlin, an Irish Catholic from Boston;

- Brandon *'Doubtin"* Thomas, a black Pentecostal from N. Carolina;

- Khan Ali *'Zai'* Yusufzai, a Muslim Pashtun from Afghanistan.

They discover that they have more in common than they first thought and make a pact that one day they'll meet up again in Jerusalem after the prophesied Six Hour War in the Middle East, taking separate ways to a common destiny.

Meanwhile, they will keep in touch with one another as much as possible and work towards making that meeting a possibility. Will these prophecies come to pass? Will Israel itself survive the coming nuclear holocaust?

This apocalyptic thriller moves from war, to a couple of budding romances in very different locations, to more war and then the ultimate Middle East war. But even in the midst of conflict, new relationships are being formed. Action, friendship, romance ... and yet more action.

Neighbours from Hell:

Israel and the coming nuclear attempt to destroy her

#2 in the Arrows bible prophecy series

Raymond McCullough

Israel has not been blessed with good neighbours!

An end time war is prophesied in the Middle East: an attempt by the Arab nations surrounding Israel – with help from other Islamic nations – to eliminate the State of Israel once and for all.

But all will not go according to their plan and in approximately *six hours* the face of the Middle East – and the world – will change forever!

- **Will these prophecies be fulfilled?**
- **Will this war involve nuclear weapons?**
- **Can Israel survive the coming onslaught?**
- **Who will survive and who will be destroyed?**
- **Will Israel control the Middle East?**
- **Could this war trigger the Ingathering of the Ten Tribes?**
- **How will the rest of the world be impacted?**

Facing the Beast:

The man they call the antichrist, and our response to him

Raymond McCullough

Will we be around to see the antichrist?

If the much vaunted *'secret rapture'* proves to be a delusion, how will we face *'the beast'?*

Are the church and the Jewish community prepared to deal with this man, who hates both equally?

The apostle Paul tells us that the day of Messiah's coming – and our gathering to him – will NOT come until the *'man of sin'* is revealed, who will set himself up in the Jewish temple, claiming to be God!

The beast is known by many titles throughout the prophets:
> the antichrist
> the prince that will come
> the little horn
> the beast
> the man of sin
> the lawless one
> Gog, ruler of the land of Magog

If we have to face this ruler and his overwhelming forces, how will we cope?

How should we prepare?

Jesus said that *'many will turn away from the faith'* – how can we ensure that we are among those who will *'endure to the end?'*

Printed in Great Britain
by Amazon

29264777R00165